PRAISE FOR *HEART WO*

"To my own surprise, I don't expect new authors to be so sly or quick in engaging, holding, and enlightening their readers. Whenever I pick *Heart Wood* up, I always regret having to put it down. Shirley DicKard is extremely good."

— Gary Snyder, Pulitzer Prize–winning poet, essayist, environmental activist

"If you pick up this book you will be reading about three related and determined women in radically different times whose decisions and fates are connected in some manner by a small oak desk. This is not a book about "saving the planet." It is a book about female energy and intelligence in multiple generations of a very American family. There are some rays of hope in their response to numerous brutish points along the way, and their individual accomplishments are impressive, but there is no golden sunset, and no utopia at the end. Nor should there be. The reader does not get off easy and will not heave a sigh of relief that all will turn out OK. We are left with a clear understanding that most aspects of existence will only get worse, but we have been privileged to travel part of the way with three brave women whose choices along the way are inspiring. That is a gift."

— Kurt Lorenz, retired educator, community and environmental activist

Shirley DicKard has created a bookstore dilemma with this story: on which shelf will it be housed in bookstores? At once historical fiction, mystery/suspense, futuristic sci-fi, and empowering feminist fiction with supernatural nuance, it could sit well on any number of shelves.

Heart Wood is a climate-change cautionary tale and a celebration of the feminine spirit of nature and the three timeless women who serve as its protagonists, past, present, and future. Each of the three eras—and indeed the characters in them—portrayed in this story is rendered artfully, with intriguing detail, captivating action, and complex human dilemmas. At first, the story seemed like a jigsaw puzzle when you first empty the pieces onto a table. As the chapters unfold, the puzzle takes shape and the picture becomes undeniably clear. This is a work of great accomplishment and a worthy read for anyone, especially anyone who cares about the one and only planet we inhabit."

— Betsy Graziani Fasbinder, author of *Fire & Water*, speaking and writing coach, licensed therapist

"In this fast-paced novel, DicKard has skillfully described the outmoded approach of building dams as an answer to water shortage crisis that is worsened by climate change. She then gives a highly technical issue a human face by illustrating the fight through the collective power of women working to protect the earth. It's the bittersweet and inspiring novel all future environmental activists need to read."

— Ashley Overhouse, California Water Policy Professional

". . . a provocative journey through multi-generations of women, compelled by a mystical force to disregard the status quo and do whatever they can to make things right—for life, for the environment and for the survival of everyone."

— Jenifer Bliss, Felix Gillet Institute,
author of *Grandma Bunny, Forest Herbalist*

"I was contacted by the author as she researched the California Federation of Women's Clubs (CFWC), and specifically her Great-Grandmother Emily Hoppin, who had been involved in CFWC and was elected President of the state federation in 1915.

The California Federation of Women's Clubs is affiliated with the General Federation of Women's Clubs (GFWC), an international women's organization dedicated to community improvement by enhancing the lives of others through volunteer service for more than 126 years. The Clubs of CFWC are located throughout California with the primary purposes of carrying out charitable service programs, providing leadership opportunities, and enriching the lives of its members through personal growth.

Founded in 1890, GFWC's roots can be traced back to 1868 when Jane Cunningham Croly, a professional journalist, attempted to attend a dinner at an all-male press club honoring British novelist Charles Dickens. Croly was denied admittance based upon her gender, and in response, formed a woman's club—Sorosis. In celebration of Sorosis's twenty-first anniversary in 1889, Jane Croly invited women's clubs throughout the United States to pursue the cause of federation by attending a convention in New York City. In 1890, sixty-three clubs officially formed the General Federation of Women's Clubs.

I was struck by the similarities of women in *Heart Wood* with all the women involved in the CFWC from the beginning—women like Emily Hoppin. They were and are the backbone of every part of our lives, be it home, business, social, or political. In the early days, women were considered second-class citizens, but Emily rose above the norm of her day and was a shining star. Shirley has brought to life three strong women. It was a privilege to be involved with this book."

— Deborah E Bushnell, state chair,
CFWC Women's History and Research Center

"*Heart Wood* is a journey through time connecting three women, their deep relationships to the natural world, and their struggles to survive in a world being destroyed by men's actions. Part historical, part futuristic, and part mystical, the heartwood of the mighty oak is a portal through which the women of one family find strength to speak to the issues of their times."

— Sushila Mertens, co-author of *A Women's Guide to Sacred Activism*,
a living room conversations library partner, and end of life doula

"First, do no harm. As a physician, I know these ancient words apply not only to healing people, but also to the environment. Almost daily, we witness the mounting climate crisis through visual evidence and indisputable facts. As an eco-novel, *Heart Wood* goes a step further and immerses us in what it might be like to live in a future world where children live in chronic respiratory distress because of polluted air, where they can't tolerate most foods, where it's impossible to stay hydrated because of excessive heat and the lack of clean drinking water, and where human fertility plummets. *Heart Wood* is a cautionary tale, yet one of unexpected insights and hope. You'll find yourself asking what you can do right now that your great-grandchildren will thank you for!"

— Christine Newsom, MD and environmental activist

"*Heart Wood* is a compelling family saga set in the foothills of California's Sierra Nevada. Its characters shift from one generation to the next, as do the struggles they face in saving their homestead from the ravages of climate change, fire, and human greed. But it's time that poses the most dire challenges to the land and to those who seek life upon it.

Shirley DicKard deftly weaves the worlds that time turns up, from the pastoral world of the 19th century to the menacing environment of the future that transforms the homestead into a refuge. She writes from a knowledge of California's hills and rivers, and with a fine eye for detail. Heart Wood's fluid journey into both the past and the decades yet to come should not be missed."

— Leslie Rivers, actor, director, teacher, and
author of *Fiery Star: The Journals of Emma Rose Lightfoot*

HeartWood

Shirley DicKard

Cover design, family tree, and map by Mariah Lander, Blue Avocado Design

Interior design by Joan Keyes, Dovetail Publishing Services

Excerpt by Gary Snyder from his *Good Wild Sacred* chapbook, Five Seasons Press, 1984.
Used with permission of author.

Author photos by Lisa Redfern, Redfern Studio

Printed in the United States of America
First Edition

Sierra Muses Press
Nevada City, California

One must learn to listen. Then the voice can be heard.
The nature spirits are . . . alive under our feet, over our heads,
all around us, ready to speak when we are silent and centred.
So what is this 'voice'? Just the cry of a flicker, or coyote,
or jay, or wind in a tree, or acorn whack on a garage roof.
Nothing mysterious, but now you're home.

— Gary Snyder, *Good Wild Sacred*

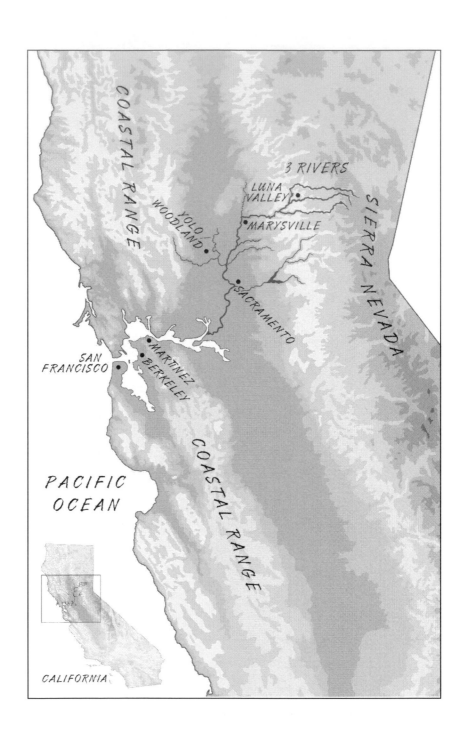

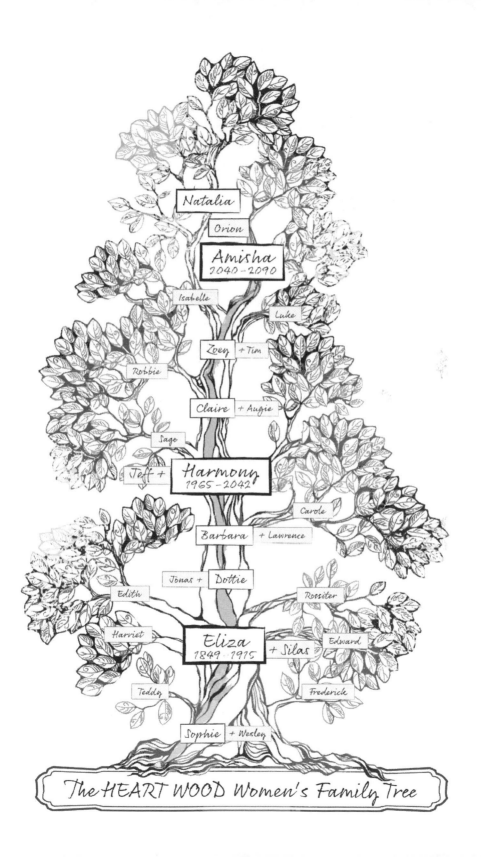

Natalia

Orion

Amisha
2040–2090

Isabelle

Luke

Zoey + Tim

Robbie

Claire + Augie

Sage

Jeff + **Harmony**
1965–2042

Carole

Barbara + Lawrence

Jonas + Dottie

Edith

Rossiter

Harriet

Eliza
1849–1915 + Silas

Edward

Teddy

Frederick

Sophie + Wesley

The HEART WOOD Women's Family Tree

SHIMA'A

An ancient woman knelt by the shallow grave she had prepared for herself, her breath faint as the rustle of dried leaves. Shima'a knew it was time. She had lived her long life on this great river. From the hushed moment when she entered the world with a birth veil covering her face, her people had treated her differently. As a child, she saw what others did not see, heard what others were unable to hear, and knew what could not be known by mind alone. Her people respected her guidance, yet when she spoke as she had last night, they kept their distance.

Shima'a thought back to her final words to her people. With her frail shoulders draped in fox pelts, she stood on trembling legs to speak through the spiraling smoke of the evening circle. The men had completed their talk, and all was quiet. She searched the faces of her people, but not one would return her gaze. As smoke drifted across her eyes, clouding her sight to this world, Shima'a cried for the earth's future one last time.

I see rivers that hold only death in their waters and children who cannot breathe the air. Fire will blacken great mountains and wide valleys, leaving the earth parched and angry.

With a hushed voice she continued.

One by one, our plant, fish, and animal brethren will slip away and disappear forever. Even the seed of our people will no longer make life.

1

When at last her sight returned to the fire circle, Shima'a saw only confusion and concern in the faces of her people—not for the future she foretold, but for her. With a heavy heart, she motioned to be led back to the sleeping lodge, but sleep would not come. She feared her words would wander unheard and prayed for a way to reach through time to touch the hearts of women.

In the dark of night, lit only by a sliver of moon, Shima'a slipped out to the river while her people slept. She followed the path along the riverbank until she came to the circle of stones she had hidden in leaves, knowing this time would come. She waited until she knew the crackling of footsteps around her arose from woodland animals and not from her people. She must not be disturbed.

Alone now by her grave beside the great river, Shima'a brushed aside the raven feathers she had woven into her hair and went over preparations for her last breath. All was complete: an oblong depression within a circle of river stones, a long band of white doeskin, and the acorn she held in her hand.

Shima'a had searched many days for this very acorn—a smooth, dark amber shell that contained the strength of an oak tree—one whose spirit could travel for generations. Now, under cover of darkness, she sang to the acorn, her voice rising and falling like the earth's heartbeat even as her own heart slowed its fragile rhythm. When she had infused the acorn with the power of what it must do, Shima'a wrapped it securely into the middle of the doeskin band and tied the band around her chest so the acorn rested over her heart.

As the night wind caressed her cheeks, pale and cold, Shima'a lay down within her earthen bed and closed her eyes, feeling a deep murmur grow beneath her as if the earth was shifting to welcome her home. She folded her frail fingers around the acorn bound securely over her heart, then, slipping out with the last exhalation of the new moon, she offered her final prayer.

Mother Earth,
Let me be as mist floating above the river of time.
Let me guide distant generations to
Listen to the silence,
Hold the earth in their hands,
Gather the women,
Then do what must be done.

AMISHA

2075
San Francisco, California

San Franciscans were surprised by water falling from the sky. Most water crept in at them from the sea. On Tuesday, September 24, 2075, the shift in the weather came fast and unexpected.

Unanticipated rain today! Nib.news streamed into Amisha's dreams through the miniscule implant behind her right ear, rousing her with its 7:00 a.m. newsfeed. She scrunched the thin blue quilt close to her neck and rolled over.

Get your buckets out! continued Nib.news, glibly ignoring its failure to predict the downpour that now deluged the city.

Orion tugged the quilt back over his bare shoulder. He appeared to sleep, but Amisha knew he was deep into his own newsfeed—street closures, soccer schedule, power quotas, outbursts, followed predictably by a round or two of gaming. She waited until he got the weather.

"What the . . . ?"

She nodded to the rain pelting the bedroom window and, with a right-flick of her eyes, queried her Nib: *Didn't it already rain twice this year?*

Last rain: April 14, 2075. Four point six inches of precip in one hour temporarily raised the Bay five inches. Seawall was moved back two feet. Your closest umbrella stand is corner of Grove and . . . Amisha halted her Nib feed with a left-flick of her eyes.

"No solar. You won't make it across the bridge today," she said. "You should get home and cover your truck bed."

Orion grunted and pulled her across his chest so they were eye to eye. "*Should* go home." He gave a playful tug to the long, sand-colored braid draped over her breast. "But let's stay, try again?"

"Hey," she walked her fingers across the tanned chest of the only person she allowed close enough to touch. "You've cum twice this month. Let the sleeping dog lie." The truth was, Amisha didn't want him to waste himself on her. Healthy, strong, hardly twenty-eight, he could still be a father. When's the last time her Nib gave a fertility nudge? One year, five years ago? It didn't take long to notice that, childless when she turned twenty-four, Nib nudge images of cuddly babies ceased. She turned to Orion, but he was already lost in his game.

Propped up on an elbow, she studied Orion's face as his eyes darted back and forth beneath the lids. He was still the same Orion she met when she moved across the street from him three years ago. Bald, muscled, taller even than she, he had appeared out of nowhere to help haul boxes up to her apartment. The first time he draped his arm around her shoulder, it felt like the brother she wished she'd had. Orion was different—she didn't recoil from his touch.

Maybe she didn't try hard enough to get pregnant. The first time they came together, it didn't feel like mating, not in the *we're-trying-to-make-a-baby* way. It was easy, like an antistress infusion from her Med.pak. Conceiving proved harder. She tossed the quilt around her shoulders and slipped from the bed. Anyway, her life was filled with children at the medical center, though by the time they got to her they were in rough shape. How the hell was she supposed to keep children alive, as her Nib reminded her every morning, when the list of foods they could tolerate kept getting shorter?

Her up-energy tune, "Gotcha," streamed in her head. A minor earthquake temblor passed beneath her feet. A thread of a dream floated up then disappeared.

While she slipped on a white work tunic over her long pants and pressed the "Dr. Hoplin" sticki-label onto her top pocket, she listened to her day's schedule: **In Person office hours 9 a.m. to 2 p.m.**

Food break. Update on Pharm.food advances at 3 p.m. Various recommended hologrammies 6 p.m. to 9 p.m. Sleep at 10 p.m.

Amisha liked being called "doctor," liked being an authority. While Nib.med analyzed children's symptoms; prescribed and monitored treatments with scans, Med.paks, and Pharm.food; the non-responsive cases were given "I.P." time with doctors. Her training was virtual, bodies were not, and the prospect of touching patients made her chronically tense jaw clench even tighter. At least she wasn't expected to embed Nibs behind newborns' ears.

Outside the bedroom window, rain pounded on the sidewalk, overflowed the gutters, and spread over the street in sheets of precious water. A distant wave, like the unrest in last night's dream, pushed against her chest. Amisha rounded her rigid shoulders and waited for her Med.pak to infuse her heart with its blessed relief. Deep breath in, out, in, out.

"Orion!" she called from the bathroom. Of course, he was still gaming. She sent him a mental message but got no response to her ment. Breathe in . . . out . . . in . . . out. Where did she learn to do this? Certainly not her training. She left Orion an urgent ment to contact her.

I.P. hours in thirty minutes, reminded her Nib. **A pedi.cab is passing in eight minutes.** Amisha dropped a handful of general-purpose Pharm.food packages into her aquamarine crocheted bag for her midday food, then checked her route for shootings and outbursts and decided it was safe enough to walk. She needed to clear her head from last night's dream.

Grove Street was clogged with people holding buckets up to capture the rain. Like the rare, clear nights when hundreds flowed from their homes to witness the sight of stars, people were fascinated by water falling from above. Ignoring the "Disperse and Be Safe" warnings that flashed above every corner, pedestrians collected like drops into a slow-moving sea of faces turned upward to the wet sky. Cautiously weaving through the crowd with her long legs, Amisha turned onto Ashbury and headed toward the park. At the curb, an elderly woman wrapped in a ragged shawl tugged at Amisha's soaking wet tunic and pointed her cane at the falling rain. *Milagro*, she croaked. Amisha stared at the old woman, then moved on.

A string of pedi.cabs drawn by thick-legged young men passed by. Amisha shook the muddy spray from her pants and mented Hailey that she'd be late. Her efficient assistant mented back the records of her first patient, Ravena, to review on the walk over, but Amisha closed them down with a quick left-flick of her eyes. She preferred to feel the rain and think about stars.

Come . . .

What?

North Star will come onto the horizon at 10 p.m. this evening, her Nib filled in.

Something about her dream welled up again, distant, uneasy. Within seconds, a surge of well-being spread through her body, and Nib.know launched its predictable commentary for this intersection: **Entering Golden Gate Park. Once called "The Panhandle," Golden Gate Park is a nine-block strip east of the original Golden Gate Park's entrance, and the location of the famous "Human Be-In" and "Summer of Love" of 1967.**

Amisha tried not to think about the original park, but it was too late; her Nib continued: **The original Golden Gate Park, built in 1871, was three miles long and a half mile wide.** A vitru.pan popped up showing the original park—miles of green rolling hills, museums, lakes, shaded trees, and open meadows—even a moving ring of bobbing animals, children, and music.

"Now, nearly two hundred years later," Amisha recited out loud with the Nib, "its three-mile-long tent city generously houses Oceania's Pacific Rim immigrants."

"Because," Amisha added, "most of Polynesia, Micronesia, and Melanesia are under water."

Set my pace to be at work by ten, she directed her Nib, then matched her stride to the internal clicks and quickly moved away from the tent city. Perched on the hill across the park, the University Hospital sat humped like a headless Mount Rushmore. Rubble from both Great Quakes was piled high behind it, ready to be hauled down to the Embarcadero Seawall to keep the encroaching saltwater at bay.

Half the city's rubble had already been dropped into the Financial District's Seawall to no avail. The sea slipped in like a thief in the night.

Amisha stepped around a pedestrian waiting for his directions to download. *Raindrops are like falling stars*, she mused. She'd seen stars before. Night skies full of them.

Order an imprint of *The Starry Night*, one of the Dutch painter Vincent van Gogh's most famous paintings . . .

No! With a sweep of her eyes, she L-flicked the image away. Where had she seen stars? She couldn't remember.

Perhaps you're seeking vintage films. *Star Wars*? *Star Trek*?

No!

Movie stars? Tom Hanks in *Forrest Gump*?

No!

***The Green Mile*?**

No! Wait, it had been a while since she viewed that one. OK then, tonight, after food. She picked up her pace so she didn't dawdle in the old Haight-Ashbury district with its broken windows still boarded against a bygone era.

Was it at Gramma Claire's? Stars and green hills . . . She tried to focus on her memories, but the Nib imposed its own version of everything green.

"Green, oh shit." She retrieved Ravena's report with an R-flick, then overlapped it with the other reports of Herbie with his newly dyed black hair, Allie with her sweet, crooked smile, and frail little Christophe. There it was in plain sight: a new intolerance—this time to chlorophyll. With a quick L-flick, she closed the records and squeezed her lids tight, preparing for the wave of anxiety to spread across her chest. *Closest bench?* she queried her Nib, then sat down as the light-headedness came on.

"Dr. Hoplin?" The pedi.cab driver stood by his open passenger door. "Dr. Hoplin?" he repeated. Amisha accepted the ride without a word and crawled onto the plastix seat and closed her eyes.

Hailey stood waiting by the front door of the University's Pediatric Clinic. She took her boss's bag and guided her upstairs past the exam room where Ravena and her parents waited, to her office across the hall. With her white plastix spectacles conveying more authority than she possessed, Hailey smoothed back her curtain of black bangs and gave her boss a brief but penetrating look.

"I sent the pedi.cab when I detected you hadn't moved for a while. When you didn't reply, I figured you were either hypnotized by the rain or having another spell."

"Good call, thanks." Since the last big quake, everyone was tied into the Omni-Alert System. Amisha knew there was no place where she couldn't be helped.

"Give me a few minutes." Amisha closed the door to her private office, swept aside a stack of small paper notes, and propped her head in her hands. It was so obvious—why hadn't chlorophyll intolerance already been picked up? From her pants pocket, she retrieved a string of cobalt blue beads and untied the loose knot. Antique Turkish worry beads slid one by one into the metal bowl on her desk, ready to be restrung for the zillionth time. They rattled in unison as a small earthquake temblor shuddered the earth.

Amisha pulled the silk cord through the eye of the largest bead. What the hell am I supposed to do? Ravena's parents are waiting for me to wave a magic wand, but I haven't been given one yet.

You'd like to order the newest fantasy wand? Amisha rolled her eyes and deleted with an L-flick.

She mented Hailey to bring her hard-copy records of today's patients. No, she didn't have authorization to print. Do it anyway. Half an hour later, with a look of exasperation, Hailey dropped the papers onto her desk.

"Next time, send me to the moon."

Amisha spread the records out side by side. She first detected Herbie's and Allie's intolerances to soy ingredients when they were two months old, Christophe at four months, and Ravena at six months. Ravena's mother was allowed to breastfeed her for six months, as her milk had tested low for toxic accumulations. When switched to Pharm.milk after six months, Ravena's troubles began. Amisha prescribed each of them the Red Pharm.food regimen for soy intolerance. A year later she prescribed the Pharm.food regimen for wheat intolerance, with its bright gold wrappers. Ravena became uncontrollably irritable. Her only relief came from the Med.pak cartridge inserted in the right lower quadrant of her abdomen that continually infused smooth muscle relaxants into her irritable intestines.

Intolerance to corn, rye, lactose, tree nuts, peanuts, wheat, gluten, glucose, lysine, and tryptophan followed in turn, accompanied by shredded intestinal mucosa; angry, blistered skin; massive headaches; gradual deafness; and sores that didn't heal. With each emerging intolerance, Pharm.food developed a new regimen in a unique color-coded package, as well as an expanded array of related Med.pak cartridges. But for chlorophyll, they had nothing. And chlorophyll was present in most everything that was still safe to eat. With a quick stoop before the hallway mirror to see that her name tag was on straight, Amisha entered the exam room.

"Hail, Ravena!" She held up her palm in mock salute but backed off when she saw the eight-year-old child propped between her parents. "Whoa," she softened her voice. "What's with my little girl?"

Mr. Belange cleared his throat. "Nib.med instructed us to give her nothing but Soothing Pink Pharm.food, but she won't eat. *Can't* eat." He cleared his throat again. "Look at her."

Eyes listless and sunken, Ravena tried to follow Dr. Hoplin's instructions to move her arms or turn her head, but her muscles couldn't obey.

"Lips coated with minute pustules," Amisha mented her observations then, after using a tongue blade to inspect Ravena's oral cavity, added, "pustules coat oral mucosa and presumably the length of her intestinal track."

"How often does Nib.med track her?"

"Every day," her mother said. "But when the results come back, it tells us to continue as prescribed."

The flatness in Mrs. Belange's voice bothered Amisha, as if she already knew her daughter wasn't going to make it. On the wall behind Mrs. Belange, a verdant green poster with a spinning earth touted Pharm.food's mission—*To Feed the World.*

Yeah, but how can you feed the children when you can't keep them alive, Amisha wondered. She wished at once she could retract the thought, but it was too late.

"Shit." Amisha slumped against the wall to wait out the light-headedness.

"You OK?" Hailey mented.

"Yes," she mented back.

"No, you're not."

The door to the exam room flung open and Hailey rushed over. She was used to answering Nib.alerts when her boss was having an episode, but this time, her armful of Pharm.food samples fell to the floor like mice skittering for cover.

"Number three this week," she said under her breath as she whisked the Belanges out the door. She felt the back of Dr. Hoplin's neck. "You've gone dry again."

Amisha turned her head.

"I'm getting you water," Hailey said out loud for emphasis and slid her card into the Water.well's receptor.

"Not from your allocation." Amisha nodded to her purse hanging on the wall. "Mine's in there."

"Forget it," Hailey said. "I've drunk enough today, and unless you get enough water in you, your episodes won't stop." She set her boss's amber measuring glass under the spigot and filled it with the murky, menthol-enhanced water from one of the few sources available to San Francisco: a mixture of water reclaimed from old fracking wells and low-salt sea water.

Amisha kneaded the clamped muscles around her jaw while waiting for the restless particles to settle into circular grooves along the bottom of the glass. After drinking the top two-thirds, she handed Ravena's report to Hailey. "Another one."

Hailey scanned the rows of numbers and words with glazed eyes.

Amisha snatched back the report. "Here, look, bottom of the page . . . Chlorophyll Intolerance."

"Chlorophyll?"

Amisha sighed. Every time she got close to improving a child's symptoms, something new got in the way.

"Isn't chlorophyll green? I mean, aren't plants green?" Hailey retrieved a food sample from the floor. "Gluten, Soy, Lactose,

Fiber, Sugar, and Nut-Free. "Will Pharm.food make one for chlorophyll?"

"My hands are tied until they do." An image of S-M leather popped up.

Are you fit to be tied? ran the subtitle. Disgusted, Amisha whisked it away.

"It's all there in the reports—this manufactured food is killing our kids."

Hailey put her finger to her lips to silence Amisha. "What are you gonna do?" Hailey returned to menting as she collected the rest of the samples and stacked them next to the canister of bamboo pencils.

"Wait to see what they're going to come up with next." Prepared now for the familiar pressure that swelled beneath her breastbone whenever she questioned Pharm.food's practices, she exhaled with pursed lips, inhaled, exhaled again, waiting for Med.pak to do its trick. Nothing.

Empty rebalancing cartridges can be refilled tomorrow at 7:00 a.m., her Nib informed.

"No! I need it now!" Amisha shot back an Urgi.ment. The reply was obscured with static. Options? She'd popped her last nitro tab years ago, and what were probably the last two aspirins in the world were in her medicine cabinet at home. She L-flicked away the offer for a perfusion of nanobot scavengers and refused to zombie-out on the Pharm.pain regimen. But it wasn't just pain. A deep foreboding rose up like waves washing over half-built seawalls.

"I'm calling a pedi.cab," Hailey said. "You're going home."

Amisha raised her hand in protest, then dropped it as Hailey grabbed her crocheted bag and guided her downstairs to the waiting pedi.cab.

"Reschedule Ravena for tomorrow," she wheezed.

"No," Hailey snapped. "You're taking tomorrow off, and I'm getting Dr. Bruno to order a work-up for you."

"Nonsense." Amisha waved her off.

As the pedi.cab pulled onto 7th Avenue—clogged with a steady stream of cyclists, high-speed pedi.cabs, and occasional solar-paneled sun.autos—Amisha settled back into the open-air seat and mented the cyclist to take the back route to 1228 Grove Street. "They must have moved the seawall back again today," she said as he pushed through a crowd burdened with their worldly belongings.

The cyclist grunted and changed gears.

"Why do people wait 'til saltwater licks their front door before they evacuate?"

"Dunno." He extended his left hand to signal his turn through the maze of travelers then pulled up to her faded pink Victorian, paused for a temblor to pass, then helped her up the steps to her front door.

Simple and functional, her second-floor apartment offered a reprieve from the world, with water and food prep in one corner, a double futon bed in the other, a five-drawer dresser against the wall, and, in the center, a table and two chairs for when Orion came over. Behind a narrow door was her bathroom with its dry compost toilet and sink, and a mirrored medicine cabinet mounted so low she rarely saw above her chin unless she stooped. Decorating with what bits of color she had, she hung her aquamarine bag on a wall hook, propped Gramma's old red vase between two books on her dresser, and covered her bed with great-grandma's faded blue quilt.

From the front window, Amisha noticed that Orion's truck hadn't moved, meaning he was still home. Too weary to even ment him, she finished off yesterday's nut butter sandwich, stripped off her clothes, pulled the quilt over her head, and dropped into an exhausted sleep.

The old vase on her dresser was shimmering red the next morning when Amisha raised her head from the pillow. Most days started this way. Though the rising sun was rarely seen, its warmth caused micrometal particles suspended in the air to scintillate in a vague morning glow, casting a sense of dawn across the city.

"Red, first to show. White, last to go." Memories of Gramma's deep raspy singsong circled up like smoke rising from last night's dream. She'd been there, wandering among the flowers at the old place, searching for dawn's first red petals. Another world.

Seven a.m., rise and shine. A new day. New children to keep alive.

Dreams and distant memories rose like mist before her eyes, nudging her back to the other world.

Your schedule is . . .

Amisha dropped her feet onto the bare floor as Nib.news relayed her schedule. Her chest felt better. Sleep must have done her good. An old place in the mountains. Had she visited? Or was this wishful thinking? She'd been very young.

Ten to noon, meet with Dr. . . .

She'd lost track of the place since Luke. All she had left was Gramma's chipped red vase with nothing to fill it.

I.P. hours now 2 to 4 p.m. due to unscheduled power save.

Another temblor rippled across the room. Would the aftershocks ever end?

Avoid corner of Hayes and Filmore, shooter outburst, six injured and . . .

Amisha reached for the plastix sandals she left on the floor. Something changed the year she turned twenty-five. Not just her fertility. Like something was . . .

Your role now is not to have children, but to . . .

Amisha tried to close down her report.

. . . keep them alive.

Something swelled from beneath the Nib drivel. Something wandering through her memories, calling, stirring up fragments, like tendrils of dreams beckoning her down. Some she knew, others—well, it wasn't unusual to cross over anymore. Last week she awoke thinking she was in Orion's dream, shared it with him, scared him. Was her Nib beginning to fragment already?

She slipped a work tunic over her head and dropped her braid down the outside. Her pants lay crumpled on the floor where she had tossed them yesterday . . . something uneasy about yesterday. She reached down . . . Ravena . . . chlorophyll.

"Shit!" She flung her pants across the room. "Shit!" The red vase tottered. She lunged, arm stretched out, stop, please, shit! Pants collided with glass, glass collided with floor, shock waves exploded the vase into a thousand pieces, a distant echo shattered free, so faint she almost didn't hear.

It's time.

Sharp glass pierced the soles of her feet.

Come home.

"I am home."

May we offer you the comforts of homecare cuisine? Delivered to your home in . . .

"Shut up!" she clapped her hands over her ears. "Leave me alone!"

It's time . . . Come.

Amisha collapsed to the floor. "I can't!"

Come home.

She rocked. Pain splintered her knees.

Floating homes are now available in the freshly renovated City Harbor. No need to ever evacuate again.

Amisha pounded her fist into the mound behind her ear as if she could break it.

Never evacuate again, again. . . . Static emissions continued.

"I am home!"

Your home is 1228 Grove Street, San Francisco, California.

"Stop! I'm trying to hear . . ."

Hearing tests are available free to medical staff, you have only to . . .

Amisha grabbed a sharp glass taper and stabbed at the mound behind her ear. Red dribbled. Deeper. Pain frizzed through her neck, down her arms. She dug at her Nib from below, from above, circling around the edges, lifting, leveraging it open like a manhole. Her left arm twitched. She couldn't see her bed across the room.

Code Red, Code Red!

She was going to die. Not the long, slow walk into the waiting sea she'd imagined. This might be easier.

Unable to stop, she tunneled the shard deeper beneath the pulsing Nib, prying at the thin bioelectric-gel rootlets until they snapped in an unbearable firestorm of pain. Her stomach contorted. Partly digested nut butter heaved onto the floor. She dug until she could no longer feel, until she no longer cared that this was the end. With the last of her will, she twisted the taper into the quivering circuitry and popped out her Nib. It slid across the floor in a slick trail of blood and settled beneath the chair. She was too weak to pursue it.

Frozen in a vacuous silence, she drifted for hours, possibly days. A voice wondered if she was alive, could she move, where she was? No, not a voice, threads of thoughts—her own thoughts. She heard what she thought. She was inside. What was outside? Her finger wiggled against the floor. Someone had lit a searing fire against her neck. Then nothing. Again, that voice thinking thoughts in her head. What's today? No calendar appeared. Disconnected, deaf inside, underpants wet.

She should move. Breathe in. Breathe out. Deeper. She lifted her lids, a hairline of light, morning shimmer. She raised her hand before her face. Fingers appeared then faded. She heard her voice outside her now. "One, two, three, four, five." Then nothing. A knocking outside, over there, her door. Louder, then gone. She mented Orion, but something was very wrong. She covered her eyes and tried to cry.

It's time.

Amisha squeezed her lids shut. Please, no more! Blood oozed down her neck. She rocked, unable to stop. Then she saw them. Long, birdlike bones and blue veins hovered over her curly blond ringlets, then reached down through the shimmering green to gather her tiny fingers.

Come home.

"I don't know how." She curled in tighter.

We're waiting.

"Then help me."

ELIZA

1849–1861
Niles, Michigan

Long ago, a young oak spread out her leaves and settled her roots into a wide meadow on the bank of the Saint Joseph River. For over three hundred years, she offered her acorns for food, her branches for shelter, and her green canopy for shade. But her final offering was yet to come.

Eliza loved Grandmother Oak—the landscape of her life since birth. While the whole world seemed to be rushing off for California's gold, she lay beneath the oak tree's shimmering green, imprinted forever with shifting light and shadows.

Eliza's mother Sophie discovered that her infant would rest content for hours beneath the oak tree, and soon a path the width of a baby carriage connected the front porch of the two-story brick house to the big tree across the meadow. While Eliza's older brother Frederick tossed stones down by the water's edge, Eliza rested in her carriage, mesmerized by the dancing greenery overhead.

By the time her younger brother Teddy arrived, Eliza was no longer content to merely observe. She discovered her own river stones circled around the base of the trunk like the ring of pearls around her mother's throat. She explored the trunk, so large that not even Papa could fit his arms around it, and searched for short snags and small crevices that would fit her hand or foot. High over her head,

19

four large branches came together over the center of the trunk forming a hollow, and she wanted up!

On a windy January afternoon, the day before her seventh birthday, Eliza slipped out of the house alone, determined to reach the top of her tree. She pulled off her black boots and stockings, tucked the bottom of her blue calico skirt inside her bloomers, and climbed up to her last-known toehold. With her left hand clutching a stubby snag and her right hand dug into a crevice, she scoured the trunk for a toehold for her left foot. Her eyes were almost level with the top of the hollow when she felt her skirt slipping from her bloomers. Without thinking, she released her left hand to grab the skirt. As her left foot scrambled against the trunk, she grabbed higher for balance. As if lifted by a gust of wind, Eliza fell headfirst into a nest of soft dried leaves and green moss that filled the hollow.

From that moment on, Eliza and her Grandmother Oak were constant companions. After school, with books bound in a leather strap, she rushed across the meadow and settled into her nest, always facing west into the setting sun—the only direction she could stretch out her legs in comfort. Over the years, the books she brought changed from children's pictures and poetry to Emerson and Shakespeare. Later she borrowed Papa's *New England Journals* and the letters from his friend Silas in California. She read and reread the descriptions of life in California until she felt transported there.

A rhythm developed in her afternoons with Grandmother Oak. With a book propped against her upturned knees and her head resting against a large branch, she read until, lulled by the shimmering shadows overhead, her eyelids closed and she drifted into a slumber. At first her dreams flowed with softness: lush meadows filled with songbirds and green forests that went on forever. But as she grew older, she would awaken from her dreams feeling uneasy, as if whispers hovered about her shoulders and plucked the hairs of her neck. She was glad when the dinner bell called her back to a world she recognized.

Eliza's father, Wesley, drew back the lace curtain from the window on the stairway landing and squinted at the oak tree across the meadow, a habit he developed when he and Sophie discovered where their daughter passed her afternoons.

"It's not natural, her spending so much time in that old tree." The judge released the curtain and continued up the stairs to the bedroom, his wife trailing behind him.

"Give her time, she'll grow out of it," Sophie said. "And it's not an *old* tree, it's an *oak* tree. And for some reason, it's her special tree."

"Either way, makes me uneasy."

"At least Eliza is reading. We can't say that about . . ."

"Give the boys time, too," Wesley snapped. "They'll catch up."

"I'm not so sure about Frederick," Sophie said. "He'd rather be down at the river with his friends."

"That's precisely my point. Eliza should spend time with young girls, have other interests, something more ladylike."

"She'll come around." Sophie rolled her eyes and handed Wesley a white shirt, still warm from the iron.

"What do you think? Gray tweed or black suit? I've got the McKinley land case to settle this afternoon."

"Black, definitely." Sophie folded his favorite threadbare sweater and put it on the dresser. "The postman delivered another letter from Silas. Are you going to read it at supper?"

"Why not? We all want to know how he's getting by since he left the mines for farming."

"I thought we weren't going to talk of California. It gets her so wound up."

"Sophie, you worry about her friends, I'll worry about California."

Sophie removed his black trousers from where they hung in the closet. "Does she still take your *Atlantic Monthly* up to the tree?"

"Sometimes before I get to read them myself. What the devil could—" He sucked in his waist, fumbling to buckle his belt, then threw the belt on the floor.

Eyebrows raised, Sophie handed him his black suspenders. "Stop by the mercantile after the hearing," she said. "Ask the Vardells for a belt two sizes larger."

With a snap, Wesley set the suspenders on his shoulders then slipped his arm into the jacket that Sophie held for him. "That's most likely where she gets her peculiar questions—from your periodicals," she continued.

"Last week, she wanted to know when our river is going to run dry."

"Whatever did you tell her?"

"About the river? Oh, I assured her our river's far too big to dry up. There's always more rain to keep it flowing the way the good Lord intended." He placed his hand on Sophie's shoulder. "It's not her question that disturbed me. It's that she insisted I wasn't telling her the truth."

The dinner bell rang three times before Eliza registered the sound.

"But I just got here!" She wrapped Emerson's poetry and her father's journals in her leather strap, bunched up her skirt, and backed down the six feet of tree trunk. As the sun dipped beneath the horizon, Eliza slipped into her seat to the right of her father and bowed her head.

"We thank thee, Lord, for all thy bounteous goodness bestowed upon us." Wesley paused to raise his eyebrow at Teddy and Frederick's fidgeting.

Please let this be his short version, Eliza prayed, but her father droned on.

"Bless the hands that have prepared this food, for we are nothing but humble servants in your sight."

Eliza drifted back to Emerson, her day's companion.

> *The word unto the Prophet spoken,*
> *Was writ on tables yet unbroken;*
> *The word by seers or sibyls told,*
> *In groves of oak, or fanes of gold,*
> *Still floats upon the morning wind,*
> *Still whispers to the willing mind.*

She imagined herself a sibyl, long flowing white robe beneath an oak, or even Queen Califia, ancient ruler of California.

"Amen!" Wesley boomed.

Sophie passed a rose-point dinner plate for him to fill with thinly sliced pork roast; then she added boiled white potatoes and end-of-season string beans and passed the plates to Frederick, Eliza, and Teddy, in order of their age. After the perfunctory sharing of the day's news, Wesley cleared his throat and pulled out a yellowed envelope from the inside pocket of his vest.

"Received another letter today from our friend in California. Seems he's now gone back to farming."

Eliza looked up. "Read it, Papa, read it!"

Wesley removed the thin parchment pages from the envelope, mumbling that it hardly seemed twelve years since Silas had left for the goldfields.

Cache Creek, California
October 13th, 1861

Dear Wesley,

I write to let you know that I am well, and to inform you of my new business raising cattle and growing barley at my Cache Creek ranch across the valley in Yolo. There promises to be a good market. Quite a number of old bachelors here think of returning home and getting married. Although I am doing fairly well, California is making a few rich while it impoverishes the many. You may think me strange, but I have been thinking of living in this country for some time. I think it one of the most delightful and healthy climates in the world.

Wesley took a sip of water.

"Go on, Papa, go on!" Eliza urged, her chin resting in her hands.

As to this new war, I see no end to it, and unless the Federal forces succeed in some decisive hard-fought battle, the chances are about equal for the dissolution of our Republican form of Government. Yet I hope that day may never come, as with it goes man's best hope of civil law on earth. It would interest me to hear how people back home view the institution of slavery.

"Slavery!" Eliza jumped from her seat to read over her father's shoulder.

Wesley brushed Eliza's hand from his shoulder and continued.

> *For my own part, I think it will be a long time before the American slave will have bettered his condition. I now believe the only practical way the North will ever succeed in conquering the South is in giving freedom to every slave within reach of its armies. That will eliminate the labor of millions of slaves, making the South's cause almost hopeless.*

"What does he mean, 'conquering the South'?" Eliza asked.

"He's being practical, not philosophical." Wesley folded the pages and slid them back into the envelope. "He most likely sees it as a good military strategy for the north—has nothing to do with whether slavery is right or wrong."

"But it *is* wrong," Eliza retorted. "People can't own people—even Africans."

Wesley's eyebrow shot up but before he could respond, Sophie rose to clear the dishes.

"Politics!" She grunted, as the kitchen door swung open. "Eliza, I need your help in here."

"May I have the letter to read again?" Eliza whispered as she bent over her father's shoulder to clear his plate.

"When I'm finished replying, I'll let you know," he said, sucking in his lower lip. How could his daughter be so perceptive when his boys were so oblivious?

HARMONY

1985
Berkeley, California

I know what I want—I've dreamed it a thousand times: Carnegie Hall, my shimmering blue silk gown flowing across the stage as I approach the Steinway. Seated with my fingers poised over the keyboard, a deep inhalation to quiet my pounding heart, and a slight nod to the conductor, the audience will disappear as I enter the world that Chopin composed just for me.

Back in 1981, I was Debbie Durrell, the performing arts music major at UC Berkeley. For seven hours a day, I'd cloister myself in one of the music department's practice rooms and fall so deeply into my music that I'd lose all track of time, only to emerge from the windowless basement amazed it was already dark.

Even at the tender age of eight, my first piano teacher, Mrs. Furnoy, noticed my tendency for excess and, in contrast to her other students, made me set a timer to actually stop playing the piano and take a break. "What eight-year-old has to be dragged away from the piano to eat!" I overheard my mother, Barbara, complain to her bridge group, though I suspect she might have been bragging.

After reading Chopin's life story in Mrs. Furnoy's music library (she had underlined the passages of his stormy affair with George Sand), I fell deeply in love with his music, at once romantic and baroque. After school, I'd drill into my Hannon exercises until my

25

fingers ached, but I knew Chopin awaited me with the seductive harmonies of his nocturnes. Relentlessly, I'd dissect troublesome technical passages until they flowed like warm honey. To me, Chopin offered sweet perfection.

At Piedmont High, my piano teacher, old Mr. Petroff, said my proficiency merited applying to the prestigious Berklee Conservatory of Music in Boston, but Mother and Father wanted the *other* Berkeley, the one close to their home in the Oakland-Berkeley hills, with its familiar sunset view of the Golden Gate Bridge and San Francisco skyline. After all, as a third-generation Californian, I should consider nothing less than the University of California.

I also happened to know Mother considered private college tuition too expensive, although it shouldn't have been, not for an ophthalmologist's family in upscale Piedmont. But the Great Depression had left deep scars in Mother, who still had shelves of tinfoil pie pans from every frozen chicken pot pie we'd ever eaten. I loved my parents, but not their world of appearances, security, and bridge games.

"Work diligently toward your music degree," Mother instructed me as my father dragged the last box of books into my freshman dorm room on the Berkeley campus. "Don't marry a Catholic or Jew, and please don't do anything to tarnish the family name. Remember, you're third-generation Californian."

But I knew what I wanted. The basement practice room became my sanctuary, my house of prayer. Yet, it didn't take me long to realize that on ground level, students who once protested the Vietnam War now shifted to protesting pollution of the planet. Something nagged at me—a vague feeling there was something I should be paying attention to. I bought a copy of Rachel Carson's *Silent Spring* at a student booth in Sproul Plaza when I stopped to sign their petition protesting coal companies and their role in acid rain. It sounded bad, whatever it was.

Then a gust of wind turned my life upside down.

The music department had moved a piano outside to the quad for the free concert I was to perform, a requirement for my performing arts degree. I called it *Chopin for the Planet*!

"How could anyone poison the planet with a heart full of music?" I asked the tie-dyed students sprawled on the grass in front of the piano. Wearing a white peasant dress, my unruly curls cinched with a blue paisley scarf behind my neck, I performed *Chopin's Nocturne, Opus 72, Number 1*, so moody, yet gentle and powerful at the same time. Just as I turned the last page, a gust of wind blew it onto the grass. A passing student ran to retrieve it for me. As his sun-tanned hands placed the page back on the piano, our eyes met, and, shamelessly, I allowed the last note of the nocturne to linger way too long.

"Can I help you pack up?" he asked after the applause subsided, the crowd of students dissipated, and my professors finished their appraisal of my performance. With movements so gentle yet decisive, he lifted my music satchel. As the always-cantankerous latch flipped open, *Silent Spring* fell out.

"Really?" He brushed the grass off the book and handed it to me. "You're into this?"

I nodded at his curly-topped brown mullet, acid-washed jeans, and peace-symbol necklace swinging across his blue T-shirt.

"Coffee?"

He carried my satchel down Telegraph Avenue to the Mediterranean Café, where we ordered two cappuccinos and took a seat in a dark corner of the smoky room.

"By the way," he said extending his hand, "my name's Jeff. I'm in environmental science."

"Debbie, performing arts, but I guess you know that." I slowly released my hand from his. "I've never heard of that department. What do environmental science majors do?" I asked. "Is Rachel Carson a professor?"

"How I wish!"

Casually tucking a wayward lock of curls behind my ear, I leaned in. "Do you really think we're being poisoned? I mean, pesticides and herbicides sprayed all over our food. That's outrageous!" He moved in close, engulfing me in the warm aroma of English Leather.

"Three years ago, I was headed for a business degree."

"Your parent's idea?"

He nodded. "When I realized I couldn't save the planet with that degree, I changed my major to environmental science. Got an interview with the Environmental Protection Agency next week."

"I want to save the planet, too!"

"Really? With music?"

I fell back in my seat. Words eluded me, yet familiar images flooded my mind as if borrowed from another time.

Jeff tilted his head, waiting for me to say something.

Slowly, words emerged from my lips. "I know the music I play may move the soul, but what the earth needs is my feet on the ground." I stopped short, pondering what I had just said, like Mary when the angel announced she was going to give birth to someone really important. We gazed at each other like actors when the orchestra swells and the couple is ready to kiss. Only we didn't. Instead, Jeff reached for my hand.

"Life with feet on the ground means getting dirt on these professional fingers, you know."

I pulled my hand back. I'd have to think about that.

On the way back to my dorm, we stopped by Cody's Books to browse the used bookshelves for earth science books. Downstairs, in the newly expanded science department, my eye caught a dark green leather book lying flat on top of a table of children's books. I picked it up and flipped through the blank pages, but when I tried to place the journal back on the table, my fingers wouldn't let go. I purchased it on the way out and dropped it into my satchel.

Over the next few months, Jeff and I spent so much time together, it was clear we had become an item. I spent most mornings alone in the basement practice room working on my audition selections for graduate school. Afternoons I'd meet Jeff and our friends at Peet's Coffee on Vine Street for caffeine-fueled sessions on how we should react to recent environmental outrages: close call at a nuclear power plant, industrial-waste spill in a major waterway, or reports of the growing hole in the ozone layer from use of chlorofluorocarbons. Evenings we'd retreat to Jeff's apartment where, unbeknownst to my parents, I practically lived—thank god for the pill. With one hormone pill a day, I could cross pregnancy off my list of worries.

A month before graduation, we sat at opposite ends of the avocado-green couch rubbing each other's feet and talking over our day. Jeff was unusually quiet. I tickled his foot to get his attention.

"Hey, you've hardly said a word all evening."

"Don't have much to say."

"Really? Didn't you have another interview with the EPA today?"

He shifted his position to watch kids playing basketball in the park across the street.

"Wasn't it today?" I tried again.

Amid wild shouts, someone made the winning basket. Game over, the group dispersed. Jeff turned back to me.

"Yep."

"And?" I raised my eyebrows, feeling my heart sink.

"Game's over there, too." He started to get up, but with me holding down his foot, he flopped back on the couch, arms crossed tight against his chest.

"Filing papers isn't exactly what I had in mind." He yanked the offer letter from his shirt pocket, balled it up, and overshot the wastebasket by a foot. "No master's degree, no work experience, I've got to work my way up from the bottom. The bottom! Hell, I'm pumped up and ready to fight for the planet right now."

"It's their loss."

"No," he shot back. "My loss."

"How long would you have to file papers?"

"If they like me, most likely until a position opens up."

"That doesn't sound too bad."

He pulled his foot from my grasp and headed to the bathroom. The door slammed behind him. When he returned, he slouched across from me in the mustard-yellow chair from the thrift shop.

"What about you?" he asked at length. "I'll bet you nailed your audition at Mills."

I took a deep breath, unsure how to describe what transpired. "Oh, the performance went well enough. But I'm not so sure I want the graduate position."

Jeff bolted up from his seat. "You what? That's the most prestigious, career-launching graduate music program on the West Coast," he said. "You're insane."

Out the window, a new group of kids was break dancing on the basketball court. While one kid in a big afro spun on his shoulder, another kid in white gloves moonwalked behind him to their cheering friends. I turned my attention from their fun and continued.

"I went into the audition feeling prepared and confident. The music department's chair, Susan Porter, introduced me to the other faculty at the table. Just before I sat to play, they wheeled in this elderly woman with thin reddish-gray hair, all wrapped up in a saffron-colored jacket. She looked like one of those Hare Krishna people only, of course, she wasn't. Susan apologized, saying Ms. Caitlin Lyons is the retired dean of student affairs and requested to be part of the panel."

"That's curious."

"I know, but what could I say? Susan and the other faculty probed me with the usual questions about my strengths, weaknesses, and what I would bring to Mills Liberal Arts Women's College. Then she told me to proceed with my prepared repertoire."

Jeff sat up and leaned forward. "Then what?"

"By the time I completed my repertoire, the old lady had fallen asleep in her wheelchair!"

"What? But that wouldn't impact your score, would it?"

"Wait. There's more. During the discussion afterward, she informed me my playing was not sufficiently passionate."

"How could she know if she was asleep?"

"She then announced that since the graduate positions were almost filled, she personally would not recommend me. Jeff, I nearly burst out in tears."

"I can't believe this." Jeff crossed the room, his jaw as tight as his fist, and pulled the curtain over the window. "Both of us in one day."

"Maybe it's something astrological, like a bunch of planets lined up wrong."

"You've got excellent grades and reviews. And passion? My god!" He yanked down the roller shade on the other window with such force, it released back up again with a loud whirr and flew off its mounting.

"Here's the crazy part," I said, ignoring his ongoing fumbling with the shade. "After the interview, she asked to be wheeled over to me at the piano, then beckoned me closer with her knobby finger—like this," I said, curling my finger like the old woman with the apple in Snow White. "I thought she said she was ninety years old, but her voice was so thin and wobbly I had to lean in even closer to be sure I heard her correctly."

"You didn't take a bite of her apple, I hope."

"She told me she wanted to see me in person because she had such admiration for my great-grandmother. To tell the truth, Jeff, I was taken aback. I asked if she meant my Great-Grandma Eliza, who was just a farmer, or my other Grandmother Rachel, who I hardly knew, but I thought she was a librarian.

"'Eliza Baxter was a woman of deep passion,' Mrs. Lyons told me, 'but she ran out of time.' Then she made some comment about how I've got my great-grandmother's eyes. Her driver came to pick her up, but she waved him away. She still had something to tell me.

"Then she took my hand and whispered under her breath that I truly did play beautifully, but she believed my real passion wasn't here, but somewhere else! She told me to follow the music of that other longing instead.

"Jeff, I've got this eerie feeling deep down that she knows something."

"You told me you'd never give up your music."

"I know. But these thoughts are all so new. I just want to sit with them awhile."

A month later, still needing something to lift our sagging spirits, Jeff treated me to dinner at Chez Panisse for my twentieth birthday. It was a new restaurant near his Shattuck Avenue apartment, and we'd been hearing a lot about its signature of serving only organically and sustainably grown food, like homemade ciabatta, goat cheese marinated in olive oil and herbs, even salad greens grown in the restaurant's garden—their very own garden. I was stoked.

Jeff, too. We talked all the way home about what it really meant to "think globally, act locally"—a phrase we'd been hearing a lot about recently.

"You know the saying that when one door closes, another door opens?" Jeff asked.

I nodded, noticing the glint back in his eyes.

"Well, I'm looking through that new door, and instead of a desk at the EPA or a concert piano, I'm seeing rows of corn and tomato plants, and chickens, and a huge compost pile. I can almost smell the manure heating up the compost." He took a deep breath like he was smelling a sweet rose.

"How about a tool shed for you and a cellar full of canned food for me," I added, my excitement growing as hot as his compost pile. "This is something we can do right now. Hell, I've browsed through enough issues of *Mother Earth News*—it's full of information on how to get back to the land." With Jeff's arm draped over my shoulder, we continued down the sidewalk, dodging kid's bicycles and trash cans waiting for tomorrow's pickup.

"You know," Jeff said as he unlocked the front door and held it open for me. "If the EPA wants work experience, well, this is real-life experience that will work."

"Clever," I said as I kicked off my sandals and set them inside the front door. "We'll just be saving the planet from the ground up!"

After a good laugh, Jeff turned serious. "I know *I* can do this. It's a sidestep from what I set out to do. But I'm concerned about you. Can you really give up your music?" To make his point, he turned the AM/FM radio to the classical station and upped the volume. I retreated to my favorite chair next to the window and rested my head against the top of the cushion, so I was staring at the white speckled ceiling.

"Ever since my audition, I've been thinking about what Ms. Lyons said." I closed my eyes and drifted with the music until a man's voice broke in to announce we'd been listening to Bach's *Two-Part Inventions*. "I want to make a difference in the world, Jeff, and I think what the earth needs now is people willing to stand up and do what's right to protect her. I don't think I'll have to give up my music. I may not make it to the concert stage, but there'll always be pianos around I can play on. I may even teach children to love music. I can easily do that from our homestead. *Our homestead,*" I repeated.

"Are you sure? Turn your back on four years of college just to live in harmony on the land?"

He was playing the devil's advocate to test me, but something he said caused me to jolt. I felt an urgency behind this decision that wasn't there before. A feeling it was time to *come home.*

AMISHA

2075
San Francisco, California

Veiled in San Francisco's early morning mist, Orion's tall, ghostly figure loaded cargo boxes onto "Blue Sky." Each box landed on the rusted blue truck bed with a hollow thump, sending reverberating waves down the dilapidated row of Victorian homes.

Go. Now!

Amisha pulled herself up. The room swirled around her bed. She staggered to the window and clawed back the cardboard patch taped over the glass shattered during the last large quake.

"Orion." Her voice was thin and faint.

Orion looked up.

"Here," she waved. It was too much effort to say more.

He cinched his cargo and meandered across the street.

"Thought we were doing food Thursday night," he called up.

Thursday? Thursday night? Nothing came up from her Nib.

"You've been ignoring me. Did I do something wrong?" he continued.

Amisha had no clue. She waited, eyes searching left and right.

"First you send an urgent ment, then don't answer, not even my knock. You OK?"

Now.

"Take me with you," she whispered.

"But you don't even know where I'm goin'."

35

"You always go across the Bay and upriver."

"Yeah, but . . ."

"I have to leave."

Orion studied her for a minute, then gave his *I've given up trying to make sense of you* shrug. "Sure, come along. I can use the company. Make it fast. Light's finally coming through and I need power to make it back before dark." He started to cross the street but turned back. "Hold on, aren't you working today?" But Amisha had disappeared.

With the room swirling, Amisha dragged her old wheeled backpack out of the closet and opened the top drawer of her dresser. What to take? She grabbed handfuls of underwear, tops, and bottoms. Sweater? Were mountains cold? Shit. How would she know? Wetness dribbled down her neck. When she brushed it away, her fingers returned red. Her head was empty, silent, but she wasn't dead.

The floor buckled as a temblor rippled through.

"Amisha! Light's up. Hurry!"

She swept the contents of her medicine cabinet into her crocheted bag—hairbrush and ties, frayed toothbrush, and a small metal box with her last two aspirin. Vision wobbly, stomach clenching, she vomited the last vestiges of nut butter into the sink. Above her, a stranger with coppery-turquoise eyes faced her in the mirror. Eyes still darkening, she noticed. No commentary, no suggestions followed. Red oozed from the ragged gouge on her neck. She yanked a wide teal-colored ribbon off its hook—the color of her eyes before they changed after years of breathing the nanometallic-saturated air—and wound it twice high around her neck, then into a loose knot.

The Med.pak embedded in the curve of her hip was useless without Nib sensors. No estrogen, mood stabilizers, anticoagulants, beta blockers, thyroid, epinephrine, or antiviral-bacterial-carcinogen factors. This didn't bode well. She slipped a half-used bar of soap into her bag. In the kitchen, she passed over the nut butter and grabbed some crackers and raisins. What else? She topped her backpack with packets of Pharm.food.

Orion banged on the fender. "You still comin'?"

She held five fingers up to the window. Money? No Nib. Can't exchange credits. From under the bed, she retrieved an antique Macy's box and dumped her collection of old Sally Ride coins into a small pouch and stuffed it into her backpack.

One hand on the doorknob, Amisha scanned the tiny room, her home for the last three years. Her head throbbed rhythmically as if in time with—the Nib! She raced across the room and dug her heel into the baby-fingernail-sized tangle of metal and silicon, grinding until she was certain the Nib was pulverized. "Don't think," she said and closed the door for the last time.

"What's going on, Mish?" Orion dropped her backpack on top of his crates and pulled her toward him. His eyes narrowed as he searched her face for clues. "Hey, what's with the ribbon?" He flicked off a spot of dried blood from her neck. Amisha pushed his hand away.

"Whoa. You don't look so good. You're sick? Is that why you're not menting?"

She pulled the ribbon down, exposing the crust of coagulated blood behind her ear. "Dug it out."

"Holy shit!" He exploded. "You'll die without it!"

She pulled the ribbon back up. She knew now this was a lie.

Orion grabbed her shoulders, forcing her to look at him as his eyes searched right and left. "You can't ment, can you? You're cut off from everything now. Can you hear me? Can you think?" He was practically screaming. "What about your balancers? Your heart?"

"Look, I dug it out. I'm still alive."

"Yes, but for how long?"

Amisha shook her head. She had no answers.

"You were fine yesterday morning."

"I wasn't—haven't been for a long time."

"You wandering again in your dreams?"

She was afraid to say more.

"Tell me!"

"Something wants me to go," she said reluctantly.

Orion's eyes widened. "Something at work, Mish? Somebody wants you out? I can check for you."

Come. Home.

She looked up, startled. "Did you hear that?"

"Look, I'm getting you up to Emergency."

"No!" she pulled back, her breath fast and jagged. "I've got to get . . . home."

"Mish *this* is home. You and me and . . ." He knew that by now, her Medi-Pak should have balanced her with an infusion of Calming. As if smelling her fear, he drew her close, his voice low and soothing. "You're scared again. Something happened."

"Come with me," she whispered.

"No. This is from your dream, not mine."

Amisha didn't resist as Orion folded her into his arms and held her close like her mother used to do when she was dizzy with the flu. Mother's chest . . . rising and falling in peaceful silence. She hardly remembered the time of silence, before her parents took her to the tall building, the line of other little children, the sharp stab in her neck, the prickles that grew behind her ear beneath her skin, and the new voice she began to hear. Not like her mother or father's, but just like her old Auntie Su's voice. Before they left the tall building, her father had gently removed the black cord with its metallic square medallion from her neck and dropped it into the receptacle for outdates.

"Now you can hear Auntie Su all the time," he said. "Much nicer than having that old thing dangling from your neck, getting in your way. She'll always be there to help you." Grandma Claire cried when she showed her where they had put the new Auntie Su. "It's called 'Retrofit.' Mother and Father have one, and so can you," she had told Grandma. But Grandma turned away, like she had lost a big battle.

Now the voice was gone. Not Auntie Su, who she had first upgraded as girlfriend Talia, then briefly Jordan, until she got tired of hearing a man's voice. Eventually she installed a nameless voice, programmed to be both competent and comforting to her. Over the last few months, however, she had detected something new, a murmur so faint she thought at first it was static from her Nib. Now and then, a word would break through, then just as quickly be covered over by a wave of Nib drivel. Something was weaving through her dreams at night like a root tip seeking water, seeking her. She'd wake up shivering.

"Amisha?" Orion pulled wisps of long hair away from her face. "Hey, you've gone somewhere. I can't reach you."

She looked up at the squint lines radiating from his dark brown eyes. Grin lines, she called them. "No, not grim lines," she had laughed at him. "Grin, from the silly smile you always wear." Could she live without Orion? San Francisco, yes, even her little patients. But Orion? If she left, he might find someone to have a baby with. He could do it; the world desperately needed more children, but not from her. She was like one of those old salmon fighting her way back upstream one last time, only she had no eggs to offer.

Orion squinted at the sun already moving well across the morning sky. He motioned for Amisha to jump in, then deftly adjusted the angle of the dozen new tech-fit solar panels on the roof as he waited for Nib.check's confirmation that the battery pack was fully charged. Blue Sky started up with a familiar hum; Orion slid into the driver's seat and pulled away from the curb.

"You can ride with me across the Bay. Maybe you'll come to your senses before we reach the Martinez dock."

Neither spoke on the drive down Grove to Market Street, which by midmorning was clogged with cyclists, pedestrians, pedi.cabs, and a few sun.autos. Amisha hunched down into her silent world.

The top half of San Francisco's buildings were nothing but skeletons. After surviving the Big One in 2025, the hundred-year quake, people were understandably taken by surprise when another once-in-a-lifetime quake rolled over the city in 2052. Power was reconstructed once again, but came only in short daily allotments, except for a few undisclosed locations dedicated for emergency services, so they were told. Nib communications resumed—people were freed from the terror of disconnection and not knowing. Rubble that wasn't hauled into the ever-moving sea walls of the Embarcadero, Mission Bay, and Financial Districts was piled high, casting shadows over surrounding buildings.

Orion pulled into line at the portable ticket booth, once called the Ferry Building, and mented his arrival. He turned off the engine to wait.

"Are you ever going to tell me what's in your cargo?" Amisha nodded back to the wood, plastix, and metal boxes stacked in the truck's bed.

"Can't."

"Is it legal?"

"Should be," he replied. "Doesn't much matter."

Amisha felt herself losing ground. "How much longer 'til the ferry?" she asked, reflexively waiting for Nib's reply, but getting nothing.

"Forty minutes, at least."

"Let's walk then." She struggled out of the truck and started down the street toward the old Financial District but didn't get far. The district, once a vibrant collection of purposeful high-rises, was now a forest of toppled buildings standing like barren tree stumps in a swamp. The street ended abruptly at lapping water. Boats floated in front of each building. *When did electric power start failing?* If she couldn't remember on her own, then how was she going to know things now? She reached for Orion's arm, feeling a queasiness return. She could still stay. He'd cover for her.

"Eight minutes," Orion said, and guided her back to the truck.

When did the sea invade the ground floors? she wondered, unable to stop thinking about the inevitable.

Orion started the engine and steered the truck onto the waiting ferry.

The old ferry boat puffed, sailed, burned, or sunned its way across the bay twice a day, using the most available form of power. After circumnavigating the hazardous underwater mausoleum of piers and old Bay Bridge pilings that circled Treasure Island like a coral reef, the pilot maneuvered through the congestion of small sail and rowboats until it reached the aquatic houseboat village of Emeryville. Most passengers disembarked to make the arduous journey up into the Oakland-Berkeley hills. Orion continued up the Bay through the Carquinez Strait to Martinez.

Amisha hung onto the railing of the passenger deck, relieved that most people were menting so she didn't have to suffer random eye contact. She sat next to Orion and, with a vacant expression, also bowed her head.

"What?" she said, startled.

"I said, do you even have a plan?" Orion repeated, seeming irritated at having to talk out loud.

"I'm going to Sacramento. It's where I last saw my brother."

"The one you never talk to? The crazy one you cut off a long time ago? The one who . . ."

"I need something from him," Amisha interrupted. She turned her back and peered down into the rubble bobbing in the murky water. Once the memories were called up, she couldn't suppress them. "'Lukie.' He hated me calling him that. Image was everything to him; 'Lukie' belittled him. It was my only way to get back at him."

"For . . . ?"

"For destroying everything he touched, including my little sister." Her voice turned bitter. "Lukie always had this filmy blackness surrounding him. Something wasn't right, but our parents were too distracted by the collapse to care." Amisha retrieved the cobalt worry beads from her pocket and ran them under her thumb, one by one.

"You're leaving everything to search for a brother you hate? Amisha, it's not just crazy, it's dangerous. Stay away!" Orion threw his hands up in exasperation.

"I think Luke holds the key to where I'm going . . . somewhere in the Sierra."

"You're kidding."

"He owns, no, he stole the old family place from me and Isabelle. It's up in the hills. I think that's what's calling me."

"Amisha, look at me." Orion held her by the shoulders and searched her face. "You're sick. You've got no Nib. Hell, there's no way I can find you." He wiped his sleeve across his cheek. "Even if you find this place, the mountains are dangerous—burned up, no water, no food, maybe ferals. You won't survive."

She blinked back her tears. "In my dreams I'm sitting at a little desk by a window and the sky's actually blue and . . ."

"Amisha!" Orion squeezed her arm until she winced.

She flung off his arm and covered her ears.

"Stop being stupid and come . . . back . . . with . . . me." His words reverberated like distant thunder.

Amisha hid her face and turned away.

The afternoon air shimmered a bronze-gold as the assumed sun made its descent behind the humpbacked tanks that dominated the Martinez hillside. Orion drove a mile back into the abandoned refinery, zigzagging around fallen pipelines, upturned asphalt, and massive black patches of oil-soaked earth.

"I'll take you to the dock. If you're still determined, you can ride upriver with the cargo." He maneuvered the truck around a two-foot pothole, narrowly avoiding breaking an axle. "That's new," he muttered.

As they neared the floating dock, Amisha was assaulted by the foul smell. Orion waved at the waiting sailboat, a young man jumped up, and the two men shifted to the rhythmical flutter of sign language. The young man looked at Amisha, considered, nodded, then continued negotiating in their silent conversation.

"I've told him what he needs to know," Orion said. "He knows you don't have a Nib and it's not safe for him to use his. There won't be much talking either—he's one of the deaf corn cereal kids."

Amisha sighed.

"He knows to drop you off in Sacramento."

"How long will it take?" She eyed the oars and sail.

Orion signed her question. "Two days, depending on wind. Tides are good."

"There is a tide in the affairs of men, which taken at the flood leads on to fortune, omitted . . ." Amisha stopped, unable to recall the rest, weary now with the weight of her decision. She slumped onto a cargo box and studied the man she'd be depending on. A red rash covered one side of his round face and continued down under the neck of his grayed T-shirt. The same rash covered his thick fingers.

"It's the water," Orion offered, interpreting her gaze. "Not contagious."

"His name?"

Orion taught her how to sign "Caleb," then added, "He's also got paper and pencil if you can still write."

Amisha shrugged.

"He's a good man," Orion reassured, but his voice was tight.

Several gulls circled overhead. Their eerie squawks pierced the silence.

"They'll come looking for me when I don't respond," Amisha said. "Please, you've got to tell Hailey I'm OK. I'm taking a vacation. She'll know how to cover. Dr. Bruno can look after my kids . . ." Her voice broke off. "Tell her it's all fine."

"You can still change your mind."

Amisha pressed her face into the familiar muskiness of his chest as if trying to inhale him into her memory.

"Please, tell me this is just a bad dream," Orion said.

"Then come find me."

"How?"

"Hoplin. Luke and Monica Hoplin. That's all I know."

For the rest of her days, Amisha would remember the sounds of waves sloshing against the dock, the bell ringing from Caleb's boat, the heaviness of Orion's footsteps walking her to the boat, the shuffling of boxes as Caleb arranged the cargo for balance, the thump of her backpack landing on the empty bench. But she had no parting words to remember. Orion spun around and jogged back to Blue Sky without a goodbye.

Caleb motioned for her to sit and, with her backpack tucked beside her, she turned for her last sight of Orion, his head slumped against the steering wheel in his truck.

"Oh, Orion," she whispered.

Silently, Caleb shoved off from the dock and guided the boat into the dark strait.

ELIZA
1863
Niles, Michigan

Silas Baxter slid the sharp tip of his pocketknife under the nail of his index finger and removed the last traces of dirt. Fingers spread wide in front of him, he examined each nail once more before returning his knife to the pocket of the first clean pair of pants he'd worn in four months. Mrs. Osborn expected him for dinner at six. Fourteen years is a lot to catch up on, he thought. It'll take more than one dinner to tell all that's happened in California between my letters. Do I look successful? He tilted his head in the mirror, reached for the scissors, and trimmed the edge of his mustache one more time.

Sophie circled the table, placing small, pewter salt and pepper shakers above each place setting. "Eliza, put your book down and help me with the table. And where are the flowers? I asked you hours ago."

"In a minute," Eliza called from the parlor. She closed *The Deerslayer* and set it on the sofa. She was almost fifteen, and dying to find out how Judith Hutter planned to rescue Deerslayer from the Hurons.

"Eliza! And please . . . don't make the arrangement so big we can't see over it. Reverend Foster is short, and I want him seated in the middle." Sophie removed nine crystal water goblets from the hutch and began cleaning them with the soft flannel cloth draped over her shoulder. "And none of your dusty, dried weeds in the arrangement or we'll have Judge Rochester's wife sneezing all evening." She scanned the table with a scowl. "Now where am I going to set the ninth chair? Without so much as asking me, your father invited Silas Baxter who's recently back from California. Eliza, did you hear me?"

Flower arranging was Eliza's favorite thing next to reading. She started in the cutting garden with snapdragons, bleeding hearts, delphiniums, and peonies, but always ended up in the meadow picking dried seed heads on contorted stems and tangles of red berries that she wove into the arrangement. Mother called them weeds but, to her, like the umbrella of dried seeds in Queen Anne's lace, they were the beginning and end of life all in one.

As the grandfather clock in the hallway chimed six, Sophie tucked her hand into the crook of Silas's elbow and guided him into the formal dining room with the rest of the guests following behind. Beeswax candles at either end of the table cast a soft glow over the crystal glasses and brightly polished silverware, each engraved with an ornate letter "O." Eliza had constrained herself with a modest arrangement of pink and purple delphiniums. With an imperceptible nudge, Sophie recentered the vase on the white linen tablecloth.

Silas took his seat to the right of Judge Osborn and waited until his hostess seated herself at the end across from her husband. Following her lead, he unfolded the linen napkin across his lap, his rough fingers catching the fine threads like sandpaper. Better to keep his hands safely concealed on his lap.

The judge lifted his small glass of red wine to his guests. "Welcome Judge and Mrs. Rochester and Reverend Foster. Good to have you back home, Silas."

Silas clinked glasses with a polite smile. Judge Osborn had helped bankroll his first headlong rush to California in '49. In return, Silas tried to keep up a regular correspondence, only asking for financial assistance when he had no other options.

"How long are you staying this time, Silas?" Mrs. Osborn asked.

"Long enough to select new breeding stock for my Holsteins," Silas replied. "A month at best." The starched white shirt borrowed from his younger brother itched against his neck. He paused, waiting to see which of the three spoons Mrs. Osborn was going to use for the creamed soup. *Only need a fork, spoon, and a bowl in California.*

He wasn't used to all the children either, made him nervous. Three of them now. The two boys were probably waiting to bolt from the table soon as they were allowed. But the girl had hardly taken her eyes off him since he arrived. *Is something in my beard?* He ran his fingers through the loose hairs beneath his chin.

"Yes, Ma'am, I would like some potatoes, thank you." Silas glanced at the girl across the table as he dropped a spoonful onto his plate. *Something's familiar about her. Maybe those eyes, the way they squint together under her brows.*

Judge Rochester's booming voice interrupted his thoughts. "How do you aim to get cattle all the way back to California with so much of the country in upheaval with the war?"

"You're right, sir." Silas swiveled in his seat to face him. "I'll admit this is a hell of a, I mean, an inopportune time to be moving cattle. Most able-bodied men are either fighting the war or are a casualty of it."

"Why didn't you join?" Eliza interrupted.

"Eliza." Sophie cast a warning look. "Let the men talk."

"Go on," Wesley said. "I'm interested. Why didn't you?"

Silas shifted in his seat. "After fourteen years out west, I consider myself more a Californian." He took a sip of water. "Washington and Virginia patriots are swarming all over the West, pushing their agenda, recruiting for their armies. Personally, I think they're more interested in our gold than our men."

"You didn't *want* to fight?" Eliza asked.

Silas was quiet for a minute, then answered politely. "Fighting doesn't interest me, Miss Eliza. Farming and cattle do." He leaned toward Wesley. "Anyhow, I think I can hire plenty of men from Niles who still want to try for California's gold."

"Why'd you stop mining for gold, Mr. Silas?" Eliza peered at him, chin cupped in her hands, her elbows propped casually on the table.

"That's enough, Eliza." Sophie grabbed an empty bread plate and rose from the table. "Boys, you are excused to go upstairs, and Eliza, when our guests are finished, please help clear the dishes. I need time to prepare the dessert."

"Mother, *please*. He's from *California*." Eliza glanced sideways at the dinner visitor. "I'll be quiet. I promise."

"I don't mind, ma'am." Silas looked to Wesley for assurance. "It's not often I have the opportunity to be interrogated by a young lady." With a quick wink, he continued. "Actually, Miss Eliza, it wasn't anything like I expected. Too much cold and disappointment. I only lasted a year."

"You said mining was too hard."

Silas raised his eyebrows.

"She reads all your letters. Probably knows each one by heart." Wesley patted his daughter's hand then returned to Silas. "You opened the general store at Goodyear's Bar instead of mining?"

A tree. Silas sank back in his chair. *I remember now. I was saying goodbye to Mrs. Osborn on the front porch before heading west. Why was I holding her baby girl?* He looked to the ceiling, trying to piece together the events of so long ago. *The baby was crying, but her brother was crying even louder inside the house.*

"Sorry, sir, could you say that again?"

"The general store. You gave up mining . . . ?"

"Right," Silas said, collecting his thoughts. "I stayed around the diggings for a while but found delivering supplies to other miners much more lucrative." He looked back at Eliza remembering how she was abruptly thrust into his arms while her mother rushed away to take care of the wailing brother. *I walked her out to that big oak— that's when she finally calmed down. Had the same squinty eyes even back then. Made me laugh. I teased her I'd come back and marry her someday. But here I am, a confirmed old bachelor at forty-one and likely to remain so.*

"Your letters didn't sound very happy then." Eliza's tone was serious.

Silas refocused his eyes at the girl across the table. "Well, Miss Eliza, I finally got smart and left the store *and* the goldfields. The Sacramento Valley was warm and dry with plenty of pristine water and excellent growing soil. I decided to do what I knew best—farming."

Eliza scooted over to the vacant seat next to the dinner guest. "Please, tell me *everything* about California."

As the other guests turned to discussing Lincoln's new Emancipation Proclamation, Silas hunched down eye to eye with Eliza and whispered, "You can hardly walk across a meadow without crossing elk tracks or brushing against wildflowers or finding . . ."

"Gold?" Eliza asked.

"I wish," Silas sighed. "Miss Eliza, California's absolutely the most beautiful place in the world."

"Does it sparkle?"

"Oh, yes!" he said, sweeping his arms open wide, almost spilling his water glass. "When the sun rises glowin' pink over the steep mountains east of the valley or sets all red and orangey behind the rolling hills to the west, it's almost magical." Silas felt a rosy warmth rise in his cheeks and returned his outstretched hands to his lap.

"And in between is all the gold?" Eliza asked.

Silas laughed. "No, that's just where I live in a valley stretched far as you can see with tule marshlands—some reeds as high as my armpits," he said, stretching out his arms to show how tall the stalks were. "I have to wade through a sea of marsh grass on horseback to find the little calves hiding in its tall stalks."

"Are there oak trees?"

"Oaks?" Silas rolled his eyes. "Lord knows, we've got oaks!"

"What kinds?"

Silas thought a minute, then listed the ones he knew from around his house. "There's valley oak, black and canyon oak, and shrub oak. The rolling hills are full of them."

"Like wildflowers in a meadow." Eliza sighed.

"There's also pine, cedar, fir, and madrone. You could build an entire town from the lumber around just one meadow," Silas added.

"No!" Eliza shot up. "They're going to ruin it!"

"Ruin what?" Wesley joined in.

"The meadows . . . they're all going to be gone."

"Eliza, sit down." Wesley commanded, his clenched jaw rippling under his beard. "You have no idea what you're talking about. Our guest is talking of building townships for all the new Californians."

Eliza slumped back in her chair, tears building in her eyes. "But that's how it starts."

Wesley leaned toward Silas. "Don't mind her. She gets these ideas sometimes, but they pass." Wesley nodded toward the kitchen. "Eliza, best you go see how you can help your mother."

Eliza didn't move.

"Now!"

The kitchen door slammed behind her. "Now, Silas," Wesley continued, "what are your plans to develop the four hundred acres you intend to purchase?"

"I'm thinking wheat, barley, and grapes," Silas said. "With Cache Creek down below and the Sacramento River weaving through the whole valley, I've never seen such fertile soil."

Eliza entered and silently gathered a plate, fork, and knife then retreated into the kitchen. With each trip, she slipped quietly around the table as the men deliberated their business. A few minutes later, Sophie swished through the kitchen door and the room was filled with scent of warm, spicy apple cobbler topped with fresh whipped cream. "I hope everyone has room for dessert."

"After eating alone in my wagon for four months, this meal has been a real pleasure," Silas said.

"We were just discussing his plans to expand the ranch," Wesley said to Sophie.

Eliza looked up. "Who lived on your land first?"

"You mean people?" Silas replied, a bit taken aback. "I guess you mean the Indians."

"Are they still there?"

Silas glanced at Wesley as he leaned back against his chair. "Well, miss, when I bought the Harbin grant, there wasn't anyone living there," he said, choosing his words carefully. "I built in an open part near Cache Creek. There weren't signs of Indians, except maybe a few grinding stones down by the water. Don't know I thought much about it, to tell the truth."

Eliza put her spoon down. "Why is it people who are there first always get pushed out? It's true, Papa, isn't it? Who lived here before you built our house?"

Wesley tossed his napkin on the table. "I don't know where you get these far-fetched ideas, but I've had enough. It's just the way the world works."

"But, Papa, I know there were Indians here once."

"Potawatomi," Sophie chimed in. "You still see some around. Mainly downriver."

"Yes! Why'd they leave?" Eliza asked.

"Men wrote up agreements with the tribes," Wesley said. "It's a civilized way of working together."

Eliza jumped up, knocking a spoon onto the floor. "Does that mean if someone came and wanted to live here, we'd have to leave?"

"Enough of this worrying," Wesley said. "No one's going to be chasing us away. Now sit down, young lady, and finish your cobbler. We men still have business to go over."

"Well," Eliza said, not letting the subject drop. "I don't like how the world works. It's *not* civilized. It's like being wild animals."

Silas thought a bit. "Wild animals seem to have their own rules about territory." He tilted his head toward Eliza. "They're pretty smart, you know. When a young mountain lion grows up, he gets kicked out and has to find his own territory."

"There's mountain lions in California?" Eliza's eyes widened.

"Cougars, we call 'em. A young cougar will spend months wandering around like this," Silas maneuvered his hand among the glasses and plates. "He's looking for a new piece of land that doesn't belong to another cougar 'cause he knows he'd be run off if he tried to stay."

"That seems better," Eliza said.

"Well, it's a lot more work." Silas let out a deep growl and clawed at the plate of sugar candies in front of Eliza.

"No!" Eliza giggled. "That's mine." She pushed a bowl of chocolate-covered walnuts toward him. "Go get your own piece!"

As was the custom after dinner, the men followed Wesley to the parlor for a bit of brandy, while the women retired to the sitting room for tea. Eliza pressed her hand into the crook of Judge Rochester's arm and walked him to the parlor.

"Are you *really* against President Lincoln's proclamation?" she asked.

"My dear," he bent toward her as if to whisper a secret, "I'm not against freeing slaves. But I'm not certain it's the thing to do to save the Union, despite Mr. Lincoln's opinion."

"Only *Confederate* slaves would be freed," Reverend Foster said as he held back the deep maroon drapes for Eliza and the Judge to enter.

"So the Confederates won't have their slaves to fight for them?"

"Or cook or repair equipment or work in their factories and farms or build their fortifications or tend their wounded," the Reverend added. "Slaves are their workhorses."

"Thousands and thousands of Africans suddenly free?" Judge Rochester said. "I'm anticipating utter chaos."

"Eliza." Sophie's voice rang from the dining room.

"But isn't it just the right thing to do?" Eliza asked, ignoring the call.

Her father tilted his head. "Which? Preserve the Union or end the institution of slavery?"

"Papa, it's not right for people to own other people like they're a cow or a dog."

Reverend Foster raised his eyebrows. "You may be right about that, young lady, but this matter is quite a bit more complicated."

"Eliza!" Sophie pulled back the parlor curtains. "Mrs. Rochester and I are waiting for you. Tea is getting cold!"

"But this is more interesting to me!" Eliza pleaded. "Father? Reverend Foster? Mr. Rochester?" Silas parted his lips then closed them again.

"Next time, I'm sending Frederick in with the men," Sophie muttered.

Back in the sitting room, Eliza flopped into the chair next to Mrs. Rochester.

"Louisa announced her engagement yesterday," Sophie said as she added two sugar cubes to Eliza's teacup and placed it before her.

"Congratulations, Mrs. Rochester," Eliza said without enthusiasm. "When do they get married?"

"In about a year and a half, as soon as Timothy takes over his father's import business."

"Timothy's been her beau since she was fifteen," Sophie added.

"I know, I know." Eliza slumped farther into her chair.

Sophie pursed her lips. "Why don't you bring down your sampler, Eliza, and we'll all sew a spell."

"I'm sorry, Mother. I'm not up to . . . all this. May I please go upstairs to my room to read?" Before her mother could reply, Eliza turned to Mrs. Rochester with a quick curtsy. "Good night, Mrs. Rochester. Tell Louisa I'm very happy for her." Eliza brushed her lips against her mother's cheek then retreated upstairs.

Sleep didn't come easily that night. Every blink was wet with tears. Eliza pulled the quilt to her neck, then threw it off, aching with such longing. But for what? A white wedding dress like Louisa? No, that's not what she longed for. Eliza extracted herself from the tangled covers. Shadows of branches arched across the wallpaper as if caught by the moonlight and held prisoner against the wall. She pressed her forehead to the windowpane, vowing she would never live out her life here like an old spinster in her solitary room. Outside, moonlight washed the meadow into an unfamiliar landscape.

"What is it I want?" she asked herself. "Sometimes it's this big . . ." She stretched her arms wide as if making an offering to the heavens. "I think I feel it . . . and then it's gone." She dropped her hands and gazed out to the meadow. "Grandmother Oak, you must know what I feel. It's there every time I curl up with you."

At the breakfast table the next morning, Eliza poked at her egg yolk. Yellow oozed between the tines of her fork.

"You could have been a little chick if a rooster had found your momma," she sighed. "But look at you now—broken, cooked, and goin' to be eaten up." She sliced the egg white into thin strips then stirred them into a pool of yolk until her plate looked like straw from the barnyard. "You should be scratching around in the yard like your sisters."

"What are you mumbling about, Eliza?" Sophie removed the salt and pepper shakers and returned them to their tray at the end of the table.

Eliza lurched forward. "I need those, Momma. I'm not done yet." She shook them until her plate was speckled black, then pushed the mashed egg in circles around her plate with a corner of her toast.

"Do you ever feel like someone's right behind you, watching you?" Eliza asked. "Then you turn your head and . . . poof! They're gone."

"What do you mean, watching you?" Sophie raised her eyebrows.

Eliza looked up quickly, then back to her plate. "It's nothing, Momma. My mind just won't stay still sometimes." She thought of the men bantering about important ideas after dinner.

"Momma, what do *you* think about owning slaves?"

The dishes clinked in the sink as Sophie washed then rinsed them in a pan of water.

"Momma?"

"I'm thinking." Sophie sighed, then threw the wet dish towel onto the counter and reached for a fresh one. "You know we don't tolerate slavery here." She put a dried plate on the table, then added quietly, "Free men, yes. Slaves, no."

"What do you mean?" Eliza asked.

Sophie tapped her toe against the pine planks as she thought.

"Momma?"

"Eliza," she said after a long silence. "What I'm going to show you, I cannot even show your father." She opened the back door. "Come out to the porch with me."

Eliza maneuvered around the laundry barrels and brooms stacked in the corner and followed her mother to the railing by the back steps. Sophie pulled back the white quilt hanging on the clothesline suspended between two posts.

"Have you ever wondered why I never take this quilt down?"

Eliza shook her head no.

"Ever notice the design?"

"You told me that's the bowtie pattern."

"See how they all form a line? Which way are they all pointed?"

Eliza pulled the quilt taut then shrugged. "I don't know."

"Well, if you were coming up from the river, and needed to get over to the Foster's barn, which way would you go?"

Eliza pointed north. The Foster's barn? She thought a minute. Why would anyone from the river want to go . . . She grabbed her mother's arm. "Momma!"

"Sushhh." Sophie put her finger to her lips.

"Reverend Foster?"

"No, his sister, Miss Foster."

"And the Rochesters?"

"Mrs. Rochester has her own quilt hanging."

Eliza's thin eyebrows squeezed together as she took it all in.

"It's best if the judges don't know what's going on."

"But they must know!"

"Of course they do, but nothing specific." Sophie shook the quilt, releasing a cloud of dust.

"How many? I mean, they come up from the river?" Eliza asked.

"Usually around dawn. Several a week."

"The biscuits and gravy you took over to the Foster's last week. You said it was for the needy. And Papa's old belt and jacket?"

"Food, clothes, whatever the operators say their passengers need." She took Eliza by the arm. "We better go back inside now."

"And my outgrown dresses you gave away?" Eliza asked as she slipped through the open screen door.

"For the ones with children. To blend in better when they get up to Detroit or Canada, or wherever they're going."

"Momma, I can't believe this has been going on right under my nose!"

"That's exactly how it's supposed to be." Sophie held Eliza at arm's length. "There are many ways to do what's right, Eliza. It doesn't always take words."

HARMONY
1985
Berkeley, California

High in a ceremonial meadow in the Berkeley hills, Jeff and I gaze into each other's eyes and recite the vows we wrote, pledging our commitment to each other and to our new life as caretakers of the earth. I wear an old-fashioned, floor-length, emerald-green dress custom made by the White Duck boutique on College Avenue. No white virgin bride for me—I'm the Renaissance Queen! For Jeff, I picked out a muslin peasant shirt with rainbow suspenders and asked him to keep his sideburns long so he looks old fashioned, too.

My parents are giving their best shot at looking proud, but frankly, I think they're baffled by the churchless ceremony led by a lay minister with his guitar, the wildflower bouquet I picked that morning, the plate of potluck food awkwardly balanced on their laps while seated on Mexican blankets in the grass, and the roving tambourines and jugglers. Jeff and I walk hand in hand among our family and friends. It's all so perfect.

After the cutting of the two-layer, whole-wheat carrot cake, I announce that, as a new feminist, I'm keeping my maiden name. Jeff's parents seem as perplexed as mine. I'm sure they hope this is just a phase and when the reality of raising a family hits us, Jeff will return to pursuing his MBA and I'll change to the rightful family name. I'm sorry, Mr. and Mrs. Clarence Linderman, but Mr. Jefferey

Linderman has no interest in the new corporations sprouting up all over South San Francisco, nor will Ms. Debbie Durrell follow as his chattel.

With the last of the freeze-dried food left over from our Yosemite backpacking honeymoon returned to the storage locker, I pick up the phone and dial home.

"Mom! Didn't someone in the family have land up in the Sierra?" I ask.

"What, no, hello, or how's the new bride?"

I know I'll get nothing from her until I complete this conversation. "Sorry, Mom. Yes, I'm fine. How are you? Did you miss me? Of course, you're the first person I called. No, I didn't get any tick bites . . . nope, no bears either. And yes, it's nice being home again, though Jeff and I loved being in the Sierra. Now, is it my imagination, or did you once tell me some family woman had a little cabin in the Sierra?"

Mother paused as if surprised at my interest in anything family. Or maybe she was hoping I was thinking of starting my own family.

"You might be thinking of your great-grandmother Eliza. I was told she once had a parcel up by the Second River, though why she'd buy land so far across the valley from her Yolo ranch is beyond me."

"Who has it now?"

"Who knows? No one kept track of it."

Later that week, Jeff and I take a two-hour drive to the Oro County assessor's office in the Sierra foothills. Jeff thinks we should have called ahead, but I like the idea of a treasure hunt. Inside the foyer of what seems to be the only two-story building in town, we locate the directory and head upstairs to Room 203.

Curled like a cat over a black Royal typewriter, the senior clerk, with "Mrs. Thelma Cartwright" pinned to her pink sweater, pulls the typewriter's carriage-return lever back to the left so the paper rolls down to the beginning of the next line. Only when a soft bell signals that she is near the end of the following line does she look up at us.

"Yes?" She lowers her chin and peers over her silver-wired spectacles, nearly the same silver-blue as her tightly permed hair. "You're asking for historic records then?" Like a child given an early recess, she jumps from her seat and leads us down the endless beige hallway to the last door.

"Used to be a bank vault," Mrs. Cartwright explains as her arthritic fingers struggle to turn the combination knob right, left, and back again. The foot-deep black door creaks open, and the single overhead light bulb reveals floor-to-ceiling shelves of oversized frayed red-leather ledger books.

"Since you don't know the assessment number or the exact year your great-grandmother purchased her property, you'll have to start at the year 1900 and go forward." She slips on a pair of white cotton gloves, gently blows the fine dust from the top of the 1900 ledger, then hoists the heavy book against her hip and lays it on the viewing table in the center of the vault. After repeating her instructions three times on how to turn the frail yellowed pages without damaging them, she gives us each a pair of gloves and points out the column of names.

"You've got two shelves to go through. There's no index and no shortcut to locating her name, so you'll have to be efficient readers." At the sound of her counter bell down the hallway, she turns with a wistful sigh. "If I finish my typing in time, I'll come back and lend you a hand."

Jeff scratches his head. "This could take us hours, even days. Are you sure you want to pursue this?"

I open to the first page with "January 1, 1900" handwritten across the top.

"My god, Jeff. Take a look at this fancy writing! It's like calligraphy, all curlicued."

"How'd they ever have time to write this all out?" Jeff points out the splatter of black ink in the margin. "Probably even used one of those quills and ink wells."

Much like listening to Shakespeare when at first you can't make sense of the antiquated speech, then gradually it begins to sound normal, our eyes and brains adjust to the old script and we easily scan the "Purchased By" columns book after book. I am driven—no—obsessed—to dig deeper and deeper, drawn by a knowing that something is waiting for me. Jeff isn't so patient. After two hours, I suggest he go find a café or at least a vending machine.

And that's when I find her.

Deeded from Mr. James Harwell to Eliza Osborn Baxter,
May 7, 1906.

"Oh, my god, this is it! It really happened! Parcel # 20-34-06. All we have to do is locate the current owner and buy it." It doesn't occur to me that it might not be for sale, that we can't just drive up and purchase it sight unseen. But that's exactly what we do.

AMISHA

2075
Sacramento, California

After what seemed like a week of helping row the skiff up the Sacramento River, Amisha arrived in New Town Sacramento, exhausted to the core. Legs wobbling like a drunkard, she stepped onto the gray plastix floating waterfront designed to accommodate the ever-rising river and mouthed a final *thank you* to Caleb. Her arms and shoulders were in spasm, her shirt plastered to her back in a layer of sweat, her nose and throat on fire. She'd give anything for a bed, even a bench, to sleep on.

She struggled to bring New Town into focus. East of the waterfront, the early morning shimmer cast a faint glow along the empty streets lined with one- and two-story structures. A string of flatbed wagons waited by the dock for donkeys to be hitched to them; empty pedi.cabs lined the sidewalk stands ready for their drivers; a single sun.auto was parked with its hood propped up under a peeling billboard. The city seemed to be holding its breath, waiting for that first touch of sunlight to awaken it.

Across the street, a wide-spreading tree seemed a reasonable place to rest. Amisha dragged her backpack to the patch of dried grass, lowered herself against the trunk, and, with an exhausted sigh, closed her eyes. Despite the stench, the river had been peaceful. She hardly missed Nib's commentary of street names, impending hazards, and places of interest that used to accompany her progress.

A sharp tap at her foot brought her back to the dim morning. A pause . . . another tap.

"I said, time to move on."

"I didn't hear. Sorry, I'm just resting a bit."

"Not here. Not anymore. Curfew's still in effect."

"Where can I lie down, even a short while? . . . Sir," she added, for there was enough light to see the man wore a dusty camouflage shirt and pants like it was his official uniform, though it was probably his father's or grandfather's.

"Where the rest of you people go." He waited, arms crossed.

You people?

He remained impassive. She collected her pack and crossed the street, hoping she was heading in the direction of the outer district, where she last remembered Luke lived.

A light flickered at a corner several blocks down—Daybreak Café, one of the few places authorized to open before light for early-shifters. Amisha ordered a hot brew of root coffee and wrapped her aching fingers around the cup's warmth. She dropped a Sally Ride on the counter and lifted her backpack to leave, but the double-chinned waitress with "Trina" embroidered in red on the top of her once-white apron lifted the coin with her pudgy fingers and held it to the dangling light bulb.

"Gawd, these still around?" Trina slipped it into her pocket with a grunt.

Amisha reached into her bag for another coin.

"Yur not from here, are ya?" She pointed to the line of workers waiting for the stool. "Most people know shift-workers are served first."

"I'm looking for someone," Amisha said.

"What's yur prob?"

"I'm down," she replied, giving her neck a quick tap. "Malfunction during upgrade."

"I was wonderin' 'bout the old Sallys," Trina said, her mouth curled into a lopsided smile. "Get a few like you, time t' time. Mostly helpless."

"Maybe you can query for me? The name's Hoplin. Luke."

"Sorry," she said, glancing at the tiny lens blinking over the cook's station.

Amisha quietly set another Sally on the counter.

Trina removed a pile of dirty dishes and refilled her cup. "That'll be 891 27th," she said under her breath.

Amisha nodded, slid two more Sallys across the counter. Before she could take a last gulp, she was squeezed from her stool by two men jostling for her place.

From the corner of 5th and H Street, she started walking east toward 27th. If the air was already shimmering now, by midmorning the sidewalks would be scorching. Where were Sacramento's famous sheltering trees? Oh yeah, the firewood controversy. She crossed 9th Street and hunkered under the shade of a vacant front porch to rest.

Luke . . . her stomach contorted. She wasn't ready for him—never would be. Amisha dropped her head between her knees and waited for the tightness in her chest to subside, grateful that her flood of anxiety didn't immediately trigger unwelcome memories all dutifully recorded and played back at the flick of an eyelash. Seven years older, Luke modeled his life on the vintage Monopoly game he made his two sisters play. He wouldn't free them from his locked bedroom until he controlled the entire board property, houses, bank, and . . . his sisters.

"Only way to survive is to be on top," he boasted. Amisha hated his sneer. She hated hearing his footsteps stop at Isabelle's bedroom. At thirteen, her little sister—dear, sweet Isabelle—dropped out of sight. And Luke? Amisha broke off all contact after he "won" the family homestead decades ago. Amisha loathed him, yet here she was, blocks away from begging, like asking for a loan so she could keep Marvin Gardens.

She unwrapped one of her crackers, soggy from the river. She hadn't thought about Luke in a long time. She could have monitored him but chose not to. Last time his name popped up, before she permanently blocked it, she saw his oil holdings had skyrocketed soon after the ban on extraction was permanently repealed. MBA, top of his class at Stanford. What else did she remember?

His twenty-first birthday gift to her: seven nights at Consolidated Oil's Amazonia, a five-star luxury resort in Ecuador. No ticket to get there, of course, but she didn't care. With a silent prayer for the brown-skinned children who bathed in oil-saturated streams, she shredded his gift. That was her last contact with him.

Her afternoon was a blur of sidewalk cracks, hot asphalt, swerving cyclists, and the slow, steady progression of street signs—15th, 20th, 25th. The streets were lined with decayed tree stumps and tired, workingman's houses with waterless, xeriscaped front yards, shuttered windows, and backyards overflowing with unrecycled junk. After landfills were outlawed and absolute recycling enacted, everything, even Pharm.food wrappers, had to be repurposed, for there simply were no disposal places left. Even the ocean was abandoned after it became too clogged for ships to safely navigate. At every corner were canisters reminding people to *Re.Purpose—Your Civic Duty and the Law*. What didn't fit in the canisters, well, that's what backyards were for.

Throughout her journey, she prayed she would find Luke. Now, standing at the corner of 27th, she feared she would. It was as if the street was a border—one side held tumbled rows of small houses, their unrecyclables spilling out from the yards; postured on the other side were tall, stately houses shaded by trees, a wall, and a guardhouse. She faced the guardhouse, unable to move. Without her Nib, she had no ID. Delivering goods to Mr. Hoplin, that's what she'd tell the guard. But what did she have—Pharm.food? She regretted the loss of her Med.pak. By now it would have neutralized the adrenalin flooding her system and she'd be thinking more clearly. With her pack slung over one shoulder, she walked over to the gate, hoping she'd have a better story by the time she got there. The guardhouse door flapped open on one hinge, wires dangled from the intercom, and a shade was pulled over the window. Amisha walked on through.

Inside the wall was another world. Trees provided a blessed covering of shade. Sidewalks were less cracked, paint less peeled, and the feeling was tentative green rather than unrelenting gray. Windows facing the street were small for privacy and safety, and occasional drought-tolerant bushes were planted beneath. These dowager homes struggled to hold onto their former dignity.

Amisha stopped before a vaguely familiar white Colonial-style house with a two-story portico entry and multiple green-shuttered windows. Hanging on a post, partly hidden beneath a draping of plastix ivy, were the numbers "891." She was desperate to rest, eat something, tidy up, but the afternoon light was dimming fast, and no one, not even residents in a gated neighborhood, would answer a knock in the dark.

At the front door, the doorbell and camera button were taped over, so she unlatched the patched screen and knocked.

"Luke? Monica?"

A cat meowed. A shuffling noise. After a few moments, a small peephole opened.

"Who's it?" The voice was raspy and thin.

"Your sister," Amisha said.

"I've no sister."

"Do the Hoplins still live here? I'm looking for my brother, Luke."

The door squeaked open a crack.

"If this isn't the Hoplin's anymore, do you know where they might have moved?"

The door opened farther, revealing a frail woman, five feet tall at best, wisps of bleached-yellow hair framing her weary, lined face. A threadbare house tunic of once-bold geometric designs sloped over one bony shoulder as she struggled to balance a languorous tabby cat over the other shoulder. The old woman shoved her jewel-encrusted hand in Amisha's face.

"Out!"

"I hate to bother, but I've come such a long way. Please, can you help me?" Amisha leaned against the wall in case her knees buckled out beneath her.

The old woman ran her fingers through the brittle fur of her cat's back, eyeing the stranger from head to toe as if trying to decide where this puzzle piece fit in. After a lengthy silence, the woman kicked away two cats trying to escape and opened the door.

"Might as well come in."

"Monica?" Amisha's pack fell to the floor.

By eight that evening, the cool delta breeze had swept out the stale air from the streets and, after a simple soup, the two women moved their conversation outside to the back patio.

"When's he coming back?" Amisha asked, still reverberating from the news that her brother had been living in Ecuador for the past ten years. She wouldn't be surprised if he had a whole other family there.

"Oh, he's back, just out there doing business." Monica waved her hand in the vague direction of the river. "Returns tomorrow. Stick around, you can see him yourself."

Amisha shuddered. This place hardly matched her image of him, but then, a lot had changed since she last saw him.

"He stopped mentioning sisters long ago. He's the only surviving family. That's what he told me." Monica rearranged the folds of her skirt to line up with the geometric designs of her tunic. "It's not like you or Isabelle kept in contact."

Amisha studied the primitive artwork on the patio wall behind Monica. "What did he do?"

"You know what he did."

"It was oil back then. And outrageous resorts."

Monica pushed an oversized picture book called *SpanAmerica Enterprises* toward her guest. "Sometimes he took me to South America, but most times he brought me back a trinket or local art."

"This is a multinational oil company," Amisha said.

"That's all I need to know, he informed me." She spun her heavy diamond ring against her enlarged knuckle. "Now maybe you should tell me what I need to know about you."

Amisha pushed up from her chair and walked over to the tall plastix fence at the end of the gravel patio.

"I've been in San Francisco mainly. I diagnose children's . . . well, more like find the right Pharm.food to match the symptoms created by their other foods. Hardly what I was trained for."

"Doctor?"

Amisha nodded. Though the delta breeze swept in wisps of cool air, she felt suffocated. She pretended to search the ground for something, hoping the light-headedness would pass.

"Why'd you come here?" Monica pulled the tabby cat onto her lap and picked bits of dirt and leaves from the scruff of its neck.

She's querying about me, Amisha realized. Am I still up or did I disappear with my Nib?

Monica's eyes swept side to side for several seconds, then stopped. "Sorry, can't bring much up anymore."

"Your Nib?"

"It's deteriorating, but upgrades are just as bad."

Amisha slumped into a chair, remembering all the times when the information she got didn't seem quite right. She opened her mouth to speak, but the cricket chirping at the back fence drowned her out.

"Used to be you can tell how hot it was by counting cricket's chirps," Monica said.

Amisha didn't reply.

"One, two, three, four, five . . ." Monica couldn't keep up with the fast chirps.

"I need directions to the homestead."

"Six, seven, eight, nine . . ." Monica threw up her hands. "You'll have to talk to Luke."

"You must know."

"Nope, it's been decades since he deserted it. I've no memory a'tall."

Amisha bolted up. "What?"

"Wasn't worth the bother of keeping. First, they shut down electricity to the mountains, then closed all the roads up there. It was easy to stop paying taxes and let it slide."

"Abandon it?"

"I'm sure squatters moved in."

"But you can still prove ownership?"

"I don't know. Ask Luke. He'll be back first thing in the morning."

Though bone weary, Amisha found it hard to shut down her mind that night. The short couch and musty yellowed sheets didn't bother

her. But the aching in her chest wouldn't let up, and the damn clock in the kitchen with its hideous fake ticking was driving her crazy. Not like Grandma's old wall clock with the brass pendulum that her three-year-old eyes used to follow back and forth until she was dizzy. The old clock seemed loudly important back then, announcing the hour and half hours from its station on the stairwell landing.

Amisha slipped from the sheets and felt her way down the hall to the bathroom, guided by a faint nightlight. On the way back, she passed by framed photographs of assorted people in exotic locations. One figure stared back at her: Luke. She hardly recognized him. It was as if someone had pulled the plug and deflated him into a wizened old man. Below his hairless, crusted scalp, his face was nothing more than a rumpled map of stubbled, jaundiced skin. But his eyes, dark and intimidating, still filled her with terror. That had not changed. From the room across the hall, Monica stirred, sighed, turned over. Amisha felt her way back to the couch, closed her eyes, and attempted to sleep.

Just before the shimmer, with the room still shrouded in darkness, she awoke in a sweat. She considered her options. Here she was in Luke's house, totally vulnerable, begging him for directions to the homestead—a position he always exulted in. Every cell in her body screamed to flee, but she wasn't going without getting what she came for. Amisha straightened her tunic, slipped on her shoes, and pushed the long stray hairs away from her face. Monica was her only hope.

Seated at the kitchen table, Monica nudged a cup of tea toward Amisha. "No, can't recall saving anything from the old house. Luke didn't even bother locking up. He was done with it all."

Amisha leaned forward. "But you must have saved something . . . old photos? Discs, drives?"

Monica shook her head.

Amisha took a deep breath. "Then I can't imagine you'd have brought back anything large, like furniture . . . or a desk?"

Monica removed her tea bag from her cup and dropped it into the bowl of dried-out tea bags she collected for reuse. "Who writes anymore? Why'd you be interested in a desk?"

"I'm not really, it's just a sentimental memory."

Monica gave her a sideways look. "I haven't been up there in decades. Might have seen one. Probably burned for firewood as well. Like I said, Luke didn't care anymore."

Luke. Amisha struggled to organize her thoughts. She stepped outside the patio door into the already oven-hot morning. On the top of the fence across the patio, she noticed a metal latch partly hidden by faded plastix ivy. A gate? Her hand had barely touched the latch when the patio door burst open.

"Stop right there!"

Amisha lifted her arms high in the air like a scene from an old *White Cop News Feed*. "What the hell do you have in there?" she laughed. "Furniture?"

Monica circled until she came between Amisha and the fence, her right hand hidden in the folds of her skirt. Amisha sensed she was struggling with something.

"Monica," Amisha lowered her voice. "It must have been so hard. Luke in South America . . . you here all alone with nothing but this." She took a step toward the gate. "But you've survived, haven't you? With all his power, he couldn't keep you down, could he?" She raised her hand toward the latch, but Monica's hand was there first.

"Please, he doesn't know." She stopped her plea and eyed Amisha. For seconds they stood silently under the hot sun. Then Monica made a decision and released the latch. The hidden gate creaked open. Amisha ducked under the shade cloth, and as the gate closed behind them, a vaguely familiar musky aroma assailed her nostrils. She steadied herself on the nearest planter box and looked around the small enclosure. Everywhere was green, lush green with soft red globes that dangled from thin sprawling branches. She struggled to recall the earthy aroma. A fruit? Vegetable?

"What . . ." but her question was stopped by a metallic click concealed within the folds of Monica's skirt.

"It's how I survive, my dear." Monica revealed the gun's steel barrel. "And, yes, I keep them guarded or get ripped off."

Amisha thought of Grandma Claire's stories of the old days when marijuana plantations were illegal. "You sell?" she asked.

"I trade." She fondled one of the globular tomatoes. "For water. These Golden Jubilees and Cherokee Purples are my water babies. They have it all . . . water, food, even seeds."

"But seeds are illegal, you can't save . . ."

"You've never eaten a fresh tomato, have you? People actually give me their day's water allotment for a single one of these." She pulled a deep red tomato off the vine and rolled it in her hands with great tenderness. A high-pitched mechanical buzz zigzagged outside the canopy cover as if searching for a way into the garden. Monica stashed the tomato in her pocket, dashed outside and with a long plank, swatted the metallic winged creature until its thin titanium frame was smashed flat.

"Damn droneflies. They make 'em smaller and smaller. Snoops, that's what they are. Could even be Luke's." She dragged Amisha out of the gate and into the house. "Go! Right now." She pulled Amisha's pack to the hallway and set it by the front door. "You know too much. I can't risk you being here when Luke returns."

A car engine whined into the driveway then shut down.

"But the homestead . . . Please! You've got to tell me how to find it."

"Stay away from there," Monica hissed. "Only outlaws and vagrants—you won't last a minute." She grabbed her tabby by the scruff, pushed it into Amisha's arms, and disappeared into the kitchen. When she returned, she traded the tabby for a balled-up yellowed cloth.

"Take this and disappear." She whisked Amisha out the back door and whispered, "Save the seeds!"

ELIZA
1864
Niles, Michigan

"Makes no sense," Wesley muttered as he pulled his nightcap down over his ears and cinched his robe tight against the early morning cold. "No sense at all." Alone in the meadow where the tree once stood, Wesley kicked at a clump of tangled branches and bent to examine a large, shattered limb. "Not a sound last night. No warning." His words hung in the air like fog rising from the river below the meadow. "Just look at this old tree, split apart, branches covering the meadow in every direction." He pushed aside a cluster of leaves to make room for Sophie, who arrived breathless and shivering at his side.

"Did you hear it fall last night?" he asked.

Sophie shook her head and wrapped her lambswool shawl against her petite body.

"Can't believe we all slept through it. Don't think it was diseased. Old, maybe," Wesley continued.

"Eliza," Sophie whispered. "We should wake her."

"I already sent Frederick in to get her."

"I'm afraid this is going to . . ."

"She's coming. She's coming!" As the front door banged behind him, Frederick tumbled down the front steps with Teddy following behind.

"Careful, there are sharp pieces everywhere!" Wesley boomed. "This will be a major job to clean up. It's too close to the house to simply let nature take its course."

"But Eliza. Wes, I'm afraid for our daughter."

Wesley blew warm air into his fingers and rubbed them together. "The tree was old, bound to die sooner or later. Maybe it is just as well. We have already agreed Eliza spends far too much time in it."

The front door squeaked open.

"Why does she just stand there?" Wesley took a step down the meadow trail toward the house, but Sophie held him back.

"I told you, Wes. She will be taking this hard."

Barefoot, skin pale beneath her thin white nightgown, Eliza stood transfixed on the front porch, looking as if she'd awakened into another world. She pulled a strand of hair from her eyes and blinked. Why was everyone looking at her? What was all this rubble covering the ground? Grandmother Oak? She blinked again. Where was her tree?

"Eliza, dear." Sophie extended her hand and coaxed Eliza down the stairs. "There was an accident last night. We have no idea what happened." Sophie guided her into the tangled maze of sticks and leaves that now blocked the path from the house to where the old tree once towered above the Saint Joseph River.

As Eliza approached, sights and sounds slowly coalesced into the image of the tree shattered at her feet. Her hands flew up to cover her mouth.

"We were all just as shocked this morning," Sophie said.

Teddy stopped jumping, shrugged at Frederick, then both brothers resumed walking tightrope down a long, prostrate branch.

Dazed, oblivious to the sharp wood that snagged her gown and punctured her bare feet, Eliza searched for a way to the center of what was left of Grandmother Oak.

"You're shaking, dear. Come here, sit next to me." Sophie guided her daughter onto a large mossy branch and pushed aside leaves to make room for their feet.

Eliza was overcome with an uncontrollable shaking. "I was just here."

Sophie removed her shawl and placed it around Eliza's shoulders. "You were just here?"

"Last night, before bed, I came to tell her my news, but she . . ." Eliza broke into a wave of sobs.

"You came to tell her you were going away to college?" Sophie had long accepted that young Eliza talked to this old tree like an invisible friend, but she was older now, going away to the women's seminary in Kalamazoo this fall. She should put all this behind her. It was just a tree. Yet, as Sophie formulated the words, something made her pause. A memory of her own.

Wesley worked his way through the branches toward the trunk's exposed center. Standing on tiptoe, he peered inside. "By God, this tree is as ancient as the hills." His voice boomed into the hollowed trunk. "Died of old age, I reckon. Just gave up the ghost. We're fortunate it did not fall during the day and kill someone. Could have, you know." He peered down his spectacles at his daughter.

Eliza lifted her head, but her mother intervened.

"Wesley, please be more sensitive." She dabbed at Eliza's cheek with the corner of the shawl. "Teddy, Frederick!" she shouted. "You go on back to the house and start your breakfast. Eat it cold if you have to." With an imploring look, she added, "You too, Wes."

Eliza rose, but Sophie pulled her back. "Sit a piece more with me. There's something I want to talk about." When the front door banged for the third time, Sophie reached down for a smooth twig and twirled it between her fingers like the thoughts spinning in her mind. After a long silence, she spoke.

"I have never told a soul how we really came to settle in this meadow." She took a deep breath, collected her thoughts, then continued. "I have always suspected there was something between you and this tree—from the time you were deep inside me, here," she patted her belly. Eliza stopped sniffing. "I was several months into my confinement when your father took me out in the buggy to show off the land he had selected for our home. It was a hot summer day, and on the way back home, we drove by this very spot. You started flip-flopping inside me so hard I was forced to stop and rest. That's when I noticed this magnificent oak tree out by the riverbank, like it was inviting me over to its shade. The closer I got, the more you bounced around, like you were calling to each other from across the meadow. But the strangest thing is, the minute I laid back against its trunk, you quieted down as if it was singing you a lullaby."

"She sings to me all the time," Eliza whispered. "Not with words, but in ways I can feel."

"I am sure she does, dear," Sophie said, thinking of Eliza's unusual behavior after spending time up the tree.

"I announced to your father that this is where we should build our home. And for once, he listened to me. It helped it was near water and was a tad closer to town than what he had selected. You grew under the shade of that tree even before you entered the world. After you were born, I could leave you for hours in your baby carriage just staring up at the light shining through the leaves. And when you were old enough to walk, I would sit on the front steps and watch you go back and forth across the meadow to the tree. When you were fussy, I knew I could always settle you down in her shade." She dabbed at Eliza's nose with her handkerchief.

Eliza nodded, her tears coming slower now.

"After school, the first thing you would do was run out to the tree and spend the rest of the afternoon up in her branches."

Eliza's eyes widened.

"You think your father and I didn't know about your little hideaway up in the tree? You were hardly seven when we first noticed."

"You were watching me?"

"We thought it was sweet at first and didn't want to spoil your secret. But as you got older, your father was concerned it was not ladylike to be spending so much time alone in a tree. You would come back to the house, well . . . changed."

"I am changing, Mother. Look at me!" She pointed to her full bodice.

"It was your thinking that changed, and all your talk of strange things."

"What is strange about California? Everyone wants to go there."

Suddenly, Eliza wanted to ask her mother if she had seen the woman . . . the woman writing by the window, but she dared not.

Sophie gave her daughter's hand a pat. "Let us go inside or you will catch your death of a cold. You need to eat too, dear. I am sure there will be lots of talk about what happened here last night."

For the rest of the day, neighbors flocked by to see the night's mysterious destruction. Men grouped around the fallen tree and conjectured on the cause of its sudden demise. Women sipped cups of tea and shook their heads at a loss of such beauty. Eliza sat on the porch steps and watched it all, vacant-eyed.

"It's a shame there's not much salvageable wood," Mr. Jenkins said, as he placed his saws back in his cart. "Except maybe a bit of the heartwood."

"Then save it!" Eliza jumped up from the porch.

"I'll come back in the morning, set aside what heartwood's still solid. But looks like you'll have a year's firewood from the remainder," the woodcutter shouted over his shoulder.

Eliza shuddered at the idea of tossing her oak tree into the fire like chunks of meat.

"We should plant a new tree in its place for shade," Sophie said. "And a maple tree will be a beautiful red in the fall."

Eliza pressed her ears closed and retreated to her room.

That evening, Sophie set a plate of chicken and boiled potatoes on a tray outside Eliza's bedroom door. "I know you're sad, dear, but you should eat. It will revive your spirits."

Eliza left the tray untouched. She had no appetite. Words blurred when she tried to read, as did the flowers on the wallpaper across the room. That night, her dreams wavered like the mist surrounding Grandmother Oak. She was curled up in a tree. She was gazing across a wide, distant valley . . . a woman at a desk—a small wooden desk with a drawer filled with fountain pens, blotters, notebooks, and whispers.

As for Grandmother Oak, time had run its course. For over three hundred cycles, she held her secret among the inhabitants of the river. But her sap had become thick and slow, her leaves brittle and few; scars of age had closed in on her. On the eve of her own demise, deep embers smoldered, for there was one thing left she must do . . . and she could not do it alone.

HARMONY

1985

Berkeley and Sierra Nevada, Northern California

Our mustard-yellow Volvo is parked outside the apartment, filled to the brim with camping gear, cooking utensils, nonperishable food, one duffle bag apiece for clothes, and three boxes of "how-to" books for our new lifestyle. I slip into the seat next to Jeff and wrap my arms around his neck.

"This is it!" I say.

He turns the key; the engine hums. "No going back," he says.

"No going back," I repeat. Not that the thought hadn't occurred to me when I dropped off his blazers and ties and my nylons and heels at the Salvation Army thrift shop in Berkeley. I'd already sold most of our wedding gifts at an upscale consignment store. The china and silver would have looked good in my older sister Carole's sophisticated San Francisco Victorian home, but I didn't have time to deal with her. We left a few belongings in my parent's garage, including three boxes of piano music.

"We'll come back for them as soon as we get you a piano," Jeff promised.

With my California map folded to display our journey north into the foothills, we start out for Great-Grandma's land in Luna Valley.

"Hey, Deb, you're awfully quiet," Jeff comments as he passes a big rig on Highway 80 along the San Francisco Bay. "Got second thoughts?"

"No, just a huge swarm of butterflies in my stomach." I wave at the massive oil refinery spewing noxious clouds into the atmosphere ahead of us. "It's like we're getting away from here just in time."

Jeff nods and sinks into his own silence. I wonder if he has second thoughts, but I don't want to hear them if he does. It's too late now. An hour passes. We stop in Sacramento for a picnic lunch at a small park near the river, then continue north to Marysville, where we buy some fresh fruits and vegetables at a produce stand and stock our chest with a block of ice.

"How'd people in covered wagons survive with no ice or freeze-dried foods?" Jeff wonders.

"If they could grow and preserve all their food, it should be easy enough for us."

"And if all else fails, we've got Safeway."

I slap my hand over Jeff's mouth and make him nod me a promise that will never happen.

Before we signed the final legal documents last week, the real estate agent had asked once again whether we'd like to see the property before buying it.

"In normal circumstances, we would, but this was my wife's . . ."

"This was once my great-grandmother's land," I finish for Jeff. "It's destiny that it is now ours."

The agent cleared his throat and advised us to keep a lookout for two big madrone trees that indicated the bottom of the road leading up to the property.

We drive past the two madrones twice before noticing that, indeed, there is a road leading uphill between them. It's heavily rutted and overgrown with brush and vines, but nothing a chainsaw and shovel can't fix—both items unfortunately still on our shopping list. Luckily, I brought father's old garden clippers. After an hour of walking and clipping, we reach the top of the driveway, where it opens into a wide clearing. Jeff stops, tilts his baseball cap back, and runs his fingers through his hair, mumbling something about maybe we should have checked it out first. But I clutch my heart and spin in circles, feeling like Maria in *The Sound of Music*.

"Come on, let's check out our future homestead!" I grab his hand. Above us, the grassy hilltop is encircled by a forest of trees (I vow to identify each type). A small gully to the east (where the sun rises) is lined with ferns and small boulders for sitting. Downhill flows a small creek that promises water for drinking, maybe even trout for eating. There's even a few gnarly apple trees on the eastern slope. I look around for where Great-Grandma might have lived, hoping for signs of a little house, but see nothing.

We set up a temporary camp in a wide space down at the bottom of the driveway, thinking we'd be hidden away. Wrong. Just about every VW bus that chugged by stopped to check out whether we were hunters or squatters.

"Nope, just returning to my roots," I explain to the flaxen-haired woman who introduces herself as Summer Rain.

"Looks like you're gonna need some help if you plan on building up there," says her husband, Nova, pointing up the jungled driveway. "How about if I round up some help for you?"

Jeff demurs. "Thanks anyway, but our plan is to be self-sufficient."

"Yeah, right. I remember starting out that way seven years ago," Nova says. "But turns out, helping each other makes being self-sufficient easier."

Jeff looks to me, I nod eagerly, and the men shake hands.

The next morning, six men show up with chainsaws, hatchets, and strange short-handled two-sided blades, one side like a rake, the other like a sharp hoe. A broad-shouldered guy in a yellow flannel shirt pulls another blade from his mud-spattered pickup and places it in Jeff's hands.

"This McLeod's going to be your best friend," Mark says. "Invented here in the Sierra for clearing, firefighting, and trail work. Consider it our welcome gift."

Two days later, we maneuver our Volvo up the dirt driveway and park below the clearing, where the men's wives have set up a picnic table from a sheet of plywood over two sawhorses. The table is covered with casserole dishes, homemade bread, bowls of fresh salad, and plates stacked high with healthy cookies. We may be late-comers to this back-to-the-land migration, but still, I'm surprised to find such a cohesive community here.

Over picnic lunch, we meet our Luna Valley neighbors. Nova and Summer Rain live across the road and sell fruit, vegetables, and olive oil at a little highway stand down by the bridge. A half mile up the road, Indigo and Lark raise sheep for wool that Indigo then spins on an old spinning wheel she found at a secondhand store. Madrona organizes a nursery cooperative for the growing number of children born in the valley, and her husband Mark works at a small family-run lumber mill just past the one-engine firehouse.

"And over there is Dora," Mark points to the stocky woman with short, slicked-back hair, tight blue jeans, and a pack of Marlboros tucked in her sleeve. "She lives by herself and she can split a cord of wood faster than any man in the neighborhood."

Dora flexes her biceps and takes a deep bow amid the group's clapping.

"No one messes with Dora," Nova warns.

This first summer on the land the skies are crystal clear, and heat rises in soft, rippling waves. We establish our home tent on a flat spot near the top of the driveway, cook rice and beans over a Cole-man stove, store food in a small propane refrigerator, and refill five-liter jugs with water at Indigo and Lark's, who already have elec-tricity and a well. When the heat becomes unbearable, we wander downhill to skinny dip in the river.

We discover that most everyone who settled here in Luna Valley wants to be self-sufficient caretakers of the earth like us. The valley is freckled with tipis, tents, trailers, half-built homes, and remod-eled miners' cabins. Just like the old barn-raising days, men help build one another's homes and women bring them food.

Jeff is chomping at the bit to start building our home and hands me a notebook full of his house-design sketches. "It's why we came here," he says. "Let's just pick out a spot and do it!" But I want the land to reveal to us where we should build. If we can just find where Great-Grandma built her cabin, that might be the site.

We agree to be more methodical. Every morning we walk a different part of our twenty acres. We follow deer trails through thick groves of madrone and oak trees, walk the fern-laden creek, bushwhack through shoulder-high ceanothus and manzanita bushes. But the land doesn't speak.

I try meditating and set a timer for twenty minutes. Swami Nada-something-or-other said twenty minutes is the minimum time needed to clear one's mind. At least that's what our new neighbors Jayati and Sagar told me when they moved here from the Indian commune the next ridge over.

This is when I decide that Jeff and I need new names, too. Something more fitting to our new lives. I meditate on that as well. With the timer ticking away across the tent, I sit cross-legged on my cot, close my eyes, inhale deeply, then let it go. Easy enough, no need for an Indian guru to show me how. Inhale, pause, exhale, pause, inhale, *RiverSong* would be a good name, or maybe, oops, inhale, pause, exhale, quick peek at the timer, only twelve minutes more, inhale, pause, exhale. Where to build? Maybe if I imagine myself in our house, canning in the kitchen or putting babies to bed. But all I get is a strange feeling of sitting at a desk by an upstairs window, staring out to the western horizon.

"Just look at us!" I write in my journal that autumn. I had washed and pinned my fifth shirt on the clothesline next to Jeff's heavy blue jeans, underwear, and socks, then smoothed out the wrinkles with my hand and left them to dry overnight. We're so blessed to be living our dream. Even hauling water and washing loads of laundry in a tub feels so rustic, like Great-Grandma must have done. But my period starts the next morning and I don't feel quite so blessed, nor much in the mood to deal with soggy, tangled laundry. That's when I discover the laundromat in town.

Jeff does his part to make our humble tent a home. "Tah dah! My first piece of furniture." He stands back to admire the two pine slabs he has measured, cut, and set atop a stack of cinder blocks. I fill the shelves with popular homesteading books from the Good Morning Food and Grain store. It is an expensive investment but sure to save us tons of money over our lifetime: *The Owner-Built Homestead* by Ken Kern, Seymour's *Farming for Self-Sufficiency*, Carla Emery's *Encyclopedia of Country Living*, *Organic Gardening* magazines and *Stocking Up* by Rodale Press, and, of course the old standby, the *Whole Earth Catalog*.

By the end of autumn, my enthusiasm tapers off just a bit. More than anything, I miss my piano. To keep in shape, I run scales up and down the tabletop with my fingers like it's a piano, but only when Jeff's not around. I don't want him to know—we've both made sacrifices. I think of Mother's promise that she'll send up my baby grand piano when I have four real walls.

Winter arrives early this year, and the beautiful snow that drifts to the ground in luminous crystal flakes also sags the roof of our tent and makes it impossible for the propane heater to keep us warm. Jeff and I zip our sleeping bags together and sleep naked intertwined. That is, when we sleep. The closeness of our bodies, all musky from sweat, turns us on something fierce, and we interrupt our sleep over and over to try out new positions in our double sleeping bag.

At last, our land breaks its silence and speaks to us. Returning from dinner at Indigo and Lark's, we walk a new route home through the snow, up the east gully and over the top of the ridge north of our tent. The snow glistens under the full moon; our breath crystallizes before us in a magical fog. Jeff is the first to notice the four right angles barely visible in the snow-covered ground. My eyes are drawn to the perfectly straight rows of stones that connect corner to corner—the foundation of Great-Grandma's cabin.

I call home from Nova's phone the next morning.

"Mother, I've got amazing news!"

"Oh, sweetie, that's wonderful. When are you due?"

Silence.

"I mean, that *is* why you called?"

I do my best to shift gears. "Not quite yet, Mother. But you will be the first to know. After Jeff, that is. But for now, I have something almost as exciting."

Silence.

"Great-Grandma's cabin! Not *the* cabin, but the foundation. She, your Grandmother Eliza, actually lived here!"

More silence, but I feel the gears moving. "We're going to move up into the foundation, pitch our tent, and begin building the four walls."

"Then those stories are true. Although Grandma lived on the Yolo farm, far away across the valley, she had . . ."

"A room of her own."

"Just a room?"

"About the size of your living room, Mom. But that's all she'd need."

"That's not much of a house."

"You should come see. You haven't been here yet." After that, I think I have her hooked. But suddenly even the remote possibility of a grandchild starts things moving. I hear my father shuffling next to her, then take the phone.

"No grandchild of ours is going to grow up in a makeshift-walled tent. How much do you need to build a real house?"

AMISHA

2075
Sacramento, California

Amisha squeezed though a wide space in Monica's back fence and emerged into one of Sacramento's narrow back alleyways. Which way? Right? Left? Hell, the air was so thick with particulates she couldn't tell which direction she'd come from. She decided left, kept her pace slow but desperately wanted to run. With a quick peek over her shoulder for Luke, she dashed across the busy H Street and ducked into a small back alley with double-wide garages that formerly held several cars but now overflowed with unrecyclable junk and garbage so bleached and old it no longer stank. Needing to catch her breath, she leaned against a patched cement wall. What if Monica told Luke she was there? Or worse, if he discovered on his own? She had no clue what to do next. Going back and asking for directions was out of the question. Head into the hills and take a chance? Where were the hills? Only a few days ago, her Nib would have instantly given detailed directions. Why, oh why, hadn't she queried directions before? She could use a little help right now, thank you.

Amisha reached into her pants pocket for her worry beads but instead pulled up the ball of yellowed material Monica had thrust at her. She imagined the tomato wrapped within, even spoke the word "tomato" aloud, waiting for the cerebral evocation of this ancient food, but her salivary glands didn't respond. She unwrapped the tomato and brought it to her nose. Old and earthy, touched with a tinge of long ago. The aroma traveled up the seldom-used corridors of her nose seeking the source of this strange memory.

A shadow drifted over head and the silent passage of a drone cam brought her back to her predicament. In one deft move, she dropped the tomato into the cloth and folded the edges to conceal it. Only then did she notice the thin squiggles inside the cloth. She ran her finger along the lines of quivering handwriting.

River north to Marysville.
At fork, go east into foothills.
Ask, but not directly.
Follow the string of pearls to La Luna.
Be careful.

Incredible! Amisha retraced the route back to the river. *String of pearls?* Before that fateful morning in San Francisco, nothing was a mystery. Now, everything was.

Yesterday morning when she arrived at the dock, the city was just rubbing the sleep from its eyes. Now it was a spectacle of sailboats, rowboats, paddle wheels, kayaks, and barges deftly avoiding the shoals of submerged sidewalks as they traveled upstream and down. Some vessels burgeoned with rusted farm equipment; others were loaded with mega cartons of Pharm.food and crates of unknown cargo labeled for the Chinese and Hmong farmers of the marginally fertile upper Sacramento Valley. Small groups arriving from out of the hills wearily unloaded their worldly goods onto the dock. A ragged cluster of migrants, mostly single men with a bedroll and rifle on their backs, negotiated for a ride upstream.

"Take me upriver to Marysville?" Amisha asked one boatman after another. They stared at the ribbon around her neck and her outstretched hand as if they'd never seen a Sally Ride, then turned back to their work. It didn't take long to learn *no nib, no ride*. At the far end of the dock, a collection of foot travelers milled around a weather-beaten sign—*River Road North*. It was a ten-foot-wide dirt path that guided pedestrians, human-drawn carts, and donkey-drawn wagons along the dusty levee of the Sacramento River. Amisha stepped in line.

The first day of walking under the blazing sun, she scrutinized other travelers for behavior cues: stay to the right, keep your head and neck protected from the sun, stop here to eat, relieve yourself in the occasional cover of meager bushes, curl up for the night in depressions along the riverbank, hug your belongings close. She was desperate to confirm this road led to Marysville but, without a nib, couldn't enter the private world of fellow travelers. Only last week she, too, might have been viewing a drama enactment, or shopping for a new work tunic, or menting Orion. She willed herself not to think of him.

On the second day, she noticed a well-maintained road that paralleled the river almost out of sight, just east of the levee. Occasionally, a soft-humming solar vehicle pulsed by—not like the sun.autos that filled the streets of San Francisco, but longer, sleeker, faster, and blacker, clearly built for those who lived in a different world than hers. She'd heard rumors of the elite—always wondered how they powered their lives. Nib.know had quickly dispelled their existence, but now her mind was free to wonder and question.

On the third day, now following the Feather River, she thought of nothing but her aching feet. How did people do this? Some had wide-spreading bare feet, some limped painfully, others sprinted as if they made this trip every week. The ones who seemed to be doing the best wore the same heavy-duty Plastix sandals she wore. It was a stroke of luck she had a new pair molded for her feet just last month.

On the fourth day, the quasi-saltwater port town of Marysville wavered ahead like a mirage through the rising heat waves of the upper Sacramento Valley. Small, flat-bottom boats bobbed in the dock's shallow waters as workers refilled cargo for the last leg of the journey up to the Oroville Dam, miraculously still standing despite three major quakes. Asian immigrants had thrown so much rock and rubble against the dam in their annual ritual to placate the water gods that, despite the second damaged spillway, it remained standing. Of course, there wasn't much water to hold.

At the town's periphery, a narrow footbridge spanned the Yuba River where it joined the Feather River. The toll-keeper accepted two Pharm.food packs and let Amisha cross into Marysville. Like an oarless boat, Amisha drifted with the other travelers into a cluster of narrow streets and disheveled brick buildings. She followed a sandal-footed woman holding a bulging plastix bag into what appeared to once have been the town's center—one-story buildings with large windows and individual doors pressed shoulder to shoulder along the street. Amisha had heard of storefronts from the era when businesses stocked all the merchandise they sold so people could touch and try things on before buying. How inefficient. The sandaled woman emerged from a door holding another bag. Shopping? Amisha was confused. Why wouldn't she ment her order? It would be there before she got home. As the woman turned the corner out of sight, Amisha realized once again that she'd have to figure everything out for herself.

A small temblor ripped the ground; metal rooftops sizzled in the searing light. Only fools, no, what was the phrase—*mad dogs and Englishmen*—are out in this heat instead of inside taking a siesta. Amisha remembered that much at least. She wiped the trickle of sweat from her forehead and turned back to the levee in search of shade.

Tucked against the crumbling dirt levee built to contain the once-ravenous flood waters of the Yuba River stood a white-squared archway with corners upturned to the sky. Beyond it rose a red-and-white gabled building, its red door framed by vertical banners with black inscriptions like the ones she once saw in old China Town. Amisha traced her fingers around the corroded brass letters to the right of the door: "Bok Kai Temple: God of the North Who Controls Water and Floods, 1880."

People milled about in the clean-swept courtyard. A few clustered under the trees in quiet conversation. Amisha appeared to be the only one who wasn't a new-wave Asian climate immigrant, come to reestablish the roots set down by their gold rush ancestors. Across the courtyard, a steady stream of people disappeared through a dark doorway and reappeared clutching small brown packets. A wizened man with dangling gray whiskers shoved her aside and hobbled in. A young woman emerged with a whimpering baby pressed to her breast. Amisha yearned to touch the baby's head, but the mother turned away. A baby. How long since she had seen one.

Amisha stepped into the dark, incense-filled room and waited for her eyes to adjust. Hovering over a small altar, a woman bowed and placed a handful of rice before a small gold figure of a deity. Red tapered candles illuminated the offerings of flower petals, nuts, and seeds. In a small room to her left, a young man and woman huddled over a counter where an old hunchbacked woman wearing a shawl held the girl's thin white wrist. The old woman reached for the boy's wrist, pondered a moment, eyed his tongue, glanced at the girl's belly and below the boy's belt. On the wall behind her, she opened one of the many small drawers, measured out a thimble of dried gray leaves, mixed it with a fine brown powder, and handed it to the girl. The boy pressed a small package of rice into the old woman's hands.

Amisha stepped to the counter. "I'm a doctor," she said, pointing to her chest, then realized it was futile to say that anymore. The old woman waved her hand as if to ward her off, then grasped Amisha's wrist and pressed her fingers up and down an imaginary line. With a deft move, she slipped the ribbon away from the crusted gouge on Amisha's neck, turned back to her drawers, and handed Amisha two packets of pungent-smelling herbs, chattering in her foreign tongue as she pointed to Amisha's chest and to her neck. Amisha handed her a Sally. The old woman shoved it back and pointed to her mouth.

OK, OK, Amisha thought. She dropped a neon-blue Pharm.food packet on the counter. The old woman swept it to the floor. *Then you can have your little packet back*, Amisha wanted to say, but something made her drop the herbs into her backpack. She placed a small handful of raisins on the counter. In a flash, they disappeared.

Outside in the blinding light, Amisha had no idea where to go. East to the foothills? Ask? She'd never had to ask—whatever she needed was always in her mind, sometimes before she'd even formed her question. But her neck hurt, her chest hurt, and her mind hurt from having to figure everything out. She leaned against an arch and closed her eyes. Breathe in, out, slow, in, slow, out. . . . From behind her she heard footsteps, then a hand covered her eyes, and another hand tore off her backpack. She fell slow-motion to the ground, her shoulder pinned down, a taste of blood in her mouth, more shuffling, then footsteps running away.

Gulping for breath, Amisha opened her eyes to see a toothless old man hovering so close that his tangled gray beard almost brushed against her cheek.

"You OK?" He extended his gnarled fingers toward her arm.

Wild-eyed, Amisha tried to scramble from under him.

"Whoa, now. Just checking for any damage."

"My pack?" She looked at the feet circled around her. A black boot kicked her bag toward her. Amisha shuffled through the contents. No purse, no Sallys. A sizable crowd now gathered in front of the temple. Heart racing, she turned to the old man, but he had disappeared.

Go! Now! Amisha grabbed her pack and backed away one step behind the other, keeping the crowd in view until she reached the corner. The herb woman appeared with a broom and swished people back into the courtyard. Amisha crossed the street into an alley and ran, zigzagging around piles of discarded plastix and furniture until she reached the end, then turned into an even smaller alley. Gasping for air, she leaned against the brick wall to catch her breath. Down the far end of the alley, canyons of dark buildings floated in and out of focus. A ragged horizon resembling mountaintops hovered in the distance. Mountains? Like a moth to flame, she grabbed her pack and headed east toward the distant hills.

By staying close to the north side of the levee, she followed the river to the edge of town, where several streets converged into what was likely the main route into the hills—a road as rough and worn as the travelers. Those trudging back into town hardly lifted their heads at her, but the ones traveling up with packs piled high and rifles slung over their shoulders approached her from behind and, with hot breath down her neck, pushed her aside with an elbow to her ribs, sometimes whacking her bum like a mule. Maybe she didn't get their ments to get out of the way. She learned to keep her distance.

As darkness settled in, Amisha started looking for a place to rest. She'd pushed herself too far—her calf muscles cramped like crazy, her feet were swollen, and a sharp pain flashed across her chest with every breath. At the next bend in the road, she turned onto a lesser-used path and collapsed against a wagon abandoned at the edge of a barren field. Pack off, she opened two blue Muscle-Repair Pharm.foods thanking any and all gods that her food had not been stolen. And the tomato? It was still there. She would celebrate with it later, even if it was to be her last meal.

Amisha peeked at the directions again: *River north to Marysville.* Yes. *At fork, go east into foothills.* She'd done that. *Ask, but not directly.* There's no one she dared to ask. *Follow the string of pearls to La Luna.* That one baffled her. And finally, *Be careful.* Monica didn't have to remind her of that. With her sweater balled beneath her head, she stretched out under the wagon. Lulled by the vestigial memory of the river lapping against the boat, her breathing slowed like water dribbling down an oar into the brackish waters. Then all was quiet.

In the faint early morning light, Amisha was torn from her sleep by heavy boots stomping inches from her head. A sharp stick jabbed at her belly.

"Get the hell out!" A deep, raspy voice bellowed. "Out!" Rough hands reached under the wagon, pawing for her neck, belly, and hips. An animal brayed in alarm. Four hairy brown legs shuffled behind the black boots.

Amisha scooted out from the other side of the wagon. "Don't touch me! I didn't mean any harm." She grabbed her backpack and turned to run but tripped over the old man's stick. Grizzly brows, like strands of metal fiber, concealed his sunken eyes. A tattered hat hid his face. His breath revealed he was hardly sober, and from his chin dangled a beard like tangled gray moss.

"Shouldn't 'a' left," he groused, inching his arthritic fingers along the perimeter of the frayed tarp that covered the wagon's contents. "What'd you pilfer?"

"I swear, I was only sleeping." With her perception keened by days of hypervigilance, she lifted her backpack and stepped back several steps, stopped, then scooted to the right. The old man's eyes remained fixed on the space she had been. Without a sound, she shifted several feet more to the right.

"You can't see, can you?"

The old man lurched in the direction of her voice, but Amisha stepped away before his hand could grab her. He fumbled and turned, sniffing for her location.

"Not much worth seein' anymore, so don't make no difference I can't see," he snorted. He maneuvered the dusty-gray mule into position and worked the buckles with his thick fingers until his mule was harnessed. "Argo here knows to always bring me back over there." He pointed with his chin to the small tent across the street.

"What's 'there'?"

"You know." The old man gave a few pelvic gyrations to make his point. "Never too old for that, are we? Gotta have my farewell plunge."

"Farewell?"

He pointed his chin toward the mountains, his beard quivering like dried leaves in the wind.

"Those the Sierra?" she asked.

He reached for her wrist. "I'm thinking maybe I should take you with me."

Amisha twisted to avoid his grasp.

"Only one good reason for a woman to be up there."

"I've my own reason for going. Don't need yours."

"Well, then," he said, smoothing the worn patch between Argo's ears. "If ya don't want my company, you should head north where it's safer."

Amisha eyed the old man. She had the advantage of sight—she could outrun him if needed.

Be careful. She remembered Monica's last direction.

It was a calculated risk.

"I'm only going one way," he warned.

"Me, too," she said.

"How old are ya?"

"Thirty-five."

"Gettin' on in years, aren't ya? Don't know as I have much use…"

"I've got food."

"What kind?" The old man perked up.

"Pharm.food mostly."

He frowned.

"Crackers, raisins."

He ran his tongue over his lips. "Get in then." He pointed to the back of the wagon. "Call me Charlie." He wavered his hand into the space between them.

"Amisha," she said, diverting her hand to avoid touching his gnarly fingers.

"Thirty-five?"

Amisha turned away. "Look, I'm here for the ride . . . nothing else."

Charlie lifted the brim of his hat. "Me too," he grinned.

Jostled on the hard seat at the back of the wagon, Amisha shielded her eyes from the scorching sun and watched the valley recede into the shimmering haze below. She was grateful for the least bit of current stirred up by the wagon wheels and grateful her swollen feet weren't still pounding the hard trail. An occasional traveler passed them heading downhill, following the mostly gravel riverbed back to the valley. Charlie tipped his hat at some; others he flashed the long blade he kept hidden beneath the seat. With the river on their right, Charlie hummed in rhythm to Argo's steady steps. It was hardly a lullaby, but curled against her backpack, Amisha drifted like a baby in a rocking cradle. Several hours later, she was awakened by stillness. Behind the wagon, Charlie was relieving himself in the brush.

"Damned buck brush," he grumbled as he untangled his pants from the thorny branches. He pulled out a metal canister from a small compartment hidden beneath the bench and passed it to her. "Have some water . . . but not too much. Next water's at Brown's Spring, if you can call it water."

Amisha held a small mouthful against her sticky dry gums before swallowing. She took another swig, then returned the canister to its hiding place. "What's up there?" she asked, pointing to the hint of peaks in the distance.

"You askin' 'bout hills? Not much."

"People?"

"They've come and gone, mostly farther north."

"Oregon?"

"Farther. Canada's still deciding its immigration policy."

"They say fires took out most of the foothills. Anything survive?"

"A structure here and there."

"Trees? People?"

"Can't say," Charlie climbed back into the wagon.

"Why are you going up there?" Amisha asked.

"Can't say that either."

Midday, Argo pulled the wagon into a small clearing. Charlie lifted the wagon tarp, fumbled for the feed bag, then filled his hat with pellets and offered it to his mule.

"Now where's our food?" Charlie rifled through Amisha's backpack, ran each object under his nose, discarded the familiar crinkle of Pharm.food packs, and pried open the bag of raisins.

Amisha opened the neon-green packet labeled "AM Push" and placed it in his palm, then opened an orange one for herself, "Gym Hour . . . for building muscle."

"Used to have one of those sun.autos." Charlie gummed at his bar. "Traveled faster then. Had to give mine up when my eyes went dim."

"You don't have to be blind," Amisha said. "Doctors can fix that."

"Not everyone who wants gets to be fixed. Anyway, I'm much better off not seeing so much," Charlie said, puffs of air escaping through his pursed lips. If he said more, Amisha didn't hear. She was lost at the mention of sun.autos and, for the thousandth time, wondered at what she had done.

When they returned to the wagon, Amisha squeezed in next to Charlie so she could see where she was heading. They passed occasional wagons and solitary foot travelers hunched under the weight of their packs. The way they looked her over made her press closer to Charlie.

"What's this about?" Charlie asked.

"Don't like how they look at me."

"And you're going up into the hills alone?"

Her eyes welled up. "I just want to make it there. After that, it doesn't much matter what happens."

"Then maybe you'd better tell me where you're going."

Amisha took a deep breath. "I'm looking for an old homestead . . . and a necklace." She waited for Charlie to say something, but he seemed deep in thought.

After hours of silent travel, Argo turned north onto a lesser-used trail, hardly wide enough for the wagon. Charlie went ahead feeling for branches grown over the path, then snapping them off or holding them aside for the wagon.

"This is such a tiny trail," Amisha said, anxious about the new direction. "Shouldn't we go back to the main road?"

Ignoring her, Charlie continued on for an hour before they entered a clearing. Charlie ran his fingers over a faded hand-carved sign and grunted for Amisha.

"Englebright Meadow?"

He cleared his throat. "We'll tie into the string here." He wrapped the reins around the post. "You can almost hear the river trickling. Almost." He held back a willow branch as Amisha got down. "We'll go by foot the rest of the way, let Argo manage the wagon without our weight."

That explains the odd, long shape, Amisha thought. I assumed it was a coffin at first.

"Your choice. Go first and bushwhack with my blade or follow in the dust."

Amisha gripped the carved-bone handle, surprised at how unbalanced she felt with the heavy steel in her hand. She threw it at a nearby branch.

"Whoa!" Charlie yelled. He grabbed the blade and sliced through the brush with long, arching strokes, continuing until she got the idea of a steady rhythm. "You haven't told me the truth yet," he said, thrashing the air with his blade as he tried to return it to her hands. "No one in his right mind goes up there anymore."

"You are," Amisha replied over her shoulder.

"I've got my business there." He moved closer. "Don't see there's any business for a lady up there."

Amisha covered her nose and continued clearing the trail.

"Raised my two sons up there," he said. "Before the dam. They never forgave me for sellin' out. Now land's gone, home's gone, even water behind the dam's gone." Charlie rambled on about all the dams built along the western slope of the Sierra to capture rain and melted snowpack. "What hurts is my boys blame me. But what could I do?" He wiped his eyes with his dingy sleeve. "Don't think I have any more trips left in me." He took the blade from her and whacked at a branch brushing his knees. "Aw, hell, don't suppose it'll hurt for you to know—there's still a few folks holding out. I run supplies up to them. It's the least I can do."

"To your sons?"

"Hell, no. They're long gone. Dead for all I know."

Amisha cupped her ear against the hot wind gusting up from the valley below. She wasn't sure she heard him right. "Who's holding out? How many?"

"Who knows? They're pocketed here and there along the string of pearls."

Amisha shot up. "What'd you call it?"

"Wasn't sure when you said 'necklace.' Thought I'd test you," Charlie said. "You got something to tell me?"

Amisha nodded. "It's my way back home." She pulled out the cloth with Monica's instructions and read it to him. "*Follow the string of pearls*—I had no idea what it was."

Charlie thumped his stick into the dirt. "You're on it right now," he hollered. "Hundred years ago, some crazy guy wanted to build a necklace of parks and trails from the ocean to the mountains. They called him both visionary and lunatic back then. But to us, well . . . he gave us a lifeline."

"Oh, my god, I can't believe it!"

"Ole John Olmsted was always in people's faces, begging money for the next trail. But he knew . . . he knew!"

"We follow this trail and we'll get up into the Sierra?"

"Or back to the ocean, if you get turned around!" he howled. "If we're lucky, we'll make it to the first dam by dark. It'll be a good place to overnight." Charlie motioned her close to him. "Walk up here with me. It's your turn to tell me what you're really looking for."

Under the canopy of tall brush that arched over the trail, Amisha unfolded the events of the last year—her failing health, removing her Nib, the family homestead—but made no mention of the voices.

"If you've come to die, that's probably what'll happen," Charlie said. "Mostly buzzards and survivors up there to pick your bones clean. At least, that's what I'm counting on."

Amisha shuddered. She hadn't thought much about the details.

"We're quite a pair, then," she said.

"Yup, the blind leading the blind, as they used to say."

ELIZA
1865
Niles, Michigan

"Come in, lassie, come in!" Douglas Frazier pulled open the heavy sliding door of his carpentry shop. "You're late, I almost started without you." Years of pipe smoke deepened his already heavy Highland brogue. Breathless from hurrying over from school, Eliza followed the strong-shouldered Scotsman to the rear of the workshop, inhaling the mixture of sawdust, lacquer, and tobacco.

"Where is she?" Eliza asked, scanning the shadowed corners of the kerosene-lit workshop for the remains of Grandmother Oak.

"Aye, the wood your father set aside for a new fireplace mantle is over there on the racks." He guided her around the long workbench that commanded the center of the room. "I don't know how you convinced him to make you a desk instead, but I'm glad you did," he said, as he brushed the powdery dust from his worn leather apron. "The wood is seasoned enough to work with, but for some unfathomable reason, I just cannot seem to get started."

"Show me."

As Mr. Frazier hung the lantern from a ceiling hook, a warm glow spread over the oak planks, making them appear to dance with light and shadows.

"Pick out the ones you want for the top of your desk. Maybe that's the best place to begin."

"The ones my hand will rest upon when I'm writing, then." She leaned over the rack to examine the grain of the top pieces.

"No. No! Feel with your hands, lassie. Your hands!"

Eliza spread her palm atop the plank closest to her. The wood felt warm beneath her fingers. She reached over for the next piece, like the branch that pulled her upward. Some planks felt anxious and cold; those she discarded. Others filled her with memories of snuggling deep down into Grandmother Oak. A few filled her with such intense longing that she quickly withdrew her hand. Then, quite clearly, she knew what she wanted.

Small enough to carry.

Eliza quietly drifted from piece to piece, setting certain ones aside for Mr. Frazier to put on the workbench.

As wide as your hips, as deep as your arms can reach.

She arranged her selections in order.

Three slats on either side, a shelf below,
and a small drawer for our journals, pencils, and pens.

Eliza rearranged the order of the oak heartwood planks.

"Aye, never ask a woman to make a quick decision." Mr. Frazier tucked his hands into his armpits.

And no nails.

Eliza stepped back from the workbench. Before her was the perfect desktop made of four three-foot lengths of heartwood resting side by side.

"Mr. Frazier, I don't want any nails in this wood."

"As in mortise and tenon joints? Now whatever does a young lassie know of furniture construction?"

Eliza shrugged and drew her hands into her coat pockets.

She stopped by every day after school, making a game of seeing how long she could watch Mr. Frazier enveloped in his cloud of sweet pipe smoke before he noticed her. Today he seemed more grumbly than usual, throwing up his hands as he measured, cut, and struggled to fit the pieces together.

"I figured it'd be time for you to be showing up," he growled without looking up. "I should be done w' this part by now, but I'm just not gettin' a good fit here."

Eliza set a wicker basket on the worktable. "Something to sweeten you up," she smiled.

Mr. Frazier popped a whole oatmeal cookie into his mouth and mumbled as he chewed. "I've never had so much trouble in my live long life. Look at this!" He held up two pieces that should have been a perfect mortise and tendon joint yet wouldn't set together right. "It's like they're at war with each other." He reached for another cookie. "Well, Liam will be back tomorrow. He'll help me figure this out."

Liam Frazier—with his coppery red hair and flashing wide grin. Like most boys in high school, he never noticed her, so, contrary to her outgoing, flirty girlfriends, she paid him no mind. "Didn't your son go back east?"

"Aye, studyin' to be an attorney," Mr. Frazier said with obvious pride. "Much too bright to be a humble carpenter. He's coming home next week for school vacation. You'll probably see him here."

Eliza shrugged an off-handed "maybe," then returned to examining the misfit pieces.

"Is this the frame that goes beneath the desktop?" She arranged the sections into a rectangular shape.

"Aye, and it's a puzzle that's refusin' to connect all its pieces together."

Eliza recalled fleeting images of women sitting at a desk. She held one of the longer pieces across her hips.

"Mr. Frazier, I see your problem. The frame is simply too narrow. It must be at least a hand wider."

"I disagree. I'd say it fits you quite well." Mr. Frazier brushed crumbs from his tangled beard and held the piece up to her again. "I hardly think a young lassie should be telling a master furniture maker how to do his business, especially when her father is paying me quite handsomely," he said with a twinkle in his eyes. "I intend to build a desk befitting the daughter of a judge."

"But Mr. Frazier, I see it quite clearly—like in a dream."

"So, now it's wood nymphs givin' me directions?" He took a long puff. "Well, I canna' afford to cross those nymphs. Last time, I ended up bottom of a creek." He lifted a new piece of wood from the stack. "If I make the pieces longer, they'd best come together like the handshake of old friends!"

The next month, Eliza's attention was diverted from the desk to packing for school. The Michigan Female Seminary's list of what students were required to bring was very specific. Every corner of her bedroom was stacked high with items from the *Student Handbook*: *towels, napkins, a napkin ring, one teaspoon, two sets of sheets and pillow cases, a blanket or a Marseilles quilt, flannel underclothing, thick shoes, overshoes, an umbrella, and a dress for gymnastic practice.*

The list of required books excited her the most. Papa had given her a modern atlas and English dictionary, and she already had all the standard poetical works. But she'd have to ask Vicar Baker for *Songs for the Sanctuary.*

"Do you think I'll need more than three fountain pens?" Eliza asked her mother. She had a habit of breaking nibs by pressing too hard.

"Why don't you just pack extra nibs," Sophie suggested. "And your desk? Will it be ready? She scanned the packing list with a scowl. "I see no mention of bringing furniture." Before Sophie could protest, there was a loud rap at the bedroom door.

"May I come in?"

"Papa, you're home early!"

"I've a message from Mr. Frazier," Wesley said, unable to withhold a smile. "Shall we go?"

The moment Eliza placed her hand upon the desktop, she knew it was perfect.

"Say something, lassie!" Mr. Frazier winked at his son Liam then looked to Wesley and Sophie for approval.

"Eliza?" her father nudged.

She was lost beyond words. It was just as she had seen it in her dreams.

"It's perfect, Mr. Frazier. Simply perfect. You are indeed a master furniture maker."

She circled the desk several times before opening the small drawer—the right size for her notebooks and fountain pens. As she closed the drawer, a pattern in the bottom caught her eye. It was a heart—an irregular yet recognizable heart made by a knothole cut in half and placed side by side.

"The wood nymphs will be proud," she whispered to Mr. Frazier.

"It's so beautiful," Sophie admired. "How ever did you get such a deep polish?"

"I canna rightly say," Frazier stammered. "I think this little desk is just glowin' to be here."

Liam nodded to Eliza from across the desk. "If you ask me, it could have been made much larger. There's hardly enough room for all the books you'll need. There's no space for studying or . . ."

"I want her small, so I can carry her with me wherever I go," Eliza interrupted him.

"You're only going to Kalamazoo. I'm sure there are workmen who could carry your desk for you."

"We're going to California," Eliza blurted. Startled at hearing herself utter these words, she retreated to a corner and waited for her father to negotiate with Mr. Frazier on the price, then hand him an envelope of money. She didn't mention California again until letters started arriving at school and her obsession became more than she could contain.

Mr. Frazier had Liam help deliver the desk up to her room (she blushed to think that Liam was in her bedroom) and set it in the open space next to the door. Not quite right, Eliza lifted it against her chest and easily moved the desk beneath the window overlooking the open meadow.

With only a few weeks left of high school, her teachers noted an abrupt change in Eliza's work. Mrs. Cutter, who rarely gave Miss Osborn more than a perfunctory "very good" on her English papers, started using phrases like "clear, concise, masterful vocabulary." Mr. Hubert wrote in the top corner of her civics and government report that while he disagreed with her premise that Manifest Destiny did not give "patriotic pioneers" permission to destroy everything that got in their way, including "heathen" Indians, he noted that her argument was well-executed and insightful. Eliza set the page facedown on the desk. "I think it is *we* who are the heathens in the Indians' world."

Deep in thought on her walk home from high school that afternoon, she didn't notice Liam until he tapped her shoulder from behind.

"Miss Osborn?"

"Hello, Liam." Normally, she felt self-conscious around Liam, with his red hair curled about his ears like a Greek Adonis, but since the desk arrived, she felt unusually emboldened.

"Don't you think America should lead by example, not by conquest?" Oh, how she wished she had smiled instead, or blushed, or asked after his father, but those were the first words that left her lips.

"May I lead you by example?" Liam took her arm and guided her through the group of classmates that stopped to watch their encounter.

"What I mean is . . ."

"I understand your concern, Eliza, but without conquest, there would be no America. It's the nature of how we grow and expand." Liam firmed his grasp on her elbow and steered her across the street. "It appears we are walking in the direction of your home. May I continue with you?"

Mrs. Osborn placed another setting on the table that night, a practice she adopted for Liam's entire semester break. Liam infused Eliza's life like a drop of ink in a glass of clear water. Liam, the boy who never noticed her a whit in school, now waited across the street to accompany her home, strolling right past Ruth and Sarah, the most popular girls in her class.

Although Liam and Papa did most of the talking at dinner, Eliza remained in awe that tall, handsome Liam was sitting next to her. Liam dabbed his full lips with the linen napkin just like Papa, and when Papa leaned back to unbutton the top of his vest to make room for his dinner, so did Liam. He even sipped red wine from the crystal goblet, leaving the same amount that Papa left in his glass.

In three more years, he would be an attorney and, he pronounced, someday a judge like her father.

Later that night, Eliza sat at her desk and wrote his name in her notebook. She added an extra flourish to the "L" and extended the "m" into a curl. She continued writing until "Liam" filled half of her page, then added "Liam Frazier" all the way to the last line. Did she dare? Just one line then. She held her breath as "Mrs. Liam Frazier" appeared on the page. Her insides quivered as again and again she wrote . . . "Mrs. Liam Frazier."

When Liam returned to law school, Eliza wrote to him every other day describing her studies, quoting her favorite Shakespeare sonnets, and sharing her dream of graduating from the seminary in four years and emblazoning her students with her love of English literature. Liam wrote lengthy letters back, expounding on torts, courts, and laws. One letter made her heart leap, for though it may have appeared to her they were courting, this was his first mention of matrimony.

"It may please you to know that as an attorney, my wife should have a prestigious education. She should be learned in the arts and literature and uphold any parlor conversation but, of course, will never need to work herself."

Eliza put his letter back in the envelope. Not work? Perhaps love of learning would be sufficient for her. She would hold salons, invite prominent artists and thinkers, be sought after near and far. "Mrs. Liam Frazier's Sunday Salon," she wrote across the page. "Mrs. Liam Frazier, Mrs. Liam Frazier." She stopped; the "L" was looking oddly like an "S." She deliberately formed an "L," but again her hand wrote "S," then "Silas," "Silas Baxter," and "Mrs. Silas Baxter."

Wherever did this come from? Eliza dropped her pen and pushed back from the desk. Mother and Papa's old friend from California? This was silly. She shuffled the papers into the drawer, capped the nib of her pen, and went outside to get some fresh air on her hot cheeks.

HARMONY
1987
Luna Valley, Northern California

"One, two, three . . ." Jeff pulls the lever of our new meter box on the temporary power pole. The disc starts whirling and, voilá, we're connected to the grid. I feel a bit decadent. Neighbors on either side of us still live in trailers and half-built cabins with noisy generators they run until bedtime. But with unlimited electricity now, we can install a well, recycle our five-gallon water jugs, and get on with the real reason we moved up here—building our home. Well that, and the baby the midwife announced is due in seven months!

Jeff is stunned. I guess I am, too. I thought condoms and a diaphragm were as good as the pill but without the risk of artificial hormones. Perhaps they're not as effective inside sleeping bags? It didn't take us long to get excited. Or our parents. Dad sent us another check to get the house finished faster. Can we do them both—a baby and house in seven months?

I assume we'll build on Great-Grandma's foundation, at least make it into a room, maybe our baby's nursery. Wrong. Jeff and I walk the neighborhood men around possible building sites. They're stoked to have a new house to help build, but according to the guys who know such things, Great-Grandma's hillside is too steep to cut a road up to the old foundation.

"Don't get blinded by sentimentality," Mark chides, and guides me back down to level ground where our car is parked. Lark and

Nova pull out their tape measures and start marking the best position for solar gain in winter and shade in summer. That night, Jeff pours over *The Owner-Built Homestead* so he can keep up with the guys.

The first month, our two-story hand-hewn, Woodbutcher-style home rises from a newly poured concrete foundation a short walk up from the driveway. We use local cedar and pine from the mill where Mark works. A work group hauls our hand-selected round stones up from the river for the fireplace. From salvage yards down in the valley, Jeff scavenges an old claw-foot tub, windows, and French doors. Oli, the stonemason from an older settlement down toward the valley, builds a curving stone staircase from the driveway to where it meets the wooden staircase leading up to the front deck.

Five months later, the house is nearly ready to move into. The old 1934 white Wedgewood cook stove commands the kitchen to the right, ready to cook with propane or heat with wood. At the other side of the main floor, the black cast-iron wood-burning stove will heat the rest of the house with oak and madrone we cut from our land. Upstairs, a long hallway connects two bedrooms and a bath.

My sister, Carole, wants to send us some furniture as a housewarming gift—a telltale sign she's redecorating again.

"Your rustic country home is perfect for these antique pieces," she tells me over the phone. I'm silent. I know what she's up to.

"Then let me give you just one piece," she cajoles.

"Grandma Dottie's old desk?" I suggest. Now she's silent. "Look, I appreciate the offer, but you should see how small our house is. Maybe you could keep it in your basement?"

We sigh in unison, mindful of our promise to mom.

"Then I'll just send you some flowers. Do they deliver out in the wilderness?"

Just as the house is completed, my new women friends surprise me with a "Blessing Way" baby shower. They festoon our living room with candles and incense, drape my belly with lengths of colorful gauze, and adorn me like a goddess with flowers and a necklace of beads imbued by each woman with positive energy for the new baby. It's all so earthy and ethnic. How could life be so perfect, so creative, so filled with harmony?

And that's when I know my new name—*Harmony!*

Jeff and I work like crazy over the next four weeks to get our self-sufficient garden and orchard established before the baby comes. Over dinner, I make a two-page list of the vegetables and herbs I want to grow. Jeff estimates we'll need twelve raised beds and calculates whether there's enough lumber left over from the house construction to build them. He wants to build them himself despite the cherried thumb he got from helping build the small woodshed.

While he's hammering away, I borrow Nova's truck and head to town to buy fruit trees. How many will we need? One dozen? Two dozen? Which fruits keep best? Before checking out, I sweep through the rows of seed packets and drop one of each type in my basket. I'm too exhausted to look at my list. I return with the truck bed filled with bare-root spindly trunks of Arkansas Black and Sierra Gold apples; a Bartlett pear; Italian prune; Babcock peach; Rainer and Bing cherries; three types of almonds and walnuts; twenty blueberry bushes; and three dozen strawberry plants. I have a vague memory of stories of Great-Grandma farming in the valley. Someday, I'll have to research that.

At home, I wait outside the truck door for Jeff to come down from the garden to help me unload. He removes the tarp and looks at me incredulously.

"Do you realize how many holes we'll have to dig? I'll still be shoveling dirt when you're in labor."

I stand there, teary-eyed, rubbing circles around my melon-ripe belly.

"Oh honey, I'm sorry." He enfolds me in his arms and gently rocks. "I'm just so happy to be here with you, and the garden, and the baby." He reaches around and presses his hand against my tailbone, something he knows gives my aching back relief. "We should go over names tonight. Maybe shorten our list?"

"As long as it's a nature name." I sniff.

But something gnaws at me.

Next morning over breakfast of homemade biscuits and fried eggs, I take a deep breath and say what I've tried so hard not to let bother me.

"Jeff, honey," I put my hand over his, "I can't be Harmony without my music. I miss my piano desperately." I shove my plate back and tap out the first measure of a Chopin polonaise on the kitchen table. "My heart aches and my fingers are getting stiff."

"That's your pregnancy, dear."

"I don't want to sound whiny, Jeff, but music's been a part of my life since I was a little girl. I worked hard getting my degree. Now I'm going to lose all my proficiency."

"I understand, Harmony, I really do, but we both agreed—"

"But it's just a piano. Everyone has a piano."

Jeff pops the last biscuit in his mouth and grabs the Volvo keys from the hook. "I'm sure the school must have a piano they'll let you play on. When I get back from this short job in Sacramento, you can take the car and go talk to the principal."

"But what about our garden? What about all our new fruit trees? I can't dig holes in my condition."

"I'm finally getting in with the EPA," he says. "Even a two-day consulting job is a foot in the door and it's money. Not much coming in otherwise."

I reach for a tissue. He reaches for his city jacket.

"When I get back, I'll dig you an orchard full of holes."

On Friday nights, we rotate houses for a neighborhood potluck dinner. The unwritten rule is the main ingredients in your dish must be organically grown in your garden, which means lots of tomato spaghetti sauce, zucchini, and salads. Of course, I love this idea, but I realize that while shucking off the old ways, we've created new standards of "good and bad." If it isn't organic, it never makes it into our homes. Brown rice is good; white, not. Cotton clothes, natural; poly is petroleum. Recycling, saintly; garbage, sinful. Sugar is out; honey in (however, since peaches and pears never can well with honey, I decide a little sugar won't hurt anyone and keep a secret container just for canning). I brag about growing and eating our own food like we invented this lifestyle ourselves. *Listening to Mother Nature* is our new religion, and aside from a few chainsaw accidents, marauding bears, and botched canning jobs, this is a golden era—at least that's how I record it in my journal.

During our communal dinners, we first catch up on each other's week, then turn the conversation to what's happening in the outside world. Last week we brainstormed how to eat lower on the food chain to avoid the accumulation of man-made toxins in the fish and animals we eat. This week we're back to the prophesized great collapse of all society due to the impending depletion of oil.

"Life as we know it will be over," Indigo pronounces in somber tones. "No one knows how soon, but Swami says to start preparing for the worst."

I sigh. No sooner do we connect to the electric power grid than we obsess with finding ways to do without it. Jeff fills the tool shed with long-bladed scythes, saws, and mauls suggested in *The Whole Earth Catalog*. I keep my cantankerous old sewing machine because it can be retrofitted with a belt and foot pedal for power when the time comes. Our electric grain mill also comes with a hand-crank, and although I love my new blender, I keep Grandma's old eggbeater hanging on a hook. We store kerosene for lamps, save seeds for next year's garden, and are thankful for wood from the surrounding forest to heat our home, even if it means laboring with a handsaw. We're so prepared for the prophesy that lack of oil will be civilization's downfall, that I ignore my dreams where it's always the lack of water.

But right now, water is plentiful. We pump water from deep in the earth, water splashes over granite river boulders, and, one night, in the middle of the night, it trickles down my legs.

"Jeff!" I fling back the quilt. "Drive over to Indigo's. Call the midwife." I start panting my Lamaze breaths as he fumbles with his inside-out jacket. "No!" I grab his arm and pull him back. "Don't leave me. I think it's coming!" By morning, our house is humming with women, including Dora, who refuses to come in but keeps busy chopping wood outside until it's all over. With Jeff holding me in his arms, I am the center of a universe filled with chanting, massage, raspberry-leaf tea, encouraging words, and a hell of a lot of pain.

"Back labor," Morning Star, the lay midwife calls it. She reminds Jeff how to apply pressure to my tailbone. I hear him wish he could take my pain away, but I'm in too deep to even grunt back. Twenty-two hours later, pushing the last two hours on my hands and knees, Morning Star guides little Claire into Jeff's trembling hands and now it's Jeff who's crying. Two years later, baby Sage does the same. Small wonder my favorite herb is clarey sage!

AMISHA

2075
Sierra Nevada, Northern California

Lost in thought, Amisha followed Charlie and Argo into the shadows of the deepening river canyon. Argo navigated the seldom-used trail with ease while, behind her, the two-footed travelers struggled over the sharp rocks that jutted beneath their feet. There was water—a little, anyway—enough for Amisha to soak the kerchief Charlie gave her and tie it around her sweltering forehead. Charlie never complained about the heat. She never saw a drop of sweat on him.

Though enough daylight remained to travel farther up the river canyon, Charlie halted the wagon in a rocky outcrop below the steep walls of the aged dam.

"Tired?" Amisha asked.

"Nope, just don't like sleeping in a bed of mercury 'n arsenic." Charlie unhitched Argo and with a light whack, sent her out to forage for her dinner. "Do ya see a cracked cement wall up there? Did a damn good job of holding back all the poisoned dirt from the gold mines, but once you've got it all held back, what do you do with it?"

"You're talking two hundred years ago, Charlie. It's gotta be gone by now."

"Well, I'd be mad as a hatter to touch the earth behind it. Get it? Hatters all mad from using mercury to make their felt hats!" He chuckled at his cleverness, ignoring Amisha's silence. "We'll overnight here like I always do and get an early start tomorrow."

As the cool night air slid down the face of the dam and settled in the riverbed below, Amisha snuggled into Argo's thick, rough coat. Charlie's raucous snoring rattled into the silence from the other side of the mule. Sometimes silence hurt Amisha's ears and made her jumpy. Other times, the silence lined her mind like soft moss. The strange call of a night bird or the trickle of water against rounded river rocks wasn't enough to fill this new emptiness. And the night sky—far too dark without its familiar night glow.

The next day the threesome trudged up the trail and crossed over the top of the dam, then continued under the scorching afternoon sun along the high ridgetop.

"Taking the high route's a calculated risk. We could be picked off for target practice," Charlie warned. "But it's easier traveling up here. Brush 'n' rocks all cleared away. Still, you never know who you'll meet around any bend—most not worth spittin' at. Stick close to me, keep your head down, and you'll be . . ."

"Snake!" Amisha screamed. Charlie held up his boot midair, waited for the four-foot reptile to slither by, then set his boot onto the ground and continued.

"Charlie! Snnnnnake . . . huge . . . you were going to step . . ."

"But I didn't, did I? What color? Black, brown, yellow?"

"Don't know. I've never seen a snake before. Like dried leaves maybe."

"Did it make music?"

"Huh?"

"Music! Play its rhythm instrument," Charlie snapped. "Was there a rattle at the tip of its tail or did it taper off in a point?"

"I didn't see."

"Well you better start to see 'cause your life will depend on it."

Amisha wiped the sweat from her forehead. Her Nib would have alerted her. Or would it have? Nudged from behind by Argo's nose, she started back up the trail, glad for the mule's sympathetic company. When Charlie caught up with the wagon, he stopped Argo at a fork in the trail.

"Which way?" he asked Amisha. "Your call."

"Which way's the string of pearls?"

"Both, for now." Charlie tied the reins around a thick manzanita branch and hobbled over to her. "Once we get 'cross the meadow, you'll have an important decision—right or left fork? But right here, Missy, it's only this way or that." He jutted his chin up and down the path.

"I've no idea."

"And neither do I 'til you tell me exactly where you're going."

She closed her eyes. She had no idea, really. String of pearls, somewhere in the Sierra. She slumped onto a rock, eyes welled with tears. "When I left, all I wanted was to get to the homestead. Now I just feel stupid and helpless." Her pent-up tears gave way to sobs. "Tell me what to do, Charlie."

Charlie felt his way onto a rock slab across the trail from her and waited.

"Tell me!" she pleaded.

Unmoved like the rock that supported him, Charlie stared into the space between them.

"I can't do this anymore. Please! I can't go backward . . . I'm afraid to go forward."

Charlie waited.

Her chest squeezed so tight, she could hardly get air into her lungs.

Charlie closed his lids.

Adrift in the surrounding silence, Amisha's only option was to wait for Charlie to do something. Behind her, Argo shifted in the brush, oblivious to her plight. High above, a rock tumbled down the embankment and rolled across the trail. She moved her foot to let it pass. In time, the tight band around her chest released, her breathing slowed, and a tear slipped down her cheek and into her open hands. She studied the tiny pool of water spread out in her palm, then lifted her eyes to the silvery full moon floating in the late afternoon sky just above the horizon.

"Moonlight," she murmured.

Charlie lifted his head. "What'd you say?"

"Moonlight," she repeated. "Luz de la luna."

"Are you sure?"

Amisha nodded. "Yes, la luna . . ."

"As in Luna Valley? By god, ya should have said so!" Charlie shot up. "I know that place. Doubt there's any folks left, but there's only one way to get there."

"Turn right, then," Amisha said without thinking.

"And you knew that all along," Charlie said. "Let's see what else you remember."

The travelers continued along the high ridge that paralleled the dry lakebed below. As Charlie warned, three armed vagrants appeared out of nowhere, blocking their trail. The lead man, whose chalky skin was indistinguishable from the dusty trail, singled Amisha out and, pointing his long blade, commanded her to uncover the wagon.

"Just give 'em your food packs," Charlie whispered as he pretended to unfasten the tarp. "I'm old and blind, but you need to be strong. Tell 'em you're carryin' the dead up to be buried. That'll scare 'em."

Amisha lowered her eyes so she wouldn't be unnerved by the two men whose rifles were pointed at her, then lowered her voice in warning. "The man in this coffin is too infectious to be buried in Marysville. Do you really want to see?" She motioned for Charlie to loosen a corner tie.

"Hell, no!" the lead man jumped back, nearly knocking the other two over. "Just give us your food." Amisha tossed four Pharm.food packs to the ground, then slipped over to Charlie while the men snatched up the neon packs and scrambled back down the trail to the valley.

"Hope they choke on 'em," Charlie grumbled.

Once they were safely past the dry lakebed where most of the mining contaminants had collected, they dropped downhill into a long meadow and stopped at another fork.

"Got two choices here," Charlie whispered into Argo's long ear. "If we stay on the necklace along the First River canyon, we'll end up a long way from Luna. But, if we drop the necklace and stay left, we'll follow the Second River past Rice's Crossing and maybe make it to the base of the next dam. What do ya' think?" Argo stretched her neck back like she wanted a scratch, then reached for the green-tinged brush to Charlie's left and pulled off a twig with her yellowed teeth. "Left? Good choice, girl!"

At their next camp, Amisha caught her foot in a deep hole in one of the smooth granite rocks in the dry riverbed.

"Hey, you're walking in someone's kitchen!" Charlie warned. "Course, you probably don't know what a kitchen is!" While Amisha rubbed her ankle, Charlie pointed to the six-inch hole. "We've been traveling an old Indian trail, and that hole you stepped in was one of their mortars for grinding food. Means this was once a good place for gathering food and water." He picked up a stone and hurled it down toward the dry river. A small furry rodent skittered under a charred tree stump. "Used to be common to find miners' cabins nearby, too, sometimes built right on top of the mortars. Those miners were smart. They knew to look for where the Indians lived and erect their tent cities smack on top of them."

"And what happened to the Indians?"

"Wasn't pretty," he shrugged.

Charlie instructed Amisha to search the brush for something edible, like red berries or pine nuts. She returned with a handful of hard red manzanita berries but spit them out. No wonder the Indians didn't last, she thought. Or maybe the heat got to them. She hunkered down under the wagon's shade and nibbled on a gooey clump of raisins.

Early the next morning, Charlie roused Amisha from her sleep and, with hardly enough light to see the trail, they continued up the river canyon into the hills, barren from decades of fires.

"Don't need eyes to know when the sun's up," Charlie said. "I can feel the heat waves rising ahead of me!"

Like the rodent scurrying from cover to cover, Amisha scanned the trail for the next boulder or bush that might offer shade. After stopping to eat under the eaves of an old powerhouse toppled by a long-ago earthquake, Amisha soaked her kerchief in a small collection of precious water, then wrapped it around her neck. They resumed their journey up the trail to the next fork.

"Right or left?" Charlie gave her another test. Amisha chose left, only to dead-end after a short distance at the base of the old Garden Bar dam. Defeated, she rerouted and they continued the rocky trail up the Second River canyon.

"Gettin' close, I can almost smell it." Charlie grabbed a stick and whacked around the brush to find the entrance to a small trail hidden by overgrown buckbrush. "Only a few know it's here." At the top of the hill, they were greeted by a pair of turkey vultures circling overhead. "Don't feel much signs of people," Charlie grunted. "Don't know if that's good or bad."

He pressed Amisha for what she remembered. They were getting close, but he needed more details.

"I've only a few fragments, Charlie. Like green—everywhere."

"Well that's no help. How about water? Had to be near water. If they didn't have a well, you're out of luck."

"All I remember is a long road winding uphill. And two gigantic red-barked trees at the bottom. I was young. I just can't remember anything else," she snapped.

"You must have at least a tiny drop of your ancestor's blood left in ya'! Which side of the road? Right? Left? Or are you too tired to listen to yourself?" He felt for an old stump and settled down to wait.

Amisha sat on another nearby stump wishing desperately she could get an infusion to lighten her chest pains, to ease her mind, to let her rest. She took a deep breath and closed her eyes. Light as a curl of smoke, her memory drifted between the two trees, up a curvy road, around a bend. Her eyes flashed open.

"Red bark. What has red bark?"

"Manzanita, madrone," Charlie sniffed. "Like this here stump I'm sitting on."

Amisha jumped up from her stump—also red. With Charlie's blade, she whacked wildly at the brush between their two trees. Despite Charlie's warning to take it easy, she chopped at the overgrowth until a path began to appear.

"This is it. It's gotta be!" Laughing and crying at once, she yanked at vines and pushed back the towering brush until she could see the road bending to the right.

"Come up, Charlie, you gotta see this!" she shouted, but Charlie remained below.

"I've gone 'bout as far as I can go," he said when she returned and placed the blade in his lap. "Nope," he waved her off. "It's yours now. Keep it close."

Suddenly she noticed how frail he looked, wizened almost. "Please, Charlie, stay with me one more night. I don't know what I'll find, and you should rest." Her voice was suddenly squeaky and tight.

"Sorry, time's up." He pressed his hands on his knees to push up and, half bent over, wandered back to the wagon. After fumbling under the front bench, he found the blade's black leather sheath and directed her to fasten it to her waist. This time, Amisha didn't recoil. She pulled out her backpack and, on impulse, unwrapped the tomato and held it to his nose.

"Never thought I'd live to smell one of those again." Charlie took another whiff.

"Here," Amisha pulled out the blade, but he stopped her.

"You need this tomato more'n I do," he said. Just remember to save the seeds, wrap 'em in that cloth, keep 'em dry and dark, give 'em dirt and water. You'll figure it out."

"Please, Charlie. Please come up with me. I don't want to be alone."

Ignoring her, he felt his way to the other side of the wagon and tightened the canvas cover.

"But it's getting dark, Charlie."

"Do my best traveling in the dark," he said as he settled onto the bench. With a soft "gid'y'up," the wheels started to roll.

Amisha hugged herself tight to keep from shaking. There had been no time for last words or even to thank him. Charlie was already far down the road, and when she looked up again, he was gone.

ELIZA

1868

Yolo, California, and Niles, Michigan

Fork and plate cleared from the kitchen table, Silas raised the wick of the kerosene lamp and set a sheet of ivory notepaper in front of him. Perhaps tonight he would complete the letter that had been stirring around in his head for days. Half a page later, he crumbled it and threw it into the fireplace amid the ashes of yesterday's drafts. He shouldn't be writing her. The page smoldered and burst into flames. Hell, she's probably a grown woman by now who won't even remember who I am. Could even be married. He reached over to the wobbly bookcase where he kept a cigar box of receipts, neatly stacked San Francisco newspapers, a clay cup of pencil stubs and fountain pens, and an 1860 directory of Kentucky horse breeders. Last time he saw her was when he was back purchasing Holsteins. He flipped through his dog-eared journal of farm records. There . . . 1863. Why, that'd make her eighteen or nineteen now.

He set another oak log on the fire. Something had lit his melancholy streak. Maybe too many days of gray overcast sky. In the pasture outside the kitchen window, calves bawled for their mothers, and mothers returned their calls. Nobody to talk to, maybe that was it. He pushed an ember back into the flames with the poker. He didn't mind the women dropping by with jams and pies, but they conversed outside on the porch. It wasn't proper to invite them in.

Still, it was a good life here. The farm was a manageable eight hundred acres of grain, fruit, cattle, dairy, and his prize, Yolo Maid—the finest three-year racehorse around. What more could a forty-six-year-old man need?

Oh, hell. He reached for another page of stationery. He'd just write that girl a simple little letter. Maybe elaborate more on the questions she'd asked him at dinner back in Niles. She'd made him think, he chuckled, which was more than he could say about any woman he'd met out here. Miss Eliza was interested in hearing about California once. He'd start with that.

Michigan Female Seminary, Kalamazoo, Michigan

The headmistress, Miss Parmalee, lifted a crumpled ivory-colored envelope from the day's mail basket, held it up to the light, turned it front to back several times, then peered over her wire-rim spectacles at the twelve dinner tables of chattering young women.

"Letter for Miss Eliza," she announced. With a heavy trail of flowery perfume following in her wake, she stopped at Eliza's table.

"From California?" Eliza reached for the letter, but the headmistress did not release her grip.

"This must have slipped by me. I don't remember anyone from California on your parents' list of acceptable correspondents." Miss Parmalee turned to address the growing curiosity in the room. "It is my responsibility, young ladies, to see that you are protected from unhealthy contacts." With a dramatic sweep, she lifted the letter back up to the light and read the upper left corner. "'S. R. Baxter, Cache Creek, California.' This appears to be a man's penmanship, Miss Eliza. I cannot permit you to read this without first contacting your father."

Mr. Silas? Eliza ignored Franny's elbow nudging her in the ribs. Why would he be writing her? She stood to face the headmistress. "He's just an old friend of my parents. A farmer from my hometown. He lives in California now."

"And looking for a woman, no doubt. Don't trust anyone from California." Her voice rose shrill above the growing murmurs. "Uncivilized men looking to snatch up a wife to do their cooking and cleaning and," she paused, "have their progeny." Eliza stared at the floorboards beneath the headmistress's black boots. "We are educating you, my dear," Miss Parmalee lifted Eliza's chin to look her directly in the eye, "for a wholly more dignified life." The headmistress stashed the letter in the bottom of the basket and with a brisk turn, distributed the remaining letters. "Miss Katrina," she nodded in approval, "here's one from your mother, and Miss Portia, a letter from your sister."

Two weeks lagged by before Miss Parmalee called Eliza to her office. Deep burgundy drapes held back all but the slightest shafts of natural light. Eliza brushed past the black woolen cape hooked on the coat rack and took a seat across the desk. Other than the kerosene lamp and a few pieces of paper resting under the headmistress's clasped hands, her desktop was bare.

"Good morning, Miss Parmalee."

"And to you, Miss Eliza."

"You've heard back from my father?" she asked politely, so as to keep any excitement from her voice.

The headmistress studied Eliza's face, then looked down at her desktop.

Eliza gasped. Under the weight of the headmistress's folded hands was the open envelope, two pages of handwriting, and a small pile of dried leaves.

"What are these?" The headmistress nodded to the desiccated foliage.

Eliza peered closer. "You opened my letter?"

"I took it upon myself to investigate. I've learned there are some things that even a parent lacks awareness of." Miss Parmalee leaned forward. "Had your father allowed you to read this letter without my oversight, you might have unknowingly been led astray."

"But those are leaves. Pressed specimens."

"Do you know what he means by these?"

"That is my personal correspondence."

Miss Parmalee glanced at the first page. "Would you like to read it?" She moved the letter toward Eliza, then pulled it back. "How old is this man?"

"I really don't know. He's old, though younger than my parents. I recall him to be a rather pleasant gentleman." Eliza scrambled to remember him—brown beard, blue eyes with squint lines when he smiled. She liked his laugh. Polite. He mainly talked politics with her father, but he always stopped to answer her questions about California.

With her fingers tapping against the elbow of her folded arms, Miss Parmalee looked Eliza directly in the eye. "May I remind you," she began, her voice slow and controlled, "that upon graduation you have an obligation . . ." she cleared her throat and continued, ". . . to teach high school in Niles. I've worked very hard to procure that position for you—a very prestigious appointment for a new teacher." Her eyes loomed wide behind her thick spectacles. "I can't have you doing anything that would jeopardize this."

"I always honor my commitments," Eliza nodded. There was a period of silence when neither said a word; then Eliza leaned forward. "May I please have my letter now." Without further word, Eliza picked up the ivory pages and dried leaves, slid them into the envelope, and left.

That afternoon, Eliza did not attend class, nor did she show up to supper. She spent the day at her desk reading and rereading the letter. Something made her feel jumpy inside. Here was someone who really cared . . . she didn't know how to put it into words, so she read the letter one more time.

February 21, 1868, Cache Creek, Evening

Dear Miss Eliza,
I find myself compelled to write you a letter this evening, although I imagine you are wondering what would prompt me to do so. Your father said you read all the letters I sent to the family. Forgive me if I am too bold, but I imagine you are now old enough to correspond directly. I find myself in a state of melancholy this evening thinking fondly of my family and acquaintances in Niles and missing contact with them.

I remember the dinner conversation at your parents' home and how when you asked me questions, I found myself at a loss to answer. This wintry evening in my walk through the woods beyond my house, I noticed how many types of oak trees live on my land, and as I picked up some well-preserved leaves, I thought of your question—"Are there oaks in California?" As you can see, I have sent you a collection of pressed leaves from around my ranch.

The small blue-green lobed leaf is from the low-growing Blue Oak that dots the hillsides and gives my cattle welcome shade. The small pointed leaf with the toothed edge is the Interior Live Oak that grows low and wide and keeps its leaves year-round. The deeply lobed leaf is the massive Valley Oak which is probably akin to the big oak near your house. The largest leaf is from the Black Oak that turns a brilliant yellow in the fall behind my house.

I hope this letter finds you in good health. I understand from your father that you are completing your liberal arts education at the Female Seminary in Kalamazoo. I hope that the four years will provide you with an understanding and appreciation of the arts and culture of this world. I must admit that California is sadly lacking such refinements. For all its youth, the west remains a very uncultured place.

I would be pleased if you would care to write me at my Cache Creek address. I have much I could tell you of California. It is both a difficult and a remarkable place to live.

> *Sincerely,*
> *Silas Baxter*

That night, while her classmates slept, Eliza sat at her desk and replied.

Kalamazoo, Michigan
April 15, 1868

Dear Mr. Silas,

Is this the correct way to address you? I am not quite sure, but I seem to remember we called you Mr. Silas at the dinner you wrote of. Of course, I was only a child. Perhaps I should call you Mr. Baxter?

I must confess I am at a loss for how to properly reply to your correspondence, but I feel I must try. My heart stirred when I saw the return address from California. At night I dream of that distant place and, even in daytime, my imagination wanders among the rolling hills of California, quite forgetting that I am in class, studying, and soon to graduate as a teacher myself. I have pressed the leaves you enclosed between the pages of my favorite Emerson poems.

I just knew that California would be filled with so many oak trees. If there is one thing I am certain of, I shall not be content to live under the shade of any other tree. You may not have heard, but tragically, my favorite tree (I called her Grandmother Oak) suddenly collapsed and split in four directions. I cried for days. She was over three hundred years old! Can you imagine anything that old? The desk I am writing on was made of her heartwood. It's all I have left of my dear Grandmother Oak.

Would you like news of the family? Mother and Father are both well. Frederick will soon be taking his Bar exams—sure to follow in Father's footstep. Alas, poor Teddy might not continue his studies— I do not think he has the mind for it and hopes instead to apprentice with the riverboat captain. After graduating, I will be returning to Niles to replace stern old Miss Henson, who taught Geography and History since I was a student at the high school. I can still see her marching all those dates and historical events across the chalkboard as she dissected history into daily doses. I would much prefer to teach English but have been informed by Miss Parmalee it is an honor to be accepted there at all.

Oh, Mr. Silas, I would make a confession to you, but I fear those who would lay their eyes upon these pages before they reach your hands. I would be ashamed of anyone thinking I am ungrateful for the education I have received at the seminary. Now I have said enough.

My imagination hungers for details of California life. It is the only way I can escape the path I see laid out before me. I do hope you will write more.

> *Your friend,*
> *Miss Eliza*

HARMONY
1988
Luna Valley, Northern California

"I thought we moved up here to avoid all this." I lower a quart of pickled beets into the canner and wait for Jeff's response, but he doesn't look up from the letter that came in yesterday's mail. He opens a map and runs his finger along the road that runs through Luna Valley. The furrow between his eyebrows deepens.

"Looks like they're planning on spraying the entire road."

"They can't, can they? I mean, that's what Rachel Carson was all about—long-term consequence of synthetic pesticides."

"County's using herbicides."

"Makes no difference. They're all chemicals. And, for god's sake, she died of breast cancer. How ironic is that?"

Jeff pulls a little curl of hair from behind his ear and twirls it between his fingers.

"OK, I'll call the county, find out what herbicide they're planning on using, then check it out with Chris at the EPA."

That afternoon, he contacts his friend, and the news is not good. The Department of Public Works is going to use glyphosates.

"Don't worry," says the gravelly voiced foreman over the phone as he reads the product information label to Jeff. "Toxicology tests show glyphosate-based herbicides to be environmentally friendly and biodegradable. We wouldn't use it otherwise."

Deep in my gut I know it's not true.

With a nod from Jeff, I know it's time to act. I pull out my grease-stained phone-tree list and call neighbors. Everyone's concerned but can't seem to find a time to meet before next week when the spraying begins. Indigo and Lark have two ewes ready to drop, Mark's working on a big order at the mill, planting by the moon means Nova and Summer must get their succession crop of beets and carrots planted right now, and Dora? Well, Dora's ready for a fight anytime.

That afternoon while I finish canning the last of the beets, Dora and Jeff hunker down over the kitchen table and work out a short-term strategy. Jeff will type up a list of the potential harm this new herbicide will create if sprayed in our community. Dora will photocopy the list at the town's library and put one in every mailbox on the road. We'll ask the neighborhood kids to make "No Spraying Here" signs to post where our private property meets the county road. And last, I'll call the Department of Public Works and tell them not to spray between signs.

"Now tell me again why you folks don't want all those noxious weeds killed along the road?" the gravelly voiced man at public works asks me for the second time.

"It's not about the weeds, it's about the poison you're using." My voice rises to an exasperated pitch. "Why can't you mow like you've always done?" He patiently explains about spraying being state of the art and more cost-effective, but says he'll pass the word along to the road crew. He doesn't. They spray and, for the first time, we have a huge die-off of our bees. I can't prove a connection, but I make extensive notes in my journal.

AMISHA

2075
Luna Valley, Northern California

Utterly alone, Amisha unsheathed her blade and sliced into the tangled branches cascading over the road, but the approaching night made it difficult to see. Too exhausted even to flinch at the small snake that slithered past her feet, she stopped at the bend in the road to catch her breath. Charlie chose a hell of a time to abandon her. Now she had nothing to quell the fear that rose from its hiding place deep in her belly—no infusions and no distracting banter.

Arched high overhead, an oak tree's long mossy branches bowed almost to the ground. She recalled moonless nights when Luke brought her here just to frighten her. But maybe the long branches had only been protecting her. She closed her eyes, imagined holding Grandma Claire's hand, and drifted into a white fog. Beating against time, her heart slowed. *Let go, let go, so easy to just let go.* A branch snapped. Amisha opened her lids to a thin shaft of moonlight filtering through the leaves overhead. If I'm going to die, please, please, let me see if the homestead is there before I go.

Amisha loosened her grip on her backpack; it fell to the ground, and the strange packet of herbs from the old Chinese woman slipped out and landed at her feet. She'd forgotten about them, wasn't even sure what they were for. But the old woman had put them into her palm and pointed to Amisha's chest with an insistent nod. Without much thought, Amisha unwrapped the packet and spilled the contents into her mouth, coating her dry tongue like a bitter poison. She didn't care.

When at last she found the strength to move, the road seemed to expand and contract one step ahead of her. Winged creatures fluttered overhead and, although her head spun, her heartbeat was strong. Moving with borrowed strength, Amisha pushed herself to the top of the road, where she imagined the house might be. Moonlight glimmered through the shadows of a tall madrone tree on her right. Across from it, a different light caught her eye. Another moon? She spun around. A window. A moon reflected in the window. The broken window of the old house. Silent and dark, the two-story homestead appeared like a lone ship in a sea of fog. A distant owl hooted and, as her world flickered, Amisha collapsed to the earth.

Night closed its blanket of darkness. Nothing stirred. Long shadows drifted overhead and passed on into the night. Owls and nighthawks muted their calls. Bats diverted their flight. A black beetle dug out from underneath the weight that had suddenly entombed it. There was nothing more . . . no desires, no distress, no dreams.

Does she know she's home?
Not yet.
A temblor shuddered the earth.

From the upstairs window, two women watch and wait.

It's too cold for her, says the one with an amethyst broach pinned high at her neck. Her long skirt rustles as she shifts her weight to peer out.

She should have come earlier. We waited too long, says the one in a paisley peasant blouse.

Raven appears high on the madrone. Her iridescent purple-black shimmers in the moonlight. She fluffs her feathers to gather in warmth, lifts her wings, and with a single swoop circles the body. Raven cocks her head at the face of the human on the ground.

Is she breathing? the women ask.

Raven nods and considers the woven hair resting along the curves of the figure's spine. She pulls the teal ribbon from the end of the braid. It slips snakelike onto the earth. With her thick black beak, Raven grasps the braid, pulls the top strand to the right to expose a flat band of hair beneath. This she lifts and pulls to the left. Over and under, she unweaves each layer until the body is blanketed with thick waves of sandy hair. Raven jumps back.

She'll need more warmth to make it through the night, says the one with the amethyst broach. The room sparkles in purple moonlight as she pulls a down comforter from the bed. The other removes the window screen and together they toss the comforter out the window. Millions of downy feathers billow and float, gently enfolding the body as they come to rest.

From that night through the night that follows, Raven remains at Amisha's side, while below, the trembling earth cradles them against her spacious breast, lulling them with the rhythm of her ancient pulse.

ELIZA

1870

Niles, Michigan

How quickly everything happened. With hardly a year of correspondence between them, Silas informed Miss Eliza he was coming back to Michigan to get acquainted. Get acquainted? She had no idea what that meant until he was at her doorstep, shifting on one foot then the other, his beard tinged with gray. Had he really proposed with an oak leaf? No mind that he was twenty-seven years her elder; she was going to California!

The entire Osborn household was aflutter. Silas announced he must start for California by end of the week, giving them time for a simple wedding in the parlor with tipsy Reverend McClaren, the only minister available on short notice. Sophie deftly fashioned a short veil from the English tulle she had bought when it appeared Liam was a prospective son-in-law, but Liam had returned to law school alone the day before Eliza announced her engagement to Mr. Baxter.

The Methodist ceremony was brief, and after an awkward kiss on the lips, they were soon chatting in the parlor as if, Eliza thought, nothing terribly important had just happened. Silas set his teacup on the table, cleared his throat, reached into his pocket. Eliza held her breath. A wedding gift, perhaps? But, no, Silas unfolded his carefully written packing list for her. In five days, she must be ready with clothing for California's hot and cold weather, dishes, sewing machine (if she liked), and even a few books. He was leaving for Kalamazoo in four days to procure some specialized farm tools. When he returned, they'd load up and head west. It wasn't until he rode off that she noticed her desk was not on his list—even after she'd insisted a dozen times that it come with her. That's when she had the first of many regrets.

The morning of their departure, wagon all packed, Eliza stood on the porch in her best blue traveling dress and wide-brimmed bonnet tied with blue satin ribbon and waited for her husband to set out the hitches for the oxen, Zion and Beulah. With sleeves rolled to his elbows revealing dark curly hair on his forearms, his sun-browned hand slid along the curve of Beulah's flank with ease. Eliza noticed her desk was still on the porch.

"No room. I'll send for it later," Silas said, returning to test the last buckle.

"There's been some mistake." Eliza threw off her hat and rushed over to the wagon.

"Did you see a *desk* on the packing list I gave you?"

Eliza yanked back the wagon's cover and climbed inside. Silas had everything tightly packed like a puzzle: white sacks of flour, sugar, and salt; farm tools; sewing machine; her trunk of clothing; and a box of china. Near the entrance was a crate of all she'd need for cooking—cast-iron pots, enamel cups and plates, utensils, paper, and matches. Water barrels were strapped on the outside; the mattress and bedding roll was tied on top.

"I made this trip to California in '49 and '63. I know exactly what we need and where everything fits. There is no place for your desk, Eliza," Silas said, standing behind her with a broken buckle in his hand.

"We can put it there." She pointed to a crate with nothing on top.

"That's where the oxen feed goes."

Eliza held up a cast-iron pan. "The desk can be a table to cook and eat on."

Silas replaced the pan. "No."

"But you promised."

"You assumed. Listen to me," Silas said impatiently, "it may be made from your old oak tree, but there's plenty of oaks in California. I'll make you another desk soon as we get to the ranch."

Eliza climbed down from the wagon and marched over to her desk.

"That thing stays here," Silas yelled after her as he turned back to the barn.

"You have no idea," she yelled back. "No idea at all." With an imperceptible wave, Eliza motioned Teddy over to the wagon. Within minutes, her brother had removed the sewing machine and replaced it with her desk. Silas emerged from the barn just as Teddy's wagon and the sewing machine disappeared behind the house. Ignoring her husband, Eliza continued stuffing small items into the open space between the desk's legs.

"You told me you need the sewing machine to make the ranch more livable," Silas said.

"I need the desk more. I'm sure there are sewing machines in California."

Silas drummed his fingers on the side of the wagon, thinking it would have been a damn sight easier if he had sent them both on the new intercontinental train. But she wouldn't have it—had to travel the old way. Well, wagon travel may be a lot easier than it was in '49, but the desert crossing hasn't changed a bit. He threw his hands up in the air.

"It's your decision. But I take no responsibility for what may happen."

HARMONY

1994
Luna Valley, Northern California

Jeff maneuvers the two oversize boxes up the stairs and carefully lowers them onto my worktable, positioning them so the Apple logo faces us. He's as excited as a kid at Christmas although, in fact, it's *my* birthday present. I glance at my trusty old Smith Corona electric typewriter unplugged on the floor. I'm not too sure. After three hours of tinkering, Jeff's ready to show off the easy-to-use, platinum-gray appliance that now commands my worktable like an alien ship.

"Wait 'til I show you what this baby can do." He reaches behind the fourteen-inch-high box and switches it on. It comes to life with a cute little jingle sound. From the back, an intricate jungle of cords connects the computer to a separate keyboard, something called a "mouse," and—you've got to be kidding—a printer? Right here in our house? He's got my interest in a big way.

"Once you've used word processing, you'll never go back to your typewriter," Jeff promises. "It's all they use down at the EPA. No carbon paper, no white correction tape, no trips down the hall to the mimeo machine. Secretaries are practically seducing their bosses for one."

Three thousand dollars is a lot to pay for a fancy typewriter, and I hold firm against it until Jeff explains how this thing called AOL will let us instantly send messages to our friends who also have America Online.

"With AOL, you can write one email and notify everyone all at once instead of spending hours on the phone."

When I learned what this little box could do, I became as giddy as Jeff. If everyone connected this way, we could live the simple life on our land, yet be linked to the rest of the world. Everything was coming together.

In all my excitement about our new computer, I lost track of the garden. This evening, the full moon starts waning and once it's down, I can only plant underground vegetables like beets and carrots. The pressure's on. Before breakfast, I've got my homesteading books out on the kitchen table, each one open to planting requirements for a vegetable that must get in the ground today: summer squash, green beans, soybeans, chard.

I spread out three years of garden notes and planting maps, cross referencing so I don't plant the same plant in the same place as last year to avoid disease, and so that each vegetable is paired with the right companion plants for mutual support. Next, I list the supplements needed for each vegetable. "NPK: nitrogen, phosphorus, and, shit, what's the 'K'?" I ask Jeff, who's pouring his first cup of coffee.

"Potassium."

"Why 'K'? Why don't they make it something obvious like 'P'?"

"That one's already taken," he laughs. "Hey, why don't you make a computer chart of all this mess. We've got Excel now. It'll be easy."

By early afternoon, I emerge from the office elated. I've now got a two-page Excel spreadsheet for this year's garden with columns of what, where, and how to plant each vegetable along with little boxes for each bed. I can't wait to get out in the garden and start digging. But now the afternoon is blazing hot and I'm exhausted. I scowl at the old Chinese saying posted over the door:

Do Not Miss the Planting Time.

AMISHA

2075
Luna Valley, Northern California

Amisha opened her crusted lids. Her cheek stung with the imprint of tiny sticks and stones from the ground. How long had she laid there? Uphill, wings flapped away. She squinted to focus. Images, like leaves tossed by a whirlwind, slowly settled into place. She had found the homestead.

Moving in slow motion, she approached the two-story wood house. It felt vaguely the same as she remembered from summers with her grandparents. Narrow wood stairs curved upward to the large deck by the front door—certainly it was much wider and taller than this! Grandma Claire always sat on the deck, sometimes reading, but mostly staring off into the distant forest.

Amisha carefully tested each step for rotted wood or missing treads. A jumble of dead pine boughs covered the deck. She remembered playing there with Isabelle. Sometimes the deck was their Jupiter explorer station or a covered wagon. But her favorite was the underwater mermaid cave with blue ribbons waving from the railings. Luke. Why did he have to ruin everything, even her memories? He always found a way to crash in. With his hand over her mouth so she couldn't yell, and Isabelle cowering in the corner, Luke twisted their play into a sadistic world where he forced them to trample the evil flowers in Grandma's garden or feed him cookies stolen from the kitchen.

Amisha raised her hand to the door. Should she knock? Shout hello? It was her house, wasn't it? With a single push, rusted hinges gave way and the door opened.

"Hello?" With the sound of her heart pounding in her ears, she paused for a Nib.alert. But no, that was the past. "I'm here, I made it!" A bat flapped past her face as it escaped out the open door. "Hey!" She slid her pack from her shoulders and dropped it to the floor. "Something called me here. Tell me!" She stepped inside. The house smelled stale, dry, dusty, and . . . smoky.

"Hello there," she called again, this time more cautiously. If someone lived here, she wanted to know first before confronting them. She looked around. The ceiling seemed much lower than she remembered. The living room should be on the left and the kitchen and dining area to the right. Yes! A table pushed against the front window held a brown pottery vase stuffed with dried flowers laced with filmy cobwebs. Knives, forks, and plates were set out as if the next meal would be soon—as if someone had expected to stay but didn't. Water? She turned the kitchen faucet as far as it would go. Not even an empty hiss.

What about food? Ravenous as she felt after two weeks of travel, she wanted to save the last six Pharm.foods in her pack until she knew she could survive here. Otherwise, they would be her lifeline on her retreat to the city. Then she remembered the tomato still wrapped in Monica's cloth. She had removed it so many times to check the cryptic instructions, it had become soft and bruised, but when she slit it into quarters with her blade, thin, red juice trickled down to her elbow. Quickly lapping it from her arm like a cat, her nose nearly exploded with the scent of warm tomato. She stuffed one, two, three quarters into her mouth before remembering about the seeds! What the hell, she squeezed some juicy, seedy pulp from the last quarter into the yellowed cloth and stuffed it in the bottom of her backpack. The last piece she chewed slowly, savoring the fleshy texture, indescribably earthy aroma, and unbelievable juiciness.

Amisha opened the warped doors to the old pantry cupboard. Six shelves were filled with glass canning jars, mostly empty, but some contained foods too shriveled to identify. She sniffed the brown powder in one. Better not. The middle shelf was covered with empty seed shells and fine wood dust. On the bottom were several large cloth bags. She pulled one toward her. Its sides split open and long, tapered nuts spilled across the floor. They are . . . she tried to ID them with a right-flick, *Shit*. How would she know what they were? She tried to bite one, but it refused to break open. She smashed it with a heavy pan until the cream-colored nutmeat separated from the smooth shell. Foul and bitter, she spat it out. Squirrel food. She'd toss the nuts outside later, because right now she really, really needed something liquid. Nothing in the kitchen even hinted of water.

On the other side of the kitchen, an old white stove with a "Wedgewood" medallion on the oven door was hunched back against the wall. It looked so tiny. The stove Grandma had presided over was like an old steam engine, with six cast-iron burner covers she would hoist up with her black handle, then light the burners with a swoosh. Grandma, with her fresh tomato sauce simmering on the back burner next to a tall pot of salted boiling water for pasta. Right now, Amisha could drink the whole pot, salt and all. The stove was covered with crusty blackened pots and rodent droppings, but someone had cooked here.

She didn't notice the broken chair pieces strewn on the floor next to the stove's trash burner until she tripped on a wood leg and landed on the floor next to a small hatchet. Someone could cook with the trash burner if they had wood. She dug what was left of a furniture leg out of the trash burner and turned the singed piece over and over. It could have come from anything—chair, table, but please, not the desk.

Increasingly weak and woozy, Amisha knew she had to have water. She remembered how Grandpa Auggie watered berries and fruit trees in the orchard—there had to be more faucets outside. She stepped toward the back door and, without noticing the footprints on the dusty patched linoleum floor, went outside to find the orchard. The stepping-stone path between the house and orchard was obscured by a packed layer of dirt, but she knew the way by heart to the gate she used to swing on while Grandpa watered. Fruit trees still dotted the orchard—if you could call gnarly trunks and dead branches an orchard.

Surrounding the orchard, a wire fence was crushed to the ground in several places, creating an ambling pathway through the fruit trees from the small ravine below. Beneath her feet, animal droppings disintegrated into a fine powder of dried seeds. Bears ate berries. Were there still bears? She grabbed a weathered shovel handle and followed the animal trail down into the ravine, drawn by a smell she could only identify as not dry. Creeping rock by rock, she followed the scent downhill until the earth began to feel cool beneath her feet. A small patch of green grass grew squeezed between two large stones. With the shovel handle, she wedged back one of the stones then pushed the handle into the earth. It returned wet. Deeper, wetter, she dug until a small amount of water collected on the surface where she knelt. Amisha plunged her face into the water and sucked in a mouthful of wet grit. Crazed, she dug the handle back into the spring, but the more she stirred the earth, the slower the water rose. She sat back, realizing she would have to wait. Could she exist on this? If she brought back a bowl, how long would it take to fill? She pressed her open palm back into the moist earth. Water trickled between her fingers and began to fill her cupped hand. It's all she had, but for now, it was enough.

The midday sun had almost completed its arc across the bleached white sky when Amisha reluctantly left her spring to explore farther down the ravine. A thick tangle of thorny green branches revealed the source of seeds in the animal scat. She plucked a purple berry and popped it into her mouth, chewing until it released its moisture and tart-sweetness onto her tongue. She gorged until her stomach groaned a warning to take it easy.

With berry sugar coursing through her blood and lifting her spirits, Amisha didn't hear the low growl or see the movement until a brown flash charged at her, leaving a trail of blood on her arm. She jumped back from the scruffy cub, heart pounding, legs shaking. From the other side of the berries, a gaunt mother bear reared up on two legs and bellowed her warning. Amisha dropped the shovel handle and ran. Certain that the bears were at her heels, she ran faster back up the ravine, through the gate, and across the dirt toward the house.

With her hand about to push the back door open, she froze. Smoke. She smelled it before she saw the black cloud writhing out of the chimney. Inside, loud voices, men arguing, glass breaking. No warning to divert her from the outburst, no infusion of stabilizer to help her think, nothing to calm her crazy breathing. The yelling intensified. Steps came closer to the door. She turned and ran.

She escaped to the spring and dropped to her knees, shaking and gasping for breath. But she knew she couldn't stay. If she had found this water, they may also use it. She scrambled up the ravine through the thick brush to the base of an old madrone tree. From there, she could rest in its branches, watch the spring, and see the rooftop. A shot rang out, then another. More smoke. Please, please, I didn't even get upstairs. If the desk is there, please don't burn it.

Hidden high up in the madrone tree, Amisha suffered through the night, neither moving nor sleeping. Her only defense was to listen. All night long, twigs snapped, leaves crackled around her. Man? Bear? Her spring was busy that night. Footsteps of all sizes quietly entered, stopped to drink, and moved on. If she had known how to check the damp earth for signs, she would have known she was not alone.

By dawn, the house was visible again. Cramped, starving, and thirsty, Amisha shimmied out of the tree and crept closer to the orchard, where she could see and hear better. Two men. The tall one, wearing only torn pants and a vest, barked commands through the black beard that obscured his face. The other, shorter and more tightly muscled, followed each order by stuffing objects from the house into their backpacks.

Amisha wrung her hands. Please don't let them come for water.

A metal blade flashed in the sun, blinding her temporarily, then the men hoisted their heavy packs onto their backs and headed down to the road.

Would they return? She was afraid. It wasn't safe to go back, but neither could she live out in the woods. Amisha returned to the spring and planted her feet into the cool earth. Hours went by. Light gave way to dark. Stars appeared—masses of stars like she had never seen.

"Orion, are you still out there?" She dropped her head into her folded arms and wept.

Footsteps approached, tiny, tentative crackles in the leaves that paused, considered, and turned away.

Here, the wind seemed to whisper.

ELIZA

1870

Nevada Desert

California! But this was not the California of her dreams. Her heart did not swell at the first sight of the Sacramento Valley below. Eliza hid in the back of the wagon, bitter and withdrawn. Silas had stopped the wagon at the top of the Henness Pass to adjust the harness away from the sore on their ox's neck.

Hardly a week ago, Eliza was standing by their wagon in the wastelands of Nevada, hands shading her eyes from the harsh sun. Before them was the infamous Humboldt Sink, where the Humboldt River fanned into a marshy flat before completely vanishing into the parched floor of the Nevada desert.

"And so, we enter the 'shadow of the valley of death.'" Silas gazed past his wife's vacant expression to the endlessly rippling desert ahead. "I wish to god I'd put you on that new train. It would have been much easier—and safer—for you." Eliza closed her eyes and remained silent. She'd resolved to get her desk safely to California, and if that meant trading a cushioned seat on the transcontinental train for a hard bench on Silas's covered wagon, well, so be it.

It would take three days to cross the legendary Forty-Mile Desert. When temperatures soared over a hundred, Silas insisted they sleep under the wagon's shade during the day and travel silently at night under the light of the cool moon. Eliza didn't sleep much the first day, for even under the wagon's shade, heat penetrated the sand beneath their straw mattress, leaving her drenched in sweat. Silas waited for the afternoon sun to start its descent toward the desert floor, then rolled up the bedding, fed and watered the two oxen, and nibbled on the hard biscuit that Eliza handed him.

As they traveled deeper into the desert, Eliza willed herself to keep her gaze straight ahead, for discarded on either side of the trail were trunks, rocking chairs, wagon parts, and tragically empty cradles that rattled warnings of what was to come. She clenched her stomach, for the pervasive stench of dead ox and mules left her without appetite. She was afraid to sip their meager water, yet afraid not to.

For two nights, they walked alongside Zion and Beulah, leading the oxen over endless mounds of shallow graves purposely dug into the middle of the trail. Eliza winced at Silas's explanation that by rolling over the shallow graves, it compressed them into the earth and made it harder for coyotes to dig them up.

During daytime heat, they stopped to sleep near scalding hot springs or an occasional deserted settlement, but these were few and far between. After the Transcontinental Railroad was completed the year before, there was little incentive to improve the desert passage since emigrants could traverse the desert and the formidable Sierra Nevada in relative comfort. The desert continued to remain a test of man's will and fate. Eliza shuddered, for there was something deeply familiar about this dry, barren landscape, like the visions she dreamed up in Grandmother Oak.

At first, Eliza wasn't sure she liked traveling in the dark, but she gradually came to a different way of knowing. She learned to recognize the bristly sage brush by its shadowy filaments. She sensed the dark smoothness of stones against the snowy white sand. The nearly full moon cast a curved line into deep wagon ruts as if lighting a pathway ahead. What her eyes couldn't decipher, her brain filled in until she hardly noticed the lack of light. The desert had its own sounds as well—small grains of sand crunching under the wheels, the creak of wood swaying against metal, a coyote's distant howl, even threads of melody beneath Silas's droning hum.

They followed the moon until it slipped beneath the horizon, leaving them within a canopy of shimmering stars. To fill the endless night, Eliza named mythological Greek persona and drew Silas into a conversation by asking him to search for its constellation overhead. When he couldn't find one, he pointed to a collection of stars and suggested Eliza tell her own story for it. After all, wasn't she an educated lady now?

Eliza pointed out the five brightest stars that stretched from the eastern horizon to the west, naming them "The Five Siblings."

"Looks like the oldest is trying to escape his family," Silas said, his voice lighter than it had been for days. "But they are relentless in pursuit."

"Each night," Eliza continued, "the oldest slips beneath the horizon, sneaks around the planet hoping he'll lose them, but they're on his tail the next night."

"Hah!" Silas blurted. "Must be that bag he carries. See that little star next to him? Full of gold."

"No! You mean he didn't return home and share it with his family? Shame on him," Eliza giggled. "He deserves to run forever." For such a serious Scotsman, Silas could still be playful. She loved this side of him, the one that pressed oak leaves into his letters, the one that reached tentatively for her hand that night walking next to the wagon, the one that drew her close to him as they prepared their straw mattress for sleep in the heat of the next morning. Lifting under her long skirt, Silas apologized, then apologized for apologizing.

"A man should know these things," he mumbled. "But forty-seven years a bachelor, I haven't had much practice."

Eliza grasped his hand and led him to the soft place between her legs—the place where Momma said a woman must open to her husband. She had no idea what this meant and did her best not to jump at the sharp pain or the slight trickle of blood. Silas started to apologize again, but she put her finger to his lips and nodded with a smile that she was all right.

"Perhaps it's best we wait until we're finally home," Silas said, taking her hand in his. Eliza nodded yes and stretched out on their mattress next to him, not quite touching, for the sweltering heat was unbearable. She had crossed the matrimonial threshold.

Fueled by the desert heat, Eliza's dreams became increasingly intense: always an old woman, a fire, and, through the smoke, her desk. Late that afternoon, Silas gently rubbed Eliza's shoulder to rouse her from her heavy sleep. It was time to start the night's travel. As he set the oxen into their yokes, Eliza examined the long gash on Zion's front leg, split open by rusted wire and now oozing with blood and pus. She fretted as he winced with each step. Eliza bound his wound with a long rag, but she couldn't bind his suffering.

Silas walked beside Zion, relieved that the swarm of flies attracted to the breeding ground of the ox's wound were quiet at night. Silas removed the bandage every few hours, but each time, he slowly shook his head and rewrapped it.

"This doesn't look good," he muttered. With each step, sand trickled into Silas's boots, sinking him deeper into a brooding silence.

Zion struggled to stay upright, unable to lift his hooves from the bottomless sand. Silas examined the bloody foam in Zion's nostrils and heard a new lament in Beulah's moans. He matched each step, stroking the animal's sweat-drenched neck and offering small drinks of water from a bowl. Then Zion stopped, his front legs buckling beneath him.

"Silas!" Eliza screamed.

Silas released Zion from his yoke and urged him to the side of the trail. "Get my rifle, Eliza."

She didn't move.

"Now! Get it now!"

Silas urged Zion to the side of the trail, where the ox collapsed onto the sand behind an accumulation of dried sagebrush. He placed his weary hand on Zion's brow, held it there for several long breaths, then reached for the rifle.

"Get back to the wagon, Eliza."

"Silas?"

"You heard me. Now!"

She stumbled back through the brush but stopped short as the dry desert air resonated with the deep murmurs of a soothing lullaby . . . then . . . the mercifully cruel blast of the rifle.

She buried her face in her apron and collapsed against the wagon. It was a long time before Silas returned. Wordlessly, he slid his rifle beneath the bench. Inside the wagon, Eliza huddled against her desk. Silas dropped onto a sand bank and buried his head in his hands. Then all was silent.

The deathly quiet was interrupted by a resounding thud as a heavy box dropped to the sand behind the wagon. Silas looked around for Eliza.

"Help me out. It's obvious what we've got to do." Eliza steadied a box of pots on the edge of the wagon before tipping them off. As they worked together, Silas pointed to what was absolutely essential: water, food, a few cooking implements, rifle, ammunition, dried grass for Beulah, bedrolls, and the lightest trunk of clothing.

"Best not to think about the rest," he said as he unloaded the box of heavy tools he'd purchased for repairing fences back at the farm. Eliza handed him two rolls of amber broadcloth for making curtains. "California's not a wasteland," he said as he dropped them over the sand bank. "We can replace most of these in Woodland or Sacramento."

He pulled the desk forward. "This too, Eliza."

Her head filled with a terrible rush that incinerated Silas's words. She forced her way past Silas and hid the desk with her skirt. "No! You promised me!"

"Things are different now." Silas seized her wrist and pushed her back as his other hand rose up. Eliza reeled, expecting a slap that didn't come, lost her balance, and grabbed the wagon's edge to keep from falling.

"Never!" She flung off the lid to the kitchen box and hurled a pot into the sand, followed by plates, cups, and knives. "Take the whole kitchen. I'll eat sand rather than leave my desk." She buried her face in her apron and turned away.

"You're out of your mind," Silas shouted as he replaced the kitchenware. "You think I'm happy leaving my new tools? I say what's important. The desk goes."

"You don't understand, Silas. I *can't* leave it." Her words halted between sobs. "I can't explain . . . it's . . . not . . . just . . . a . . . desk."

"This trail's salted with women's tears, Eliza. Be thankful you're not burying a child. Or me." He lifted the little desk over his head. "It's a *desk,* for god's sake, a piece of furniture." He carried the desk to a small knoll far off from the trail and dropped it onto the sand. "There's plenty more oaks in California. I'll make you a new desk when we get to the ranch, I promise."

Silas allowed Eliza a few short minutes alone with her desk while he hitched up Beulah for the final leg of their journey home to California. Eliza bundled a few things out of the wagon—a piece of paper, a pen, and a cloth to shroud her beloved desk. As she slowly caressed the fine oak heartwood, she felt as if her own heart would shrivel and die. But time was running out, and snow would soon blanket the pass over the Sierra. Lacking all will for life, Eliza returned to the wagon.

HARMONY
1996
Luna Valley, Northern California

Jeff is away for a week. The EPA called him in for a marathon push to complete the Environmental Impact Report on the proposed nuclear power plant south of Monterey. He calls from his hotel room overlooking Monterey Bay.

"I'll never get tired of watching those ingenious sea otters. You know how they get inside the clam for food? They float on their backs in the kelp beds, hold a large rock on their chest, then bang the clam against the rock until it shatters open. I could watch them for hours."

"Never get tired," I repeat to myself after I hang up. And I realize deep down, that's what I am. Tired. Tired of doing everything myself. While Jeff's out using his skills to save the world, I'm here watering, weeding, planting, picking, canning, feeding. There's homework to be done, play groups to organize, sewing to finish, and endless laundry on the clothesline. Can't think of the last time my fingers touched piano keys, though the music still streams in my head. I'm surprised how quickly my eyes fill with tears. It's not that I don't want this life. I'm grateful, really. But my tears are more honest than my words, and they push through the dam that's been holding them back.

Claire stands by the kitchen table and waits for me to finish crying.

"I'm all done, Mommy." She places a sheet of plywood with her big California map on the table.

Back on duty, I wipe my cheeks and inspect the three-dimensional map every fourth grader in California has to make. Globs of papier-mâché form the two white-painted, snow-covered mountain ranges that run north–south with a wide Central Valley between.

"Did you know that when settlers first came to California, this valley was covered with reeds as tall as my armpits? It took them days to chop their way through."

"How do you know that?" Claire asks.

"My grandma told me. She heard it from her mother, who was alive then. She lived on the other side of the valley from us." I trace the route she would have taken to visit her property in the mountains. "And this is us right here."

The map is too big for the bus, so I drive the girls to school. On the way, I reconsider the principal's offer. The school's piano is badly out of tune and has a few sticky keys, but he'd be happy to get it fixed if I'd be willing to accompany the students for an occasional performance. He'd give me the keys to the music room so I could play on it anytime after school hours. My heart lifts at the thought of playing again, then I wonder how I'd ever have time to add piano to my busy day. Still, the idea hums through my thoughts, and I decide to give it a try.

AMISHA

2075
Luna Valley, Northern California

From across the ravine, Amisha watched and waited, but after two days, the men did not return. Gathering what was left of her courage, she retraced her steps to the house. Berries and a trickle of water had kept her alive, but her body desperately needed real food. She couldn't wait to get into the Pharm.food stashed in the bottom of her pack.

The shambled kitchen reeked like something had dragged itself inside and died. Next to the stove, more furniture was broken apart for burning and the floor was splintered with glass from the broken window. She lifted a tapered shard like the one she'd held in her hand what seemed a lifetime ago and set it on the table. Oh shit! She raced to the front deck where she'd left her backpack—the contents were strewn about the deck: comb, extra shirt, underwear, lip sunscreen. The yellowed cloth was balled up in a corner of the deck and the last of her Pharm.food was gone.

"I give up," she shouted. "Why'd you call me up here if I'm only going to starve? If you want me to stay, then give me something to eat!" Breathe in . . . agonizing pain in her chest . . . breathe out, fire creeping down her arm, breathe in, slow, slow. She knew too well what would happen without food and water. It was the End-of-Life Doula's little trick: do nothing, just stop eating and drinking. The euphoria was pleasant, and the end would come soon enough.

A waft of something on the stove tickled her nose—a cast-iron skillet filled with a jumble of small white bones—a long tail on one end, a shriveled, blackened head at the other. Although her stomach convulsed, her body was desperate for the meat. She tore dried flesh from each bone, then broke the long bones in half and sucked out the marrow. She had tasted her first squirrel.

Fueled by the bit of food, she decided to look for the desk before something else got in her way. To the left of the front door, the living room was strewn with a sagging leather couch, partially unstuffed by mice, several cracked white plastic chairs, a metal garbage can with a musty quilt inside, and, on a small table, two heavy paper books like the ones she remembered high up on Grandma's shelves.

On her way upstairs, she checked the bathroom on the landing—the one she and Isabelle had posted "Girls Only" until Luke had peed on the door and Grandma made them remove the sign. Oddly, the bathtub that had served as both ocean and boat was now filled with a tangle of old fans, phones, mixers, and laptops, all trailing useless black cords.

At the top, the room down the hall to the left was almost empty save for old mattresses, threadbare quilts, and a few sheets strewn on the floor. A few coat hangers dangled in the walk-in closet. No desk.

The door to the right of the stairs was ajar. Amisha hesitated briefly, for it was Grandma Claire's private room and you had to be invited in. But once inside, oh, how she had loved the tall shelves filled with books and boxes of old jewelry. If she was quiet and promised to be reverent, Grandma would open the long wooden box of nature's treasures inherited from her mother, Harmony. Inside were polished stones, nautilus seashells, sugar-pine cones, bleached white coral, petrified wood, starfish, heron feathers, and sand dollars. They really existed. She had actually touched them.

If the desk was still here, it was certain to be in this room. She opened the door a crack, half expecting to see Grandma bent over her tiny desk. But, of course, Grandma was not there. Amisha explored the boxes stuffed inside the closet, piled haphazardly against the walls and stacked three-high in the middle of the room, but no desk. Inside the box labeled "Children's Books," she lifted out *Wizard of Oz* and *Good Night Moon* with their once-colorful pictures. The others were just boring children's schoolbooks with pages of writing. As her despair intensified, she tried to imagine any other place the desk might be besides charred in the woodstove. Looking outside the west-facing window, she stopped dead in her tracks with a feeling so familiar it sent a shiver up her spine, then, just as quickly, the feeling dissipated. She closed the door behind her and waited for her heartbeat to return to normal before going downstairs.

ELIZA
1870
Sierra Nevada, Northern California

Journal Entry: September 27, 1870

*At last I am alone, and I can finally write my thoughts into this
journal. After enduring five miserable months on the trail with my
husband, then forced to abandon my desk in that dreadful desert of
death, I am left without will to speak. Yet my thoughts smolder and
surface here in my journal.*

*We ascended the imposing snow-capped peaks of the Sierra
Nevada, our final passage into California, and all the while Silas
nattered on about the pounds of dynamite and the number of
Chinese it took to blast the pass through the sheer granite mountains.
I heard his voice but didn't listen to his words. My heart was sunk in
a deep well of misery.*

*As we started our descent into California, and without
explanation, Silas diverted our route to the Henness Pass used
mainly by teamsters. Under his breath, he mumbled that he had
a moral obligation to deliver a small packet to Nathaniel, his old
mining partner in Gold Ridge. He and Nathaniel had both arrived
in 1849, and although Nathaniel had promised his wife he would
return to Michigan the next year, one year became five, then ten,
then twenty. His five children, none of whom he has any recent*

memory of, sent their mother's obituary and portrait with Silas to deliver to their father. Another woman dead of a broken heart.

I have cared about nothing since the desert—not the distance, not the discomfort, nor even the anticipation of finally seeing my new home in California. Unexpectedly, this diversion near Gold Ridge has been a blessing, for finally I am alone. While he conducted his business in the mining settlement, Silas left me encamped overnight in a little valley just beyond the road to where the Chinese are obliged to live.

I am grateful for the quiet, but I am hardly alone, surrounded as I am by forests of thick pines and fir with trunks so wide, I can hardly reach my arms halfway around them. To pass the time, I wandered down to what miners call the Second River, but it is so muddied from mining that nothing grows on either shore. With good fortune, I found a little spring uphill from my camp to supplement my water needs.

At night, settled on my mattress under a hill of stars, I listen to the wind sifting through the pines. It sounds so much like women's voices. I strain my ears hard as I can but cannot get the sounds to make any sense. Yet somehow it feels deeply comforting, like I belong here. Perhaps there is a way for me to remain behind, let Silas move on down to his ranch in the valley. I am sure there are those who would help a lone woman. Perhaps that wispy shadow of the young girl who wandered down the hill. Not Indian, not Chinese, more like a dark-haired wood nymph. I was ready to call out to her, but before I could say anything, she gave me a mischievous grin and disappeared.

Silas returns for me this afternoon. I will have to decide.

E.O.B.

HARMONY

1999
Luna Valley, Northern California

I can't sleep. Jeff's curled up under the down comforter like an old cat, while I've spent the night twisting and turning so much my nightgown's all roped up around my legs. Outside the open window, crickets chirp, a distant owl hoots, down the hall Grandfather clock chimes one . . . two . . . I hold my breath . . . three.

Then whispers, faint at first, as if from the walls. I'm an eavesdropper in conversations that don't belong to me, a private viewer of a flickering homemade film that moves through the night uninhibited by my presence. An old woman digs her grave, wheels groan, water trickles, a lone woman pleads, seeds struggle, men return, a baby is born, someone dies, women gather and disperse, always in endless conversations.

Jeff coughs and turns his back to me, taking the comforter with him. I pull the cover back over my bare shoulder and stare at the ceiling. Overnight, something has changed. Maybe I'm going crazy. I try to remember some of the signs. Hallucinations? Voices? But the voices aren't telling me what to do. They're more like fine dust stirred up by the currents of nights long past. Or yet to be.

I get up and slip a robe over my cold shoulders. All the hallway doors are closed. I fill a glass of water from the bathroom faucet but can't return to bed. I glance at the closed study door.

No, this is not the time, I tell myself. I need sleep. Yoga breathing—that's what I'll do, but I can't remember how. I close my eyes, inhale to the count of seven, hold four, exhale seven, or is it eight? Shit, where's that book? I reach up to the bookshelf. The study door is open.

"Don't do this to me," I whisper, as the open door draws me in.

Huddled beneath the window is the oak desk illumined by shadowed curtains of moonlight. I step closer. "You've got something to do with this. I can feel it." The desk seems small and frail, frightened even. I pull out a chair and sit at the desk, remembering the unannounced visit from my sister Carole yesterday.

"It's your turn, Harmony. Really, you've got to agree I've kept the old desk long enough."

"You mean your interior decorator says it doesn't fit in anymore."

"Not with vintage vinyl and Scandinavian chrome. No use me keeping it. The boys will never be interested in it. Anyway, Mom was adamant it had to pass only to women in the family. She promised Grandma Dottie, took her turn . . . "

"And then you promised Mom."

"*We* promised Mom. Your turn now." She glanced over our ersatz collection of living room furniture, mostly salvaged from secondhand shops. "I think it will fit in perfectly."

"Did Mom ever tell you why the promise?" I asked.

"No, not really. Only that after Grandma Dottie's mother died, Dottie hastened down to San Francisco. Lots of soldiers at the Red Cross centers back in 1915. When she and Grandpa Jonas got married later that year, she returned to sell the ranch and retrieve a few pieces of furniture."

"Like the desk."

Sitting in the dark, I rub the musty desktop in slow, circular motions while I think. Had I forgotten to welcome it?

"OK, this is my study—it's where I work." Aware that I'm talking to a piece of furniture, I press my middle finger to my forehead and continue. "You should feel right at home—there's lots of old family stuff here." I sweep my arm along the bookcase. "Great-Grandma's scrapbook, but it's nearly falling apart, and here's part of Grandma's library—Emerson, Shakespeare, and Thoreau—all pretty faded, but I love the feel of old leather. I've even got Great-Grandpa's letters home from the Gold Rush. You're surrounded by family."

I return to bed, snuggle against Jeff's back for warmth. Outside the window, stars drift in and out of the clouds. Crazy? I wonder. Nah, probably not. Reassured by the deep rhythm of Jeff's breathing, I let go and fall asleep.

The next morning, I return to my study and watch a shaft of sunlight move imperceptibly across the dull striations of oak grain. If this was mother's desk, I wonder why she rarely talked about it. I vaguely remember a family rumor—something mysterious about it. Probably over the years, the magic's all dried up.

I take a closer look. It's a tiny little thing, I muse. Perhaps two-by-three feet, simply designed with three vertical slats on each side, spanned by a narrow shelf beneath. Remarkably, there are no nails because the pieces fit together like a puzzle. Beneath the desktop is a small drawer that slides out reluctantly, each corner interwoven by the clasped hands of dovetail joints. Someone had tacked down ugly blue and white shelf paper on the bottom of the drawer, a relic of the '60s.

I imagine the oak heartwood may once have been polished into a deep luster, but along the way, dust settled into the small grooves, leaving a feeling of tired brittleness. A circular watermark mars the back left corner where someone carelessly placed a hot drink. Small chips, like rodent teeth, pock the base of two of the legs.

I settle into my chair. Most mornings I begin with a simple meditation, but today I'm distracted by sunlight drifting across the desktop—the turning of the earth, the turning of time. I focus on my breathing—in deeply, out slowly, in deeply . . . slowly. The hallway clock accompanies with a steady tick, tock, tick, tock, as its pendulum sweeps each second into the past. Last night's voices hover at the edge of my memory, like they're living in the books, whispering through the spines.

Then from that still space that has eluded me all night comes a voice of remarkable clarity. *Now. It's time.*

The sun pauses at the edge of the desk. Dust motes are suspended midair.

It's time.

A sense of silent expectation fills the room and I inhale, part my lips as if to speak, but in a flicker of hesitation, my lips close and my hand falls away from the desk.

"I'm sorry," I say, surrendering to the waiting emails, phone calls, and gardening column I promised to write for tomorrow's paper. "Maybe another time. I've simply got too much to do today."

AMISHA

2075
Luna Valley, Northern California

That first night back at the house, Amisha dragged a mattress and thin quilt down to the front deck and set her backpack next to her bed. If the men returned, she'd hear them in time to escape out the back door. Too hot and exhausted to sleep, she found her forgotten Turkish worry beads and gave the cobalt bead closest to the knot a twirl.

"It's come to this," she said to the first bead. "I abandoned everything I know." Next bead: "I worked my ass off to get here, and what do I get?" Small white bead: "I'm going to die of hunger and thirst or some animal's going to get me." She continued around her cobalt rosary: "I've no reason to be here, but I can't go back, not without a Nib. Orion's gone. Charlie's gone." Back at the first bead, she started again: abandoned, thirsty, hungry, danger, no reason to stay, can't go back, no Nib, no Charlie, no Orion. Round and round she went until at last, she worried herself to sleep.

Shortly before dawn, Amisha was startled awake by voices down the hill. She crouched below the railing with her fingers clutched tight around the backpack's handle and strained to hear who was approaching. The voices were muffled, hard to distinguish, but she could make out several people—deep voice of a man, softer shushing of women, and a blood-curdling wail. Someone held up a small flame; thin shafts of light flickered between the slats of the deck railing. Amisha lifted her pack and turned toward the door but stopped dead in her tracks as another stabbing cry rose above the clamor.

"Get her up there quick."

"Get her arms. Carry her up. No, wait!" More shuffling, yelling.

Amisha slipped the front door open a crack.

"No, please, no." A young girl's plea dissolved into a tortured moan.

Amisha froze.

More shuffling, groans. The group ascended the staircase.

That sound! Holding breath then exploding. She could not mistake the sound of a woman pushing her baby into the world.

Amisha dropped her pack onto the deck and cautiously approached the railing to look down at the group coming up toward her. Impossible! Hardly any births at the hospital last year, yet one was about to be born here in no-man's-land. She stepped down toward the struggling group. Swiftly from behind, Amisha felt the pressure of a stick across her throat. A large man held her back as the group pushed around her. Amisha made eye contact with a gray-haired woman whose arms encircled the girl.

"Get her on the bed," Amisha coughed behind the stick. "I'm a doctor. I can help."

With a jut of her chin, the woman motioned to the tall, pencil-thin man to release his hold. In a frenzy of shouting and effort, they were able to get the girl to the bed. Amisha rolled the girl on her back and placed her hands along the base of her contracting belly.

"No, don't push. Not yet." She scanned the girl's face. Maybe eleven or twelve, much too young to be having a baby. Amisha glared at the man standing over her with the stick ready in his hand. "She's just a child," she mouthed. The woman whose face was obscured by a cloud of frizzy gray hair pulled Amisha's hand off the girl's belly.

"We had no choice," the woman mouthed back.

With a terrified moan, the girl bore down, and from under her skirt, a dark mound of wet hair emerged between her legs, then receded back. Gasping for air, the girl fell back into the arms of the woman holding her from behind. Again, she pushed, more hair, then back in again. There was enough light now for Amisha to see the girl's bulging, bloodshot eyes and sweat pouring down her forehead.

"She's exhausted. The baby will die if she doesn't push it out soon!"

"Don't tell us what to do!" snapped the older woman. "The baby's small. It'll come."

"She should squat," Amisha said. "Let gravity help."

After short consideration, the woman nodded and Amisha lifted the girl's skirt. The labia were swollen from the pushing. She felt the top of the uterus at the next push. There was hardly any muscle tone. She guided the girl onto her hands and knees and knelt behind her. With each push, Amisha gently smoothed the vaginal opening around the dark head. The mother, too weak to cry out anymore, could hardly push.

"Please," Amisha was desperate. "She's too swollen. I need a knife to open her up."

"Back off!" Two hands grabbed Amisha's shoulders and yanked her away. Pinned against the railing, she watched helplessly as the woman slid her fingers inside with the next push and tried to pull the head out. The girl screamed then collapsed back as a dark wrinkled scalp emerged into the woman's hands.

"Push, more!" commanded the woman, who by now was tugging at the dusky-blue head to deliver the body. Frantic, Amisha elbowed her way back to the mattress and ran her finger along the neck, where the cord was tightly wound.

"Stop! Don't push!" She slid her finger between the cord and the baby's neck and, in slow motion, rolled the cord up and over the baby's face. "OK, now!" Within seconds, the body slid into Amisha's hands, exactly like all the simulations she had practiced so long ago. With the slippery infant stabilized along her arm, she quickly scanned the body, front and back then, with an imperceptible shake of her head, wrapped the limp infant in the sheet and handed it to the young mother.

Amisha wiped her hands on the sheet and backed away as the group circled around the girl. Her body trembled with adrenaline. Her lungs squeezed so tight she couldn't breathe. Without her rebalancing, she could only wait it out. Breathe in, wait, breathe out, in, out. Around her, the muffled cries, murmurs, angry outbursts faded to the background.

"You killed my baby!" The man came at her with his stick.

"Get Trev inside," yelled the gray-haired woman, who was obviously in charge. From the shadows, another tall figure with a long scarf wrapped around her head took Trev by the arm and led him into the house.

"The rest of you, too!" When the last figure was gone, the woman glared at Amisha as if waiting for her to answer the obvious question. "Well?"

Amisha eyed the woman's thin sandals, baggy pants with haphazard pockets sewn from the knee to the drawstring, her blood-tinged arms and hands, sloping shoulders, and the frizzy gray hair that surrounded her deeply lined face like a lion's mane.

"Who are you?"

"Amisha."

"No. Who . . . Are . . . You?"

Amisha had endured bears, men, these latest intruders, and delivering a baby. But now, unable to answer this simple question, she broke into tears.

The woman pulled back the loose hair from the left side of Amisha's neck.

"I suspected as much." She lifted her own hair to expose a similar inch-wide scar on her own neck, its ragged edges red but long healed.

Amisha's eyes widened.

"Now, again, who are you?"

Amisha flinched. Trust or fear? She didn't know which way to go.

"You're new here," the woman answered for her. "And you know about babies."

Amisha nodded. "I'm a children's doctor—or was one." She inched her way up to stand face-to-face, her voice remarkably intense and steady. "And now I want to know what you are doing in my home."

"I'm Dar. We're migrants, and this is *our home*." She held the door open for Amisha. "I think you'd better come inside."

ELIZA

1870
Yolo, California

By the time Silas steered the wagon between the two sentinel palm trees that marked the driveway to his farmhouse, the afternoon sun had already slipped behind the black green backbone of the Vaca Hills.

"End of the trail? Home at last?" Hands pressed against his aching back, he stepped down from the wagon. "After three trips east, I still haven't come up with the right words." He gestured to the diminutive two-story house standing like an afterthought next to the oversize weathered barn.

"End of the trail will do," Eliza murmured. She had neither the will nor the energy to engage in conversation. She had so wanted to feel something—anything—to mark her arrival, but now all she longed for was to fall into bed. A real bed. Silas warned her not to expect much—just the modest house of an old bachelor: kitchen, bedroom, and a seldom-used parlor. Even so, she was unprepared for the boarded-up shutters, peeling white paint, and a fenced-in weed patch that might have once been a garden. Hardly what she'd imagined. But then, this whole journey was proof that her imagination was woefully misguided.

Eliza followed Silas up the three wide steps to the front porch and stood behind him adjusting her frayed and dirt-stained skirt as he fumbled with the doorknob. Neither spoke.

"I sent word for my foreman Miguel to light a fire so the place would be warm when we arrived." He tossed his hat on the coat rack in the entry as he had for the last twenty years. "But he was expecting us yesterday. I fear it might be a bit cold by now."

Cold was manageable, Eliza thought, but the smell of stale, musty old tobacco reeking from the walls was intolerable. She pulled her apron over her nose and stepped into the entry hall.

"Over here's the parlor." Silas swung his kerosene lamp into the doorway to the right of the entry hall, lighting the three chairs stacked against the bare wall. "Not much furniture, but I imagine you'll be putting your woman's touch on it."

Eliza mustered a weak smile.

"We'll make a trip to Sacramento to replace the furniture we had to leave behind."

She looked away.

"You're probably more interested in the kitchen." Brushing aside the cobwebs dangling from the ceiling, he led her down the central hallway with its pine-plank floor, bare walls, and two closed doors on the left side. "Might make a dining room, maybe even an office in those two empty rooms, but for now, the kitchen's where I . . . where we will eat," he corrected himself. He shifted the light to the makeshift shelf in the far-right corner stacked high with newspapers, eastern farm journals, books propped by size against a cigar box, writing tablets, a tin can of pencils, and a framed daguerreotype portrait of a stern-looking couple. "This is also my office of sorts. Do my reading, writing, and recordkeeping here." He picked up the picture. "You might remember my parents from Niles?"

Eliza looked closely.

"Actually, you were probably just a baby when they passed on." He set the picture down, walked over to the kitchen sink, and jiggled the window back and forth until it opened. "House needs some ventilation—been closed up too long."

Eliza searched the room for something hopeful, but the best feature was a deep porcelain sink under the kitchen window. Otherwise, there was a single open hutch filled with mismatched plates, bowls, and glasses. There were saucepans below, cutlery lined up in a wooden tray, and two black frying pans hanging on the wall. She pulled a chair to the table. "There's a bedroom?"

Silas studied his wife, elbows propped on the table, head cradled in her hands, unruly strands dangling from what was left of her bun. He leaned over her shoulder to raise the wick of the flickering kerosene lantern, enlarging the circle of light that enveloped them.

"Look here, Eliza, I really don't know how to do this. I mean, being a husband. All I know is what a bachelor does." He ran his fingers along the back of his neck. "You'll have to be patient with me."

Eliza gave a prolonged sigh.

"When I left for Niles this time, I really didn't know I'd be returning with . . . I mean, didn't know I'd come back married. Sure going to be a few surprised faces around here!" A touch of color softened his leathered cheeks.

"It's all been so much harder than I thought. I need time." Her voice trailed off to a whisper.

The kerosene lantern sputtered. Neither spoke for a long time.

"You're exhausted," Silas said at last. "Come along upstairs, I'll find you some clean sheets." Lantern held high, he led her back into the hall and up the narrow staircase, then paused outside his bedroom door. "I feel I should be giving my bride a better welcome." She followed him into the room. "Perhaps you'll let me start over in the light of day."

Silas lit the small lamp on the bedside table. A shifting pattern of shadows and light danced over the red wool blanket that covered the single bed. Across from the bed was a wooden chair next to a chest of drawers with a stack of clothing neatly folded on top. Two mismatched wool slippers sat side by side beneath the curtainless window, and an open book had been left facedown on the bedside table as if waiting to be picked up and read.

Eliza lowered herself into the chair with a sigh. Folded deep in the one remaining trunk was the dress Momma had made to mark the momentous occasion of her arrival: a skirt of gold broadcloth, lace gathered around the neck, and a pale brown belt. But now, all she wanted was to disappear and be alone.

Silas pulled off the red blanket and made the bed with the clean but yellowed muslin sheets.

"I reckon you'll feel better after a good night's sleep . . . up here by yourself." He wanted to make the last words into a question, then thought better of it. "I'll put my bedroll down in the parlor if you need me."

Eliza did not protest.

When the door clicked shut, she tugged off her shoes, dragged the tired, threadbare dress over her head, and, wearing only her dirt-stained petticoat, slipped beneath the sheets and descended into the blessed forgetfulness of sleep.

All night long her bed swayed along the wagon trail between Michigan and California. Momma rocking her cradle with her shoe. Momma humming in the kitchen. Squeeze eyes shut, don't open. Itching everywhere. Momma rustling in the hall linen closet. A slit of light between her lids, don't open. Hold tight. Too late. Somewhere along the dark trail, her two worlds overlapped then separated forever. She was in California.

Squinting at the morning light, Eliza shifted up on her elbows. Her stomach still rolled from the trail, her muscles ached, and every movement made her lungs seize in a fit of coughing.

"Eliza?" A gentle tap on the door. "Are you up? May I come in?"

She slipped back under the covers, held the sheet up to her chin. "Yes."

With a slight tinkle, the door opened. Silas entered balancing a small teapot, cup, and saucer on a tray.

"May I give you a more formal welcome to our new home?" With a tentative smile, he placed the tray on the table next to the spent kerosene lamp.

"At least I had the foresight to fold up my clothes before I left," he laughed, gesturing to the perfectly aligned stack of flannel shirts on top of his chest of drawers. He rubbed the back of his neck, giving her time to speak. "Did you sleep well? I mean, was the bed comfortable enough? Not too lumpy or hard? Can't say I favor sleeping on a bedroll—too much like the trail. First thing, we'll have to get a full-sized bed. Can't have us . . ." He stopped, face flushed. "Here, let me pour you some tea."

Eliza propped the pillow behind her back and tucked the sheet and blanket under her arms. Silas poured the amber liquid into a white teacup, set the steaming cup in her hands, then returned with a plate of dry toast. "Got the bread from Miguel but won't have butter 'til we go to town tomorrow." He pulled a red-speckled apple from his jacket pocket. "Here, still some left on my tree out front." He opened his pocketknife and cut the apple in quarters, then peeled each section with a single deft stroke and placed them on her tray.

Eliza turned the cup around to where the rim wasn't chipped and sipped in silence. The tea lifted her mood but left the deep hollow inside untouched. She gazed down at her cup to keep her tears from spilling over.

"Can I get you something else?"

She shook her head no.

Silas ran his tongue over his upper teeth as if preparing to say something but didn't.

"Then I'll just let you drink your tea in peace," he said politely, his voice resonating with a new edge. "There's a lot of work calling me outside. Miguel and Josepha did a fine job with the animals, but I didn't think to have them ready the house for me . . . for us." He stepped backward toward the door.

"I brought your little trunk up. It's outside in the hallway. We'll find a place for it," he looked around, "somewhere here in the bedroom," he mumbled as he backed out the room. He had almost closed the door behind him when he poked his head back in. "I reckon you found the chamber pot in the corner?"

Eliza nodded.

As the door clicked shut, Eliza set the teacup on the floor and pulled the blanket over her head.

For two days, the sun offered, then withdrew, its light from the window, but Eliza would not leave her bed. Muscles that had labored for months to steady her over the uneven trail now screamed in misery. Her stomach churned as the bed seemed to pitch from front to back and side to side. Her wedding band hung limply on her finger.

She smothered her face in the pillow, but tangled images of her dreamworld found her there too: Flames leapt from a fire fueled by the crackling of Grandmother Oak; wheels bumped over the graves of babies; the drip, dripping of water; her desk abandoned and alone.

Something tugged at her arm.

"Eliza, whatever are you doing?" Silas's face materialized in the dark, lit behind his lantern.

"Help me get up to the attic." She stood on top of the bed, hands outstretched toward the top of the wall. "My desk, it's . . ."

"There is no attic, Eliza," he said, helping her back down from the bed. "Would you like me to sleep up here, keep you company? No? Then I'll just leave the lamp on the chest over here," he said and closed the door behind him. Downstairs in the dark, the mantle clock chimed three.

When the sun warmed the room on her third day home, Eliza made a feeble attempt to get out of bed. Had there been a mirror, she would have seen brown sand still crusted around her nose, ears, and eyes, dark blotches across her cheeks, wrists etched the color of the trail, and long hair covering her shoulders in unruly strands.

She opened the trunk on the landing and searched for her yellow dress. It still smelled of Mother. She pulled it over her tattered petticoat. The leather waist band was way too constricting, as was the lace collar. She coiled her stiff hair atop her head and tucked the ends in, hoping they would stay, then peered down the narrow staircase at the coat rack. Empty.

"Silas?" She placed a foot on the first step. "Silas?" She called louder and descended two more steps, clutching the banister with her shaking hands. Supposing he's gone? He wouldn't leave me here all alone, would he? The entryway echoed as she crossed into the parlor. Silas's bedroll was nowhere to be seen.

Following the smell of bacon wafting from the kitchen, she found a half loaf of brown bread and a jar of blackberry jam with a handwritten label: "To Silas, From Miss Ida." Eliza cut a thin slice, covered it with jam, and filled a cup of milk from a pitcher in the cooler. Outside the window over the sink, black-and-white cows grazed in the field.

"Silas?" she called into the empty house. Her call was answered by a distant neighing outside. From the parlor window, she caught sight of Silas hauling crates from the wagon into the barn. Following closely behind him, a gray-tinged sorrel mare nipped at the hem of his canvas jacket. He nudged her back with his shoulder. She followed him into the barn and back out again. Empty-handed now, Silas stroked her sleek neck affectionately, then reached into the pocket she was so interested in and pulled out a red-speckled apple. He shooed her back with his elbow, then with his pocketknife, sliced the apple into quarters and offered them in the palm of his hand.

HARMONY

2000
Luna Valley, Northern California

I love this Internet thing! Whoever invented electronic mail was a genius. Email is like having a direct line to my neighbors down the road and to my friends back in the city. No more calling people one by one with the same news. I just type all their names in the top line that says "To," and their email address magically fills in. After typing something catchy for the "Subject" line, voilà, I've got an electronic phone tree! I even have a direct line to Sierra Club—*link*, I mean—and they send me email alerts along with the exact email address of people to put pressure on. I just type up a letter using the word processor installed on my computer, hit "Send," and I can be back in my garden in no time. Futurists are right. Who knows what other time-saving inventions are in store for us!

"Guess what's in my hand?" Jeff tiptoes behind me and opens his palm over my desk to display a miniature brown egg. "The Rhode Island pullet laid her first egg this morning!" When I don't look up, he says, "Hey, I thought you'd be excited. Why the scowl?"

I hand him the email letter I printed out this morning. Now he's scowling. "The janitor, school bus driver, two parents, and three kids? What's all this?"

"Jenni's been collecting names of people at all the schools up here. She said it's not her job as school nurse, but she couldn't help noticing how many people around here were coming down with big-time stuff like cancers—prostate, leukemia, breast, lung—a horrendous smorgasbord."

"Why?"

"We don't know, but I suggested she start making a list. Maybe we can get someone's attention." I cup my hand around the still-warm egg. "It's sweet, isn't it?" Late that afternoon I take a bucket of kitchen scraps out to the chicken yard and watch the hens peck through the greens from last night's dinner. I've always believed if we keep eating from our organic garden, we shouldn't have to worry. But I'm not so sure anymore. The more time I spend on my computer reading emails from environmental groups, the more alarmed I feel. I'm beginning to wonder if it's enough to simply demonstrate how to be earth friendly.

I vow to take it up a notch and get more involved with what's happening to the environment. Jeff works at the EPA; I can work from my computer. I start by creating manila folders for "Earth," "Air," "Fire," and "Water." These go into cardboard file boxes which I stack neatly on top of the old desk. To save paper, I create similar files on my computer. I'm also determined to recycle more of our garbage and set out a fourth tub for recycling plastics.

Late that afternoon as the dreamy orange sun descends behind oaks and pines on the western horizon, our family gets a surprise visit from our neighbors—Indigo on her sorrel mare and Lark leading their new pony, Oaxaca. Claire clamors relentlessly for a ride on the baby horse. Sage hides her face in my skirt. Lark scoops up Claire along with her very reluctant sister and leads them up and down the driveway on the pony.

"This is what we came here for, isn't it?" Jeff wraps his arms around me in one of his huge bear hugs.

"They'll remember this little horse ride for the rest of their lives," I comment. I slip my arms around his waist and snuggle into his bear hug.

"Yeah, but they'll remember for different reasons," Jeff chuckles. "Claire's our little country mouse, but Sage? Wouldn't be surprised if she ends up in the city."

AMISHA

2075
Luna Valley, Northern California

Amisha followed Dar into the cool, dark living room where figures were sprawled about on the furniture and floor. Lying on the couch, the young mother, her damp blond hair pulled back from her childish face, held the motionless baby blanketed in her arms. She in turn was held in the arms of a stocky, curly-haired woman. Crouched beneath the window in the far corner, the man called Trev rocked into his folded arms while, seated cross-legged at his side, a turbaned woman hummed an eerily soft melody.

"This here's Amisha," Dar announced and nudged her into the center of the room. "Says she's a baby doctor."

"Baby killer!" the man cried out.

"Enough, Trev! Let her speak for herself."

Afraid her legs wouldn't hold, Amisha found an edge of the couch by the mother's feet. "I'm so sorry." She lifted the cover from the infant's head. "There's nothing I could do—or anyone could do."

"The baby was going good 'til you laid hands on it!" Trev shouted.

Amisha took a deep breath. "No, it wasn't. The problem wasn't in the birth. It was . . ." she unwrapped the blanket and, with a moment of hesitation, placed her hand on the baby's abdomen and spread its legs.

"What the hell's that?" Trev peered over Dar's shoulder.

177

"Could be penis, could be clitoris," Dar said.

"But looks like he's got balls."

"Or enlarged labia." Amisha pulled the blanket back over the infant's abdomen. "There's no way of knowing what problems are inside because I can't scan, but I know it didn't die from its ambiguous gender."

"But we did everything right." The curly-haired woman hugged the young girl tighter. "My daughter never touched plastic in her life!"

"You can't avoid it," Amisha said. "Plastic deteriorates so small it floats everywhere, from high in the stratosphere to miles deep on the ocean floor."

"We needed this baby!" The man covered his eyes.

Dar elbowed Amisha aside. After examining the child herself, she looked up questioningly.

"Ages ago, hermaphrodites ended up in a circus," Amisha said. "Now intersex is so common we hardly even blink. When the child's ready to decide, all it takes is a little surgical intervention and hormonal redirection."

Yet Amisha knew this wasn't why the baby didn't survive. Babies were hardly born intact anymore. Hell, babies were hardly conceived. Just because Nibs directed men's Med.paks to pump infusions of aphrodisiacs into their blood didn't mean that men had enough interest in sex to make it happen. Women's hormones were just as deteriorated. Even with biogenetic engineering, nothing could coax mankind's DNA into replicating life. Over time, the alarm of overpopulation dropped from newsfeeds.

On the rare occasion when babies made it to birth, parents sequestered them away. That's when they came to her to find something their child could tolerate. Everything from breast milk to milk alternatives had become toxic or indigestible. Until Pharm.foods. Those turned out to be lifesavers. Amisha reached for her Turkish beads, heavy in the bottom of her pocket, and ran her fingers along the string. Had this baby been born at the university, she would have scanned it for inborn metabolism errors and started a strict Pharm.milk regimen.

"How long since you've had a baby survive here?" she asked.

"Eleven and a half years. That was Glory." Dar nodded to the exhausted young mother quietly sleeping in her own mother's arms.

"Glory?"

"We named her after the flower. Morning Glories are hearty, beautiful, grow everywhere. We like things that reseed easily."

"But she looks hardly eleven!"

"She started her menses at nine. We waited long as we could. And Trev was gentle with her."

Amisha swallowed hard.

"Does it appear we had a choice?" Dar demanded.

Amisha looked around the room. The scarf-turbaned woman next to Trev had the same long, sloping nose as he did. Both were thin, tall. Siblings? Dar's ashen-gray hair conveyed the authority of her age. Glory's mother was technically a grandmother, making her beyond childbearing as well. Like herself, all had neck scars. Surely, these weren't the survivalists she'd been warned about.

With a nod from Dar, Trev and his sister went upstairs to arrange mattresses on the floor. The grandmother extracted herself from her sleeping daughter and set out plates on the table, filling each one with fresh dark greens and walnuts.

Dar pulled Amisha aside. "You can stay a few days, sleep on the deck. But if we add to our clan, it has to be someone fertile." They were interrupted by a wailing from the kitchen.

"They're gone!" Glory's mother pointed to the empty bottom shelf of the pantry.

Amisha froze. "I thought squirrels had gotten into the house and stashed their nuts. I tossed them outside."

"You tossed the acorns? How stupid are you?" She pleaded to Dar. "They were to last 'til this coming harvest. What are we going to eat?"

"Clarissa, calm down, let her explain."

"You eat those? I've never seen anyone eating acorns here before. Just squirrels, maybe deer."

"What do you mean, 'before'?" Dar moved closer.

"This is my family's place." Amisha hesitated, unsure how much to reveal.

"*Was* your family's place. It belongs to whoever is here now," Dar said with finality. "It's a way station. We use it on our travels between the high country and the coast. When we return, there's usually evidence others have been here."

"Like you," Clarissa glared as she passed by with a metal bowl and plate of food. Amisha followed her into the living room. Glory should be checked for bleeding. She found Clarissa kneeling beside her sleeping daughter, gently washing dried blood from her legs.

"Hey!" Amisha pushed Clarissa's hand away from the bowl of water. "That's precious drinking water!"

Clarissa dropped the cloth back into the water, wrung it out, and without looking up, continued bathing her daughter.

"Dar!" Amisha yelled.

In an instant, everyone was in the room. Dar reached for Glory's pulse.

"Look at what she's doing," Amisha shouted. "That's drinking water for staying alive!"

"We'll just get more," shrugged the woman whose scarf was now off her bald head and draped around her long neck.

"But it will take half a day to get that much again." Amisha was almost in tears.

"At the pump?"

"Pump?"

Trev and the scarf woman led Amisha out the back door and down a narrow path behind the house to the rusted red hand pump covered by a metal enclosure. Trev gave two easy pumps, and an inch of water splashed into the bucket beneath.

"Oh my god, oh my god, oh my god!" Amisha fell to her knees and scooped the water in her hands, gulping until she nearly choked.

"Someone had the foresight to install this old workhorse," Trev said. "Even Sharome can pump it. Here, show her how easy it is." He gestured toward the silent woman.

Sharome gave a few pumps then glanced sideways at Amisha. "Now you know my name."

"She doesn't talk much, but she has a lot to say." Trev placed his arm around Sharome's shoulder and gave a reassuring squeeze.

Back inside the house, Amisha brought a fresh bowl of water into the living room where Dar and Clarissa were talking quietly in the corner.

"We'll bury him . . . or her out in the bone garden," Dar whispered. "On the northwest hill, there's four stakes that mark the wire blanket we put over the graves. Keeps the critters out."

"There's others?"

Dar nodded.

Amisha turned back to Glory, checked her pulse, then felt that her abdomen was firm and wasn't bleeding. The whole group was now stretched out on the floor, arms and legs straddled over each other like a litter of sleeping puppies. She felt comfortable enough with Dar, but Sharome's penetrating orangy-brown eyes made her feel sticky, like she couldn't disengage. She looked away but felt the heat of Sharome's gaze follow.

"You met Sharome?" Dar asked.

"Doesn't talk much. Doesn't need to," Trev repeated.

"'Til the acorns come on," Clarissa added. "Food-gathering seasons used to be predictable. So were our travels. Now all we have is Sharome to tell us when it's time to move on."

"I heard you singing for Glory just now. Your voice is beautiful." Then Amisha nodded at Trev, seated with his long legs extended into the room. "He's unusually tall."

"Yep, that's Trev," Dar sighed, "our little rooster."

"Doesn't look too little to me," Amisha said.

Dar grinned. "Trust me."

"We usually stay here at least a full lunar cycle," Clarissa said. "Time enough to gather acorn, madrone berries, whatever's ready. We'll stay until Sharome knows it's time."

The group waited for Sharome to open her eyes.

"It will be another moon," Sharome pronounced. "Unless the currents shift again."

"Seasons used to come straight and predictable. Now they wobble," Dar said. "We'll make do with whatever you've been eating."

Amisha swallowed and considered her position. They knew how to survive here. She could learn from them—perhaps even go with them if she didn't find the desk. Did she dare ask?

ELIZA
1870
Yolo, California

Over the next fortnight, Eliza and Silas passed like ships in the night. Silas worked out in the barn. Eliza wandered the house. Neither spoke unless it was unavoidable.

To Eliza's relief, Silas was gone on frequent trips to restock the farm. When he returned, he was preoccupied working with Miguel, replenishing hay and feed, repairing the smokehouse and fences, and relocating some of the smaller stock Miguel had moved closer to his cabin at the far corner of the ranch. New animals appeared daily—a herd of Holstein cattle claimed the field east of the house, horses filled the stalls, geese and ducks were released from their crates with quacks and hisses and quickly found their familiar pond behind the barn.

From her vantage point at the window, Eliza watched the ranch come to life, grateful for the time to settle in at her own pace. She hadn't regained her appetite and, when she wasn't sleeping long hours, she wandered the rooms, opened drawers and doors, peered behind furniture, moved stacks of old newspapers and books, always searching for something she could not name.

The morning sun streamed through the kitchen window, illuminating a cobalt-blue bottle filled with dead flowers. Spiders had woven webs throughout the desiccated petals, making the flowers difficult to identify. Lupin perhaps? Or cornflower? She sneezed and dropped the flowers in the trash.

She scanned the rest of the kitchen to see what she had to work with. Aside from meager dishes and cooking pots, there was so much she hadn't noticed that first night. Such as the cooler that pulled cold air from beneath the house and circulated it up through wire shelves to help keep the butter, block of yellow cheese, apples, and dried jerky from spoiling.

She removed a page from Silas's tablet to make a shopping list based on what she remembered in her mother's kitchen: flour, salt, baking soda, sugar, lard, eggs, milk, oats, cornmeal, meat, fruits, vegetables. She dropped the pencil and held her stomach. Enough on food. She started a utensil list on the next page: dish and hand towels, breakfast bowls, mixing bowls, measuring cups and spoons, and—looking out the bare kitchen window—she added curtains.

At the far side of the kitchen were the bookshelves Silas had called his office. "Not in my kitchen," Eliza said as she lifted off a stack of dusty old journals and dropped them on the floor with a sneeze. She set to work consolidating his books, pencils, and tablets, even the half-empty stationery boxes. Curious that one box was exceptionally heavy, she lifted the lid and was surprised to find her letters bound in thin rawhide strips. He'd saved them all. Every bundle was labeled by the month; each letter had a number written in the bottom right corner. She slipped number "12" from the "January" packet. It began:

> Dear Mr. Silas,
>
> For the topic of my last elocution, I took your advice and spoke on the benefits of physical exertion to one's health, though I am hardly a good example—a point that was not lost on my classmates. I resolved to take up walking into town rather than riding in the carriage. This I did for six days, then, alas, I forgot . . .

Distracted by a light breeze that brushed a wisp of hair against her neck, Eliza tucked the strand back into her bun and went in search of the window left open by mistake. Although all windows in the parlor were closed, she noticed a slip of light in the west wall between the two bay windows. Silas had stacked crates high in the space between the tall windows, but as she pushed the boxes aside, she discovered a third window, still shuttered from the outside, but with a crack that allowed a small shaft of light to slip through. Eliza stood outside in the flower bed and pried the nails out with a kitchen knife. The shutters swung open.

"Now, let there be light!" she exclaimed, then hurried back inside, blinking to accustom her eyes to the dark again. Seated at a desk beneath the window was a woman with short brown hair curled around the nape of her neck. The figure swiveled to look Eliza in the eye, then faded away until only the desk remained. Then it too disappeared.

Silas found Eliza standing transfixed in front of the parlor window.

"You promised no fluffy curtains now," Silas said, relieved to see his wife finally moving about the house. "You know what the sight of lace does to me." He gave a nervous chuckle.

Eliza paid him no mind. She pushed a crate away from one side of the window and a wicker chair from the other, then pointed to the four-foot expanse between them.

"Don't put anything in that space," she instructed. "It's for my desk."

Silas's eyes brightened. "So! You want me to build you a desk after all? Something that fits right there?"

But Eliza was transfixed by the shafts of sunlight slipping over the dark green hills, moving slowly as if in search of something beyond the window.

"No," she said, "just give my desk time to find me."

HARMONY
2005
Sierra Nevada, Northern California

A super-storm is projected to hit the Sierra Nevada sometime by evening—it's about the only thing on the news, keeping me on edge all morning. Out on the front deck, I scan the southwest skies where storms usually originate. Only a few gray clouds darken the horizon behind the forest. The phone rings again, neighbors checking in.

"No, we're all set," Jeff's deep voice booms from his office upstairs. "But I'm heading over to Nova's to help her get more wood in. You might check over at Indigo and Lark's. They're in the city this weekend. Their goats may need extra feed." He gives the window latch an extra crank and lowers the insulated curtains behind his computer.

I dump an armload of firewood into the wood box on the entry porch, kick off my mud boots, remove my wool cap and shake out my curls, then go upstairs to check the National Weather Service. As my old Mac G3 starts up with a hum, an old oak tree flashes briefly like an after-image, then resolves into my familiar screen saver of a magenta sunset over the ocean.

"Come take a look at this," Jeff calls from the next room. "Storm's just been upgraded to severe." He points to the giant white spirals amassing over the Pacific. "Could pack more destruction than the '76 storm that took out the road and both bridges."

I zip up my "Save the Redwoods" sweatshirt and peer over his shoulder. "Both radio stations are going crazy, warning everyone to stay home and get prepared." The furrow between my brows deepens. "Do we have enough food? Dora says grocery shelves are stark empty. You've checked the generator?"

Used to my excessive worrying, Jeff uses his low, soothing voice to report he has everything under control. "Propane tank's full, I brought up extra wood, and the cellar's full of your canned tomatoes. We can eat spaghetti sauce for days if we have to." He taps his fingers on the counter. "I'm still waiting for parts to come for the generator, but it should be OK. Wish I'd started sooner though."

Like the rest of the folks in Luna Valley, we learned from grueling experience that when a storm knocks out the electricity, we're the last to get our power restored—the trade-off for living in a hard-to-reach river canyon. It didn't take long to figure out that a sturdy stand-by generator and a week's supply of food and water were as essential as a good pickup truck. But I worry if that will be enough this time.

After checking the day's action-alert emails, I go downstairs to the kitchen to distract myself by cutting up carrots, onions, and garlic for the chicken stock simmering on the woodstove. I'll add seaweed and brown rice later. Should last a week.

Throughout the afternoon, dark cumulonimbus thunderheads build to the southwest. By evening, they've coalesced into a smoldering black wall. But no storm. Before going to bed, Jeff checks the satellite image for areas of dark red that signify heavy rain, but the storm has been delayed. He joins me in bed, commenting that it looks like I'm reading the same page over and over.

"I can't shake off this ominous feeling." I close the book and snuggle up to him. I wish I felt more like a capable, independent woman, but tonight I feel like a little girl wanting to be taken care of.

"It's a winter storm, Harmony. We go through this every year."

"Yeah, but last year, a pine crashed onto your truck. Could have been the house."

"Would you rather be back in the city worrying about muggers and rapists?"

"You know my answer."

"One must embrace all of Mother Nature, as someone I know likes to say."

A melodious ringing from the wind chime drifts up from the chicken yard.

Jeff reaches over for my book and sets it aside.

"You're getting too obsessed. Back off and get some perspective or you'll have permanent furrows in your brow like your mother." Totally ignoring my dirty look, he clicks off the light, draws his arm around my shoulder, and circles my breast with his fingers. "How about a little loving? It'd be good for you and, hell, I'd do anything to make you happy," he grins.

I'm really too distracted, but I give it a try. Jeff kisses my lips, my neck, and coaxes my favorite spots, but my engine simply idles and I get no lift off. With a quiet sigh, I turn on my back and let him finish.

It always amazes me how easily and soundly Jeff falls asleep. Tonight, I'm too wired to sleep, so I go over our storm preparations: flashlights by each bedside, candles in every room, a propane lantern on the kitchen table to use until we get the generator turned on, dry firewood stacked on the porch, jugs filled with water stored beneath every sink, stockpot simmering on the woodstove, and the pantry filled with nonperishable foods. Outside, treetops sway ever so slightly as a distant rumbling rolls through the hills to the southwest. The room feels small, like the walls and ceiling are being sucked in. I close my eyes but still can't fall asleep.

Outside, the wind picks up, twirling the towering tops of pines in ever-widening circles. A branch scratches against a window downstairs. A couple of ravens squawk and fly off to more protected perches.

I hope the storm is overrated, like Jeff says. In our twenty years here, we've endured some awful storms. Like the time I was stranded alone with Claire and Sage, who were only six and eight. With Jeff away at a consulting job in Berkeley, the girls and I lived a whole week without power or phone. No generator either. The storm kept coming for days until the snow was too deep and dangerous to walk in, so we pretended we were camping. We melted buckets of snow for water and told stories by the light of the woodstove. But it hardly snows much anymore. I yawn and drift off into an uneasy sleep.

I awaken to a dark room and dead silence. Power's out—that didn't take long. With my head pressed back into my pillow, I listen. The wind has picked up and changed direction. Rain smacks against the window. "Jeff?" I try to waken him, but he snores with his back to me, oblivious to the power outage or the arriving storm.

A white, electric flash from down the hallway fills our bedroom, and immediately a blast of thunder rattles the windows like an earthquake. This is strange. Storm's coming in from the east. Storms never come from that direction! Jeff situated the generator on the east side for that very reason—to protect it, but now it'll face the brunt of the storm. "Jeff!" I shake his shoulder, but he doesn't rouse. I rip out of bed and practically fly down the hall so I can get there before the next flash.

In my study, my shaking hands grope for the window, but I can hardly see because of all the file boxes I stacked up on that little desk. Steady rain beats like gravel tossed against the windowpane. An aged mustiness suffuses the air. I feel for the top box and lift it from the desk and onto the carpet, continuing until all the books, boxes, rolled maps, and files are circled on the floor behind me. Next flash, I lean over the now-empty desk to watch the forest, quivering bright as daylight. My hand rests upon the desktop. Heat builds beneath my fingers.

Outside the window, wind gathers force and whips the pine tops in arcs so wide I fear the trees will snap. Massive oak limbs groan under the ponderous weight of wind-swept rain, and the forest lights up in a symphony of flashes and cracking thunder. In a sudden chaotic crescendo, a cloud bursts open, gutters fill, downspouts overflow, rain cascades from the roof, a massive waterfall roars. My ears hurt, my heart aches, I forget to breathe.

Groping for my sweater on the chair behind me, I find it draped instead across one of the wooden packing crates piled high to the ceiling. Another flash lights the forest: one one thousand, two one thousand, three, and deafening thunder explodes over the metal rooftop, roiling in my ears and *I am drawn to a fire, swirling sparks, an old woman's furrowed face, hands clutching a round object over her heart. The old woman casts the fiery amulet to the heavens. I reach out* and the hairs on my arms prickle. Another flash, the room is empty, the crates gone. With a deep shiver, I pull my sweater tight and wait for the blast. Like ancients dwelling in caves of unspoken fears, I dread its power.

I pull a chair to the desk. Outside, a volley of waterlogged branches snap and crash to the forest floor like gunshots ringing through the hills. I press my cheek against the desk and cover my eyes. The oak is warm beneath my face, almost comforting. I ride the storm on through the night until, in a blinding flash and deafening roar, something massive splits asunder and falls to the earth in an agonizing crash.

And then it is over.

With my heart pounding wildly, I release my fingers, white from gripping the edges of the desk, and peer out the window. Lightning flickers against the distant hills like a cat that has become bored with its prey and is moving on. Shafts of moonlight slip between the opening clouds and catch the underside of broad madrone leaves, flashing them from white to green and back again, slower, slower, until they come to rest. As the wind pushes the storm clouds forward into the night, muffled voices emerge through the silence.

Teddy, Frederick, be careful.
Footsteps crunch over tangled branches.
Better get Eliza.

AMISHA

2075
Luna Valley, Northern California

Dar's clan moved into the sleeping room upstairs, following their seasonal ritual of transferring clothes, bedding, and belongings from the storage room to the large room across the hall. Amisha followed Trev and Sharome from room to room under the pretext of helping, but mostly she wanted to learn more.

"What's in all these boxes?" Amisha asked Trev as he handed her a lightweight box to take across the hall with the others. They couldn't all contain books.

"Stuff we've collected. Can't carry it all with us, so we only use it here."

"That's a lot of boxes."

"Not the ones stacked along the wall by the window. Those aren't ours."

Amisha pursed her lips, changed her mind, and pushed an empty box over to the closet.

Now!

Amisha turned her head toward Trev and Sharome to see if they heard. Seemingly not. She took a deep breath. "How about furniture?" she asked. "Was there ever a desk here? Just a little one, nothing special."

Trev scowled, shook his head, and headed into the other room.

"Why?" Sharome asked.

"Nothing. Just an old memory. I thought maybe it might still be here."

Sharome stuffed the clothes back in the box and turned from the room.

Unsure, Amisha continued to work alone until all the empty boxes were stacked against the wall. As she headed downstairs, she caught the end of a whispered conversation from the partly closed door of the sleeping room.

"It *is* her."

"Don't you say nothing."

In the peak of midday heat when it became almost life-threatening to be outside, the group converged in the cooler living room, sinking comfortably into each other's company. Clarissa and Glory napped on the couch. Tipped back on a plastic chair, Trev whittled a stick into a sharp point. Sharome sat on the floor at Trev's feet, eyes closed as usual. Amisha took the empty place on the floor next to Dar.

Dar nudged Amisha's arm. "Tell me about your Nib."

"I just dug it out one day."

"Why?"

"Why don't you all have Nibs?"

Dar shrugged. "Same as you, probably."

"Mine was getting strange. I couldn't trust it."

Dar raised her eyebrows. "That's all?"

Amisha looked down at her interlaced fingers in her lap, wondering how to find the right words. "I just had to get out of the city. I'm not sure why."

"Sounds a bit risky. Was there another big quake? Tidal wave?"

Amisha shifted the conversation, hoping to quell the clenching in her chest. "I thought maybe you had different types of Nibs, like the older, pocket-insert style."

"With no electricity? No, things weren't going well for us in Berkeley. We knew we had to drop out. That was almost ten years ago."

"And you've been OK without a Nib?"

"Enough to survive."

"Well I had no clue how to find my way without one. If it wasn't for Charlie, I'd never have found my way up here."

Sharome opened her eyes.

"Who's Charlie?" Dar asked.

"A crusty old man I met up with in Marysville. I swear I had no idea where this homestead was. He and his mule brought me up here."

"The old blind prospector?" Sharome crawled over to join the conversation.

"Yes! You know him? Argo was amazing. She knew the way up here all by herself."

Sharome retreated to her place against the wall.

Amisha looked from Dar to Sharome, then to Trev and Clarissa, who were now listening.

"What?"

"Charlie and Argo died years ago," Sharome said cautiously.

Amisha laughed. "Can't be. I was with them. We talked, slept under the stars, he even showed me . . ."

"They're buried side by side in the old cemetery outside The Forks. You can see it yourself."

After a painfully long silence, Dar spoke.

"I didn't pay much attention to your saying this was your family's place, but maybe it's time you tell us more." She waited for Amisha to collect her thoughts.

Amisha pointed to the woodstove. "Grandpa Auggie used to build a fire in that stove on winter mornings, though I mainly visited in summer. Grandma Claire always read on the front deck, even when Isabelle and I turned it into a space station."

"This was your grandparents' homestead?"

"Actually, Great-Grandma and Grandpa built it a hundred long years ago. I never knew them, but I was told the room upstairs was originally Great-Grandma Harmony's room." She looked at Trev. "Where all those boxes are now."

Trev and Sharome exchanged glances.

"The truth is, I came up here prepared to die. I'm smart enough to know my heart's giving out. I didn't think about it—I just moved in sort of a dream."

"Whose dream?" Dar asked. "Yours or your Nib's?"

"I don't know anymore."

Dar leaned back against the couch. "Doesn't matter. This place belongs to whoever is here."

"And we're here now," Trev said as he flipped his knife at a knot-hole on the wall across the room and hit it dead center.

ELIZA

1870

Yolo, California

"Silas Baxter!" A volley of thunderous knocks nearly shook the house off its stone foundation. "Come out here, Silas. You've got some explaining to do!" The front door flew open, and a voluminous woman dressed in a whirl of peach and blue pushed her way into the hall.

Wiping his hands on his pants, Silas scurried down the hall from the kitchen. "Mrs. Dosmar, has something happened? You've given me quite a fright."

"I gave you a fright? Nothing like what you gave me."

He knew her scowl—knew he was in for trouble. "I'm hardly home a few weeks and already you have an issue with me. What have I done now?" He asked as politely as he could, having learned over time that it never paid to tangle with his closest neighbor.

Berta leaned out the open window to get a better view of the backyard, but the object of her concern was out of sight behind the house.

"Women's undergarments," she said with her thick arms crossed over her farm woman's chest.

Silas blushed.

"You'd better have a good explanation, Mr. Baxter."

Silas peered out the window for as long as he could. "Looks like in my absence, someone's been using my clothesline. Miguel's wife, perhaps?" he turned with a shrug. "Now as long as you're here, would you pass on my message to Horace that I'm just getting around to stopping by?" He took her by the elbow and nudged her toward the door, but she wouldn't have it.

"Your clothesline is filled with women's undergarments—too small for you, even if you were so inclined. Or . . ." She gave him a dubious look. "Maybe you have a live-in housekeeper?"

Silas glanced upstairs. Why did Berta always have to boom like she was calling children in from the field. "I . . . I . . ." he hesitated. What else could he say? Swinging both arms to the ceiling in surrender, he pointed upstairs. "I went and got myself married."

"Married? You'd be the last bachelor to get married before hell freezes over, Mr. Baxter. You'd better come up with a better explanation than that!"

"Her name is Eliza."

Berta's eyes narrowed. "How old? Girl? Widow?"

"I don't know. Twenty maybe."

"You don't know? Where'd you pick her up then?"

"I've known her since . . . well, since she was almost a baby, back in Niles."

"A baby?"

"Berta, I didn't know I'd actually bring a bride home with me from Michigan. Something just got into me."

"Does she have a last name?"

"Osborn, I guess it's Baxter now. She's educated, well-bred. . . ."

"And you've kept her hidden for weeks?"

"She hasn't been well."

"Well I do hope she has not brought cholera upon us."

"No, no, I'm sure it's not, or she wouldn't have made it as far as California."

"When do I get to meet this woman responsible for the fall of Yolo's last confirmed bachelor?" Berta boomed.

Silas put his finger to his lips. "She's resting upstairs. Perhaps tomorrow," he whispered.

"I won't leave until I see her with my own eyes." Berta settled into one of the wooden chairs in the parlor, opened her needlepoint purse, and gave her nose a powder.

The last thing Silas wanted to do was disturb Eliza from the rest she seemed desperately to need, but after taking as much of Berta's glaring as he could stand, he relented.

"It's important," Silas said as he helped Eliza to sitting.

"Neighbor?" Eliza murmured, groggy from being pulled from her sleep. "You've not mentioned neighbors."

Silas exhaled. "Try your best to make a good impression. You'll want to be on Mrs. Dosmar's good side, believe me."

From her vantage point in the parlor, Berta watched two stockinged feet cautiously descend the stairs, then the hem, skirt, and bodice of a wrinkled yellow dress—without collar or waistband, Berta noted—and finally the rather confused, sunburned face of Silas's new bride.

"Berta Dosmar, please meet my wife, Eliza Baxter."

Eliza extended her hand with a little curtsy, but when Mrs. Dosmar didn't react, Silas drew up two more chairs and suggested he make some tea while the two of them got acquainted.

With Silas gone, Berta rose and took Eliza's chin in her hand and turned her head this way and that, as if examining a horse at auction. "He says you've not been well?"

"I haven't quite recovered from the long trip out," Eliza replied. "It was more challenging than I anticipated."

"I see. I see." Gathering Eliza's left hand into hers, Berta gave the loose gold band a twist, then stood back. "Well, I've accomplished what I need for now, and it's nearly milking time. Tomorrow we shall get better acquainted at my house. Please have Silas bring you by for afternoon tea at two." And as abruptly as she had arrived, Berta left out the front door.

Silas entered with a steaming pot of tea and, with a deep sigh, set the tray on the side table. "Looks like my peace and quiet have come to an end," he said.

HARMONY

2006
Luna Valley, Northern California

Had I realized how useful the little family desk was going to be, I wouldn't have waited so long to take my turn with it. With every inch of my long worktable buried under my computer, printer, file boxes, tangled cords, surge protector, external hard drive, speakers, and books, I can hardly find an empty space to write. But now, the desk has become my annex. Everything I don't currently use—news clippings, magazine articles, maps, books, notebooks—goes into one of four boxes I've stacked on top of the desk or on the little shelf below.

Today I'm going to "browse the web" about raising chickens. Like browsing dress racks? Who names this stuff, I wonder? With our brown and black-speckled hens pecking around the garden, I feel such kinship with women all around the world. We raise our vegetable greens. Our chickens peck the plants down to stubs, then leave their poop to fertilize the next sowing. It's all part of nature's cycle of life. But there comes a time when I need to know more than the books cover on chicken raising. That's when I discovered the joy of "googling." There are websites filled with information on just about anything—like the off-color poop my leghorn hen is dropping. I just type "chicken poop" in the long, narrow bar at the top of the screen and a dozen websites pop up. After clicking on one, I "drill down" (must be a guy who named this!) until I get into "abnormal poop colors." Not only do I get access to expert advice, but I can instantly purchase other relevant books just by typing in my credit card number—not that I'd ever divulge such personal information.

After deciding the poop color is normal, I continue browsing to see what else I can learn about chickens. I find fascinating information on debeaking egg peckers, artistic chicken house designs, photos of exotic show breeds, and warnings about hormones in commercial chicken food. My god, I had no idea. From there it's a quick shift to the atrocities of the commercial red-meat industry. An hour later, I've added my email address to five animal-activist alert lists to get weekly updates. How connected our world has become!

In this summer's intense heat, my chickens huddle under the broad clary sage leaves, panting with their beaks wide open to cool themselves. I turn on the hose and give them a fine spray, but recently I've noticed a hissing sound just before water emerges from the hose, and the bottom of their water dish is covered with a fine layer of silt. Should we be concerned?

AMISHA

2075
Luna Valley, Northern California

That evening, Clarissa took Amisha outside and pointed to the quarter moon overhead.

"We leave at the full moon."

"That's in three weeks." Amisha didn't need a Nib to count the moon's quarters. In the city, she rarely saw the real moon. Here, she was awed by the sterling crescent or brilliant white globe that journeyed across the sky most every night.

The group now shifted its focus to gathering food. The stash of acorns that Amisha had dumped outside had long since vanished, so she offered to gather more with Clarissa—it was the least she could do.

"There's two main oaks we harvest: black and valley," Clarissa explained as they climbed the hill above the house with large muslin bags tied to their waists. "Blacks taste best and keep well, but you have to go higher and higher in the hills to find them anymore." She stopped beneath a massive trunk of a wide-spreading oak and held up a long, pointed acorn. "But more of these valley oaks are moving up from below. They can't take the heat!" She instructed Amisha on how to avoid buggy ones, how to stoop to save your back, and how to carry a song of thanks in every breath.

A week later, after the back porch was filled with sacks of acorns, Clarissa announced it was time to start processing them. Half would be leached in water, ground into meal, and stored in glass jars. The other half would be left whole in muslin bags for when they returned.

"This time, I won't touch them," Amisha promised as she loaded the bags onto a pantry shelf. That is, if she was still here.

With the acorns safely stored, Amisha helped Glory gather the red berries hanging in clusters from the bushes with red bark, then spread them out to dry on a screen with another screen on top to keep insects and debris out.

"These manzanita berries get ground up then sifted for sugar. We'll trade some for sea salt at the coast. Dar pointed out the two large screens set up on the large expanse of dirt and dried weeds outside the back door.

A memory flashed: *A green lawn was once there with rolling croquet balls. "It's a strike," Grandpa heartily bellows. Laughter. Luke sulking behind a tree.* Amisha ran her fingers through the layer of crusted berries. Fine sugar dust sifted below to the dirt.

The idea of abandoning the house and traveling with the migrants was a recent thought. Frankly, Amisha was terrified at being alone again. Except for Sharome, she was comfortable with these people. They knew how to find food and survive without Nibs. *Come home to what?* she wondered. She had searched and searched, but no desk. Three times at dinner, she had asked directly if they knew anything about a little desk, but they'd shrugged and continued eating their salad of wild dandelion and succulent purslane. It was futile. Coming up here wasn't her idea. It could easily have been planted in her mind. Same with the stories about keeping the desk in the family.

Three days before they were to leave, the group's rhythm shifted again. The food supply was laid out on the table and sorted into what they would take for eating and for trade, and what they would store for their return. They filled muslin bags with yellow meal for baking acorn cakes, manzanita sugar for energy, dried Saint-John's-wort flowers for calming. Clarissa packaged jerky from squirrel and rabbit that Trev caught in a snare. Trev gave all the pocket tools a last sharpening with the whetstone. Amisha pumped water, filling their plastix and animal-hide containers until they bulged.

As the full-moon departure approached, a silence fell over the group. Sharome became fidgety and clung to Trev. Her orange-flecked brown eyes followed Amisha's every move. Amisha distanced herself whenever she could.

"You sure about coming with us?" Dar looked up from the table where she had spread out the packets of dried pennyroyal for one last count.

Amisha waved her off. "Nothing to stay for, nothing to return to."

"You're giving up finding that little table then."

"Desk," Amisha corrected. "Have you ever thought you knew something then realized you didn't understand at all? There's no desk and I don't want to be here alone, that's all." She opened the back door to leave but stopped at hearing Sharome's and Trev's heated whispers on the back porch.

"She's got to know."

"Shut up, you."

"I won't keep her from it," Sharome snarled.

Amisha quietly closed the door. She was afraid to ask.

The morning of their departure, Amisha folded the last of the grease-stained cloth towels and stacked them on the shelf, aware that Sharome was watching her from the shadows behind the pantry door.

"What do you want, Sharome? Come on, spit it out."

Sharome slipped from behind the door.

"You've been watching me." Amisha pushed the door closed.

"I know it's you," Sharome whispered, half-hidden in shadows.

Amisha's arms pricked with goose bumps. She didn't trust her or her brother, but if they were going to be traveling together, she wanted to have it out before they set off.

"You're the one."

"The what? Come on, make sense, Sharome."

Sharome slapped one hand over Amisha's mouth and pulled her upstairs by her braid to the room with all the boxes. With the frenzy of a madwoman, she slammed the door closed and pulled two large boxes into the room's center. Afraid to move, Amisha watched

Sharome set four smaller boxes atop those, then cover them with a large piece of plywood. After testing the platform for stability, she motioned Amisha over, pointing to the crumbling white ceiling panels above the boxes. Seeing Amisha didn't understand, she pointed harder.

"Up there. It's you."

Amisha looked to the door to escape, but Sharome had already climbed up and lifted a three-foot section of ceiling, causing a shower of crumbled sheet rock and shredded yellow insulation to fall to the floor and block her exit.

"Give me a hand." Sharome pulled Amisha onto the wobbling platform. Using Amisha's knee as a step, Sharome hoisted herself up into the attic, then reached down for Amisha's hand and pulled her into the dark. "Feet there, and there," Sharome instructed. Disturbed by the commotion, bats flew in circles overhead, disrupting decades of dust. Amisha couldn't stop coughing. Sharome guided Amisha by the hand along the ridge beam until they came to an obstacle straddled over the beam. Sharome placed Amisha's hands onto the flat surface.

Trembling uncontrollably, Amisha inched her fingers in opposite directions along the front edge until each hand came to a corner. Turning the right angle, she continued toward the back. When her hands met at the center of the back, she gasped.

Sharome gestured for Amisha to back down to the room below, then she rotated the desk, angled it leg by leg through the ceiling hole, and lowered it into Amisha's outstretched hands. Amisha jumped back, her fingertips nearly scorched from the desk's heat. Sharome wiggled back down from the attic and landed beside the desk with a loud thump. Coated in fine dust, sheet rock, and insulation, the two women faced each other, the desk between them.

"There *is* a desk." Amisha could hardly speak.

Sharome nodded.

"So small."

"Strong enough to call you here," Sharome said.

Amisha extended her hand, then quickly withdrew.

"Go ahead." Sharome motioned to the desktop.

As if reaching out to a wild animal cornered and unpredictable, Amisha gradually settled her hand on the top of the desk. A warmth spread beneath her fingers. Her heart's wild thrashing calmed. Tears spilled from her eyes.

"I never imagined . . ."

"Now you can stop imagining and start listening," Sharome said.

Amisha eyed the gaping hole in the ceiling. "How?"

"Trev and I hid it up there. Too many wayfarers looking for wood to burn. If you were going to come someday, it had to be protected."

"You knew I would come?"

Sharome gestured to a large box marked "Garden" in the closet. "It's all in those boxes. We were looking for books about growing food but found only boxes of scribbled notebooks. It was winter, we had nothing to do, so I started reading them. Some were easy enough to read, but one fragile book filled with long curvy lines and letters all bunched together was impossible." Amisha reached for a box but Sharome held the lid down. "Later," she said. "There'll be time enough when we're gone."

"How did you know it was me?" Amisha asked.

"At first, I wasn't sure, but when you said you were *called* to your family's homestead and asked about a desk, all this had to be about you."

Amisha later remembered the outpouring of words from the women, the thoughtful silence, the parcels of food returned to the pantry shelf. This time, no one asked if she was certain. She remembered their words of encouragement, their promises to return, and the gentle hugs that didn't make her flinch. But mostly she remembered Dar's final words of warning or consolation, she wasn't sure.

"You won't be alone, Amisha. You'll find out soon enough."

As the last person closed the door behind them, she *was* alone . . . with the desk.

ELIZA
1870
Yolo, California

At two o'clock the next afternoon, Silas guided Eliza up the stone walkway of the Dosmar farmhouse and knocked on the door. Eliza smoothed the folds of her blue calico skirt, hoping she had pressed out enough wrinkles to make the dress decently presentable. It was the only other dress she had.

Berta Dosmar appeared, her dark brown hair neatly spiraled in a bun, a berry-stained apron tied around her large midriff. With a peck on the cheek for Silas and a polite nod to Eliza, she invited them inside.

"I thought I'd be finished with my pies by now," she said, removing her apron. "No mind. Have a seat in the parlor. This is a good time for me to stop for tea. The twins are napping, and the older children won't be home from school until four. You'll have time to tell all." Seated in a commodious armchair across from the couple, Mrs. Dosmar nodded toward Eliza and pronounced in a tone decidedly more serious, "You must understand, Silas, that this changes everything."

Silas switched his hat to his other knee. "I was hoping I could find Horace...."

"He can wait until I'm done with you." Twenty-five years of bringing this man pies and setting a place for him at Sunday dinners . . . what were the women going to do now? She took a hard look at the woman who had snatched away their beloved bachelor. His young wife had obviously found a mirror since yesterday and fixed up her hair, though her dress was shamefully rumpled and lacking a belt. Such a specter of sadness. Maybe a bit of tea would brighten her up.

Berta leaned forward. "Do you need some tea, dear?" Before Eliza could reply, Berta was clattering teacups in the kitchen.

"What do you think?" Silas asked under his breath.

"I'm not sure what she and I would talk about. I see no evidence of books or newspapers."

Berta swept back into the room with a tray of flowered cups and saucers, a tea pot covered in a quilted cozy, and a plate piled high with slices of white cheese, red apples, and molasses cookies. She nudged the plate toward Eliza.

Eliza took a single slice of cheese and apple while Berta poured their tea.

"Now, Silas," Berta settled back into the chair across from them, "you must start from the beginning."

Silas had no choice but to sink back into the corner of the sofa and tell their story that by week's end every person in Yolo would have formed an opinion about. What could he say? Their families were old friends back in Niles, they'd corresponded for a time while Eliza was in school, and last trip back east he'd stopped by and, well, made her a proposal. "Probably the most spontaneous thing I've ever done," he confessed with a blush.

A bit of fire rose in Eliza's eyes. "Mrs. Dosmar, you must understand that I became acutely interested in all things California. Silas had written so many letters to Papa describing California, I just knew this was where I must be." She took a nibble of cheese, then discreetly dropped the rest into the napkin in her lap.

"Well, the real California's a far cry from the version sold to Easterners," Mrs. Dosmar said.

"I see that now, but I had other reasons for coming out here."

Silas rose and brushed the crumbs from his pants. "Now if you ladies don't mind, I've shared our little story and now I have some business with . . ."

"Sit! Silas. I'm not quite done with you." Berta refilled his cup and added two sugar cubes. "Just how you like it." She noticed Eliza's untouched cup. "You're not hungry?"

Eliza shook her head.

After a long sip, Silas added in a very quiet tone, "She's not been well since we arrived. Nearly three weeks and I don't see she's getting any better."

"Good Lord, three weeks!"

"She's in bed most of the time or staring out the parlor window talking to herself. I'm fearing she's not been happy since we arrived home."

"Since the desert," Eliza said, averting his eyes.

"Ah, yes." Silas slumped back in the couch, discomforted at having revealed so much.

"Well?" Berta broke the long silence.

Silas cleared his throat several times and looked away.

"We were down to one ox and little water," Eliza jumped in.

"I warned her about the desert."

"He forced me to abandon her." Eliza's voice quivered. "Left alone in the desert!"

"Oh, my poor, poor dear." Berta reached for Eliza's hand. "What was your child's name?"

"No," Silas blurted. "Her desk."

Eliza swung around to face Silas. "You picked my desk up and tossed it against a hill of sand like it was rubbish. Well, you got what you wanted."

Eyes narrowed in concentration, Berta followed the conversation back and forth.

"I warned you I wouldn't live in California without my desk," Eliza nearly shouted.

"No piece of furniture is that important," Silas shouted back. "But who am I to know women's needs?"

"Surely you could purchase or have one made when you arrived?" Berta asked.

"Not like this one."

"She just plain won't let go of it," Silas groused. "She sits for hours in the parlor talking to her desk like it's sitting under the window."

"My desk is coming back, I tell you. No. I promise you!"

"I see." Berta nodded to Silas. "Maybe now *is* a good time to find Horace, give me and Eliza a little time together." She pointed to the back door. "Try the north barn. I think he's working the new mare in the back corral."

As Silas slipped out the door, Berta handed Eliza a red-checkered apron from the wall hook. "Come join me in the kitchen. I could use some help finishing my pies." Just outside the kitchen door she turned to Eliza. "Three weeks! I tell you, what woman could survive three weeks alone with any man?"

Eliza gave a weak smile.

"No offense to Silas," Berta continued as she rolled up her sleeves at the center worktable, "but he's an old stubborn Scotsman." She stopped to calculate on her fingers. "I take that back. He's only in his late forties. But he's also kind and gentle and he runs a good farm." She sprinkled a handful of flour onto the table and set a ball of dough in Eliza's hands. "You *do* know how to roll a crust?"

Eliza pressed the rolling pin into the dough, expanding the crust in ever-widening circles. With the quiet, steady rhythm of rolling and rotating, the knot in her stomach began to loosen. She reached for an empty pie tin.

"Why so many pies?"

"Most are for the Methodist social tomorrow." With a heavy metal spoon, Berta stirred the spicy-sweet mixture of suet, citrus peel, apples, animal organs, tongue, and leftover meat from butchering that was warming on back of the stove. "Want a taste of my mincemeat?"

Eliza clutched at her stomach. "It's not really my favorite."

"What kind of farm woman doesn't like mincemeat!" Berta laughed. "You'll see. Someday you'll have your own recipe for all those extra animal pieces and I'll be begging you to share it with me."

"I'm not so sure," Eliza said, giving the next mound of dough a quarter turn and rolling it into a reasonable circle. "Do you mind if I sit? It's my legs."

With a throaty hiss, Berta swished the sleeping tabby cat off the stool and out the door. The room filled with the sound of a steady rhythm as the two women worked in silence across from each other—Eliza rolling out the bottom crusts, Berta pressing them into the pan and making fluted waves around the tops.

"This desk of yours," Berta said without looking up. "I want to hear more about it."

Eliza stopped rolling.

"Seems you're quite attached to it."

A tear rolled down Eliza's cheek and onto the empty pie tin.

"It was like a piece of home for you, wasn't it?" Berta sighed. "We all missed our home when we arrived."

Eliza nodded, dabbing at her cheeks with the hem of her apron. "Men just don't understand."

"Berta, my desk is going to return. Of that, I'm certain."

"Well, dear, I hope it does for your sake, and Silas's too." She pulled Eliza's bottom crust in front of her to be filled. "But let's talk about why you're not eating."

"I've had no appetite since I arrived. To tell the truth, I'm sickened at the smell of food. Silas pressured me to see Doctor Wesley, but I told him all I need is my desk."

With a loud thump, Berta dropped her rolling pin onto the table and rounded the table to Eliza.

"My, my, my! Why didn't I see this sooner? When was your last flow, my dear?"

Eliza shook her head, confused.

"You know, your monthly?"

Eliza blushed. "It's been a while. The trail was hard on my body. Everything just came to a halt—eating, sleeping, my monthly."

"And did you and Silas?" Gertrude put two fingers together with a shy smile.

Eliza slowly nodded yes.

"Well, that settles it. Tired, tearful, queasy. Silas, old boy, looks like you brought back more surprises than a bride. You brought back the wee beginnings of a family!"

That night at supper, Silas noticed Eliza's untouched plate.

"You're terribly quiet."

Eliza nodded.

"Did you like Berta? It looked like you two were getting up a good conversation."

"Yes, quite," she was quick to respond. "I didn't realize how much I miss women's company." Eliza took a few nibbles of bread. "Berta says I'm going to have a baby."

Silas stopped midswallow. His fork clattered to his plate. Like a wild bird, his eyes darted around the room landing on everything but his wife.

"Silas?"

He folded his napkin, set it next to his plate, then unfurled it, dabbed at his mustache, folded it again. He lifted his fork, stabbed a chunk of potato, then positioned his knife and fork across the top of his plate.

"I . . . I don't know what to say."

Eliza pressed her palms over her eyes and broke into sobs.

"At least I know what's been wrong with you."

"Wrong?"

"You not being able to stomach food, I mean." He rose and pushed his chair against the table. "Just one more thing I didn't think through."

"You're angry?"

"I don't know what I am right now." He stood at the window for what seemed to Eliza to be a dreadfully long time. Without warning, Silas pounded his fist on the wall. "Hah!" He turned back to Eliza. "Just wait 'til Horace hears about this. He had six foals while I was away. But *I'm* going to have a baby!"

Tangled in a blanket of confusion in her bed that night, Eliza waited for her feelings to settle. For the first time since she arrived, she thought of Silas alone downstairs on the hard parlor floor.

Was he sleeping? He wasn't the only one who didn't think things through. Everything was coming on much too fast and not at all like she imagined. She looked out the open window at the clouds. Did her longing for California override her good judgment? She hardly knew Silas, hardly knew California, hardly knew anymore why she came there. And now, she pressed her hand against her belly, a baby she hardly knew.

That night she fell into a dream, one she would have again and again, with endless fields of freshly plowed earth and tall stalks of grain that brushed against her legs as she floated through. Luminous seed heads ripened, spilled to the parched and barren earth where only fire can grow. She searched for water. Always water.

HARMONY

2008
Luna Valley, Northern California

Outside on the driveway, two men stand beside the unmistakable green U.S. Forest Service truck and wait for me to emerge from the house. The Forest Service is offering voluntary fire-safety inspections. With my blue sweatshirt zipped up to my neck against the late spring morning, I wait for the one with "Mike Ferris" pinned to his green wool jacket to write our name and address on his clipboard.

"WUI," he says solemnly.

"What?"

"Woodland-Urban Interface. With so many folks building houses in the middle of the forest," he says, handing me a colored brochure, "it's getting mighty difficult to manage public lands with all your private residences mixed in."

"We're working to get homeowners to help by reducing the fire danger around their private property," says the shorter, stockier ranger. His voice is familiar. I'm wondering if he was the one inside the Smokey the Bear suit at the last fire department picnic but decide not to ask.

"Too many houses, too close to wildlands, too much potential for wildfires," Mike explains.

They ask permission to look around. Forty-five minutes later they return and hand me a copy of their checklist. #1 Remove all vegetation and flammable material within 100 feet of the dwelling.

#2 Limb up all branches six feet from the ground. #3 Eliminate all trees and brush ten feet either side of the driveway and where the property meets the county road below. They give us an "A plus" for the metal roof, then dock us for the wood deck and siding.

This is ridiculous. We didn't move to the forest just to cut it down! I start my rebuttal. "We can't remove the greenery along the roadside because it's our privacy screen from neighbors. We'll limb up some of the tall trees we can't see from the house, but not the shorter dogwood and lilacs—that's just not their natural shape." I ask them to show me how far a hundred feet is from where we stand. This is stupid. "We can't just move the woodshed," I tell them. "We need it near the house in the winter to get wood for the woodstove."

"This isn't just for your own protection," Mike says with a new tone of exasperation. "It helps protect your whole neighborhood and the entire forest."

Smokey points to the thick manzanita and brushy Scotch broom between our house and the road. "Indians and old timers used to light fires every year to keep this looking like an open park. Can't do that anymore. Too many people." He shakes his head. "You folks out here are living in a tinderbox. It's only a matter of time before it ignites."

Mike hands me the clipboard and points to the signature line. "We'll return in thirty days."

Upstairs in my study, I toss their inspection on the little desk by the window. It lands atop the stack of far-fetched dystopic novels which I'll get around to reading someday. "What?" I glare back at the desk. "Of course, I'll get it done, but I'm not happy about cutting back my trees. We didn't settle up here to live on a dirt parking lot."

That summer we took in two families who were evacuated because of wildfires in the foothills. Lightning strikes burned twelve hundred acres and destroyed ten structures the next ridge over. Word is that a hunter's campfire caused the second fire just east of us. Only two houses burned, but it took ten smoke-filled days to control the fire that ravaged five thousand acres of national forest. I thought that summer was an aberration. It wasn't. Dealing with wildfire would soon become a way of life for us.

Amisha

2075
Luna Valley, Northern California

After waving goodbye to the migrants as they disappeared down the dirt driveway, Amisha returned to the house. The kitchen table overflowed with food packets Clarissa had generously left her. She knew she should store them away in the pantry, but she couldn't wait to examine the desk and assure herself it wasn't a dream.

The desk stood in the middle of the room just as she and Sharome had left it. But her heart sank. Such a frail little thing could hardly have the power to call her up here. She gave the desk a gentle shake. Its joints wobbled and creaked. She drew her fingers through the dust. Tiny splinters stuck in her tingling fingertips. She pushed the desk against the window, pulled up a chair, and sat in front of the desk. Her long legs narrowly fit in the space beneath; her outstretched hands filled the width of the desktop with ease. Beneath her palms, the wood grain appeared dusty-gray and tired. She waited for something to happen. Two ravens scolded from their perch on an oak branch.

Amisha traced an "A" in the dust. "Seems we're both old ladies in exile," she said, surprised at the tears falling onto the oak grain and quickly disappearing. "You must be thirsty." She fetched one of the bags of walnuts Clarissa left her along with a heavy rock and a block of wood and cracked the walnut shell in half to expose the oily nutmeat. After wiping the dust from the desktop with a cloth, she drew another "A" with the nut piece. The oak eagerly absorbed the trail of oil. For the rest of the day, she rubbed nutmeats into the desktop, moving side to side in a gentle rhythm until the bag was empty and the desk, warm and glistening.

Tired, but feeling a small sense of accomplishment, Amisha collapsed into the chair. She pulled a sliver from her thumb and sucked on it until it stopped hurting. Her shoulders ached terribly. She shifted her chair to catch a bit of the late afternoon sun on her shoulders. The warmth felt good. As her eyes drifted around the room, she noticed as if for the first time the boxes stacked two, three, four high in the corners, in the closet, and along the walls. She pulled the closest cardboard box toward her, careful to protect the crumbling corners. Disregarding the scribbled writing on top, she opened the flaps. Inside, wedged shoulder to shoulder were books—old-style books with numbers across each spine. Curious, she lifted out the farthest one with a red-paisley design and flipped to the last page.

> *February 7, 2042: Wisps come and go all the time. I turn my head—they're gone. Who else lives here now? Claire and Auggie. Who else?*

"Claire, my grandmother?" Amisha squinted at the unfamiliar handwriting.

> *My arthritis is so bad I can hardly hold the pen. When did these hands get so bony and crawling with veins? A wisp of a child tugs at my skirt. "Come," I try to lift her but can't. "Come, this is your desk too." She crawls onto my lap and grabs a pen, makes tiny, tiny circles all over the page. She feels so light against my chest, I can hardly tell where she begins and I end. She holds up my journal, shows me what she's made. Seeds? With a shy giggle, she touches her chest, then mine, then returns to filling the page. Yes, we are each other's seeds. I want to keep her forever, but my arms won't hold. I . . .*

"Oh my god, I feel like I know this!" Amisha circled the room. Pushed against the wall were boxes of books with hand-printed numbers starting way back in 1985. Words were written on top of other boxes: "Homesteading," "Food Storage," "Gardening," "Animals," "Wind Power," and "Solar Energy." What else? Stacked on the closet shelves behind her were metal canisters stuffed with envelopes labeled "Seeds" and other small, unidentifiable matter. Behind the canister stood a box half-filled with small slips of papers—receipts for eggs, embroidery, and a used piano made out to Harmony Durrell. My god, these weren't Grandmother Claire's boxes; these were from Great-Grandmother Harmony!

Amisha's mind raced. Great-Grandmother couldn't have known she'd be here someday. In what remained of the fast-fading light, Amisha read until her stinging eyes forced her to stop. As she drifted into sleep that night, she was filled with an indescribable sense that all she needed was *here*.

The next morning, Amisha awoke to a new chill in the air. Winter? Before leaving, Dar warned that cold times were coming. Winter is unpredictable, Sharome added. Seasons have their own reasons. They touch down in a fury of wind and rain, return for a deep spell of snow, then bounce off somewhere else, leaving us all sweltering and dry. Before last night, Amisha had no idea how to prepare for this new season. Nib alerts always instructed what to do for rain, snow, floods, freezing ice, mudslides, rising seas, or hurricanes. Now she had Great-Grandmother Harmony's books to help her.

After gulping down her morning dandelion-root tea, Amisha was back in Gramma Harmy's room, as she now called it, but soon became discouraged at how hard it was to read.

"How to prepare for winter?" she said to the room, half hoping one of the books would spontaneously fan open with the information she needed highlighted in yellow. She picked out a small book from the "Homesteading" box. Its pages were thick with black writing, but no pictures. How the hell was she supposed to find "winter" in all those words? She tossed it back and returned to the boxes of Harmony's journals—much more interesting. She selected 2017 and opened to the first entry.

January 7, 2017: Big storm took out the electricity again which means no power to the well pump and hence no water. Ironically, I'm also out of propane for the back-up generator, and Jeff's fancy solar water pump stopped working a month ago. Wouldn't you know it, the repair person can't make it out here until next week.

But I outsmarted them all. Jeff said I was crazy for wanting an old-fashioned hand pump for the well—probably not techie enough. But now I get to decide, and some overpowering feeling nudged me to get one of those red-handled water pumps installed. Even did the research myself. If it worked for Great-Grandma, it would work for me.

"Oh, my god—the hand pump. Yes! It saved my life." Amisha was nearly in tears.

Outside, the wind picked up, tossing dried leaves against the window and reminding Amisha of her task at hand—preparing for winter. But she kept thinking about what she had read. Gramma Harmy lived here even before her grandparents, Claire and Auggie. How did she survive? These boxes might hold other clues if she could just figure out how to find what she needed. She took a blank notebook and a yellow pencil stub and wrote in simple block letters across the top of the first page: "Winter—How to Survive." She started a list of what she knew: #1 Wood—stack high, #2 cover windows, #3 store food—lots.

She clenched and released her fist to ease a cramp from holding the pencil. Writing was so awkward. Why write when your Nib recorded and retrieved anything you could ever want? Mom insisted she take block printing in school—said it was like learning Latin. Well, no one uses Latin and sure as hell, no one writes.

She started with the "Food Storage" box and after sorting through books on canning, dehydrating, saving seeds, and root cellars, decided the tattered book *Putting Food By* held the most promise for ways to make her blackberries last the winter. Did it ever! Pages and pages, thick with words, but how the hell was she to pull up the data she needed? Amisha closed her eyes, thought of the word "berries" hoping something would pop up. But it didn't.

She lifted out the next book, careful to keep it from falling apart at the binding. *Gardening by the Moon* was filled with drawings of moons in all phases. This was more like it. She pressed her finger against the line under the words "Root Crops"—an archaic way of being directed to more information, but maybe it would still work. No. This book was absolutely dead. She certainly couldn't read through every page—that's way too much work. She wanted to know right now! A sweet scent blew through the room, like the promise of grandma's apple pie cooling on the kitchen counter. Apples? Didn't she see a picture of apples at the beginning of one of those books? She dug deeper into the boxes.

ELIZA

1871

Sierra Nevada, Northern California

"Trails are gettin' picked over and my legs are gettin' stiff." Scrabby scoffed the last of his whiskey and tossed the empty flask in the back of his wagon. This trip east he'd gambled on a less traveled route used mostly by cattle drives. It paid off. He'd found some decent items set back from the trail: china dishes in their original shipping crate, hard-to-find fencing tools, and a massive claw-foot table that would need some work to bring back the walnut luster. Those would be snatched up first, he figured. The other goods, like the butter churn, kitchen chairs, hoes, and rakes would be easy enough to sell to the mercantiles sprouting up in California's valley towns. Even the little writing desk he found covered up with a tattered blanket would go fast. He passed it over twice before deciding on impulse to take it. Satisfied, he arranged his wagon so the less expensive household items were in the back and turned the wagon west to San Francisco.

Lady Luck's finally on my side, Scrabby mused. He could have used her help twenty years ago when he near broke his back, prodding gold out of freezing water. Yuba, Feather, American Rivers—hell, didn't make no difference. Back in 1851, whatever gold glinted in his pan ended up in the saloon. All he wanted was to impress Meghan's father with his new riches. So much for that. Meghan went off to school, never even said goodbye. That hurt. Ah, to hell with them both.

1852

Hardly two years after arriving in the gold fields, Scrabby had sold his pick and pan and turned his mule Rosie and his rickety wagon back east to Ohio. The first night he camped at the far end of Bear Valley, making it easy to get a head start over the steep pass. The wind quivered through the yellow aspen grove, reminding him just a flicker of Meghan's laughter. He spit a wad of tobacco juice into a nearby manzanita bush. He swore he'd never return empty-handed. Maybe he just wasn't meant to marry.

Over the next days, Scrabby worked his way down to the base of the Sierra's eastern slope, noting how much settlers left behind as they lightened their loads for the final ascent over the pass into California. He hadn't thought much about it until he stopped to let Rosie graze and started poking around. Most of the furniture was worn by the elements, but some was protected enough to be of interest. Like the ornate cherry headboard resting against the base of a sugar pine or the upturned treadle sewing machine hidden behind it. Such a shame, he thought. So many abandoned dreams.

He traveled slower the next few days, taking stock of the potential riches left along the trail. Clothes trunks he ignored, but the box of woodworking tools with oak handles burnished to a deep sheen and blades sharp enough to carve aged hardwood gave him reason to dance a little jig. Some German probably brought these from their homeland. Must have been awfully hard to leave them here. He rubbed his calloused hands together and lifted a blacksmith's hammer and bellows. Might be useful back home, he thought and hauled the oblong box over to his wagon.

As he was leading Rosie back to the wagon, a bright flash behind a juniper grove caught his eye. Hidden by a tall manzanita bush, he found an iridescent pink lantern shade decorated with hand-painted cherubs, remarkably still intact. He thought of Meghan and the furniture her parents brought over from Ireland. Maybe he should bring this home to her. Would she be happy or disappointed to see him? He wasn't sure. He wrapped the delicate shade in the remains of a tattered quilt and bundled it safely in the wagon.

He removed his pipe and tobacco pouch from his jacket pocket, tapped a thread of stringy leaves into the bowl of the pipe, then lit one of his precious matches. After several puffs to freshen his head, he reflected on his immediate surroundings. There were still valuable possessions everywhere he turned. It'd be a shame to leave them here to rot and ruin. Hell—wouldn't hurt to put a few more things in the wagon—he had the room. For the rest of the day, he halted Rosie whenever something caught his eye—furniture, mirrors, tools, and trunks. By the time he left the Truckee River on the eastern side of the Sierra and started into the Nevada desert, Scrabby's wagon was bulging with treasures.

Scrabby stabbed a potato with his knife and pulled it out of the fire. Something else nagged at the back of his mind, and it wasn't about facing the desert crossing. It was more like something growing into a whole new idea. Why not turn around, head back west now? He could make it easy back over the pass before the snow. He'd bypass the gold fields and head straight for San Francisco.

Over the years, Scrabby developed a new enterprise: bringing riches *into* California. He ignored the shrugs and folk's foul-spirited remarks as he crossed through the Humboldt desert, Salt Lake plains, and eventually Fort Laramie, venturing farther east each trip with his empty wagon. He soon traded his old wagon for a larger one, added three mules to help Rosie. He traveled east until his wagon was full, then turned back west with his payload. While others were still sweating for gold or blasting hillsides away with water shot from massive monitors, he was drinking imported Costa Rican coffee and haggling with San Francisco merchants over prices.

In the city, he was known by his proper name, Charles Lyons, dealer in fine wares. Some trips he'd stop in Sacramento to repair broken pieces, then he'd wash, shave, and don his three-piece suit and bow tie. He liked his business. He liked the solitude and the independence. And he liked the money.

1871

Twenty years later, he still never took the ocean view from the Cliff House for granted. Scrabby checked his pocket watch. His merchants had another five minutes. With the brandy snifter held to the window's light, he gave the rich amber liquor a swirl then took a long, satisfying swallow. This moment was made for lingering. Tomorrow he'd be back in Levi pants and leather jacket, headed to the Sacramento Valley to make his rounds of smaller towns, where he'd easily unload the butter churn, wash tub, tools, and small kitchen items.

Scrabby didn't find the note right away. Only a few items of minimal value remained in the wagon when he started for the eastern part of the valley. But that small desk at the back of the wagon perplexed him. To date, no one even made him an offer. He'd watched folks check it out, run their hands across the top, take mental measurements, confer with heads together in quiet corners. But not one offer.

He tapped the tip of his boot against the wagon and weighed his options. Give it away? Leave it by the roadside like he found it? He hoisted himself into the wagon and approached the little desk, now scrunched alone in the back corner.

"Sorry, but I gotta get going." He pulled the desk forward with his weathered hands. "Maybe I'll just take you along for my campfires." He reached for the ax stored under the bench. "Just a piece of junk—been nothing but a bother to me." He gave his ax a practice swing. "I could almost take you apart by hand." He yanked the small drawer out to test how easily it would come apart and noticed, for the first time, a wrinkled fan of paper stuck in a crack at the back of the drawer. Careful not to tear it, he extracted the brittle page and smoothed it out against the desktop. In the most delicate of penmanship he read:

> *To whomever finds this note, please have heart. I have been forced to abandon this desk under great duress. If you should find space to bring my precious desk to California, I beseech you to deliver it*

to: Eliza Anna Osborn Baxter, Cache Creek, Yolo, California. I promise you compensation worthy of your efforts.

Sincerely, and with greatest gratitude,
Mrs. Silas Rossiter Baxter

The small desk's fate hung in balance as Scrabby read and reread the note. Yolo was a full day's journey out of his way. He should make headway to the base of the pass before dusk. No, there'd be no detour. Not for a useless desk. No matter how much he was paid, it wouldn't be worth it.

His thoughts drifted to Meghan and her parent's parlor filled with small, treasured pieces from Ireland, hand-carried to America. Women liked such things. He'd been gone so many years, for all he knew, she was already married. He wished he'd been a better writer.

Scrabby turned the note over in his fingers. All this thinking was wearing him out. Across the valley, the horizon filled with dark masses of billowing clouds, the kind that usually brought rain. He watched them build against the coastal range until they formed a dense blanket overhead that extended for miles up and down the valley. With the sun obscured, it was hard to keep track of time. Was it still early afternoon? Two ravens cawed to each other flying low across the field, then with full swooping circles, landed on the top branches of a valley oak. Rosie looked up from her grazing, then settled back, unperturbed.

Scrabby knew he'd better get going, but the truth was, he felt too depleted to move. With arms crossed over his chest, he leaned back and stared at the changing pattern of clouds drifting across the darkening hills. In the distance, a thin shaft of sunlight slid between the layers of gray, seeming to search the valley floor. The rays swept across the landscape first highlighting a tree, a distant hill, then picking up a bit of sparkle from a small stream before disappearing into the clouds again.

He blinked and refocused his eyes. He couldn't put it into words, but he knew with absolute certainty that something in his world had just shifted.

From her front porch, Eliza, too, watched the dark clouds billow and drift along the hillside darkening the late afternoon sky. Something was coming. She tapped her fingers along her crossed arms, then returned inside to the parlor. She had not protested when Silas placed his bookcase under the middle window, but now she felt an urgent need to make room. As she dragged the bookcase to the opposite wall, the air snapped with static electricity. She swept away the dust on the floor, then stood back from the empty space and took a hard look out the window.

Eliza felt a deep knowing—even when there was just a small spec at the end of the driveway. She pushed Silas aside as he hung his hat on the hallway rack and flew down the front stairs to wait for it.

"Mrs. Baxter?"

Eliza was already in the back of the wagon with the desk enfolded in her arms.

Silas followed her outside, not believing what he saw. He stepped forward to greet the itinerant merchant.

"Silas Baxter," he said. "And my wife—"

"Mrs. Eliza Baxter. I know." Scrabby eyed the farmwoman hugging the desk.

"Eliza?" Silas called.

But Eliza either didn't hear, or she refused to let go of her desk until she was ready. When at last she lifted her head, Silas helped Scrabby carry the brittle desk into the empty space beneath the parlor window.

Being who he was, Scrabby felt he had no choice but to accept their offer of a fine, farm dinner with the couple and their little girl, a shot or two of whiskey, and, as it was already dark, a warm night's sleep in the room set aside for unexpected travelers. After dinner (had he talked too much?) and a trip to the outhouse, he walked back very slowly through the house up to his room. Not that he was drunk, just that this was all new to him—a family home, children's toys, warm kitchen, books, even laughter—like nothing else in his life. And the little package wrapped up in brown paper and twine? The Mrs. had placed it in his hands after he'd gone on and on about

Meghan. Told him to listen to the silence of his heart. Just maybe he'd follow her advice.

In the master bedroom, Silas turned over and stretched his arm out across the empty bed. He knew where Eliza would be. Perhaps now with the miracle of her desk's return, she would settle down at last. He had carried such guilt over what happened although he knew he'd done the only thing he could. With only one ox left, he was terrified they wouldn't make it out of the desert. For the first time in over a year, Silas felt immense relief and hope that their marriage would work out.

Eliza, of course, didn't sleep. With a quilt wrapped around her shoulders, she spent the night gently rubbing the desk with a flannel dipped in oil pressed from their olive grove. When she had caressed every inch of oak, she tucked another quilt around the desk and spent the night with her head pressed against the warmth of the heartwood.

HARMONY

2009
Luna Valley, Northern California

"What's this expense?" Jeff points to a line in my check register. "NEDF for $30?"

"They're doing so much. It's the least I can do."

"NEDF?"

I sigh, not ready for another lecture about saving our money. "NEDF is defending the environment on a national level. They rely on us small donors. I can't be a watchdog for everything myself, so when they send an appeal, I try to tuck in a check."

"Sierra Club, $25; World Wildlife, $15; Elephant Protection League, $12; Friends of Farm Animals, $10?" His voice tightens. "Have you added these all up?"

We launch into our familiar argument about how to change the world. We're trying to make our homestead a model for how to live lightly on the earth, but Jeff also has contract work with the EPA. This is my way of working globally. We agree to set a budget for environmental donations and make them only after we've paid into the girls' college savings. But when I see photos of volunteers cleaning oil-soaked birds, I need to help right now, not wait until next month. Jeff says I'm obsessive-compulsive. When it comes to the planet, is that a bad thing?

A whole morning spent scanning through email alerts and reading Dora's endless summaries of county supervisors' meetings gives me little more than a headache. Time to escape to my favorite place—the river. Like a homing pigeon, my old yellow Volvo glides down the switchbacks of the narrow mountain road until I enter the Third River canyon. Here the road parallels the shallow, trout-filled water—shallower than normal for spring runoff, I notice. Should I be concerned? I hang right into the parking area, where I can pick up the river trail.

Sandals off, hiking boots on, I find the dusty trail head and start walking. The first part is rocky and unstable, but I know it will smooth out around the bend and I'll soon strike a cadence. I grab a handful of tiny red berries from a silver-leaved manzanita bush and pop them in my mouth. They're crunchy, slightly sweet, but I'd hate to have to live on them. I spit them into the bushes.

My boots pick up a deep, thudding rhythm alongside the steady flow of the wild-rushing river. Each step drops me deeper into the mindless presence I came here for. My forehead smooths, my jaw loosens, my breath deepens. River's good medicine.

Around the bend, the trail dips down and I pick up speed. Got to call Senator Bailey's office when I get back and . . . stop . . . I quiet myself . . . just breathe. Farther down the trail, wafts of tropically sweet-smelling native azalea tickle my nose, and sure enough, the trail is lined with branches of white blossoms nodding and bending along the path. Heavenly! I breathe deep. So much of the world needs protecting now . . . rivers, forests, fish. Am I doing enough? Oil spills, clear cuts, and pipelines all must be stopped. Trafficking, sweatshops, overpopulation, and gender equality . . . we've got to get more women elected. I kick a rock from the trail, watch it tumble down the bank and splash into the river. I work my ass off, sign email petitions, mail donation checks, listen to phone pleas, call my senator. I'm so in touch, I know what's happening around the world minutes after it happens—not like Great-Grandma, who had to wait to get her news at the mercantile. But recently I've begun to wonder, even as I read that our oceans are fast becoming cauldrons of plastic soup—do any of my efforts really make a difference?

I return home ready to do a little housecleaning in my study upstairs. The river cleared my mind a bit. Time to clean up my office. I consider my long worktable. There's no way I can get everything off for a good dusting, so I start with the small desk—all but disappeared under the storage boxes. I drop everything to the floor and stand back. How small it is. How dry the wood has become. With a rag dipped in environmentally safe lemon and walnut oil, I start rubbing at the back corner, working my way toward the front. The oil soaks in readily, leaving my hand pleasantly warmed. By the time I reach the center, I can hardly touch the wood, it's so hot. I sit back to let it cool. What's the big mystery here? Someone should have written a story about this desk so family women would know what to expect when they inherit it.

I finish rubbing the top, legs, and shelf more slowly so I don't build up so much heat, then neatly replace the files, boxes, and books on the desk. I'll tackle the worktable another day.

That night, the dreams return—water trickles, fire hisses, seeds struggle, a baby dies, women gather and disperse, always in endless conversations.

AMISHA

2076
Luna Valley, Northern California

The more Amisha read Great-Grandmother Harmony's journals, the more perplexed she became. Where was Great-Grandfather? And a dam? She found other clues stuffed between the pages: a water-stained envelope from Jeff in South San Francisco, an offer to buy the property (torn in half), and a canceled order for piano repair.

June 7, 2016
I wish I was strong enough to shove the piano down the front steps—
that worthless pile of shit. Instead I throw an old white sheet over
it and spend afternoons up at the school where they finally have a
decent piano. Just wish it didn't remind me of him whose name I
shall never say again. Playing on Nova's old guitar gives me some
solace. I'm glad the girls grew up with music in the house, though it's
damn near impossible playing Chopin on a guitar. Up at the school,
I still warm up with exercises and scales, but my fingers are stiff
from years of disuse. I'm so discouraged. I hear the music in my
head but can't play it anymore.

August 21, 2016
I miss my neighbors. I can't believe they all took the money and
moved on. Construction continues daily, big rigs kicking up dust,
making noise like bellowing dinosaurs. About once a week, some

heavyset man in a dark suit knocks at my door, always with a larger cash offer or a larger threat. But there's nothing they can do. My land is just beyond the condemnation zone. Now they're calling me that "crazy old lady" because I scream in their faces and slam the door on them. Next time I'll answer with a pitchfork! I'll never, ever, ever give up this land. It's all I have left. The girls come visit, Claire more than Sage, but that's because Claire also feels the urge to come home and dig in the dirt. Of the two, I hope she'll keep the land in the family. The desk too.

February 17, 2020
Winter. There was a time we used to shovel three to four feet of snow. Now it's just a few days of cold interspersed with rain, then back to the warm Mediterranean climate.

Sometimes Mother Nature throws us a curve ball, like the thirty-day rain last year where water cascaded in a huge rooster tail over the dam's spillway. Below the dam, people scrambled to collect the water with huge storage tanks in back of their trucks. They got water, but they also got stomach aches and skin rashes from it.

Amisha found it hard work reading Great-Grandma Harmony's journals word by word. When she reached an impasse, she did what Harmony did—went outside and took a walk. Starting on the overgrown trail behind the house, she ambled up the hill not thinking of much, just listening to crackling leaves beneath her footsteps and the slight wheeze of her breathing. When was the last time she had strong chest pains? It's been a while, she noted.

Had Amisha looked slightly uphill to the right, about forty steps beyond the house, she might have noticed a crumbling rock foundation covered over with brambles and, just beyond, a small grove of gnarly trees. But she was distracted by what her foot scuffed up under a mound of dusty leaves. Bending closer, she discovered a stubby white stalk topped by an upside-down cap that emitted a very peculiar odor, like old leather. She brought the mushroom to her nose, inhaled the muskiness, and felt herself instantaneously transported back to Orion, her head pressed against his chest. She had tried so hard not to think of him this last year. Her memories of leaving him only brought despair. Yet one whiff held more strength than any memory could.

Now Orion dominated her thoughts. As she hiked up the hill, her breath quickened; sliding downhill, she remembered relaxing into his arms. Low-hanging leaves caressed her bare arms, breezes teased her lips. And cupped gently in her hands was the closest thing to being with him—the only man she felt like touching. With the mushroom carefully settled in the bottom pocket of her tunic, she turned back toward home. Even the house seemed to sigh as she entered, as if it had been waiting for her.

Before now, she hadn't paid much attention to her sense of smell. Her Nib had only directed her attention to ways her mind could see or hear. Now she wanted to open her nose to everything! The kitchen smelled of the earthy mushroom on the counter. The living room smelled of pungent smoke from the woodstove. Each packet of dried foods had its own unique odor. She remembered from medical training that a long, long time ago, doctors used to do that—smell for putrid, pungent, or sweet smells on their patients. So primitive. She'd never have gone into medicine if she had to smell and touch her patients. Thank god for Insta.scans.

Along with her scent discoveries, Amisha also began to listen in new ways, as if awakening from a long sleep. It was natural to hear sounds immediately around her—a plate against the sink, her footsteps on the stairs, water tumbling into the bucket. As her listening expanded outward to animals rustling the leaves uphill or wind weaving through the needles of tall pines, it dawned on her that she could actually hear much farther than she could see. She began to listen for what was beyond sight. That's when she heard the bell ringing from down the driveway.

ELIZA
1880
Yolo, California

With brisk strokes, Eliza swept the leaves off the back porch, stopping occasionally to squint into the bushes behind the house. She was being watched again—the same woman as yesterday and the day before. Probably one of the Patwin Indians from down by the creek. Irritated that someone was sneaking around her house, and despite Silas's warning to steer clear of the heathens, she put the broom down, pushed a hair pin back into her tight bun, and stepped off the porch.

"Who's there?" Eliza called in the authoritative voice she used for her children. She waved slightly, but the woman remained partially hidden in the bushes like one of those statues in a city park. Eliza stepped toward her. "What do you want?"

The Indian adjusted the bark apron covering her thighs and dropped her head so that her round, dark face was obscured by thick strands of black hair.

"What are you doing here?" Eliza asked.

The Indian woman raised her head, revealing three vertical tattoos from her lip to her chin. Her deep black eyes met Eliza's.

"Waiting for man. Work here," she said so quietly that Eliza could hardly hear.

"The new hand, helping with fencing?" Eliza closed her fists and made the motions of pounding in a fence post.

241

A wide grin spread over the woman's broad face, then quickly disappeared. She held up a small, woven grass basket, and with fingers to mouth, made the motions of eating.

"Ah. Food." Eliza nodded and repeated the eating movement.

The woman swept her cupped hand from side to side.

"You're waiting for the dinner bell?" Eliza relaxed. "I'm just about to ring it."

She motioned for the woman to follow her down the garden path to the cast-iron bell mounted on a wooden post, but the woman didn't move. Eliza traced the raised words, "Crystal Iron Works, Saint Louis, Missouri," then pulled the rope, and a thunderous clang reverberated into the crisp autumn air.

"Time for dinner," Eliza shouted, then turned back toward the woman, but the Indian was gone.

That night, with the children already fed and in bed, Eliza unfolded her white linen napkin and turned to Silas. "You didn't tell me you hired one of those Patwins. I thought you said it's best to keep our distance from them."

"At the moment, I've got no choice." Silas smeared the last of the butter in thin streaks over his bread. He looked at his wife, then to the butter crock.

"I'm sorry we're about out of butter," Eliza said, peering into the nearly empty crock. "The Palace Hotel wanted a double order for this morning's train. I think there's a convention in San Francisco." She looked back at him. "No choice?"

"Slim hasn't come up from the south yet, and I'm short a hand. I tried, believe me, but everyone's tied up." He pushed the last of the crust into his mouth. "He seems to be working out well enough, considering."

"Considering the man's an Indian?" She knew people held Indians in low regard, enough so that bounty hunters got paid by the head for Indians to be either forced into labor or killed outright. But she couldn't understand why. "Does he understand English?"

"Enough to follow instructions."

"Is he from the Patwin tribe down by the creek?"

"That's where I found him." A small muscle rippled under his brow. "Why are you asking about him?"

"I think I met his wife or, rather, his woman, today behind the house." Eliza scanned Silas's face to see if she should continue. "She brought him his dinner."

"Don't encourage anything, Eliza."

She took a deep breath. "Why?"

Silas pressed his back against the wooden rungs of his chair. "It's an agreement we men have settled on. So far, these people have been peaceful here. But we've all heard stories. I've got nothing against them personally, Eliza, but the truth is, Indians are unpredictable heathens."

He laid his hand over hers. "As soon as Slim returns, I'm letting the Indian go. I want you to do the same—leave them alone."

The following afternoon, Eliza swept the porch and called the hands to dinner, but no sign of the native woman. The day after, the bushes behind the house were empty, and the dinner bell brought no sign of life.

On the third day, Eliza discovered a small spiral-woven basket made from willow and redbud tucked into a corner of the back-porch steps. She lifted off the cover of green oak leaves to reveal a flat, light-brown cake with slightly crumbled edges. It was too small to be the Indian man's supper. Accepting the obvious, she broke off a few crumbs and put them in her mouth. An earthy nuttiness flowed over her tongue. She waved toward the bushes and carried the basket into the kitchen. Midmorning the next day, Eliza returned the basket to the steps, now filled with a small loaf of cornbread. Two days later, it returned with four acorn cakes inside.

Monday was laundry day. The morning sun felt warm on her shoulders as Eliza lifted the heavy wet sheets from the wicker basket and pinned each one with wooden pegs onto the line between the porch and the back fence. Humming her favorite hymn, she pegged the corners of sheets together into a wall of flowing white muslin. Eliza tilted her head, for behind the sheet was a new sound. There again, a faint crunching in the dried grass. As if a game, the Indian woman's round face and toothy grin popped through the opening in the sheets. She motioned with her hand for Eliza to follow her down the narrow trail that led to the creek.

"Wait!" Eliza shouted, as a mouthful of clothespins fell to the ground. *Leave 'em alone*, Silas's words echoed. She shook her head and removed another sheet from the basket. "I'm sorry, but I can't." She pegged up the next sheet.

The Patwin woman sat down on a flat stump near the edge of the yard and arranged the long strips of dried grass and beads around her thighs. Eliza untangled the wet sheet, folded it over the line, and smoothed the edges so they were aligned. The woman picked at the dried leaves stuck to her bare feet, folded her hands in her lap, and continued watching.

Whatever does she want? Eliza considered the food baskets they'd been exchanging. Certainly not friendship with a white woman. She knew she should turn away, but curiosity drew her nearer. I'm really not encouraging anything, she justified.

After Eliza pinned up the last sheet, the Indian woman slipped over to examine the laundry, first by pulling the hemmed edge to her face, her flat nostrils flaring at the smell, then running her fingers along the hem, leaving a trail of brown fingerprints.

"Sheets. For sleeping." Eliza put her hands against her cheek and closed her eyes. The woman gave no indication of understanding. Eliza made the motions of laying the sheet on the ground, and with eyes closed again, pulled another sheet on top of her. The Indian smiled and pretended to wrap a sheet around her shoulders and closed her eyes.

"Yes." Eliza was delighted with the connection.

Without warning, the Indian woman set off down the path.

Go!

Eliza untied her apron and tossed it in the basket. She did a quick calculation: the lamb stew was already simmering on the cook stove. She'd top it with this morning's biscuits instead of making dumplings. The rest of the laundry could wait until tomorrow. Sorry, Silas, but she might never have this chance again.

It was difficult to keep up with the woman, who was fast disappearing down the trail. Heart racing, chest heaving, Eliza finally found the woman waiting in the shade of an enormous oak grove. Eliza took a tentative step into the cluster of trees—a mixture of mature blue oaks laden with acorns, thin saplings, and a few older trunks with bare, gnarly branches. The understory was burned to almost bare earth. Overhead, green leaves and branches wove a crown of silent shade.

"*T'uhka*." The woman pointed to a cluster of dangling acorns, then circled her belly with her hands. From the woven reed basket propped against the trunk, she pulled a handful of acorns. "Eat for many," she said, pointing down to the creek with her chin as she let out the piercing call of a red-tailed hawk. Six children scrambled up the trail toward her. Two full-bodied young girls with the same black hair, straight bangs, and woven reed skirt as their mother supported the youngest boy with naked, pudgy legs, bowed knees, and rounded belly. Three others with berry-stained mouths, ragged loincloths, and pigeon-toed gaits followed behind. At the sight of the white woman, they scrambled for safety behind their mother's legs. Covering her smile with her hand, Eliza peeked right and left to make eye contact with the children.

"Eliza," she said as she patted her chest. "My name is Eliza."

The woman touched each child on the head, reciting names that Eliza found difficult to repeat.

"And you are the Patwin tribe." Eliza pointed to the acorns. "You eat these?"

The woman led her down to the riverbank to the five tall reed baskets—each the height of a young sapling and as wide as an arm spread.

"Many *T'uhka*," said the Patwin woman. She opened the bottom and let some acorns tumble into a small basket. With a motion to come along, she walked to a flat rock outcropping near the creek where her daughters were pounding peeled acorns with long stone pestles, crushing them into a fine powder. Eliza moved in closer to watch.

The tallest girl then gathered the acorn powder into another basket and placed it into a hole dug in the earth lined with pine needles. Eliza followed the mother to the fire pit and watched her extract a hot rock with two sticks and place it into a basket of water. The stone sizzled; the water bubbled. She poured the boiling water over the acorn meal in the hole, repeating this many times.

"Now not bad," the woman said, screwing up her face to show how the acorns tasted before her treatment. The youngest boy burst into giggles, then sought refuge behind his mother's skirt.

"Now we eat." She reached for an acorn cake that was cooling on a rock by the fire and with great care placed it in Eliza's hands. "*T'uhka*. Our food. Our life."

Eliza wasn't sure what to do. She held the warm cake to her nose and sniffed the earthy fragrance. She looked at the six pairs of expectant eyes waiting for her to eat it, then popped it in her mouth. Can one really subsist on eating these simple acorns?

After that, Eliza never actually *saw* the Patwin woman, but every few days a small basket of acorn cakes waited for her on the back porch. Eliza continued to refill each one with cornbread, biscuits, or whatever she was cooking, and placed it in the niche behind the back-porch steps.

Little Harriet, tall for her nine years, reached across the table and grabbed a handful of soft cake to share with her brother. Only four, Edward eagerly devoured the "mush cakes," but their father never saw a crumb. Silas would only disapprove, Eliza thought, as she took one for herself then pushed the cakes to the back of the cooler. How quietly the Indians live and move just beyond our land, as if in a parallel world.

Over the next few weeks, Eliza noticed that the exchange of baskets had slowed. It had been five days since she picked up the last basket of acorn cakes, and her cornbread remained unclaimed for two days. One morning as she reluctantly lifted her basket to bring it back into the house, the Patwin woman appeared out of nowhere, speaking in a voice so urgent it startled her. In a move so swift that Eliza had no time to react, the Indian grabbed Eliza's wrist and dragged her down the steps toward the path that led to the creek. Fighting to keep her balance, Eliza pulled back, but the Indian's strength overwhelmed her and she tumbled forward.

"Stop! Please stop!" Eliza cried.

With a flurry of fiery words, the Patwin woman jerked the white woman farther down the trail. In Eliza's struggle to keep from tripping over the rocks, her boot caught the hem of her long skirt and both women fell to the ground. A metallic fear flowed over her tongue. She should have listened to Silas. She should have shouted for help. She *should* have been more careful. Eliza pulled herself to her knees, found a firm footing, and stood, ready to run.

Then she saw the woman's eyes.

The Patwin woman held her palms over her heart. Her eyes pleaded, *Come.*

Eliza looked back at the children playing on the front steps and without thinking, followed the woman. But instead of going to the tribe's acorn grove, the Indian turned west and proceeded through the dried grass along the creek and stopped at a fence post. Eliza recognized the post that marked the boundary between open and private land. In the open land beyond the post, a massive blue oak tree had been cut down. Its green leaves and mossy branches lay crumpled around the remains of the enormous trunk.

Hands over her heart, the Patwin woman approached the tree, gathered an armful of leaves to her breast, and rocked back and forth as if holding a child who had died.

Eliza struggled to unravel the path of destruction. As far as she could see upstream, not one oak tree remained standing. She turned in circles. *Who cut these? Why?* Her head spun. Someone cut down *everything.*

The Indian motioned for Eliza to follow her back to the tribe's grove of blue oaks. There, she circled her trees three times then stopped in front of the largest one and addressed it in rising and falling wails. She pointed west in the direction of the fallen oaks, then back to the grove of trees in front of her, her hand making a slicing motion across her neck.

These oaks will be next.

"No!" Eliza said. "This can't happen." She circled the grove like a needle weaving between two worlds—farm woman, mother, wife—and who she would become if she did not speak up for the Indians. She turned back to the Patwin woman, but the woman had vanished.

HARMONY

2009
Luna Valley, Northern California

Yesterday, while sipping a mug of hot French-roast coffee (fair trade, bird friendly, shade grown), I opened an email alert on elephant poaching. Before I could look away, I was captured by the YouTube video of a baby elephant nudging the tuskless body of his dead mother. I immediately clicked to donate fifty dollars. Next click, I signed their petition to "Save the Elephants." Third click, I forwarded it to my friends with a personal message.

Outside, a few ravens converse almost humanlike from the top of a ponderosa pine. Until a few years ago, I rarely saw ravens here, though I noticed them amassing in the valley below. Now they're migrating to higher ground. Intelligent settlers responding to the changing climate, I think. They band together, snatch meals from songbird nests, then toss the spindly bones to the ground like toothpicks. *Shoot 'em*, some say—as if they're the main reason our migratory birds are dwindling.

I turn back to my computer and scroll down the list of alerts that came in overnight.

Jeff sticks his head in the door.

"Hey! You gonna get outside today? It's the last day of the moon for potato planting and I've got them cut and ready for you. Garlic bed is—"

"I know, I know," I cut him off. "Just a few more and I'll be out." I continue my morning routine of pressing for clean-air standards, food security, and women's reproductive rights. My blood boils—the gall of men dictating what women can do with our bodies. If those men don't like abortions, then they should stop getting women pregnant! I stretch my arms and push away from the table. I need to feel I've accomplished *something* for all my morning's work, but all I have is a sour stomach and stiff shoulders. Stop whining, I tell myself. In the early '90s, we didn't have all this Internet, yet we saved the river.

The potato bed resists my efforts to loosen it. I jam my hoe into the packed dirt and make three trenches I know are too shallow, but I fill them with compost anyway and lay potato pieces every twelve inches. My iPhone vibrates in my thigh pocket. It can wait, I tell myself, but without thinking, I scrape the dirt from my finger and open it, leaving the screen smudged and gritty. It's a text from Sage, who loves, loves, loves her Gender in American Politics course. I send her a smiley face by typing a colon and then a parenthesis.

The lunch plates gurgle as I drop them into a pan of soapy water. A large iridescent bubble, multicolored like the earth, floats up and drifts over the counter before it pops. I rinse off the soapy plate with cold water and turn to Jeff.

"Are we ever going to get one of those hand pumps for the well? You know, with the long lever you pump up and down. You said you'd look into it."

Jeff rolls his eyes. "I already told you it makes much more sense to install a solar assist to the well. We'll put the panels on the south-facing hill, extend a long line to the well, route it up to the house."

Here we go again. Technology versus simplicity. I dream of pumping water like Grandma did. No electricity, no wires, no worries. I give the cold-water faucet a twist, and cool water from our well splashes into the sink. Reflexively, I slip a glass beneath to collect the water. Whoever said you can save the world one cup at a time was crazy.

AMISHA

2076

Luna Valley, Northern California

A bell clanged again from below the house, followed by footsteps clamoring up the front stairs, then a wild tugging at the screen door. Amisha clutched the metal rod from the woodstove in her sweaty hands and hid behind the front door.

"Hey, let us in! Let us in!"

She gripped the rod tighter.

"We're here!" As the clamor of high-pitched voices intensified, she cracked the door open and peeked through. Four sets of small eyes peered back.

"We're home!" A small throng of tiny bodies pushed their way past her and dropped their packs onto the kitchen floor. If adults had suddenly appeared, her adrenaline would have been out of control. But, oh, these were children!

"You're real?" Amisha didn't know what else to say. She'd never seen so many healthy children. At least they seemed so. She did a quick assessment, noting first off the absence of detectable Nibs. Except for the one clubfoot, their legs were well-muscled and strong, though their arms were long and underdeveloped. No swollen bellies. Their easy smiles revealed yellowed teeth, but no missing gaps or ugly dark spots. Faces were in good proportion, no low ears or wide-set eyes, and they all had similar thin-ridged noses. Children! Four of them! The oldest girl was already blossoming. Amisha hoped the toddler that the girl balanced on her hip wasn't hers. She would have been too young to bear children.

What appeared to be a young boy hardly as high as her armpit, with short strawlike hair sticking out in all directions, limped forward. "They sent us first to see who's here."

"They?" Amisha dropped to her knees in front of them. "Who's *'they'*?"

"The rest of us," answered the tallest girl, clothed in a simple brown shift. The bare-bottomed little girl she carried squirmed her face tight against the girl's shoulder.

Amisha stretched out her arm, wanting so badly to touch them.

In the middle, the fourth child, dressed in dirt-stained overalls, wrinkled his round nose and backed away.

"You know who we are?"

Amisha shook her head.

"Didn't you hear the bells?" The oldest girl looked aghast.

"No. Yes."

When she first arrived, she heard what sounded like a bell, but she had brushed off the strange ringing as a remnant echo in her head. Later, she thought she heard a single ring, followed by two. The third time she heard the distant sound, she recognized it as the deep clanging of a bell, like a ship announcing its presence across the foggy bay. She noticed a large black bell out by the old woodshed but had dismissed it.

"Why didn't you ring your bell?" asked the tallest of the ragtag assemblage.

"I didn't know," Amisha said. "Why should I?"

"We tell you we're comin' and you tell us you're here. No surprises."

Somewhat relieved, Amisha asked for their names.

"I'm Pacifica." The oldest girl stepped forward. "And this is Arctic and Malibu." She pointed to the middle boys, then lowered the toddler to the ground. "And Tibet here's my youngest sister."

"Names of old places?"

"Gone but not forgotten, Mums always say."

"Who is 'Mums'?" Amisha reached to touch Tibet's straight black hair, but the toddler turned to hide between Pacifica's legs, revealing only her short blue shift that covered the top of her speckled, tanned back.

"Mums," Pacifica said. "Like you."

"Women? Mothers? More than one?"

Arctic held out six fingers.

"Fathers? Dads?" She glanced at Malibu. "Like him, but older?"

He held out three fingers.

"I see." Amisha brushed away a stray hair from her forehead. "Then you are many families."

Pacifica shrugged as she opened the pantry door and divided a bag of crystallized manzanita berries among the group.

Amisha bit her tongue. In less than a minute, a quarter of her winter's supply of sweetness had disappeared.

"They're coming!" Malibu jumped at the ringing from down the driveway. "Where's your bell?"

Amisha pointed to the woodshed and shortly heard her bell ring for the first time. Three rings in a row.

"That's you," Pacifica said. "You're three bells, we're two."

"How many others are there?" Amisha asked.

They were interrupted as nine or ten adults shuffled into the house and set their packs and sleeping rolls around the living room. Amisha's heart sank. Somehow, she'd have to safeguard her room upstairs. Pacifica took her hand and led her to the tall woman with hair the texture and color of straw, who was directing the others and, it seemed, the only person who was talking.

"This is my house now," Amisha said to the woman, making her tone stronger than she felt.

"That's what Dar said." The woman looked up, then unfurled her bedroll against the west wall.

"Dar?"

"Yep, we usually follow in their wake. News of you traveled fast."

"You travel like Dar's group?"

"Except we tend to stay longer. At least 'til the next crop comes through." She scooped Tibet into her arms. "She was born on the coast. But I think we've traversed across that fire-devastated valley for the last time."

Amisha plopped into a chair. It was obvious there were too many to fit in the house, even if she had invited them to stay. Yet, they had children—healthy, lively children. She had to know more.

The woman was already directing people to prepare the rooms upstairs.

"Wait, not the room on the right. I claim that one."

"The one with all the boxes?"

Amisha held her breath as the group's obvious leader stopped to confer with two young women at the bottom of the stairs. All three wore similar knee-length tunics with pockets of various sizes covering the front.

"India and Oceana say we can do with the two other rooms— one for fertility, the other for meditation. You can have the cluttered one." The lead woman searched the six pockets of her tunic and handed Amisha a string of Turkish worry beads. "Here, the children found these. Yours?"

"How the hell?" Amisha grabbed at the beads trying to remember the last time she held them. Who were these people? Amisha waited for the woman to finish directing one of the men, then asked, "I don't know your names yet. I'm Amisha."

"I know. And I'm Principia. You'll not hear from me for a while. During sleep tonight, I pass the group's voice over to Montagna— she's also the only one with the green ribbon on her wrist right now. She'll be in the fertility room tonight. You'll meet the rest of us in time."

That night, Amisha couldn't sleep. Even with her mattress in the corner of what was now her private room, she heard the door to the fertility room open and close all night. By morning, she counted four visitors to the room.

Montagna greeted her in the morning with a weary yawn.

"Busy night?" Amisha raised her eyebrows.

"Yes, we did work hard."

"May I ask you . . . ," but Amisha was interrupted by Arctic and Malibu, who wanted to know what they could eat. After telling them which pack to look in, Montagna returned to Amisha. "Being the group's voice today, I have much to do. Maybe later," she said, as she nodded to Principia, who silently passed them on her way to the meditation room.

This is beyond bizarre, Amisha decided. She whisked a bag of walnuts and dried berries up to her room and closed the door. Outside the window, leaves tossed this way and that in the fickle currents of the wind. Just like me, she thought. She opened one of Harmony's journals and continued reading where she'd left off.

> *September 4, 2015*
> *It took Jeff two hours to untangle the cords, pack up his five-piece entertainment center, and haul it all down to his oversized van. Good riddance to fancy technology. I never once figured out how to make it all work. Now it's so quiet. I can hear the wind blowing through the open windows. Wish I could cover my loneliness with music, but since I don't open my laptop anymore, I can't even stream music. There's nothing to mask the sound of bulldozers working away on the road around the dam with their annoying back-up beeping. It's like a toothache that won't go away. Trucks all day, back and forth along their new road just downhill from the property line, just uphill from what they say will be the high-water line. The dust! It lands everywhere. I can feel it under my feet and in my nose. I had to dust off the desk before pulling out my journal. It's never-ending.*

Amisha left a scrap of paper to mark her place while she thought over what she'd read. Laptop? What water did she stream in? There was a dam? When she and Charlie traveled up here, the only dam was down below. There was much she didn't know about Gramma Harmy.

> *August 1, 2017*
> *Last night, the bear tore down the fence to get to the patch of blackberries we had planted. Maybe I should expand the berry patch*

in both directions, so it becomes a fence around the orchard. Might
prevent the bear from coming in and tearing branches down to get to
the apples. I should plant more of those heritage apples—they do well,
but berries? They're practically weeds.

My god, the berries and apples! Just thinking of their sweetness made Amisha salivate. Without them, she would never have made it through the first days here. She remembered her panic finding the first men in her house. She never met them face-to-face, but they left a heavy cloud of anger that took days to lift. She feared the intrusion of other wild-eyed wanderers with heavy packs and long blades, but her worries never materialized. Perhaps signs of people occupying the house was enough to send them trudging on to something more exploitable. Despite her tension with Dar's migrants, they were a relief after those first men. And without Sharome, she would never have found her desk.

She felt an easiness with this new clan settling in. They didn't talk much, only when necessary, and only through the day's designated voice who was also the day's leader. With the leader rotating every day, making decisions was disseminated throughout the group. Best of all, they respected her privacy. But there were things about them Amisha wanted to know.

Cracking walnuts at the table with Principia one afternoon, she asked about their clan. Principia closed her eyes. Amisha flinched as if an electric current had passed through her head.

"Listen to the silence?" Amisha repeated what she thought she'd just heard.

"We're all connected by the silence." Principia pointed to the scar on Amisha's neck. "We got rid of those buggers twenty years ago when we fled up here. That's when the real silence started. First, we were terrified to be cut off from our Nibs. We could see each other, but we couldn't connect."

Amisha nodded. "I still hear voices and ringing."

"Cerebral echoes. They'll stop after your nerves reintegrate. May take a while," Principia warned. "At first, there was so much emptiness in our heads, we didn't even know how to think on our own.

We clung together, started talking more, but it was hard across distances, especially when we couldn't see one another. But after we floated in our own silent worlds awhile, something happened . . . a feeling of oneness—with each other and even the plants and animals and the earth itself. Once we felt that, once it became *part* of us, no one wanted to give it up. We made a pact to keep the silence."

"But the children talk."

"Only 'til their bodies start the change. Then they join us, like Pacifica will soon." Principia emptied the bowl of cracked nutmeats into a hemp bag, closed it with a piece of twine, and stashed it behind the other bags on the pantry shelf.

Amisha was eager to know more, but with the mention of Pacifica, she finally indulged another burning curiosity.

"Your children—how do you do it?" she asked when Principia returned to the table. "I worked so hard trying to keep babies alive—the precious few even born. So much against them." She counted off on her fingers. "Men's sperm dwindled to next to nothing, women's hormones all confused, it's hard to get people to even try when their sex drive hardly exists. And when a baby is born alive? My god," her voice rose in exasperation. "Finding milk and food the baby can tolerate. But you have four!"

"I'll show you." Principia led her upstairs. "We all work together to increase the odds." She pointed out the tall, lanky man following Montagna into the fertility room. "It's simple math. Since sperm counts are low, we multiply their deposits. Men have their part figured out and know when to take their turn."

"Even when they, you know, can't get it up?"

"We have compounds."

"For what?" Amisha couldn't believe what she was hearing.

"Anyone with a chance of fertility—male and female—gets a daily dose. Mainly herbs gathered from the land."

"Like weeds? How do you know what to pick?"

"We walk and ask."

Amisha frowned.

"You look like you don't understand. Why don't you come with me and India this afternoon? We're going to take a slow walk in the forest, then sit in silence awhile. India will ask what she needs to help her procreate. We'll return when she knows. Most times it's some combination of nettle, purslane, yellow dock, yarrow, and dandelion."

"The men do the same?" Amisha couldn't imagine Orion talking to a weed.

"*Touche le bois.* That's what the men like to do: touch the wood and ask. Most times they come back with nettle, oats, dandelion. Then they stop in the pantry for pumpkin and squash seeds."

Amisha knew all about the complexities of fertility—how much could, and usually did, go wrong. Timing was everything.

"How do the men know when the women are fertile? Oh, probably those green bands around women's wrists," she answered her own question. "But how do the women know?"

"Nibs used to nudge us. But without Nibs," Principia tapped her forehead for emphasis, "we figured out how women once knew their fertility. I doubt your medical training included how to watch for changes in cervical mucus."

"Probably too primitive," Amisha said.

As they walked past the fertility room, Principia gave a high five to Henri, who sat cross-legged on the floor outside the door. "Thanks for gathering wild mint for Montagna yesterday when you were out for your own herbs."

With a wide grin, Henri held up his cup of herbal tonic in salute.

"Procreation is our highest concern," Principia told Amisha. "We all take it very seriously."

ELIZA
1880
Yolo, California

"You've been terribly quiet, Eliza." Silas waited by the end of the bed for Eliza to pull back the quilt and slip beneath the covers, then cleared his throat several times.

"You're not with child again, are you?"

"No, thank the lord. I mean, I'm just thankful for a rest from maternity." She gathered up her nightgown and moved to the far side of the bed. For the man who was surprised at his first fatherhood, he still behaved as if she were solely responsible for bringing children into this world. Harriet, Edward, two miscarriages, and baby Edith hardly ten months ago. When would his ardor cease?

"I've just been wondering who's been cutting all the oaks along the creek," she asked, striving to keep her tone indifferent. "Are the Vardell brothers selling lumber at the mercantile now?"

"Dunno. Could be." He pulled his nightshirt over his head and crawled into bed. Aroused at her breasts beneath her white eyelet gown, he reached over to bring her to him, but her lips were tight, her attention elsewhere.

"Are they free to take whatever they want?"

"Who? Vardells?" he said, voice tinged with irritation. "As long as it's not private land, why do you care?"

"You know how those brothers are. Thumb on the scale, cutting fabric a bit short. I don't like doing business with them."

"Like them or not, they're the only business in town."

"But it's so sad they're cutting down all the largest oaks. They take so long to reach that size."

Silas rolled over with his back to his wife. "We need the wood for building. Now stop worrying about such things and go to sleep."

But Eliza couldn't sleep. Just above the layer of dreams, she felt she should do something. She waited for the familiar snore as Silas entered a deep sleep, then slipped out of bed and went downstairs to her desk. Her bare feet curled against the cold hardwood as she lit the kerosene lantern and sat down to think. Beyond the window, beyond the darkness, she followed the one thought that came to her—*something should be done.*

Two days later, Eliza paced like a caged fox. Whatever had she been thinking? In one hour, women from upstream and down would be arriving for tea. The house was clean, the children were visiting friends, and Silas was in meetings all afternoon. She fluffed the sofa pillows for the third time. She had never gone behind Silas's back before these Indians, didn't know why she was now. He'd only tell her to mind her own business, to stick to her own kind.

"Well, Silas," she mumbled. "That's exactly what I'm doing— a nice social tea with women friends. I've never put on a tea before, but I've been to enough socials, I can figure it out." She rearranged the six sterling-silver spoons prominently in front of the cups and saucers following Mother's practice so guests would never know that the rest of her service was only silver plated.

At two o'clock, the parlor was filled with a heady mixture of lavender perfume, fragrant black tea, warm ginger cookies, and the chattering of five women, happy to be away from chores at home. Eliza listened politely as the conversation swirled around children, crops, flowers for Sunday's church services, and how to find a man for Miss Lindsey, the new schoolteacher. She passed the cookies (yes, she would share the recipe) without taking one herself. With her hands clutched around the plate, it was all she could do to keep her nerves and resolve from fraying. Thankfully, Berta Dosmar gave her the opening she needed.

"Eliza, you told me you have something important to discuss with us."

In a fleeting moment of hesitation, Eliza saw the oak grove, the Indian's desperate plea, Silas's angry, disappointed face, then a mighty oak chopped to the earth in a deafening roar. Eliza cleared her throat and drew her words out carefully.

"I've come to know one of the families that live on the creek beyond our property. I know some don't think too highly of them, call them heathens, but I've come to feel differently." Mrs. Houston's teacup jangled lightly against her saucer.

"They have families—children, grandparents, parents, babies." Eliza concentrated on making her voice sound stronger than she felt. "They laugh, sing, play games. They spend much of their day collecting food and cooking—just like us." An uneasy quiet settled over the group. Women sipped their tea, eyes downcast to the carpet.

Mrs. Dosmar was the first to speak. "Eliza, my dear, we have been here longer than you. We keep a respectful distance from the Indians. We don't bother them, they don't bother us."

"Until now," Eliza replied.

Mrs. Dosmar lifted an eyebrow. "Go on."

"Someone's cutting down all the oaks by the creek. Probably the Vardell brothers. I don't know if they're simply self-serving or they're purposely trying to starve the Indians out, but without acorns from those oak trees, the tribe's main food is gone. It'd be like someone burning our grain fields."

"How primitive that anyone would eat acorns," Mrs. Tuttle said.

"Let me show you." Eliza returned from the kitchen with a napkin-covered plate. "Acorn cakes," she said, unveiling four light-brown mounds of cooked meal. "Try them." All eyes were on Mrs. Dosmar, who shook her head in refusal, then, after reconsidering, broke off a small piece and passed the plate to Miss Lindsey.

"Not good, but . . . not too bad either." Mrs. Dosmar rolled the cake around her tongue. "I just can't imagine anyone subsisting on this."

"Oh my," Mrs. Houston screwed up her nose. "There's no way I could eat this. Pass Eliza's cookies back to me!"

"In a pinch, I guess I could," Miss Lindsey said, whose adventuresome curiosity had brought her out west to teach. "They make these from those nuts?"

For the next half hour, Eliza described everything she had learned about the tribe: how their life revolved around the oak grove, how they gathered acorns and stored them for the year, and how each day they prepared them for their families to eat.

"I'm curious that so much goes on just beyond my own awareness, aren't you?" Eliza circled the room and refilled their teacups. "I have so many questions. Like who has the right to the trees if they're not on private land?"

"I'd say the Lord gave men, not heathens, dominion over the earth," Mrs. Tuttle pronounced. "He put the trees there for our men to use."

"But certainly not all of the trees!" Eliza snapped.

"I don't think men even think about it. They're used to taking what they want," Miss Lindsey said, adjusting her bodice.

Eliza replaced the cozy over the teapot and set it on the table. "From what I observe, I think it's men's nature to simply eradicate whatever gets in their way," she said, waving her hands around the room. "Straighten those rivers, reclaim the swamplands, wash hillsides away, annihilate people."

"Isn't that the price of progress?" Mrs. Tuttle asked.

"Progress with an irreversible price," Eliza flashed. "Progress looks different when we women follow our own nature. Wouldn't you agree?" Her cheeks aflame, she feared she had overstepped an invisible boundary, but Mrs. Dosmar's slight nod assured her. "Isn't it our nature to protect, not destroy? Women work best when we work together—not just for our own purposes. We think of our children, our neighbors, and the future." Exhausted, Eliza returned to her chair. "Someday, we'll need the knowledge these Indians have."

The room was silent as the women stirred their tea.

Mrs. Tuttle shook her head and reached for her purse. "This is most unpleasant for me. I cannot be saving Indians when Jeremy's collecting bounty on them." She gathered her hat and gloves and stood by the front door. "I shall see you in church then." The door clicked shut behind her.

"These are not animals we're talking about," Eliza said under her breath. "And even if it were about animals, it's just not how women do things.

After a prolonged silence, Berta Dosmar cleared her throat. "I'm standing with Eliza. It's simply the right thing for women to do. If we stand together, the brothers will have to listen. And if they don't," she clicked her purse shut, "we women have our ways."

As Eliza tossed and turned that night, her panic grew like water threatening to crest over a dam. She had no idea how to stop the Vardell brothers from cutting down the oaks or from doing anything they wanted, for that matter. How could she have been so sure of herself? Who listens to women? Who cares about Indians? She kicked back the sheets. She felt awful doing this behind Silas's back, and when she thought of the women returning the next day, her heart lurched. There was still time to call it off, but something wouldn't let go. She turned her back to her sleeping husband and quietly slipped out of bed.

Downstairs, Eliza lit the kerosene lamp and waited for her eyes to adjust to the warm glow that filled the dark corners of the parlor. Sitting at the desk, she uncapped her pen and pulled several pieces of paper from the drawer. A cool draft from the window brushed past her cheek. She shivered and pulled her shawl closer around her thin cotton nightgown.

Outside the window, two owls hooted across distant treetops. Small animals scurried for cover beneath crackling leaves. Bats sliced smoothly through the darkness, their small mouths filled with gathered insects. So much goes on under the cover of night when I'm usually fast asleep, she thought. A soft curve of moonlight shimmered through the window, reflecting Eliza's face a hundred times out into the night, each face a dim shadow of the one before. "Oh, what have I started?" she whispered. "Help me . . . please."

Silas found his wife the next morning wrapped in her purple shawl, head pressed against her desk. He tiptoed toward her muffled snores and gently nudged her shoulder.

"My dear, what's all this?"

Eliza lifted her head, squinting at the room as if she didn't know where she was.

"Were you here all night?"

Eliza uncurled her back from the desk. A shadowy dissonance still lingered. "I was up in my tree . . . I heard her. . . ."

"Who? You were dreaming?"

"I don't know."

Silas waited for her to continue.

"Silas, there's something I've got to tell you. Please listen before you tell me what you think." She looked out the window, avoiding his gaze. "Have you ever felt so strongly about something that you acted without knowing what you were going to do?"

Silas pulled up a chair to the desk. "Go on." His eyebrows furrowed into a stiff, bushy line.

"You know the Indian you hired from down by the creek?"

Silas nodded imperceptibly.

"His tribe . . . his family is being run out by the Vardells. They're cutting down all their oak trees."

"Eliza!" Silas exploded. "I forbade you to get involved with those people!"

"But is it right for the Vardells to do that?" She remained calm, as if the desk had given her strength. "The Indians keep to themselves. They live so quietly you hardly know they're there. They keep getting pushed off their land, Silas, land that was theirs to begin with. I'm sickened to see how they're treated, like coyotes we don't want to have around."

"I think you'd better tell me the whole story," Silas said.

Eliza started with her visit to the oak grove, then paused. She should probably have stopped right there, but she needed Silas on her side. Gathering her courage, she took a deep breath then continued about meeting the Patwin mother, exchanging food baskets, visiting their settlement down by the creek, and learning how they made food from acorns. "Her youngest children are nearly the same ages as ours, Silas. When they laugh and play, they all sound the same."

Silas slammed his fist on the desk. "You have no business going behind my back and putting yourself in danger." He stormed to the door. "I don't want anyone knowing what you've been up to."

"It's too late," she said, spreading her hands out on the desktop. "Sit down, Silas. I have more to tell you."

Silas listened as his young wife described the outcome of yesterday's tea.

"You've got Mrs. Dosmar, Miss Lindsey, and Mrs. Houston riled up about this too? I just don't understand what would prompt you women to bother with Indians."

Eliza stood to face her husband. "Women understand things differently, Silas. What's happening is wrong. I'll do your cooking, care for your children, make sure you have clean clothes. That's my responsibility. But when something needs to be made right, I want the respect of being heard. Just like I want the Indians' way respected. But men don't care about what women think."

Silas opened his mouth to speak then silently exhaled through his pursed lips.

Eliza tugged at the sleeve of his robe. "You're different than most men. You've never been one to think only about what you want, then go out and take it. You've always said there's room for everyone. Do you really think we're better off without the Indians around?"

Silas ran his fingers through his uncombed hair. "OK, I'll agree you're right about letting them be. But I don't know how you're going to convince the Vardells." He lifted her shawl from the chair to cover her bare shoulder. "Let me talk to the Vardells. I'll see what I can do."

Eliza didn't move. "It's too late, Silas. We're handling this our own way."

Neither spoke. In the pit of her stomach, Eliza knew she was veering close to an edge that would upset their world. She wanted to pull away, yet when she closed her eyes, she felt calmly reassured.

HARMONY

2017
Luna Valley, Northern California

Dora is waiting for me at the Second River bridge, binoculars pressed to her round face, scanning the treetops on either side of the river.

"Birds?" I ask.

Unusually subdued, Dora continues to scan back and forth. After a prolonged silence, she lowers her binoculars.

"Better hold your breath 'cause we could all be underwater." She squints at the horizon, then traces an imaginary line from the top of a tall oak on one side of the river to a pine on the other. "That'll be the top of the dam."

"What dam? The county tabled putting a dam here back in the early '90s. I've got the supervisor's ruling framed on my wall."

Dora steps her mud-caked hiking boot onto a flat granite outcropping and, with a deep exaggerated voice, leans forward as if speaking into a microphone.

"Five years of drought has forced us to take emergency action. It would be unconscionable for the county to let water waste to the sea when it could be captured behind a dam. Our people must have water to drink."

"There's no way they can try this again." I can hardly spit the words out.

"New administration, state of emergency, everything's back on the table."

"They can't just say so."

"We're in new times," Dora says, rolling up her flannel sleeves. "But we can do it again. Look, Luna Valley mobilized once, remember? It was fabulous." She straightened her back, readying for another battle.

"Sure." But my voice falters. Even I can hear my lack of passion.

Twenty years ago, resistance seemed so straightforward. Pit Bull Dora had led the battle. We set up our headquarters in the one-engine fire hall the men built to protect the neighborhood. We called ourselves "FAR: Free A River." Families from up and down the valley huddled around topographical maps tacked on the walls and traced their fingers along the blue marker line that defined how high the water would go. Which side of the line were we on? Jeff and I held Claire and Sage up and pointed to our home right in the center of the water created by the blue line.

We did our homework. A handful of local hydrologists, geologists, and lawyers advised the community gratis and uncovered some scientific and legal technicalities for us. Our conversations became infused with new concepts: build-up of toxic mining-era sediment behind dams, historic salmon runs, wild and free-flowing rivers, earthquake fault lines, ecological balance. Younger then, but just as feisty, Dora installed herself in the back row at every supervisor and water board meeting and took notes. Our core committee met privately with Daryl Janson, the local supervisor—sympathetic, but overall ineffective. After all, he shrugged, "You can't deny we're in a drought. Farmers need the water. The Second River is the most cost-effective location for a new dam." Our group held press conferences. Dora and Jeff testified at public hearings and wheedled their way into closed meetings. We knew our arguments were strong and sound. But the supervisors weren't swayed.

In the end, it was the children who saved Luna Valley.

The prospect of this dam hung like a shroud over our school kids. In classrooms, bathrooms, lunchrooms, and recess, all they could talk about was that half of their friends would be flooded out, families would be forced to leave, the school would have to shut down.

Mrs. Watson, the fifth-grade teacher, understood that the best antidote for anxiety was action. She assigned her ten-year-old students the class project of creating a plan to "Save the River." What did they want to happen? Who could they approach? What would they say? Soon parents and school staff got on board and helped the class get on the supervisor's agenda. I even made sure the TV and news media were there.

At 10 a.m. on Monday, Rod, the school bus driver, dropped twenty children into a throng of reporters and cameras crowded around the door to the county courthouse. Once inside the supervisor's chambers, they quietly held up their hand-drawn posters depicting how the dam would destroy their community. One by one, each child stood at the microphone and read the speech he or she had practiced in class. How, they asked, could the supervisors just wipe out one of its own towns? Towering above them from their elevated desk, the five supervisors leaned back in their seats, taking in the children, cameras, reporters, then the children again. The children learned ahead of time that their supervisor, Mr. Janson, grew up in the area and appealed directly to him. Had he swum in the river? Ever fished or watched a black bear fish? What were his childhood memories on the river? The media ate it up.

The chairman thanked the children politely and announced they would make their final decision by end of the week. The entire Luna Valley held its breath. On Monday the halls of the school were plastered with newspaper coverage of the children's appeal. . . . The children had saved their community from being flooded.

I find a stump to sit on by the river's high-water line. Dark clouds crowd my peripheral vision leaving only Dora's suntanned face, backlit by the river. Twenty years ago, the supervisors made a ruling. We trusted them and returned to our homesteads to live in self-sufficient peace.

"Shit!" I drop my head into my hands. "I don't have the energy to do this again."

Dora grabs a long stick and breaks into song. "Another op'nin', another show, another drought, and away we go." She does a soft-shoe shuffle toward the river. "Another dam that they hope will last, will let their future forget our past. . . ."

"You're not funny." I throw a stone into the river. It skips twice, then sinks.

"We should know by now not to trust them farther than that stone."

"Well, the county's broke. There's no way they can pay for a dam."

"The declared state of emergency has opened the floodgates for funding. And not only that," Dora eyes me cautiously, "I heard the road crew starts Monday."

I jump to my feet. "Where's the due process? What about hearings and environmental reports?" I scream so forcefully I fear the blood vessels in my temples will burst.

"State of emergency—anything goes. Now who's passionate?" she mocks.

I know when Dora's mouth forms that tight, uncompromising line, she's gearing up for a fight.

"What are we going to do?" It was hopeless, and I felt nothing but helpless.

"Gather the troops, begin our battle plan."

Not for the first time, I wished for her confidence. I stumble back to the car feeling like a lizard flattened under the boots of a careless hiker.

Back at the house, I eye the computer. I should check the county's website, read the supervisor's minutes, send email alerts to the neighbors, but I turn away. Jeff's gone to town to run errands. I pick up the phone and punch in a number. It rings; I hang up. Instead, I grab a shovel and storm through the open garden gate up to the potato bed. Dirt goes flying over my shoulder left and right. Then potato pieces. I can't stop digging.

Jeff finds me curled up on the couch, shades drawn against the afternoon sun.

"What'd Dora have to say?" He sits down next to me as I repeat Dora's news.

Arm across my forehead, I stare at the ceiling. "It's all over. Great-Grandma's land—gone."

The line that Dora pointed out with her finger would for sure go straight through our homestead, I tell him. We'll be flooded out. No more garden, orchard, chickens, canned tomatoes. I bury my face in my soggy handkerchief, too distraught to continue. Jeff lurches from the couch to call Dora.

Two mornings later, I'm jarred awake by the awful screaming of chainsaws just below our property line. I shake Jeff, toss a sweat-shirt over my PJs, slip on sandals, and fly down the hill.

"What the hell are you doing?" I scream to the man revving his chainsaw, ready to cut a wedge out of a towering ponderosa pine. "Stop cutting down our trees!"

Startled, the young man who's hardly old enough to sprout a beard stops his motor, pulls up the brim of his *For the Love of Trees* work hat, and pulls a map from the pocket of his sweaty brown work shirt.

"Don't think so, ma'am," he says. "According to my maps and those red tags," he takes a closer look to be sure, "yup, U.S. Forest Service land." He sweeps his hand from the old madrone grove to Claire and Sage's favorite climbing oak. "All these go."

Chainsaws buzz up and down the ridge.

"Stop! Now!" I shout over the noise. "There's been a mistake. We never got a notice. You can't just come up here and start cutting."

He radios his boss, who says he'll be right over. I can tell by the crooked, gnarly walk that he's tangled with many a chainsaw.

"What's your problem?" he asks, eying my sweatshirt, PJ bottoms, and flip-flops. "This here's public land. Better get back to your house before you catch cold."

"Public land?" Jeff arrives breathless behind me. "Then show us your paperwork."

The boss pulls out his orders and topo map indicating where the road will be built. "Right here," he swings his arm along a route just south of our property line. "Access road for dam construction."

"But this's against the law!" I'm shivering so hard, I can hardly talk.

"Well, missy, they've finally changed our laws so we can actually get things done."

AMISHA

2076
Luna Valley, Northern California

Amisha was awakened by an unusual sensation. She couldn't point to it. There were no unfamiliar sounds—just the quiet steps of adults downstairs in the kitchen and the quick steps of children returning from the orchard with apples and berries for the morning meal. It wasn't Dar's group of migrants who returned last week and easily integrated into the household with the Silents. No, it was as if something was happening, or just did, or would soon.

The kitchen door burst open, and Artic and Malibu spilled the contents of their morning foraging onto the counter.

"Shhhh." India held her finger to her lips and nodded to the communal room, where Oceana was laid out on the floor covered in wide strips of pale blue and pink fabric.

Drawn downstairs, Amisha slipped quietly into the communal room. Three women knelt around Oceana's body. Africa dribbled oil from sesame seeds on the forehead, Principia bathed the feet with an herbal infusion, Sharome's throaty humming suffused the room.

Amisha looked to Principia, the day's "voice."

"It's her time," Principia nodded solemnly.

"Oceana? But she's not that old!" Amisha swallowed hard. She was afraid to look into Oceana's face, resting so peacefully as if she were still alive. "What happened?"

"Clarissa gave her some new herbs she found beyond the orchard," Principia said.

"She shouldn't have experimented!" Amisha cried.

"They were stronger than she anticipated."

"My god!" Amisha pressed back against the wall and covered her mouth with her hand.

"It only took two moons," Principia continued as if satisfied with the outcome.

"She intended this to happen?"

"Of course! That was her hope. And to have her cycle return after only two moons was a miracle!"

Amisha's eyes widened. "Then she's not . . . ?"

"No, not dead." Principia threw back her head and laughed. "Just not pregnant yet. She's hardly worn the green band an hour. But her egg has only twenty-four hours to live, so everyone stops to do their part." She nodded to Jacob, Xeri, Henri, and Trev seated on the floor across the room. Montagna massaged Trev's shoulders. The other men sipped the infusions that Clarissa created from what they brought back from the forest early this morning. Dar lit a bundle of dried sage and circled the room until Oceana opened her eyes and nodded that she was ready to be led upstairs to the fertility room.

Trev gestured to the men. "Anyone ready?" With a grunt, Henri unfolded his legs and stood, but Jacob stretched his arm around Xeri's shoulder and snuggled his face into Xeri's broad neck.

Principia waited as the men exchanged glances.

Henri held up his mug, indicating he wanted more of his infusion before going up.

"Would it help if India gave any of you guys a hand to get you up and ready?" Principia raised her eyebrows at Xeri and Jacob, still entwined on the floor. "Maybe not," she smiled. "Remember to wait a few hours between each of you. Give her a rest."

Henri gave Trev's shoulder a cuff and the two men headed upstairs.

Deep in thought, Amisha followed Principia to the kitchen. Despite her curiosity about these new fertility practices for making babies, something else about them made her wonder even more.

How easily they touched one another, how directly they looked into each other's eyes. She sat at the table, pulled the bowl of cracked walnuts closer to her, and deftly separated the shells to extract the nutmeats.

In her Nib world, she had little need to reach out to other humans. Nibs provided everything one could need, making asking, touching, or trusting other people totally unnecessary. When she worried about something, her Med.pak released an infusion to calm her. Didn't know what to do? Her Nib showed the way even before she asked. Touching others was awkward and unnecessary. Except for Orion. Somehow, he made it through those filters.

When Oceana's twenty-four-hour window of fertility closed, everyone except Amisha went back to their daily routines. Restless, Amisha wandered up the hill to escape all the people crowded into every room of the house: the downstairs kitchen, eating space, and small communal room, the two upstairs sleeping rooms (one occasionally used as the fertility room), and her private room. She craved time alone with the desk and journals, but even with her door closed, someone always interrupted her solitude with a knock.

She had lived in Luna Valley nearly a year and, aside from finding the desk, was no closer to knowing why she had come. She only knew that Luna Valley was a small pocket that escaped burning when so much of the Sierra and the valley was in flames, and that her house was filled with people obsessed with keeping the human race alive. But she wondered if bringing more children into this world was such a good idea now. That afternoon in her walk up the hill, she came upon the old foundation. She cleared pine needles off a wide stone and sat to think. Maybe the earth needs a rest from mankind. Maybe all they had to do was . . . *nothing*. She sat back and pondered this new thought.

Amisha asked Henri and Jacob to build her a simple shelter on top of the old foundation, which was a short walk uphill from the house. The men fashioned walls from long strips of cedar bark openly spaced for ventilation and overlapped hand-split shakes for the roof. A single door faced east so Amisha could greet the soft rays of the early morning sun but be sheltered from its savage afternoon heat. Amisha moved her little desk, a mattress, and some of Harmony's books up to her new retreat.

With her hands upon the desk, Amisha sank more deeply into the silence. She longed to write about her life and thoughts as her women ancestors had. With paper upon the desk, fingers grasping a pencil, she waited. Nothing. She wiggled her bare toes into the earthen floor and closed her eyes. Except for wisps of wind sifting through the slats in the walls and the soft sound of her own breathing, all was quiet. One by one, her fingers released their grip on the pencil. She pressed her open palm onto the desktop, caressing the heartwood in ever-widening circles until, rising from the heat beneath her fingers, she sensed a distant voice calling for help . . .

> *I dare not describe the future to these women for fear of losing them, yet I feel compelled to do so. Please, help me.*

A tingling surged up Amisha's spine. This was not from a Nib—not even her own thoughts. Something deeply familiar, yet distant and urgent, was calling to her from the past. She sensed a vast convention hall filled with the murmuring of an unsettled crowd of women's voices and answered Eliza without thinking.

Tell women that water is nearly gone, land is parched and barren, children struggle to live! They must know that everything they do or don't do today sends waves out into the future—waves that accumulate over time. Tell them it's not too late to do what must be done.

2076

In time, people of the homestead began seeking Amisha's counsel. Perhaps it was her location on the hill above everyone, or the strength of her family's roots to this land, or the transformation of her hair to silver. And though she still thought of Orion, more and more it was the women's shared wisdom and the quiet that sustained her.

Amisha had many guidelines, but only two firm rules. The first was easy to enforce: *No Nibs.* The second, *First Do No Harm*, from the ancient oath of the medical profession, was more difficult to impart. How could something that was once the basis of all healing become obsolete? She drummed her fingers along the desktop wondering how far she should take this rule. Was digging a new well into the earth doing harm to it? Or deciding a tree was more useful chopped down than standing? And *Do Nothing?* That was crazy. Perhaps she didn't understand what she was hearing. Maybe she should invite the others up to listen with her. Maybe Harmony's journals held some clues.

April 25, 2020

Got the shock of my life when two women knocked on my door this afternoon—one in a long denim skirt and a floppy garden hat over her silver hair, the younger in worn overalls and muck boots. Jenifer and Lakshmi from the Felix Gillet Institute. I'd no idea what this Gillet was, but they seemed too nice to slam the door on. Turns out they wanted my apples, that is, they wanted to include my apples in their catalog.

"We're inventorying old Gold Rush–era fruit and nut trees imported mostly from Europe by nurseryman Felix Gillet of Nevada City," Jenifer explained. "We heard you had a couple of very old trees on your land. Could we see?" Curious, I took them up the hill to the gnarly apple tree by the old foundation. Turns out Great-Grandmother must have planted a Golden Reinette apple. Very hardy, doesn't need much water. Well I'll be dammed. Here I am trying to ration water to my fancy Golden Delicious. After taking a few samples of scion wood for summer budding propagation, they took some pictures of a whole apple next to one cut in half, made some notes, then picked out some seeds. After tucking a few seeds in an envelope, they handed the rest to me. "If you want more old varieties, just let us know. We'll come back and graft other varieties onto your already-established trees."

A shiver ran up Amisha's spine. It was that same feeling that something was happening, or just did, or will soon.

The children had discovered that Amisha knew stories. This was an odd concept for Amisha, because ever since childhood, she had only to close her eyes and her Nib provided ample entertainment. She couldn't recall any of the hologramies she was raised on, but she did remember what she had just read in Harmony's journals.

After dinner that evening, Arctic and Tibet steered her by the hand into the communal room for story time. With children circled on the floor around her, Amisha waited to see which adults would join them before opening with her usual question: "What shall I tell today?"

As always, it was "Gramma Harmy!"

As always, she began, "Gramma Harmy was a powerful woman. She loved this land and her people. She knew she couldn't save the world, but she *could* save her home. Gramma Harmy made the water rise up for us to drink," Amisha made the up and down motions of the hand pump, "and planted a forest of apples for us and the bears to eat." As she waited for the children to growl on cue, she decided which story to tell from the journals.

"Now Gramma Harmy had magic in her lap. Especially the top of it! One day, while sitting at her desk, she looked down onto the top of her lap and saw pictures from all around the world. Right there on her laptop! She saw things that made her laugh, like cuddly baby kittens, but most of what she saw made her mad and sad."

"Like what?" Malibu asked.

"Well, like pictures of huge islands made of plastic floating in the ocean."

"What's plastic?"

"We don't make it anymore. It's against the law to throw old plastic away. Now all the plastic is made into other things, like chairs and roads." Amisha remembered reading Harmony's ranting about the plastic wars. The Chinese laid claim to the floating garbage island because they had produced all the plastic components, while the United States countered that they had paid for its production. Barges hauled miles-wide nets of plastic both east and west across the Pacific to be manufactured into plastix.

"One man's garbage is another man's survival," she said.

"What's garbage?"

"Hmm, I don't think we have it anymore." She looked to the adults, but no one knew.

"You'll never guess what other magic she had. She could make streams of water in her lap! Just like that, she streamed music and hologramies from the top of her lap for all to hear and see. How could she make a stream of music without getting her lap all wet? Who knows? Don't ask me how. Like I said, Gramma Harmy was a very powerful woman."

"Me, too!" Arctic patted his lap to stream some music water. Dar scooped him up under his arms and swung him around in a circle of laughter.

Amisha closed her eyes to feel this floaty expansion of laughter rising in her chest. She wanted it to last forever, to shield her from the other feeling . . . that something was getting close.

ELIZA

1880
Yolo, California

It all happened so quickly. After Mrs. Dosmar, Miss Lindsey, Mrs. Houston, and Mrs. Baxter met to develop their plan, they faced the difficult task of explaining to the tribe why long strips of brightly colored ribbons hung from the branches of all their oak trees. The people eyed the ribbons from a distance as if they held an unknown power.

"Ribbons show which trees we want to protect," Miss Lindsey explained to the attentive yet blank faces gathered in the grass beyond the largest oak. "Please don't let the children pull them off."

Not certain they understood, Eliza opened her arms wide then closed them around an imaginary tree trunk. "Protect. Guard. Like magic."

Late that afternoon, they made an unannounced visit to Jeb and Jamie Vardell's mercantile just before closing time. Assuming the women were there to order decorations for the children's Christmas party, they listened politely to the small talk until Eliza made her impassioned plea.

Jeb, older of the brothers and by far the shrewder businessman, unbuttoned his striped wool vest and took a long drag on his cigar.

"Now let me get this straight. You ladies want us not to cut that oak grove because you want to save them for the Indians? Do your *husbands* know what you're doing, ladies?"

"Of course," Eliza said, reaching for the back of a chair to steady herself.

"Silas?" Jeb raised his eyebrows at Jamie, but his younger brother was preoccupied with the blond ringlets billowing from beneath the hat of the young Miss Lindsey.

"Like us, Silas thinks we should live and let live. If you chop down all those oak trees—their food source . . ." Eliza said, eyeing the hefty waist on both brothers. "You know how other tribes have reacted. It wasn't pretty." Mrs. Dosmar's eyebrows raised at the threatening tone in Eliza's voice, but she noticed the brothers seemed to be paying attention. "In addition," Eliza continued, raising her voice so the few remaining customers were sure to hear, "we've got to think of more than ourselves. If you continue to cut down all the oak trees along the creek, there'll be no seeds for the future. We're here to make sure that doesn't happen."

"My, my," Jeb said, "I'll tell you ladies what. This is my business. I suggest you return home and mind your own business there. Now, Jamie," he said, blowing a ring of cigar smoke toward the front door, "why don't you show these nice ladies out."

But Jamie hadn't been listening. He was much too distracted by the long row of buttons flowing from Miss Lindsey's throat to her waist and the blue eyes peeking through her ringlets. "You the new schoolteacher?" he asked.

Miss Lindsey smiled and slowly untied the rose satin ribbons of her felt bonnet, taking great care to arrange the ringlets around her shoulders. "Since this fall. Miss Lindsey's my name." She extended her hand to Jamie.

Mrs. Dosmar stepped around the orange hound dog asleep in the middle of the floor and stood by Eliza. "Now we all know those oaks are not on private land, so we have a proposition that might change your mind. Shall we get down to business?"

Arms crossed over his vest, Jeb Vardell heard the women out, even nodded now and then with a purposely impassive expression. "Ribbons? That's all?" Jeb confirmed.

"The Indian's trees for a start," Eliza said. "Then we'll talk about not clearing off the whole length of the riverbank."

It had been a long day, and Jeb's stomach rumbled that it was past his suppertime. Exhaling through his lips like he was snuffing out a wax candle, he motioned Jamie over from the counter where he was watching Miss Lindsey.

"Shake hands with the ladies," Jeb muttered, "then let's close up."

The Vardell brothers waited until the buggy with four women disappeared down the street, then locked the front door and pulled down the shade.

"What the hell was that all about?" Jeb shook his head. "Even the new schoolteacher was with them."

"I noticed," Jamie smiled. "Yep, I noticed."

"I suppose she'll be teaching the children about being nice to the Indians."

"Wouldn't hurt to be nice to her," Jamie said, imagining how his hands would fit around the teacher's slight waist. "Are we really going to do this?"

"Pass by all those ribbons? I dunno, Jamie. I dunno. Being as we're the only mercantile in town, don't see how they can threaten to do without us."

Eliza bounded through the front door and tossed the last handful of ribbons into the air, showering Hattie and Edward in a cascade of rainbow colors. "We did it! The Vardells agreed to spare the acorn grove."

Silas smiled. It had been a long time since he'd seen his wife so animated and alive.

"Now the Indians will have their acorns to eat." She flung her arms around Silas's shoulders and pressed her cheek into his gray-tinged sideburns. Later that night her exuberance spilled into their lovemaking, as she opened to his touch, fully succumbing to his hands as they curled in and out of her soft curves. Without hesitation, she invited him in with every part of her being.

Silas sank back under the covers beside his wife, happy and relieved. Eliza nestled her head into the feather pillow, so they were face-to-face. "Thank you," she whispered.

"For what?"

"For letting me do it my way."

He reached over to pull a wisp of hair away from her face and said with a softness he seldom showed, "I think I've been underestimating you."

Eliza visited the tribe the very next morning after the agreement was made and did her best to explain the tribe's trees were safe as long the ribbons remained hanging. She untied a green ribbon from the tree, shook her head vehemently, then returned it to the branch with a nod. They seemed to understand.

Word spread of The Four Musketeers, as the women were now called, and what they had done—getting the Vardell brothers to alter their secondary lumber business. Mr. and Mrs. Greenwall, who had just finished their purchases, had lingered inside the front door, sensing something noteworthy was about to happen. At church the following Sunday, the Four Musketeers were the talk of the social hour. Imagine, women prevailing over the Vardell brothers!

Eliza blushed at the descriptions of her eloquent oration. At least I applied something I learned at school, she thought. Soon women approached her for help addressing the school board or to join their clubs, but she declined. What farm woman is not busy enough with her own work?

Miss Lindsey had a new beau, although she wasn't ready to give him that status just yet. Jamie was sweet, attentive, even drove her to school and picked her up at the end of every day, whether she was finished with her work or not. He just couldn't wait to spend time with her, he said, which is probably the reason he showed up at church for the first time in his life.

Two weeks later, a very serious Mrs. Royles took Eliza aside after church.

"Eliza, dear, I'm inviting you to join the Women's Community Improvement Club."

When Eliza demurred, Mrs. Royles took her firmly by the elbow to her buggy and with a controlled urgency whispered, "We need you, and you need us." Seeing that Eliza didn't understand, she continued. "It may appear that we are simply a group of women getting together to do some good. But we women know better." She glanced up at her husband waiting with reins in his hand and moved Eliza to the back of the buggy. "We can't vote, yet we have our ways. You, of all women, should know this. Unite enough women in enough clubs, and we can be a force to reckon with." She handed Eliza a list of women's clubs near Yolo. "It doesn't matter where you enter—gardening, Shakespeare, temperance, children—you will find strength being surrounded by your sisters." She folded the list and pressed it into Eliza's hands.

Later that week Eliza stopped by the schoolhouse to pay Sarah Lindsey a visit. From the doorway, she watched Sarah rush up and down the rows of desks, grab student's papers, and shove them into her satchel.

"Oh, Eliza! You startled me," Sarah said, pressing her hand to her chest.

"I didn't mean to sneak up on you," Eliza laughed. "I thought I might have a minute with you after the students had left for the day."

Sarah glanced out the window.

Eliza handed Sarah the list of women's clubs.

"You haven't been hauling the firewood in, have you?" Eliza pointed to the small round blue marks on Sarah's arm. "Aren't the older boys supposed to do that?"

Sarah pulled her sleeve down and shrugged. "I must have bumped against something."

Eliza lifted her wrist and examined the marks. "Those look more like thumbprints."

After a prolonged silence, with tears glistening in her eyes, she whispered, "I don't know how to disengage from him."

Eliza pulled the sleeve farther back to reveal more bruises. "Jamie?"

Sarah held her other hand against her chin to quell the quivering.

"You know this doesn't bode well."

Sarah nodded.

Eliza sat quietly. She didn't know what to tell her. It was beyond her experience. "Do you want to call it off?" she asked.

"He's coming to pick me up real soon."

"Then we should think of something now." Eliza checked the road for approaching dust.

"Will I ever find a man—a good man?" Sarah said between sniffs.

"You deserve better than this," Eliza said.

With Eliza standing at her side for courage, Sarah told Jamie she could no longer see him and that he was no longer to come by the school or her boarding house.

Jamie looked from one woman to the other. Although the words he shouted were unintelligible, the angry cloud that followed him down the road was not.

Eliza accepted Mrs. Royles's invitation to the Women's Improvement Club on the condition that Miss Lindsey was also included. Another slice of her time was now allocated to her club work and, with her reputation for writing and speaking, she was soon inundated with work, spending more time at her desk than ever. She would often write for an hour, then stand at the window to give her mind a break before resuming.

It was at one of those moments at the window when she realized she had not seen a new basket of acorn cakes for how long—a week? Certainly not longer!

"No, please no!" She shot down the trail. Her house slippers flew off. Stones bruised the soles of her bare feet; panic drove her on. She reached the clearing. The trees were gone. Not gone, but viciously chopped to pieces on the ground. She searched the creek. No trace of the tribe remained.

Eliza lifted her skirt and raced over to Miguel's cabin. Breathlessly, she ordered him to ride to Rachel's and Sarah's and tell them to come. It was urgent! She'd contact Berta herself.

Within the hour, four angry women assembled in the parlor. Which backup plan would they put in motion? The women weighed their options. A protest in front of the mercantile would give them immediate news coverage. Eliza could make an impassioned plea for dignity, respect, and integrity, then pass her handwritten speech to the reporters, where it was certain to make the front page. That would assuage their anger. But, in truth, as soon as the energy dissipated, people would forget, and Jeb and Jamie's business would continue as usual. The women had a better plan. One with a more lasting impact.

By week's end, a new sign replaced the French Seamstress sign two blocks down on West Main Street. A proud Henri and Jeanette Barrie stood beneath their new sign: *Barrie's French Seamstress and Honest Mercantile*. Henri had always coveted the unused square footage of his wife's seamstress business. The Four Musketeers easily convinced him it was the time to realize his dream.

"But I have no inventory to start with!" Henri exclaimed in his thick French accent.

"Our barn is overflowing with a mélange of tools and boxes you promised you'd use some day. Well, I would say that day has arrived!" Jeanette shot back.

That night, Eliza sat at her desk to record the recent events in her journal. She tapped the nib against the page. Ink flowed onto the paper as unfamiliar images and feelings arose. How naive to have trusted the Vardells at their word—to expect they would act from anything but self-interest. And yet, she had not anticipated that the women would respond with such vigor, as if they had been awaiting the opportunity to show their power. She had much to learn.

Eliza set her pen down on the desktop and pondered the peculiar images that filled her head. She saw new and used merchandise comingled on shelves, tables, and racks—clothing, kitchen utensils, farm tools, and books. If you couldn't use something any longer, take it to Barrie's and someone else might buy it. If clothing didn't fit, well, Jeanette would work her magic on it. Barrie's Mercantile would be a grand exchange center for the new and old.

"As I had hoped," Eliza later wrote in her journal, "women from all over are towing their husbands to Barrie's new business, while the Vardell brother's inventory is languishing on the shelves and orders for lumber and firewood are drying up. This is very much like last year's Irish land war, when peasants protested the practices of Captain Charles Boycott by shunning everything from his estate. And yet." Eliza drummed her fingers along the desktop. "Something has shifted. My original intent was to keep the Patwins and the oak trees from being wiped out, yet I feel this has grown into something much larger than where to purchase a soup pot—something extraordinarily critical for the future."

HARMONY

2017
Luna Valley, Northern California

Dora taps the microphone and waits for the standing-room-only crowd to quiet. As the doors to the historic hotel's conference room close, she pretends to adjust her tie, deepens her voice, and leans into the microphone.

"They say that five years of drought has forced them to take emergency action. It would be unconscionable for the county to let water waste to the sea when it could be captured behind a dam." The room erupts into a sea of boos and raised fists.

From the back of the room, I'm blown away by how much has changed in two decades. Back in the '90s when we protested a dam proposed for nearly the same location, a small trickle of people turned out for meetings. Now, hardly two weeks into mounting our defense, the room is overflowing with environmental organizations from all over the state. Ten days ago, a few neighbors held an emergency meeting at Luna Valley's one-engine fire hall. It was quickly apparent we needed to move to the main fire station for space and Wi-Fi, but even that wasn't enough to hold the flood of people responding to our email alerts. It was only when we relocated our meeting to the hotel's large conference room in town that I realized that this was a whole new game—one I wasn't sure I was up for.

A bronze-tanned young man in cargo pants and a blue "Freedom for Rivers!" T-shirt steps to the microphone.

"It's not that this particular dam is a bad idea," he says, flipping a shock of sun-bleached hair from his eyes. "The problem is that dams are a nineteenth-century solution to a twenty-first-century problem." The room fills with cheers. "And we're here to help the county get a twenty-first-century solution!" One by one, he introduces activists from the coalition of local, state, and even national conservation groups—familiar names like Sierra Club, Waterkeeper Alliance, Trout Unlimited, and Friends of the River.

I lean against Jeff and sigh. These people know what they are doing. They're organized, knowledgeable, and already have a game plan. Maybe all we'd have to do is be the human face—the local color. That I could do. Wrong. They want Dora and me onstage front and center. Dora pounds the table. I'm the heart and voice of reason. We make a good team.

The next general meeting is held the following week, giving designated committees time to develop strategies. Though we expected a typically smaller crowd, word has spread, and we had to bring in two more rows of chairs for the growing army of environmental attorneys, activists, engineers, hydrologists, foresters, university professors, and tribal leaders. Jeff sent his regrets, but he had to get his analysis for the Monterey power plant emailed by midnight. Dora and I chat the half-hour drive into town.

"But you're used to being onstage. Why not now?" She overtakes a slow truck on the passing lane, then slips back into her lane. "Jeff says you were masterful in your day."

"Performing on the piano is different." But that night, I do speak. They want the history of the 1990s dam protest and, because it's a story I know by heart, speaking comes easily. At the break, a rather good-looking man with dark, sable-brown hair tucked behind his ears and an awkwardly upturned smile moves toward me through the crowd and extends his hand.

"You're a good speaker," he says as he shakes my hand then tucks his business card for Waters United into my palm. "Very persuasive."

"Nick Sarcosky?" I turn the card over. "Water For, By, and Of the People." A Sacramento address but no website.

"I'd like to hear more of your neighbors' plights with this proposed dam. Maybe coffee sometime?"

We meet before the next meeting at the back room of a small coffeehouse where it's quiet.

"This is Dora," I say as Nick scrambles to find another chair. "We tag team everything, including carpooling." Dora takes the chair across from Nick and listens as I fill in the details of the 1990 protest.

"And are these people still in Luna Valley?"

"Just about all." I look to Dora for confirmation. "Our roots run deep here."

"And you're not about to pull up your roots for a dam, are you?"

"You got it." Sitting close like this, I notice the small, horizontal scar on the left side of his lip that pulls his mouth into a lopsided smile when he talks.

"What's 'Water For, By, and Of the People'?" Dora pulls out the card I gave her.

"We're into water rights for the little guy, starting when the city planned to cover over a little stream that ran through neighborhoods where children played. After that success, we kept going. Your situation appeals to us because your farms are the little guys."

"No website?" Dora asks.

"We're working on a new one—didn't have the address when we printed the cards. These are just temporary."

We walk around the corner to the hotel conference room where it's already standing room only. Marty, the bronzed guy who opened the last meeting, has been selected as the lead for the Luna Valley campaign. Dora stands beside him as he calls on each of the Free River Network's committees to report. It's been hardly a week and these guys are mobilized for action. They're passionate about saving another river. I'm relieved that professionals have come to our rescue. For the next hour, we hear reports from the Legal, Environmental Impact, Media, Citizen Watchdogs, Regulatory Requirements, Water Conservation, and Climate Change committees.

"Is this dam even needed?" Marty poses the question.

"Follow the money!" shouts a gray-bearded activist leaning on his cane at the back of the room.

"We'll get to that soon enough," Marty redirects the conversation. "I think all sides can agree that the bottom line is everyone needs secure water storage. The water board says we're in a water crisis from years of drought exacerbated by climate change. They propose building an exorbitantly expensive, permanent, and non-flexible reservoir to enlarge their capacity for water storage." He throws up his hands in exasperation. "But have they even considered the less costly alternatives that enable communities to be more flexible to the changing climate over time?" Marty calls on the hydrologist, Franc Beamer, to present the initial analysis of alternative solutions.

I don't recognize him from the first meeting, but I know Lark and Indigo have driven him around Luna Valley to view the layout. Tall and wiry with the frizzed hair of a springer spaniel, Franc starts by reminding us not to look for one single alternative to a dam, but to develop many smaller strategies. Maintain our resiliency! He fiddles with his PowerPoint settings while waiting for the applause to subside.

"For starters, the water board can provide water-conservation incentives, invest in sustainable groundwater storage, restore meadows, wetlands, and floodplains, fix and maintain leaky and aging infrastructure, deter evapotranspiration, and implement forest health initiatives."

My head is spinning. I do my best to keep up with what forester John Carter adds. With the microphone in hand, he opens his PowerPoint to a review of recommended forest-health initiatives and scrolls down the lengthy list.

"Forest management is a key element to watershed health," he says, "resulting in decreased soil erosion, sedimentation, decreased evaporation, but also helping with surface-level groundwater storage and maintaining healthy riverbanks with high levels of flow inundation for fish habitat."

By the heady applause, it seems everyone in the room agrees, but, frankly, my eyes have glazed over with all the specialized language. Just give me a petition to sign or a letter to write. Next to me, Nick scribbles notes so fast, I'm about to suggest he should be recording it when I notice his phone blinking away on his lap. I nudge him with my elbow.

"Will you share your notes?"

He scribbles down a few words, tears off the page, and hands it to me: *Tomorrow, lunch at The Brewery?* I nod and tuck it into my purse. He hands me another note: *Bring your husband?*

I shake my head no and whisper, "He's in San Francisco."

The Brewery is crowded as usual, but I find Nick at a small table by the door. He slides my chair in, his notes already spread out on the table before me.

"Do I have the names right?"

I quickly scan the four pages of landowners linked to parcel numbers, correct the spelling on Jayati, and add Summer and Nova, who were somehow missing on his map.

"And they all have homestead farms like yours? If there's legal action, we don't want to leave anyone out."

"Similar but different. Each of us has a different specialty crop, like olives, corn, tomatoes, chickens, but all our homesteads have the same exceptionally fertile soil."

He nods and makes a few notes, then goes on to describe a similar case he was involved in near the San Joaquin River in the Central Valley.

"There was a small town there, forget the name, but they had the most amazing little concert hall converted from an old warehouse. After being out in the field all day, I spent my evenings listening in on practice sessions for their piano weekend—Liszt, Debussy, Chopin."

"Chopin?"

"I'm a romantic at heart, I guess, but Chopin fills me with such longing." He presses his hand to his chest. "Right here."

I feel a tear build in my lower lid and will for it not to go any farther. But between sips of IPA, I'm already telling him how Chopin was my first love. How as a ten-year-old, I'd rather practice piano than do anything with my friends.

"Go on," he smiles sweetly.

"Naturally, I was a music performance major in college. But even with so much going on at the Berkeley campus, I was happy to be alone in the practice room with . . ."

"With Chopin," he finishes for me.

I sip silently, studying the rising effervescence in my pint.

"Well, we'd better be going," he says after checking his phone. He pulls out my chair and, with the lightest of touches on the small of my back, guides me out the door.

A week later, the county water board announces a public informational meeting, not up here where the damage will be done, but in some government meeting room, an hour away at the county seat. They're probably hoping there won't be much of a show. Wrong. The chamber is already overflowing when Dora and I arrive. We slip into the seats Nick saved for us near the back, where media people with microphones and cameras on their shoulders line the back wall.

"The drought is already having a disastrous impact on California's economy," begins Board Chairman Darrel Rogers. With his tweed jacket draped over the back of his chair, his long sleeves rolled up to his elbows, and the collar of his white shirt open at his thick throat, he has the casual certainty of a four-term incumbent. "California, and significantly this county, supplies half the nation's fruits, nuts, and vegetables. Some cities and farms might be able to pump more groundwater to make up for losses, but that resource is also quickly drying up. With lessening snowpack due to climate change," he pauses to see how many are nodding at this reference, then continues to make his point, "we need a form of surface-water storage that can catch all the rainfall for agriculture. We have many other dams. We know this form of storage is reliable and works."

By the nodding heads, there seems to be a general agreement in sections of the audience.

"Yes, but what are you going to do about all the sediment and toxins collected behind existing dams? And crumbling spillways?" I recognize Summer's raspy voice shouting from the front row. "Dams are not long-term solutions!"

The room erupts in clapping, a gavel pounds, the room quiets, and the chairman clears his throat and continues.

"We have determined that the proposed Luna Valley dam is a safe and viable long-term solution that will provide water storage during wet years to be used in dry years. It will guarantee clean, safe drinking water, irrigation for our farmers, and greater recreation opportunities."

I gather my courage and approach the microphone during the brief public-input period.

"With all respect, would you please clarify what other alternatives you have researched."

The room is silent as the chairman nods to the panel of experts seated at a side table. After looking at one another, the towering water resources consultant rises and takes the microphone with his long, reedy fingers.

"After two years of study, our fiscal analysts have not identified a single approach that is as direct and cost-effective as building a dam," he recites. "Within seven years, we will have a fully functioning reservoir to store and deliver water to our customers. We acknowledge the county does not have the financial capacity to finance this dam alone, but the creative public-private partnership we have developed will become a model for other counties in the state." For the next fifteen minutes, he flashes a red laser pointer over the complex financial analysis displayed on the PowerPoint behind him that justifies the county's conclusion. My eyes glaze over. I feel a headache coming on.

Dora stands and motions impatiently for the microphone to be passed to her. "Our legal advisers have determined that the county has not followed the state environmental review process, and therefore denied the public due process. We are filing a suit to demand the water board and the county set aside their sham analysis and allow the community to exercise our right to express public comment through meetings and a community stakeholder group."

The chairman holds up a one-page briefing. "You are well aware the governor has declared a state of emergency due to the extended drought. This lowers the threshold for most legal requirements so we can move swiftly to secure water for our people." He loosens his collar around his reddening face. "We can't afford to be tied down by legal red tape at a time like this."

Nick takes his turn at the microphone. "What are your plans to compensate those who are losing their land and quality of life they've worked so hard to achieve? These are good, solid, contributing citizens that you'll be displacing."

The room is spinning now as the chairman drones on and on about the common good, eminent domain, necessary sacrifices, and ample restitution for loss. But all I hear is that safeguards put in place to assure the earth's survival are being systematically dismantled.

AMISHA

2076

San Francisco, California

Grove Street was quiet when Orion returned from picking up his last load of cargo. With enough daylight so he didn't have to waste power on headlights, he pulled in front of his apartment and switched off the motor. Most people were inside taking advantage of the last allotment of electricity before power was pulled for the night, but there were still the occasional figures shuffling down the street or hunkered in a porch corner for the night, like the one on Amisha's steps, he noted. They'd all be gone by daylight.

The next morning, the figure on Amisha's steps was sitting upright, skinny legs and black boots swinging back and forth over the side of the top step, arms dangling over the rail. From his window across the street, Orion watched the small figure pull the camouflage poncho hood over his or her head, rise on tiptoes to peek in the window, then sit back down to dig in a backpack, pull out a gold Pharm.food, toss the foil onto the sidewalk, swing both legs over the edge, then pop back up to the window again like a perpetual motion machine. Innocent child? A patient? Or could be an operative checking for Amisha. He still didn't know why she had left abruptly. "I *have* to leave" was all she would say. The knot in his stomach tightened.

"Hey," he shouted from his front door. "Get moving!" He didn't like anyone poking around what he still called Amisha's place, for even after a year, he still held out hope she might return. When the figure refused, he crossed the street and cleared his throat. "What are you doing there?"

Deep within the poncho's hood, he glimpsed the upturned nose of a young girl's face and, for a brief second, he was confused. Orion steadied himself on the handrail.

"You know where she's at?" said a high, quivering voice. "Been waiting since yesterday."

"Who the hell are you?"

"Looking for Am . . ."

Before she could say more, Orion covered her mouth. "Shhh, don't say it!"

The girl dug her hands into her pockets, but her neck and shoulders twitched as if electrified.

"She's not here anymore and you shouldn't be here either. Scram!"

Orion crossed back to his truck, gave the tires a kick, and slammed the front door behind him. No more craziness today. Too many close calls during pick-ups yesterday. He stopped himself before he thought her name. Nibs transferred as much out as they did in. No thinking, no talking. But those were familiar eyes! He pulled a duffel bag from the closet. After his last pick-up tomorrow, he'd have enough to make a drop-off in Martinez, then he'd start work on the East Bay. Might be delayed. Better bring a bag.

That evening, he stuffed the duffel bag with Pharm.food packs and an extra jacket and dropped the bag by the front door next to his totally useless but favorite vintage transistor radio, so he'd be sure to see it in the morning. With a well-deserved double infusion of Drowsy, he laid spread eagle on his thin mattress and slid into a bottomless sleep.

The next morning, he was shocked as hell to find the girl seated in the passenger side of his truck.

"Scram!" Orion yanked the door open and pulled her out by the arm.

"Your truck's not going to start." The girl set her dark-teal eyes on Orion as he punched a series of buttons without success.

"What the hell d'you do? Shit. Of all days." He lifted the hood.

Sun.auto diagnostic on demand. Only $650.

Don't have that kind of credit, he replied and L-flicked the offer away.

Orion checked for breaks in the tangle of electrical wires, tested the battery, wiped the solar panels with a rag, then stood back with an exasperated grunt.

"Not down there." The girl pointed to the solar panels on the roof. "Up there."

"You still here?" he said, ignoring her comment.

"Back in there." She pointed to an exposed connection beneath one of the solar cells. "Corroded."

As he examined the wire, it snapped apart in his hand. He shot her a "how did you know" look.

"Curious about your set up. Saw it this morning. Figured better to fix it here than out there." She gave him a warped smile.

Neither spoke while Orion rewrapped the wires with electrical tape from his toolbox, made a final loop, tore off the tape, then dropped the roll back in the toolbox and shut the lid.

"Mom said if she ever didn't come back, I should go find my Auntie A . . ." The girl stopped before Orion's hand went to his lips.

"You know her?" It occurred to him she might know something important. "She never said anything about a . . ."

"Mom didn't like family." She waved her hands in circles. "Didn't like much 'cept me." She looked up at the sky, the ground, over his shoulder, then shrugged.

Orion studied the girl. A bit older but frailer than she appeared at first, but god, couldn't the kid hold still? She was like a wheel spinning in constant motion.

"Mom left a place called Detroit months ago," the girl said, hopping from foot to foot. "Looking for stronger infusions. Mexico maybe."

Orion's eyes narrowed. "Mexico doesn't let people cross the border anymore. In or out. And you?"

"Waited here, there." She pulled her hood down over her eyes then flipped it back again. "Then time to go. Now I'm here and she's not," she said, pumping her shoulders up and down.

Orion delayed an incoming ment, then asked, "Your name?"

"Natalia."

"Natalia," he repeated, then wished he hadn't as his mind flooded with old-timey Christmas trees, music, and brightly wrapped gifts.

Natalia retreated into her hood. "You're Orion."

What else did she know of him? he wondered. He L-flicked Christmas away to respond to Garth's insistent ment setting up his delivery.

Want to go to a brew house tonight?

Which one?

How 'bout Shorty's, top of Market?

Thumbs up.

Once Orion confirmed Garth was leaving the top of Market Street and was on his way to his apartment to deliver the last boxes, he clicked back into work mode. He grabbed his duffel bag from his apartment and locked the door behind him, then lifted the tarp at the back of the truck bed and rearranged boxes to make space for this last delivery. At this point, he was usually seated in his cab tapping his fingers on the steering wheel, ready to go. But waiting was a dangerous time. With nothing to fill his head but the pulse of Nib. news, his thoughts usually drifted back to her. He stopped before he thought her name—he was afraid to even remember what she looked like. Every thought, every image meant a ping out there, closer perhaps to tracking her down.

Frailty, thy name is woman! Nib pronounced in old English, picking up on his hormone-infused emotions. **Perhaps you'd like Shakespeare's** *Hamlet* **hologramie tonight?**

Garth pulled up beside Orion's truck and handed him six small but unusually heavy boxes, which Orion fit into the empty corner. "See you at Shorty's," Garth winked, and with a quizzical glance at the young kid watching from the sidewalk, he disappeared down the street.

With a quick peek at the girl, Orion dropped his bag onto the floor of the passenger side and started the motor. "If you don't know where your aunt is, I've no idea either."

Natalia stepped in front of the truck.

"Hey!"

Finger to her lips, she pointed to the back where the new boxes were stashed, then came around to Orion's open window and tugged at his arm.

"None of your business what's back there," he shouted. He was so irritated by this twitchy little kid that it triggered a dose a Calming from his med-pack. Not exactly what he needed right now. "OK, OK." He followed her to the back, where she uncovered the newest boxes and pulled the lid off the top one.

With her eyes, she directed him to a minuscule clear patch pressed into a corner of the lid.

Orion's eyes widened. He opened the others. Each had the same patch.

"Holy shit," he mouthed.

Natalia peeled off the patches and placed them in his palm.

"I should flush . . ."

She stopped him with a shake of her head, then carefully laid them out on the street curb in the same configuration as they had been in the truck, covering each with a small rock.

Brilliant. Looks like the truck is still here, but we're not. He grabbed her by the wrist and pulled her into the truck. With a quick U-turn so she could retrieve her backpack on Amisha's steps, the two headed down Market Street to the Ferry Building ticket stand.

By the time the ferry rounded the bay just outside of Martinez, the sweltering sun had started its afternoon descent, leaving the air heavy with heat. They hadn't talked much. Orion recalled when Amisha had sat across from him on this route. He'd been so stunned talking about how Luke tormented her, he'd totally forgotten Amisha also had a sister. The sister left home real early. Had something to do with Luke. Damned if he could remember her name.

Annabelle perhaps?

Orion L-flicked it off without a reply. It all made sense now—the teal eyes, upturned nose, wrinkly mouth. He stopped thinking before her face emerged. Gotta be careful.

Once inside the refinery compound, Orion guided the truck through the maze of pipes, oil-saturated ground, and empty tanks that still reeked of old petroleum until they arrived at the dock. But no skiff waited for him. He leaned across the dock railing, checked up and down river. Was he late? Early? Miscommunicated? He ran his hand over his sunbaked bare head. He dared not ment. Six months ago, Caleb had been replaced. Since then, a series of name-less faces transferred his cargo without much conversation. Some groused at the weight, others looked at him with a questioning eye, but no one spoke. Not an especially friendly lot, but someone had always shown up. Hand shielding his eyes, he checked the river again, a hard knot growing in his stomach. Should he wait? He looked at Natalia. In a flash, he jumped back in the truck and, with tires scrunching around the rusted maze, reemerged on the old free-way, heading in the direction of the eastern hills.

ELIZA
1907
Yolo, California

September 27, 1907

Dear Silas,
Once again it is autumn, and I have miraculously completed yet
another season on the farm without you. Years before you passed
away, you made all those promises to me, then you had the audacity
to keep them.

Eliza's pen scratched across the page, but her words grew faint as
she wrote. She had left the cap off too long and the nib was dry.
She tossed her pen into the tray and pushed the desk drawer closed.
Rain tapped softly against the windowpane, announcing the early
arrival of autumn. She tucked her lavender shawl tightly around
her shoulders and with long, tired steps, walked down the dimly lit
hall to Silas's office, pausing at the door to absorb the pattern of
drizzling rain cast on the wall behind his still-cluttered desk. It had
been three years since she found him facedown in the barn. Never
even had a chance to say goodbye. She hugged her shawl against her
chest. How deeply she missed him.

For the decade before his fateful stroke, Silas had methodically
tutored her in every detail of running the ranch: when to sow, reap,
and bale the hay; which Holsteins to breed for best milk production;

how to anticipate a difficult calving and when to call the vet; and how to work the market to get top price for her crops. Then, as if he knew she'd be standing here all alone someday, he left his black leather folders lined in precise order on the back corner of his desk.

"Made a few mistakes," Eliza spoke as if Silas were seated before her sipping his morning coffee, "but overall, I'd say you'd be proud of your ranch. I've been running it without you three years now and haven't used red ink once." She held his photograph to the window, tilting it to catch a bit of light. "Hattie married right after boarding school, but she lives nearby, comes 'round to see me most every day. I hope her education does her more good than mine did me," Eliza sniffed.

"Little Rossiter's not so little. A strapping twenty-one years now. Knows his way around the tractor like he was born on it. But Dottie . . ." She picked up Silas's white handkerchief she kept folded in his middle drawer and dabbed at her eyes. "You witnessed how I cried a full year after Dottie was born. Turns out my change-of-life baby did indeed change my life. Who'd have thought a little nine-year-old could be such a comfort now that I'm mostly alone. Hattie says I spoil her, but what does she know? It's like spoiling myself, I say." Eliza was interrupted by a loud commotion in the front entryway.

"Eliza! Wherever are you? Didn't you hear my knocking?" Before Eliza could answer, Berta had already stashed her wet umbrella in the hallway stand and was bustling down the hall.

"Talking with Silas?" Berta said, brushing raindrops from her sleeve.

"Don't give me that look, Berta. You know it's the one thing that gives me comfort since he was laid to rest."

"At least someone is resting around here." Berta placed her still-gloved hand on Eliza's shoulder, her tone unusually serious. "People are talking about you, my dear."

"Those university people from Berkeley?" Eliza lifted her shawl to hide the upturn in her lips.

"A *model* farm!" Berta exclaimed like she was announcing the winning horse.

"Straight furrows and contented cows do not a model farm make."

"No, but black ink achieved by a woman does. Don't diminish your accomplishments, my dear neighbor. The University of California is not considering purchasing any other farm but yours."

"And the one in Davis," Eliza added. "I'm not sure what it means to be the University's Experimental Farm. Not sure where my children would stand if I sold." She pressed a loose strand back into her bun with a deep sigh. "But maybe I'm more ready to leave than I realized."

"Leave here? Oh, I hadn't thought of that. That's a dear price to pay for fame and fortune."

Eliza dragged herself to the window, pulled back the curtain. The eastern rain pelted hard against the pane, spreading a dank coolness into the room. "Forgive me, Silas, but not having the farm would free me up for other things I've wanted to do."

Berta sank into the chair facing Eliza. "You can't be serious."

"Regardless of the university's decision, it's got me thinking of my own future," Eliza continued. "Our children are old enough. I'll divide the ranch into quarters for each to manage. I'll live with Dottie on her piece, or . . ." she said with a decisive tap against the windowsill, "I might just move across the valley to my little parcel of land in the Sierra."

"Whatever for?"

"To get some peace for myself."

"You're hardly up there a couple times a year. Why now?"

Eliza shrugged. "I don't know. Just a thought."

"I still don't see the point of you buying your own piece of land in the Sierra when dear Silas was hardly three months in his grave. Not only that, but the mountains are so far across the valley."

"There is no point, Berta. Just an idea that's been rolling around my mind for thirty years. That little piece of land was the first earth I slept on in California. Even though it was only for one night, I couldn't get it out of my mind. So, after Silas passed away, I did something about it. You should come up and see what I've done."

"Camping? Thank you, no, I'll just stay here in my feather bed."

Eliza stood looking out the window, her eyes distant. "I hired some men to build me a little pine cabin set on a foundation of stones they hauled up from the river. I bought a few apple trees from a French nurseryman who delivered fruit trees to the settlers and collected water from the hillside spring. Not many folks around, but it didn't feel like being alone at all." She gave her aching hips a rub and changed the subject. "They say the creek's going to overflow again."

"Could be." Berta had to raise her voice over the now-pounding rain. "This is day seven."

"Jeremy Kasen got Hector to print his editorial again. He's bound and determined to get Cache Creek rearranged to his pleasing."

"Well he's not the only one farming in the flood plain. You are too, Eliza. Can't call the kettle black."

Eliza turned sharply. "I beg to differ. When the creek overflows, I get out of the way, let her spread her silt over my fields. Next crop is always more vital. Besides, it's unnatural for water to flow in a perfectly straight line."

"Better tell that to the water board before Jeremy gets to them."

"Oh, he already has the wheels in motion. He professes farmers benefit because they can expand their fields farther and farther from the creek, and by better controlling the creek, there'd be no more flash floods wiping out bridges."

"You can't disagree with that."

At the window, Eliza watched the cows huddle on high ground, their pasture transformed into a shallow lake. "There's something disturbing about taking God's water and doing whatever we please with it. I can't quite articulate my thinking into words, but . . . maybe it's time to write another editorial."

"Well, you'll be pushing against the tide, my dear. Speaking of which, I'd better get my buggy across Stephens's bridge before it gets washed away." Berta pressed her black-leather glove down each finger then firmed the glove cuff with a yank. "Don't take everything so seriously, Eliza. It'll wear you out."

Eliza walked her neighbor to the front door, then went back to her writing desk and closed her eyes. Soon, the words began to flow.

Moods of the River
Like every woman, the river has her moods. Men adore her when
she flows smooth and gentle, lapping at the banks where Mallards
and Shovelers press through the rushes for food. Men are pleased
to while away the hours on her shoulders, waiting for the wiggling
worms at the end of their poles to fetch the evening's supper.

Eliza covered her smile. Something about that image. Should she keep it or . . . yes, she thought, the likeness is apt.

Yet when winter clouds break forth and spill their waters onto the land,
small rivulets join, then flow into the creek, now a foment of most fearful
energy. Gathering momentum, she overflows her banks, spreading her
dark, boiling waters across the land. Tree trunks, now half-submerged,
silently replenish themselves from the long, dry summer.

This is good. Eliza smiled. I can't stop now.

Though afraid of her wrath, man strives to control her. He brings in dirt
and builds high levees to fasten her in place like a corset.
"Reclaim the River!" his battle cry.

Eliza waited for the ink to dry before setting the page aside. She opened the stationery box and started her second page.

In the spring, he opens the canals he constructed into her long body
to siphon off her flow, directing it instead to his crops of wheat, barley,
and alfalfa. What remains of the precious liquid commodity, now claimed
as his own, he sells to the thirsty cities below.

Eliza shook her head. One could argue we wouldn't be farming here if we did not have this water, which, of course, is true. But she was left with an unspeakable uneasiness when men talked only of controlling it. She pressed her palms into her eyes and drifted back to the fold of Grandmother Oak's great branches, where she first experienced this ominous feeling.

Is it possible to live and not destroy at the same time? Farmers keep draining the swamp lands, and I hardly hear red-winged blackbirds anymore. She pushed her writing aside. Too much poetry, not enough sting. It will be laughed off. Whoever said the pen is mightier than the sword was a fool. She snapped the cap over the nib of the pen and pushed back from the desk. I should just stick with what I know.

HARMONY
2018
Luna Valley, Northern California

At Nick's suggestion, Dora, Jeff, and I arrange for all interested parties to tour our community, hoping to create the proverbial picture that replaces a thousand words. At the bridge, five cars of coalition members, all the Luna landowners, and local news reporters await the arrival of the county's white car with three brave water board officials. We chat nervously, speculating on how the newly engineered high-water mark might impact each of our homesteads.

Lacking only a hearse at the head, our procession follows the winding road up to the top of the ridge, where we gather around the revised map of the proposed reservoir that's spread out on the hood of the county's car. We're shocked. Most homesteads now sit just above the water line, yet technically inside the half-mile condemnation zone. Except for ours. We've escaped it all by a thin shave. Jeff nudges my arm; I nod back.

Disheartened, the group continues as planned, stopping at every homestead for reporters to capture the essence of our sustainable community: long, fertile rows of vegetables, fenced fruit and olive orchards, free-range chickens, and occasional cows, sheep, pigs, and even llamas. We detour down a side road to show the Native American grinding rocks by the creek (which would have been identified if a full environmental impact report had been done) and the piles of rock tailings left by gold miners and their Chinese workers. We drive by a crowded swimming hole with splashing children and picnickers on the bank. At each stop, homestead families offer snacks of cherry tomatoes, apple slices, nuts, homemade soft cheeses, and freshly pressed apple juice. Nick takes me aside.

"I had no idea you had so much to lose. This is tragic. No wonder you're all fighting so hard."

"Fighting for our lives," Jeff interjects as he joins us from the group. I link my arm in his and raise my fist. A camera snaps and we're on the cover of the next day's newspaper with a full-page feature of the dam controversy—definitely slanted in our favor. I'm buoyed by the massive solidarity building around our opposition, yet a deep chill is building in my bones.

Out of the blue, Indigo and Lark announce they sold their property a month ago. With the sizeable cash offer from a private source, they plan to buy twice as much land up in Oregon. We're incredulous. Summer Rain and Madrona admit they were also approached with huge cash offers but laughed them away.

"Too bad." Indigo shakes her head. "If this all goes through, the county will use eminent domain to take your land anyway. You'll have no choice but to accept an offer that's way under market value. You should have acted when you could." Two weeks later, we hear of three more undeveloped parcels bought up by a holding company. The rest of us dig in harder, though *digging* is fast becoming a lost endeavor. The moon goes through phases of her cycles without my notice. I buy wilted tomato and pepper seedlings from the stand in front of the grocery store and plant them in the garden whenever I can find a spare minute.

With a loud honk, Jeff announces he's arrived back from the airport with Claire and Sage, who are home to see for themselves how the dam protest is faring. The girls push the front door open with their carry-on bags and rush over to give me a hug, leaving their father to deal with his armful of groceries.

"Hey, new haircut?" I reach up to touch Sage's nearly shaved head.

"It's in support of my boss. Breast cancer, and she's only forty-two."

"Are you going to run for city council in her place?" Claire asks.

"No way! Francesca and I are getting out of LA as soon as we can and moving back to the Bay Area."

"And get married?" Claire holds up her ring finger.

Sage starts to respond, then notices the man sitting across the table from me.

"You remember me telling you about Nick, don't you?" Nick puts aside his calculations and flashes his sweet, lopsided smile.

"One of the dam resisters?" Sage gives him a high five. I notice the split-second pause before Claire does the same.

"There are two blow-up mattresses made up for you in my study," I holler as they disappear upstairs.

Jeff drops his shopping bags on the table between me and Nick and removes a four-pack of toilet paper, mumbling something about not being able to grow everything on the land.

"Jeff, honey," I can hardly contain my excitement, but I wait for him to pour a glass of iced mint tea from the refrigerator. "I've got good news!"

"We can use some good news," he says, taking a long drink.

"Nick's found a new piano for the school."

He spits an ice cube back into the glass. "That's your good news?"

"One of my elderly clients in Sacramento wants to donate her piano to a worthy cause. I told her I knew just the place," Nick says.

"And the best part is that Nick's already arranged with Mr. Johnson for me to buy the school's old one."

"The one you called a hopeless pile of shit?"

"Nick's going to have it fixed." I want Jeff to show some sign of excitement for me, but he drifts around the kitchen shelving groceries.

"That's great that Nick's finally going to get you a piano. Better than I could do. Where are you going to find room for it? Outside on the deck?" He hauls over a twenty-five-pound bag of black beans and shoves it into the bottom of the pantry with his foot.

I'm embarrassed. The least he could do is show some appreciation to Nick and some excitement for me. Nick rises and, with a nod, bows out the front door, giving us space to work this out. With a light touch on his arm, I mouth a thanks and close the door behind him.

Over coffee with the girls the following morning, I relay how my life has flip-flopped since the dam. I used to be out in the garden before the sun hit the tops of pine trees. Now I'm at my laptop or phone, checking emails, scanning news, arranging meetings, stuffing papers into my burgeoning file cabinet.

"You look tired, Mom," Claire says, hugging her white fleece robe around her long torso. Sage wears the red flannel pajamas we gave her last Christmas. She nods and sips her coffee.

I brush away a small tear before it trickles down my cheek. If Jeff had told me I looked tired, I would have bristled at the criticism, but I know the girls speak the truth. "This is your place too, girls. I'm fighting for all of us."

"You can't do this all alone," Sage, the practical one, tells me.

"But I'm not! You should come to the meetings. We have so many experts and activists, they're practically tripping over each other to help."

"Not that kind of help." Claire, the deeply sensitive one, looks me in the eye. "When's the last time you sat quietly, Mom? Meditated maybe?" I have no answer.

That afternoon, with an hour before my four o'clock conference call, and Jeff and the girls walking the trails behind the house, I decide to give meditation a try. At the very least, it might help me sleep tonight. I pause at the door to my study, already a disaster with the girl's bedding, books, and clothing scattered along the floor. How I miss those days of innocence when this was our family's norm.

At the window, I sit by the desk but can't see out to the woods. Too many files and reference books stacked on top. I remove a few to the floor and return to the window. Hands upturned, I inhale slowly, scrunch then drop my shoulders, and close my eyes. How did I used to do this? Imagine my worries floating away downstream. Wearily, wearily, down the stream. To a dam. No, breathe in, out, erase the dam, let my breath flow. Count my breaths . . . one . . .

two . . . three . . . four. I can't sit still. I'm hot. I'm filling with tears. It's like a fire across a river consuming everything in its path, consuming the wizened figure who points at me then withdraws into the flames.

"OK, enough!" I push back from the desk. This rarely worked for me back then and still doesn't. I grab my laptop and take it downstairs to the kitchen table but can't remember if I'm supposed to initiate the Skype or if Heather is. Just before four o'clock, the front door flings open and Jeff and the girls enter laughing.

"Hey, pick your hats up off the floor," I snap at them, then immediately regret my bad humor. They're only here for a few days. "Sorry," I say. "When I'm done with my call, let's just sit and have a glass of wine and you can show me pictures of little Zoey and catch me up on your lives. Enough of this dam!"

AMISHA

2016

Luna Valley, Northern California

Hunkered behind the wheel of Blue Sky, Orion concentrated on the tangle of roads entering and exiting the empty highway. It was easy not to look at the girl seated next to him, but damn, he couldn't block out her incessant noisemaking. Soon as he gunned the motor up the highway ramp, Natalia's fingers started tapping out rhythms like chaotic sparks on the metal drum of his dashboard. The faster he drove, the more intense her drumming.

He saw right away he should get off the old highway. Far too exposed. Chunks of asphalt and knee-deep potholes. Options? Take the north-south thread up the side slope of the Sierra. There'd be fewer possibilities for cover—the Great Conflagration of the mid-2000s pretty much burned the land bare—but there'd be fewer people, fewer threats. Last time he was up in the hills was ten long years ago. Things had changed.

Once on the old 49 north-south thread, Natalia nodded off—spiky, black hair hidden deep in her hood, lips fluttering in her sleep. Orion rolled his shoulders to loosen them. He needed to concentrate on the missing skiff. He'd worked well with Caleb, trusted him. But since Caleb was replaced—who knows why—Orion was growing uneasy about his plans. Smartest thing now was to skip over his connecting points and deliver directly. But what the hell to do with the girl?

Natalia awoke with a loud snort and launched into her gyrations and drumming.

"Hey, tell me about your name," Orion asked. Was she capable of a normal conversation?

Natalia shook her head as if remembering something. "Like in Christmas," she answered.

"The old holiday?"

"The dark and silent night." She whistled the first lines of *Silent Night,* looping it over and over until Orion held up his hand to shut her up. "What?" she resumed tapping on the window. "Next holiday's better—Give Away Month—make room for lots of new stuff."

"Then there's Upgrade Month," Orion added. "Can't think of the last time I upgraded anything. Don't think anyone celebrates that one anymore."

"Used to celebrate moons. Maybe see them."

"No, never heard that one." Orion checked his rearview mirror. Was that the same car behind him from an hour ago? No, he breathed a sigh of relief. It just turned off.

"Old Holidays," Natalia recited. "From Pagans, then Religions, then Corporations, but now . . ."

"Some still celebrate birthdays. You were born December twenty-fifth, I'll bet."

"Stupid name." Natalia's head bobbed to some new internal rhythm. Except for fingers tapping on the window, she went quiet. Orion sighed. Enough conversation for now. He squinted through the window. Rain? No—her fingers tapping again. By god, if she wasn't a connection to Amisha, he'd drop her off with his first delivery. He cleared his throat.

"What do you remember about your aunt?"

"Nada, nodo, nuffin'," she said, then, apparently liking the sound of it, continued with an escalating drumroll of her fingers: "Nada, nodo, nuffin', nada, nodo, nuffin'." Jaw clenched tight, Orion drove on hoping she'd wear herself out.

"In the old, old days, people drove with gasoline," Natalia said, shifting to a new subject as if she could only do one annoying thing at a time. "Fast. Old gas cars were fast—a whole week in a day."

"What I'd give to drive one of those cars," Orion said.

"Don't make them anymore." Natalia tapped the dashboard now as if to make her point.

"I know that," Orion shot back. Maybe earplugs? Immediately his Nib offered a Sound Shade to block out unwanted noises. He considered it briefly, then L-flicked it away and drove on, the tapping following him like gulls after a fishing boat.

Most days, they made good headway along the road winding up into the northern Sierra. The sun dictated their speed because the battery was unpredictable. When the sun was impeded by clouds, ash, or microparticle accumulations, they slogged along at five kilometers per hour. Other times they were forced to wait by the roadside watching little rodents scurry over the bare dirt between patches of shade until enough sun penetrated the air and they could proceed.

During one of those interminable waits, her head bobbing to a silent rhythm, Natalia pulled a round jar from her backpack and smeared some pale-yellow goop over her neck.

"Want some?" She offered him a jar with a red "Radioactive" graphic on the label.

Orion jumped away. "Holy shit, that's poison!"

Natalia laughed. "Silly old man." She screwed the jar shut and held it up. "Poison? I'd be dead now. See, I'm not," she held out her palms for proof. "Use some! Messes up the circuits. Can't find you." Before he could protest, Natalia smeared a small dab of nano-metal gel over the Nib bump on his neck. His neck tingled. It was the same tingling as when nanobots were injected to clean up his infected toe.

His Nib slurred, then went quiet.

Natalia nodded. "Magic."

"Where'd you get it?" His voice sounded loud in his head.

"A place I stayed. They liked me."

"Just one jar?"

Natalia nodded. "Best where fewer people are 'cause Nib's already weaker there."

Orion absorbed the strange quietness in his head. Who was this girl? Before he could wonder more, Natalia jumped up.

"It wears off—we gotta' get going."

After three days of starts, stops, and a few close calls, Orion recognized some familiar landmarks: deep river canyons, old arching bridges, partially burned "keep out" signs, depleted-looking settlements. Not much green; most everything was dried or burned.

"What's in the back?" Natalia asked for the hundredth time.

"You've got X-ray vision . . ." Orion mented, then wished he hadn't. "You tell me," he continued out loud.

Natalia pulled a silver Pharm.food from her bag and began munching with gusto.

He wished she didn't remind him of Amisha. It opened old fears. After Amisha had left San Francisco, he kept a close watch on her place, hoping she'd show up as abruptly as she had left. He called her clinic several times, asked after her wherever he traveled on his deliveries, but no one knew, or no one said. Then he stopped asking. It was too depressing, and he didn't want to stir anything up for her. If only he'd been able to stop her, he might have helped her. Now all he could do was worry about her.

Orion located the first delivery station—a small, brush-covered cave near the bottom of the first river canyon. He unloaded four boxes into the opening, just like he had ten years ago. He located the next two stations. Most were highly camouflaged. Twice, he passed by station number three before he saw the small hut buried within a wall of blackberry bramble. The camouflage had grown into a mound as impenetrable as barbed wire. He held the deep box topped with a jumble of old circuit boards and regarded the mound. No way to get through the tangled thorns. He tossed the box back in the truck and drove on with Natalia. The bulk of the cargo was for the final drop-off. He hoped he remembered where it was.

Exhausted after a day of dead ends and blackberry scratches, Orion was desperate to make the last delivery before night. He took a chance on the narrow dirt road that drifted downhill to the Second

River. Rounding a corner, he was startled by the sudden appearance of an old-fashioned wagon stretched horizontal across the road. He smashed his foot against the brake and barely avoided crashing into it. One wagon wheel was off and propped against the embankment. The driver seemingly asleep on the bench seat. The old man rose at the sound of their arrival and replaced his oily, leathered hat over his wispy gray hair.

"Was hoping help'd come."

"Looks like your wheel's busted off." Orion motioned for Natalia to stay in the truck, but she clamored out her side as soon as he shut his door. Damn, the girl just couldn't keep still.

"Can you help? I can't even see where it's broken." The old man stepped back next to Natalia while Orion hefted the wheel back onto the axle.

"Got a mallet?" Orion asked.

"Under the seat." The old man moved close to Natalia, but she shivered and quickly stepped to the opposite side of the wagon. "Where're ya headed?" he asked as Orion banged the wheel firmly in place and tested it with a strong tug.

"Up north." Orion knew better than to be specific. "Glad to help, but we gotta get movin' or we won't make it before dark."

"You won't, if you're thinking Tennessee Mine. That's the next stop. You're better off waiting out the night 'round here. Turn left just after the old dam, if that's what you want to call it. Head toward the sunset. You'll find a place that'll take you in for the night." The old man mounted the repaired wagon and shouted to his mule to get going.

Orion scratched his bare scalp as the wagon disappeared before it rounded the bend.

As he continued driving down the road, miraculously, Natalia was quiet, maybe even dozing. Good. He needed all his concentration to maneuver the narrow, crumbling roadway across the dam. He didn't dare look down. Only when he was safely over did he peer into the vacuous dirt basin below. Circular bathtub rings and rotted tree stumps hinted there might once have been water behind the dam.

He proceeded cautiously down the winding trail looking for signs of life. Not much, just a wheel track here and there and dozens of side roads overgrown with brush. Suddenly the detour seemed a very bad idea. It was too late to retrace his route, so he turned left into a turnout by an overgrown trail.

"Let's walk." He slammed the truck door behind him. Natalia refused to move. "Fine, then I'll go myself. Hope the bears don't find you." Ten minutes later, he was back in the truck.

"No bears," Natalia commented.

Light was getting dim. Orion drove along the narrow dirt road, wondering what the hell he was going to do. He'd slept in Blue Sky before, but now he had the girl. "Any ideas?" he asked, but she was already asleep, head scrunched in her hood against the window. He pressed on, stopping at one path after another. Nothing. Light was nearly gone. He'd continue until he couldn't see anymore, then find a turnout and wait 'til morning.

Moments later down the road, Natalia bolted upright from her sleep. "I hear them!"

Startled, Orion cut the motor and stopped at the bottom of a narrow road rising uphill through the brushy undergrowth. He had to strain, but then he heard it too—sounds of shouts and laughter. Children? Impossible—not that he knew how children sounded. He glanced at Natalia. Her fingers had stilled. She was listening intently as if the sounds were a language she might know.

"Should we go up?" he asked.

"Yes, yes!" Leaning out the window, Natalia slapped the truck door like it was a mule she could coax faster.

Orion parked the truck far enough below the dwelling that they could walk up unnoticed. By the time they reached the top of the road, both were out of breath, but immensely relieved, for it looked like they'd found one of those wayside places. Unlike his other delivery stops, this one was inhabited and free of blackberries. Watching them from the door was a young woman with straw-blond hair that cascaded over the shoulders of her brown, pocket-covered tunic.

"You one of the tinker deliverymen we hear movin' around the backcountry?" she called out.

Orion glanced back at his truck, the last of his delivery boxes crammed behind the cab. Just one more delivery and he could wipe this gunk off his neck and return to the world he knew. Natalia opened her mouth to correct the woman, but Orion was close enough to jab her in the ribs. She closed her mouth.

The woman nodded. "Haven't seen one of you in more moons than I can count. She squinted at his truck parked down under a small madrone, then eyed him with uncertainty. "Only one night and you sleep outside." Oceana led the pair through the kitchen, where several people sat quietly eating at the table. "If you have food, you can prepare it here. Otherwise, put your bedrolls outside on the patio wherever you can find room." She hesitated at bit, then left them to settle in.

The next morning, Orion quietly packed his bag before the girl woke up. She's much better here with all those women, he rationalized. Still, he was reluctant to let go of this connection to Amisha. Last night, he'd even asked the women about her but was met with strangely silent stares. No, he'd just let Natalia work it out with them. Probably best not to stop on his way back to check on her. It would only confuse her.

Natalia watched him depart beneath her half-closed lids. As the truck's motor receded down the drive, she curled in tighter against the stone wall, clicking her teeth to the rhythmic impulses flashing in her head. She'd spent most of her life dropped into strange places. No big deal here. But her head pulsed like circuits trying to ignite. With more goop rubbed over her Nib, she slipped into the kitchen, opened lids, tapped on walls, pried open doors, anything to keep her moving. She chucked a handful of crunchy balls into her mouth, spit out the sharp, hard parts. In the big room on the other side of the house, the floor was covered with bedding and snoring people. Oceana held out her arm, blocking her from entering.

"You still here?"

Natalia recoiled against the door.

"And the man you were with?"

Natalia shrugged.

"Well, Storyteller will want to know of this when she comes down."

ELIZA

1914

Yolo, California

Rossiter dropped his mother's heavy valise in the entry hall of the farmhouse and waited for her to catch up with him. Eliza's steps were slow and deliberate as if pondering a weighty load.

"It's unfortunate your meetings in Palo Alto and Berkeley weren't in the same week. You could have stayed down there and enjoyed a bit of a holiday for yourself," Rossiter said.

"And leave the farm for Dottie to run? Bah."

"She does well enough. Nothing died." He chuckled, for he knew his little sister would rather apply tint to her cheeks than throw grain to the hens. "I'll be back on Tuesday to take you to the train station again."

"If it weren't for that train station being located in Woodland, I'd be spending more time up in the mountains."

Rossiter cocked his head.

"You do know that's why the university bought the Davis farm and not mine for their new campus," Eliza said. "It was just closer to the Woodland train stop."

Rossiter put his arm around his mother's weary shoulders. "I'm glad you didn't sell."

Eliza worked late into the night on her address for the State Fruit Growers Association Convention until her eyes were too crossed to see.

Dottie nudged her sleeping mother sprawled over the desktop. "Mother, please, you should be in bed."

Squinting into the darkened room, Eliza slowly sat up.

"Come upstairs out of the dark and cold. You spend way too much time at your desk."

"Promise me!" Eliza squeezed Dottie's hands until the girl winced. "Never let this desk out of the hands of family."

"Family *women*, you mean." Dottie rolled her eyes. She knew this admonition by heart. She struggled to free her hands, but Eliza tightened her grip.

"Only until the work is done. . . ."

"Mother, your work will never be done. Now come along upstairs."

The next morning, Eliza was up at five starting the coffee and biscuits as she had for over thirty years, although now she had only Dottie to cook for. She relished her morning ritual of coffee, biscuits, and reading the San Francisco paper. She liked to sit near the window where she could hear the early morning robins. But nowadays, the news made her blood boil: Eastern syndicates buying up and consolidating western farmlands, talk of a dam across Hetch Hetchy Valley in Yosemite, and men posturing across the Atlantic in ways that could well lead to war. She folded the *Chronicle* and tossed it on the table.

Kitchen chores finally finished, Eliza turned to the mountain of speaking requests on her desk—each one an opportunity to press her views. But first she wanted to review the minutes of the most recent meeting of the California Federation of Women's Clubs. Her own treasurer's report was accurate enough—funds sifting in and out without much to show for it as far as she was concerned. She frowned. Where was her address to the board about Yosemite? She flipped through the pages, seeing her name quoted here and there advocating for physical education for girls, for stronger prohibition, and for wielding California's new franchise for women. But nothing about the proposed dam, not even in the Natural Resources division— only some talk about putting trees in city parks. *What are we about, Pink Teas?* Eliza wondered. *We've got to do better than this.*

The party-line signal for the Baxter farm rang five time before Eliza reached the phone mounted on the wall at the end of the hall and lifted the receiver.

"Yes, Violet. No, I'd not heard. Of course, I'll stop by tomorrow after church." She shook her head and replaced the earpiece in its holder. She still had not come to terms with the telephone's random intrusion into her peace and quiet. Of course, it was convenient and made it so much easier to get things done, but most times she found the telephone an unwelcome interruption. How could she think straight when she was always jumping up to lift the receiver from the wall?

That evening she resumed work on her speech about the exodus of people from farming requested by the California Fruit Growers Association for their June convention.

> *The country life needs alert men and women with minds trained to grasp not only the possibilities of the soil, but the needs and possibilities of their own lives. In this paper, I shall speak of country life from two viewpoints: the economic and the aesthetic.*

For the next two hours, her pen could hardly keep up with the words flowing in her head. If too many young people fled to the cities and no longer touched their native soil, there would be fewer people who cared for, tilled, planted, and harvested the land. People in the cities would eventually starve. What was needed was a *back-to-the-farm movement*, she decided. One that also touched the growth of the soul, the love for the beautiful and the good.

As was her practice, she ended her speech with a poetic or uplifting thought. This time, a memory of when she had occasion to take a weekly eight-mile ride over the summer.

> *There will always be in my mind the picture of those beautiful mornings when the earth was just awaking from her night's sleep, when the clouds lay in long white bars across her breast. When in the distance the snowy Sierra showed white, and crimson and gold,*

as the rays of the morning sun touched their summits. They were
mornings to remember.

A week after Eliza returned from the Fruit Growers Convention in Palo Alto, Berta, Rachel, and Jenny made an unannounced visit.

"It is time," Berta said without wasting words, "for you to run for president of the federation."

Eliza tossed back her head with a laugh. "Well, that's a good joke. Surely you came here with something more clever to say."

"We have come to the conclusion," Rachel said as she spread yesterday's *Chronicle* on the table. "We need to read more of this . . ." She pointed to Eliza's speech printed verbatim across the page in three columns. "And less of this . . ." She held up the front page with photos of mobsters hiding their faces.

"With that I would agree," Eliza nodded. "But even if I were to consider running, which I'm not, mind you, the Northern California delegation has already put up Mrs. Jennings from San Francisco as the president-elect."

"Now that's the real joke. Eudora's only interest in running is to get her picture in the paper," Rachel said.

"With three strands of pearls around her neck and a trio of pheasant feathers in her hat, of course," Jenny added. "We can't afford four more years of just planting trees in city parks."

With her hand on Eliza's shoulder, Berta sat her down at her desk. "The California Federation of Women's Clubs is our only hope to be taken seriously. We need someone to get us off the back pages and onto the front."

Eliza crossed her arms. "I'd say for a collection of women's clubs, the federation has already been quite successful. Look, we've pushed for legislation for child labor laws, juvenile courts, eight-hour workdays, Pure Food and Drug Act. Of course," she drummed her fingers along the desktop, "those are primarily urban agendas."

"Precisely!" Berta rapped the top of Eliza's hand. "That's why we need you to bring the country perspective to the table. People listen to you!"

"No," Eliza shook her head vehemently. "This country woman's life is already too busy. The nominee for president has already been made. Let sleeping dogs lie."

But sleep didn't come that night. After listening to one, two, then three chimes from the hallway clock, Eliza tossed her covers aside and flipped the switch of the new handheld electric light Hattie had ceremoniously set on her bedside. Following the circle of white light downstairs to the kitchen, she made a cup of India tea, placed it on her desk, lit the kerosene lamp, then raised the sputtering wick until a soft yellow glow suffused the desktop.

How much time does anyone have? Years? Decades? Centuries? No matter, there was never enough time. Already, she felt the minutes, hours, years slip through her fingers. What if time ran out? No, this was all foolish imaginings. She had plenty of time.

At five chimes of the grandfather clock, Eliza roused from her sleep with a stiff neck and blurry eyes. She groped along the desktop for her glasses but found instead three pages covered with her handwriting—*The Country Woman's Platform.*

HARMONY

2018
Luna Valley, Northern California

The phone rings. It's seven in the morning.

"Guess who's buying up all the land?" Without waiting for a reply, Dora launches in.

"That makes no sense. A real estate holding company?" I'm confused.

"They're the *private* part of the county's public-private partnership. Marty's got the legal team working on it. Most all the land sold in Luna Valley last year can be traced to the National Preservation Holding Company."

I slump back in my chair and think it over. With all the land that's been sold, we have yet to meet any new neighbors. I call Jeff in San Francisco, but he's in a meeting and will call back soon as he can. Nick answers on his cell. Over the crackling connection, he tells me it's the first he's heard of it but to keep him informed. He'll check in when he returns from D.C.

"D.C.? You never told me you were going to D.C."

"My great-aunt had a setback, something like a stroke. She practically raised me, so I . . ."

"I understand. You need to be there for her."

"I should be back next week."

Feeling somewhat abandoned, I navigate through the week on my own, accompanied by the distant buzzing of chainsaws still

329

working on the perimeter road around the reservoir. Dora brings over a new map with recently sold parcels dated and colored in red, making Luna Valley look like a bad case of chicken pox.

"I still don't get why this holding company is buying everything up. The parcels will be worthless if the dam is built. And if there isn't a dam, why would they want all our land?" I go over to the kitchen counter, remove the top tray from the dehydrator, and flip each tomato skin-side up. One pathetic batch is all I've dried this summer. "I assume someone's investigating who they are?"

Two days later, Dora is again at my kitchen table with the news. "Tobacco."

I snatch the report from her hands.

"This private holding company has deep ties to tobacco interests." Dora reaches into her front pocket like she's going to pull out a cigarette. Old habits die hard.

"But you can't grow tobacco here. Even though it's getting hotter, it's sure not humid enough."

"No, but what does grow exceptionally well here?"

"Marijuana," we say in unison.

"And what does marijuana need lots of?"

"Water."

It's common knowledge most neighbors have small pot gardens, while Asian, Mexican, and Central American cartels have substantial illegal grows hidden all around us in the national forest. Indigo and Lark were the first to discover a large illegal plantation behind their property when their creek went dry—diverted upstream to a hundred-acre criminal grow. We've also heard rumors that a number of tobacco corporations have already bought up massive tracks of growing land along the Pacific coast, anticipating that pot would be legalized in the future. Sociopathic corporations, I think—legally a "person," but without conscience, and only in it for their own profits.

I need time to think this through. After Dora leaves, I change into long pants, lace up my walking shoes, but am hardly out the door when the phone rings. It's Nick, back from D.C.

"Heard there was big news," he says.

I spew out our latest suspicions.

"Whoa, slow down," he says. "You're jumping to conclusions. Now tell me again just what you know and who told you."

Like a pack of bloodhounds, the next day the coalition is following every link it can find between the county and eastern tobacco companies. I bounce between incoming emails and phone calls, so focused I hardly notice the sandwich Jeff sets on my desk. He's home, but I have barely acknowledged him, I'm so deep into this.

"Another fire down by Gold Springs." He squints out the window.

The air outside is a hazy orange. I'd hardly noticed that either. "Is our fire department responding?" I fear people will be distracted at a time when we need them to focus on the tobacco connection.

"They're on alert. Depends on the wind."

"I hope they can handle it because we've called a big meeting day after tomorrow."

"Media?"

"Not yet. We want to get our facts straight and strategies down first." I bite into the cheese sandwich, and with a "thanks, dear," return to work on the meeting's agenda. Before dinner, I run the agenda by Jeff one last time—he's so good with missed details—then email it to Dora to disseminate.

Jeff serves me a steaming bowl of spaghetti made, he reminds me, with the last of our canned tomatoes. "You've hardly been in the garden this summer, and if it weren't for me, you'd hardly eat."

"Aw, honey, isn't that what partnerships are all about? We fill in for each other. And right now, I really, really appreciate that." I reach for his arm, but he pulls away and begins twirling spaghetti onto his fork.

"If you were just a little more involved in the dam . . ." I refrain from saying more.

"If you were making some money, I might have more time."

"If we don't defeat this dam, there'll be nothing to stay for."

"Harmony, you're not the only one capable of organizing."

After eating dinner in silence, I retreat upstairs and dive back in.

The next morning, Nick calls with great news. I get my pen ready to take notes on what he's found, but instead he tells me it's time to go get the piano. His client's family is moving her to a rest home, and they need the piano out of her home in Sacramento by tomorrow.

Whoa. This is not the news I expected, but I feel a tickle of excitement.

"I can't do it tomorrow because of the big meeting, but how about the next day?"

"It's tomorrow or never. Anyway, it will be good for you to take a break. You shouldn't take so much on yourself. Others can run the meeting."

Though he says the same words as Jeff, it feels different.

Nick picks me up at eleven the next morning, and we take off for Sacramento. The top of his old Mustang convertible is down, and for the first time in a long while, my spirits are up. Marty will head the meeting, and Jeff and Dora have a detailed script on what I would have reported. Nick mentions we should be back before the meeting is over, so I'll catch up on the latest in our tobacco-marijuana investigation. I'm still not sure why I have to personally accept the piano for the school but guess it's important when some-one makes a $5,000 gift.

We leave the smoky haze of the foothills and drop into the even smokier Sacramento Valley. After getting a text that pick-up time is delayed until two, Nick suggests we stop for a leisurely lunch at his favorite restaurant overlooking the Sacramento River. Calamari pasta and chardonnay on the patio, water rippling below, the day is too perfect not to indulge in a glass of wine or two.

"Thanks, Nick." I lean across the table, resisting the urge to tuck a lock of his windblown hair behind his ear. "I've almost for-gotten what it feels like to be wonderfully indulgent. I needed this."

"You deserve so much more." His fingers gently brush my fore-arm as he reaches for his cell. "Hey, time to go. It's ready."

We drive into the exclusive Marinwood Estates and pull up to a large Tudor-style house with a small ABC Moving and Storage truck parked in front. Nick confers with the driver, returns, and with a shrug tells me the piano is already loaded up. They couldn't wait.

"I come all the way down and don't even get to thank her?"

"Maybe the students can write some nice thank-you letters."

With the truck following behind us, we arrive at the school two hours later, too late to catch the end of the meeting. The principal directs the moving crew to wheel the piano into the music room.

"This beauty is a 1940s upright ebony Baldwin, recently restored," Nick tells us. While I thrill at running scales up and down the piano, they load the school's old piano into the van to take to my place.

"The school's got a gorgeous piano there," I say as I hand Mr. Johnson my $75 check for the school's old piano. "I'm dying to spend time with her and see how she sings."

"Any time after school hours," he shouts to me as we drive off.

Dora and Jeff are waiting at the kitchen table when we pull up with the van. Unusually quiet, I note. Of course, the school's old upright piano is way too large for the living room, so I have the men leave it angled into a corner.

"Hey, don't just stand there at the door. Come in and join us for a beer." I grab Nick's arm, then notice Jeff and Dora haven't taken their eyes off him since he arrived.

Jeff turns the maps and papers facedown. Nick says something about having work to do and scuttles out the door. I turn back to Jeff and Dora.

"What?" I ask.

Dora scrunches her mouth and looks at Jeff, whose fingers have been drumming the table since Nick disappeared.

"Did something come up at the meeting? Tell me!"

"You could say that," Dora replies.

Jeff pushes over an inch-high stack of papers and reads the summary report on top out loud.

"The Clear Water Conglomerate that has contracted with the county as the private part of the public/private partnership is actually SAT—the Span America Tobacco Corporation, the sole source of all funding."

"But we know this already," I say.

"Here." He pushes the stack closer to me. "You read the rest."

"As preferred parcels around the reservoir are identified and arranged to be available, they will be purchased and leased to SAT's commercial plantations."

Now it's Dora tapping the table. "Somehow they've been able to find the exact tipping point where each of our neighbors were willing to sell out."

"And that's why with all that land sold, we have no new neighbors," Jeff adds.

As I leaf through the meeting notes and maps hacked from the SAT's website, it feels like a snake is coiled around my chest, squeezing tighter with every page.

"Over 87 percent of the reservoir's water will be permanently contracted to these plantations. The remaining 13 percent will be a buffer against continuing drought and released on an emergency basis for farms and public drinking. Recreation will be limited to one designated campground. Boats will be prohibited. Swimming allowed only in the roped-off area near the campground."

"I can't believe the county agreed to this!" I bang my hand against my forehead. "Of all meetings to miss. I can't believe it!"

"The county will be paid $500 million a year," Jeff shrugs. "For that, they can buy whatever they need. Even water."

Jeff stops me from picking up the phone. "Wait. There's more." He nods for Dora to continue.

As if measuring the amount of air she'll need to tell me, she slowly inhales, opens her computer, and after several clicks, rotates it so we can both see *The New York Times* homepage. With a quick glance at Jeff, she continues working deeper into the maze until she comes to the article describing an investigation into SAT's practices dated three years prior and stops at a photo of the hearing. SAT's president is speaking into the microphone flanked by attorneys on either side and a row of five men and one woman seated behind him.

"Anyone look familiar?" she asks me. I shake my head no. She enlarges the photo and points to the second man from the right in back, slick black hair, pinstripe suit, looking down at his phone. I squint and almost recognize something familiar, but no. Not really.

Dora zeros in until the man's face fills half the screen.

"Hey, except for the black hair, could almost be Nick's brother," I say. "Got similar smiles."

Dora enlarges once more so the small scar on his lip is unavoidable.

"Nick?" Spots float across the screen.

"He's not Nick," Jeff leans over. "He's Marcus Vardell."

My vision reduces to a pinpoint. A tap on my shoulder brings me back.

"Don't say anything," Dora whispers. "We're all just pretty sorry."

Dora leaves and I drag myself upstairs.

"Shit!" I take off a shoe and hurl it against the wall. "Shitshit-shit! What a fool! I sold out my community, for god's sake—my friends!" I throw the other shoe against the door and collapse in sobs.

I hear Jeff leave a tray outside the door. "Dinner," he says. But I've no appetite.

The sun descends behind the trees. Stars fill the darkening sky.

Early next morning I call Nick, but his number is no longer in service. I send an email: no response. I call his office: there is no such number.

AMISHA

2076
Luna Valley, Northern California

Amisha rolled onto her back beneath the blue quilt, enjoying a few moments of precious solitude. Overhead, the morning sun peeked through the gaps in the ceiling logs, laying out strips of light along the floor of her retreat. Enjoy it now, she thought, because when the sun shines full on, it'll be sweltering. Right now, there was just enough soft light to read. Before entering the rhythm of the house below, she indulged herself in one of Grandma Harmy's journals.

> *May 10, 2025*
>
> *Got a voice mail from a Dr. Mubina Suharto, researcher from the University of California at Davis. She's looking for field sites for their "50 Future Foods" project, and the Felix Gillet ladies told her about the hundred-year-old apple trees on my land. Curious, I called her back. She reminded me of myself in my early days, spouting save-the-world facts and figures with such passion, like the earth will have 50 billion people on it by 2050. That's a lot of people to feed, she said. Her remedy was that people need to stop eating meat and shift to eating highly nutritious plants that are easy to grow and have seeds easy to save. Even though I'd given up on saving the planet, I invited her up. What the hell?*
>
> *The doctor arrived in crusty hiking boots and one of those wide-brim SPF hats pulled down over her long black hair. As we walked*

the trail looking for potential growing sites, she told me almost twenty groups helped develop the "50 Future Foods" concept. I could google it if I wanted to know more. I didn't tell her I rarely open my laptop anymore.

Walking up the hill, she ignored all the fertile areas I showed her but got excited at places where the earth was hot and dry and hardly anything grew. Somehow that's the point of these future foods. In order to feed the planet, plants had to be able to survive under the worst growing conditions. I wondered if it was like what my Great-Grandmother Eliza was always promoting in her speeches. "Dry farming," I think she called it. She was way ahead of her time.

Back at my kitchen table, Dr. Suharto spread out a huge pile of seed and tuber packets and suggested I try growing edibles from as many categories as I could: beans, grains, nuts, vegetables, leafy greens, mushrooms, roots, tubers—especially ones that reproduced easily. I selected ones I knew, like fava and soybeans, pumpkins, orange tomatoes, kale, and parsley. Then remembering my younger, more adventurous self, I picked out buckwheat, amaranth, and even hemp seeds. That one made her eyes light up like I'd found the hidden prize. She went on and on about how well hemp grows in poor soil without fertilizers or pesticides. When it escapes and goes feral, it's called ditch weed. People make all sorts of useful things out of it, like paper, cloth, food, ropes, medicinals, even biofuel from parts of the hemp plant—and all without the psychoactive THC.

I admired her enthusiasm but, frankly, don't have much energy for idealistic projects anymore. I tucked the seed packs into a box and placed it on a pantry shelf.

What! That canister of seeds upstairs? How alive are they after fifty years? Amisha knew seeds meant survival—that's why she tacked Monica's yellow cloth over the sink to remind everyone to *save the seeds*! For sure, she was going to look into those hemp seeds. Someday, she'd tell a story about seeds, but not tonight.

For tonight, she'd tell them the story of how Gramma Harmy built a piano with her own hands so the school children could sing her favorite Chopin song, whatever that was. Maybe Harmony sang it when she chopped tomatoes or wood. She'd just make something up if the children asked about Chopin. Maybe chop her hand on the kitchen table like a knife? She had to laugh, remembering there was a time when she'd instantly know what Chopin was thanks to her Nib, the constant informer of all things. Now it could be anything she wanted. Much more fun!

In her year here, she'd learned to stop and observe as she made her way back down the hill. Fortunately, she noted someone forgot to latch the orchard gate last night. No harm done, no wildlife got in and chomped the garden to a nub. With a quick shove, she closed the gate. She'd once survived on just a few apples and berries. Now she was part of a small community surviving on Harmony's orchard, Monica's tomatoes, and the migrants' wild plants. Maybe she'd try planting seeds from Harmony's canister. Who knows, some might still be alive.

Amisha stretched her arms to the sky and wiggled her fingertips. She shuffled through the pine needles covering the trail to the house, noting the acorns were about ready. She'd put together a group to harvest today. Or, she sighed happily, tomorrow. There was enough time.

She opened the kitchen door and paused to acclimate to the darker interior. As usual, the room was crammed with people. Breakfast was the busiest time of the day when all residents ate, organized, then scattered. Amisha nodded to Oceana, now silent, and said hello to India, who greeted her back.

"There's a . . ." India started to say.

"Yes?" Amisha selected several amaranth cakes and a small yellow pear for her early morning meal. She looked up at India, who was still struggling with some message to convey. She'd get back to her later. It sometimes took a while for the day's voice to warm up after a long stretch of being silent. The kitchen was crowded so she strolled over to the dining table, where Isabelle was holding her blue worry beads.

Isab . . .

Amisha dropped the pear, it rolled to the floor, Tibet picked it up. The room shrank to a knothole, as if she were looking through a crack in the universe. Her little sister was here, at breakfast, at Grandma's.

"Isabelle." Amisha could hardly speak. Color drained from her face as she frantically searched for Luke. What door was he behind, waiting to grab their toys, ruin their play? She reached for her beads—keep them safe, keep Isabelle safe. The beads clanged into a metal bowl.

"Auntie?" The girl lunged toward her.

Amisha took a step back. "You're . . . you're not Isabelle."

The silent ones stopped eating and looked to one another as if Storyteller had lost her mind.

Natalia shook her head, grasping for the words.

"Isabelle's my mom. I came to find you, Auntie. It's me—Natalia."

Amisha closed her eyes, opened them. The girl was still there, with Isabelle's blue eyes, freckles, and short pug nose. But this girl had spikes of coal-black hair. And a Nib.

"You can't stay!" Amisha's hand trembled so hard she could hardly point to the bulge on the girl's neck. "No Nibs here!" she yelled.

"Fah! Auntie. It's good. I've got stuff to neutralize it." She tapped at her neck. "Makes me undetectable. Believe me, or I wouldn't be here."

After Amisha calmed enough to allow the girl to stay, they spent the rest of the morning sitting outside under the shade trellis catching up. Amisha regretted she'd lost track of her younger sister. Maybe she didn't try hard enough, but Isabelle hadn't made it easy.

"Last time Mom took off, she said if I don't hear from her to come find you."

"But I was gone as well."

"I waited on your steps 'til the man across the street kicked me off."

"Man?" Amisha's heart flip-flopped.

"The one who brought me here. Kinda balding."

"Blue truck? Boxes in back?"

Natalia nodded.

"Orion brought you here? He was *here*?" Amisha jumped up.

"He split this morning." Natalia grabbed a piece of grape vine and balled it up with her fingers. "Didn't want to take me."

Amisha bolted into the house. "There was a man with the girl? Where is he?" She searched the kitchen then the living room, but Oceana held her back by the shoulder.

"He was only here a short time," India explained. "We wanted to protect you like you instructed us."

"But it was Orion!" Amisha cried. "Not my brother Luke, but *Orion*!"

"He might return. There's the girl," India tried to reassure her.

Natalia, who had been watching from the door, shook her head. "Don't think he liked me enough."

"Then find him! Does he still have a Nib? You've got yours. Bring him back!"

India's eyes widened. "Nibs are forbidden here!"

"She says she can neutralize hers. Well, I say, unneutralize it and find him!"

Oceana's jaw dropped.

"He's my . . . The only man I . . . The only man . . ." Amisha's legs buckled under, and she slid to the floor in tears.

Oceana and India nudged Natalia onto the front deck to talk with her. When they returned, India announced that Henri would take the girl to the top of the next ridge and wait for her to make contact. With her Nib unneutalized and Henri waiting at the bottom of the hill, Natalia mented over and over, but only got back unintelligible crackles, some confused directives, an offer for snow boots. Nothing from Orion.

Back at the house, with her nanometallic goop spread thickly on her neck again, Natalia did her best to repeat what Orion had told her that morning. "He said he'd return tomorrow, if I was lucky."

He didn't.

A week dragged on. The entire household was on hyperalert for this man. Amisha plunged deep into a pit of despair and couldn't be coaxed out. She asked Natalia a thousand times to describe how he looked, what he said. Did he still wear a brown vest with a big hole in the bottom pocket? Did he rub his forehead when he was think-ing? Did he hum off-key under his breath? Natalia grew weary of the incessant questions and found ways to avoid her aunt.

With everyone now bearing her same worried expression, Ami-sha knew that once again she'd have to come to terms with losing Orion. Feeling a massive headache threatening, she popped a wil-low bark ball under her tongue and took off up the hill. Instead of stopping at her cabin, she continued onto the forest trail along the top of the ridge, where she paused to catch her breath.

Come.

Feeling dizzy, she lay down on a circle of matted leaves—the bed of a sleeping animal. It was a fleeting moment, like a tingle of energy that zigzagged beneath her, like flashing rootlets that conveyed her at lightning speed, absorbing her into the pulsating matrix of roots below. She traveled knowing where water flowed, where beetles chewed, where sunlight above was clear or shadowy. She heard young saplings and ancient pines weave stories, leaf to leaf, root to root. She was entwined everywhere at once in the root web of knowing.

ELIZA

1915
Yolo, California

In the early morning light, Eliza sat at the end of her bed and opened her mother's dog-eared Bible, not to read it, but to examine the bookmark, an oak leaf dear Silas had sent her at school so long ago. She held the leaf to the bedroom window to highlight the brittle veins. *How did I get to this place in my life? I came to California such an innocent bride. I've milked, plowed, given birth to five children, all grown. I have loved and buried my husband. Yet I feel so much remains to be done.* She slipped the leaf back into its place and closed the Bible.

She felt strangely energized for not having slept much. Berta and Mrs. Royles would be here at seven this morning to pick her up. She was almost ready. For the past two days, she had washed and ironed dresses now hanging in the tall leather trunk across the room. She owned nothing fancy nor fashionable. What she wore to church would have to suffice. Beneath her dresses, drawers were filled with undergarments, stockings, and shoes. Wrapped in tissue inside her flowered hat box was her best gray felt hat, decorated with a single heron feather she had found near the creek. It conveyed its own simple elegance. On the way to the kitchen for her morning tea, she checked her brown leather satchel stuffed with papers on topics upon which she might have to speak—each topic sorted and coded with colored ribbons.

What remains? Her white porcelain cup jingled in its saucer as the hallway clock chimed six thirty. *Berta, Rachel, Jenny, Iris, Sarah. It's the women who remain,* she decided. *And the work? It's been there all along, pushing me to this point. If I'm not elected president, no harm done. I shall have given women at the convention a glimpse of what the country woman knows to be true. I'll then return to the peace and quiet of my farm or*—she smiled to herself, *at last to my place in the mountains.*

She gave the desk an affectionate rub. "Since you've been back in my life, you've given me no rest. I've held the earth in my hands. I've listened to your silence. I've worked with my women. I'm trusting that once again you'll help me know what has to be done." Eliza sipped the last of the tea and set the cup gently back on the saucer. The clock chimed seven. "It's time."

On May 17, 1915, a black Packard touring car pulled up to the carriage entrance of the Palace Hotel on Market Street. Three women disembarked brushing the fine layer of dust from their motor coats. Eliza much preferred her horse and carriage or even the train, but Mrs. Royles insisted Eliza enter San Francisco in their new automobile as a symbol of country women embracing modern technology. Eliza trusted Mrs. Royles. As the senior delegate from Woodland, Iris Royles would be presenting Eliza's name this evening at the California Federation of Women's Clubs first meeting at the Civic Auditorium. Thrilling, terrifying, Eliza tried not to think about it.

After checking into her fifth-floor room, Eliza skirted past the elevator and took the staircase to the main lobby. Such a cacophony of high-pitched voices, feathers, and furs! She found an overstuffed chair in a corner away from the registration desk, leaned back, closed her eyes, and tried to imagine the gentle sound of water lapping at the shore.

"Mrs. Baxter!" The conversation flowed over to her corner.

"Let's ask her in person."

Eliza opened her eyes to a cluster of bobbing feathered hats, like a flock of hens pecking in her yard.

"Yes?" She managed to smile so her weariness didn't show.

"We have heard," said a smartly dressed delegate with a Los Angeles Delegate pin on her lapel, "that you want to expand the federation's agenda in new directions."

"It's not so much into new directions, as you say, but strengthening our ability as women to be effective in the areas we care most about."

"You are implying that the federation has not been effective?"

A passing reporter stopped and pulled out his notepad.

"I am saying that women in California have had the state franchise for four years, and we are serious about making our new voting power an influence for good. The federation can serve to focus our new power."

"Mrs. Baxter, if I may," the reporter flashed his badge from the *San Francisco Examiner*. "With all deference to rural life, what does a country woman know of the complexities of the political realm?"

"Exactly," the Los Angeles delegate nodded to the surrounding women. "If, as you say, we are to indulge the federation in California's state politics, about which I have my doubts, then we need a leader of Mrs. Wendell Jennings's caliber."

Along the corridor, delegates stopped midconversation and moved toward the woman holding court in the corner. Eliza leaned forward in her chair.

"The country woman greatly needs the city woman's viewpoint. But no more strongly than the city woman needs the country woman's. My goal is for them to be mutually helpful." Eliza glanced at the clock on the wall and pushed herself up to standing. "You must please excuse me, for I need to make my way to the convention site."

On her six-block walk down Market Street to the Civic Auditorium, the fog spread a welcoming coolness on Eliza's flushed cheeks. This wasn't going to be easy. Thankfully, even in the heat of the moment like that, she had stopped from blurting out the blunt, terrible truth. The future wasn't about women voting or even women farming. It was about the very survival of their great-great-grandchildren and the earth itself. Not a cheerful platform from which to campaign. She had refrained from telling those delegates they were out of touch with the future. How would they know?

Dismissing the first taxicab that slowed for her, she chose to walk in the fresh air, even though it was filled with particles of black soot. She'd read about eastern cities plagued by black snow. *Are we to follow suit?* Two automobiles waited side by side for their turn to cross from 8th Street onto Market. She covered her nose with her handkerchief and coughed. At least with cars there was no manure to clean up.

All along Market Street, buildings were reemerging from the great earthquake. *Such an indomitable spirit!* Eliza thought. *Only nine years ago the streets were filled with rubble. Four years ago, women could not vote here in California. Now I'm in San Francisco running for president of an organization of women's clubs.* She stopped, struck by a passing thought. *Perhaps we should rethink our structure. Perhaps we are too aligned with the political forms that men have devised. Perhaps we need our own structure for working together and getting things done.*

Eliza moved aside so that people could pass around her. *California Federation of Women's Clubs. If we eliminated the word "Clubs," we would simply be a Federation of Women. Then everything could be on the agenda—all the work that must be done.*

HARMONY

2019
Luna Valley, Northern California

It's the silence that gets to me. The silence and the guilt that hovers like an impending storm. I was never accused. I was never challenged. John Doersch called from Rivers United and quietly informed me they need me to provide more research. I'm no longer needed to speak on behalf of the dam coalition. Dora never blamed me directly. She did comment that, of course, she saw it coming. She just didn't think my misdirected affection would create such a rift, such damage. The coalition will continue even stronger, but the Luna community is most likely weakened beyond recovery. She assured me she'd talk to me when she had her bearings again. It's been a week and Jeff has hardly made eye contact or spoken to me. I do my best to get through the day, but I feel like I'm treading water in the middle of Lake Tahoe.

I find some solace in the kitchen again. I had to buy a lug of paste tomatoes from Madrona and Mark—the only full homestead garden left besides ours. Before the sun is up, I'm in the kitchen. The canner is working up to a full boil. Quart jars, salt, lemon juice, rings, and lids are staged along the counter. There's a comforting rhythm to canning, like getting back on a bicycle after years of not riding—the body memory kicks in and away you go. I dab sweat from my forehead and slowly lower a jar of tomato sauce into the canner, remembering the visceral satisfaction of dropping jars into rapidly boiling water. Jeff comes downstairs and waits at the front door.

"Would you hand me that other potholder over there?" I ask. If he's not going to talk to me, at least he can do something helpful.

Jeff holds out the green one with burnt edges. "I'm leaving."

"Oh? Where?" I lower the next jar into the canner, relieved to hear him say a few words. "If you're going to town, would you mind picking up the book I reserved at the library—save me a trip."

Jeff is silent.

I scrape tomatoes from the bottom of the kettle and transfer the red glob into the last canning jar, then notice I'm out of basil. I consider dashing out to the garden but decide to chance asking Jeff. "Would you have time before you leave to pick me a small handful of basil leaves?" Only then do I notice the three suitcases and two cardboard boxes stacked by the front door.

"Jeff?"

"I'm leaving for the Bay Area tomorrow morning."

"That's a lot of luggage. How long are you going to be gone?"

"Permanently."

I turn off the burner.

"Come here." He motions me to the table and sits down across from me. My heart sinks like lead to my stomach.

"I've been doing a lot of thinking." He looks me in the eye for the first time in a week. I notice his eyes are tired and bloodshot.

"I've made up my mind to return to San Francisco."

"But—"

He holds up his hand and continues. "I've done as much here as I can. Or want to."

Tears fill my lower lids. I brush them away. So, I've destroyed us as well?

"Look, Harmony. When we first came here, we were Debbie and Jeff with this naive dream of changing the world by living close to the land. But it wasn't that easy, was it? And since the dam distraction, well, it doesn't look like there is much left for me or much of a reason to stay." He slumps against the back of his chair.

"Nothing to stay for?" My voice comes out high-pitched and whiny. "Our dream?"

Like water breaching an earthen dam, he continues. "I'm *tired* of this dream, Harmony. *Tired* of struggling all the time. If I'm going to work this hard, I'd rather be in a large organization with the clout to make a difference."

My ears buzz. I feel the room closing in on me.

"I accepted a position at Robert's law firm. They're desperate for environmental consultants. I'll be more effective in San Francisco than staying here planting potatoes or fighting this dam. Robert and Carole offered me their downstairs rental until I get settled."

I drift over to the stove and slowly remove tomato jars from the canner, disregarding the thirteen minutes left on the timer. With two potholders, I lift the heavy canner to the sink and dump out the boiling water. Outside, a bird flits down on the birdfeeder, but I can't see what kind—my glasses are all steamed up.

"When did all this happen?" I fixate my eyes on the birdfeeder.

"Two weeks ago."

"Then you've been planning this even before..." My voice trails off.

"It's not just the thing with Nick. It's obvious he used you."

"You know nothing happened between us, don't you?"

Jeff looks out the window, avoiding my eyes. "The attention you gave Nick left me with nothing."

I hear his words but can't make sense of what he's telling me. "Nothing!?" I turn at him with an incredulous look. "Then what were all the meals I cooked from our garden, and the nights I stayed up nursing Sage's earaches, and all the email alerts I acted on, and the supervisors' meetings I gave up garden time to attend, and all your dead-weight Levi's I washed by hand?" I grab a towel and throw it on the counter next to a half-full egg carton. "We wouldn't have any eggs if I hadn't fended off the fox, and if I hadn't baked every week, we'd be eating Safeway bread. And who had to drag the dead skunk from the cellar so you wouldn't stink at work? Me! And all the while, I worked my ass off on this fucking dam." My chin is quivering so hard I have to stop.

"You're all out *there*, Harmony." Jeff waves his arms around in the air. "Everything you're doing is out there. What about here?" He places his hand over his heart. "Us."

My eyes scan the table. I have no response. I start to say, *you know I love you*, but the words hang in the silence between us.

Absently, he sorts through the stack of mail on the table, slides the environmental appeals over to me. "Maybe it's time for you to leave all this too. I'm willing to start over with us. But not here."

Start over by going backwards? I think. *Leave Great-Grandma's land?* It's too much to get my head around.

"Think of it as creating a new story."

The canning timer buzzes from the stove. Briefly confused by the jars already cooling on the counter, I turn off the timer and turn to Jeff. "But this is my family's story. It's not finished—I mean, I'm not finished." Such an odd choice of words, as if they weren't really mine.

"Then try it out for a few months. Take a break, relax, have a little fun. I'll take you back to Chez Panisse, we'll drink lattes at Peet's, see if we can find the spark we once had."

I consider the trace of enthusiasm softening the lines of his drawn face and the searching in his eyes—eyes that once fired up when we were planning this new life together.

"There's room enough for two in their apartment," he continues, "and in case you didn't know, your mother gave Carole your grand piano. It's upstairs in her living room. I'm sure you can play it whenever you want." He lays down his final card.

"My piano? MY piano?" I grab a jar of tomatoes and hurl it into the sink. Splinters of red and glass land everywhere and I'm overcome with the urge to jab sharp glass into something fleshy.

I hardly sleep all night. With Jeff on the couch downstairs, I go over and over our conversation until I'm exhausted and confused. Am I so out of touch I hadn't seen this coming? Do I leave? Stay? What about Claire and Sage? And my piano? Soon there's shuffling sounds in the kitchen, coffee grinding, toast burning. I drag myself out of bed.

On the front deck, I stand barefoot clutching my bathrobe against the cool morning. Jeff waits below, one foot perched in the car's open door, dressed in his tweed jacket, pressed white shirt, and black oxfords, the ones too good to wear in the mountains.

"You'll have this week to think it over, Harmony. I'll be back Friday with a moving van. Let me know if I should bring one large enough for both of us."

And that's it. Jeff swivels onto the car's worn leather cushion, adjusts the rearview mirror, pushes the seat back so his foot reaches the pedal. The car starts up with a puff of exhaust smoke. He backs away, turns forward, then with tires crunching all the way down the gravel driveway, pulls onto the paved road.

Don't think. Not yet.

I find things to keep me busy: dishes, laundry, email, weeding, cleaning out the chicken house, and turning the compost pile. I jab a pitchfork into the mound of kitchen scraps, brown leaves, and garden greens, all transformed into a heavy pile of stinking compost. Smushing away tears with my muddy glove, I toss a pitchfork of hot compost into the next empty bin and continue for a half hour until my arms ache like crazy. There's good reason why Jeff did all this hard labor and not me. I fling an armful of straw to the chickens and return to the house. My shoe slips on a loose steppingstone.

That evening, my hands immersed in a sink of hot dishwater, I entertain the tiniest thought of returning to the Bay Area with Jeff. It wouldn't have to be permanent, but if we found we had enough to start over . . . I can't continue with this thought. Abandon the homestead? I can't do that to Claire, even Sage. I don't know why it should be important to keep the homestead in the family, but it is.

Then there's my piano. I'm livid. Carole can't play a note, but I'll wager her decorator has placed my baby grand in the bay window as a stunning focal point. My fingers ache to play it again. That would be another reason to return. With time and practice, I could regain my former proficiency. Lots of women resume their careers after their children are grown. I remember my dream, performing at Carnegie in a flowing blue silk dress.

I dry my hands with a dishtowel and throw it on the counter. I can hardly think of pianos without seething. How thrilled I felt to finally have a piano at the homestead. Sure, it's a gargantuan hunkered in the living room corner with chipped ivories and squiggly lines from kids' marker pens—I can ignore all those. But when I sit to play, the damn piano still has the same loose keys, ringing notes, and broken pedal—no more playable than when it was at the school.

I grab the phone and call the principal. Mr. Johnson assures me Mr. Sarcosky arranged to have it tuned, but repaired? He didn't think so. "And by the way," he says, "I thought the piano was supposed to be worth $5,000, but that's not what the sales receipt inside the bench says."

"Receipt?"

"Yes, Becker and Sons Used Pianos. $900."

"What was the sale date? Maybe it was the original sale to the old lady."

"Nope, it was dated last month."

Something snaps. I stomp upstairs two steps at a time. Show me one thing that's made a difference. I can't save the river, can't save the elephants, can't stop the oil spills. Hell—can't even have a decent piano. I kick off my sandals and fling them to the bottom of the stairs. At the doorway of my study, I stop, stunned. When did it start looking like a garbage transfer station? Topo maps tacked lopsided all over the walls, newspapers and boxes piled high on the desk, and coffee cups and red-stained wine glasses crowd my laptop. Could I leave all this? You bet I could. It'd be like returning home after a long journey. Maybe I didn't save my people, but I'd be returning wiser.

I rip off all the topo maps with their colored dots and smash them into the wastebasket, then attack what's on top of my little desk. It's heavy, but I upend the big box labeled "Earth, Air, Fire, and Water." Files slide page by page onto the floor. I glare at the empty box in my hand, dropkick it toward the growing pile, then turn to the next box and the next—my own fire sale—everything must go!

Like a switch that's been flipped, I push aside the wine glasses and wait as my computer slowly opens, stalling like a child at bedtime. Eighty new emails. I click on the first one: World Wildlife Fund. *Are you sure you want to unsubscribe?* Yes. Next, Earthjustice? Yes. The Nature Conservancy? Yes. Natural Resources Defense Council? Yes. I signed your damn petitions, sent you all money, forwarded your alerts a zillion times. Show me one thing I saved! My eyebrows twitch like crazy as I unsubscribe from my entire portfolio, even The Rachel Carson Council.

For the rest of the afternoon I purge all my files in the computer: "Endangered Species," "Weather Extremes," "Water," "Pesticides," "Pollution," "Air Quality," and "Bees." Don't think. Just empty the bulging trash bin. When I come to "Stop the Luna Valley Dam," my finger hovers over the "Delete" key but pulls back. I tap the top of my desk, look out the window, take a deep breath, and try again. But I can't . . . I just can't. I stumble downstairs through the mess of boxes and papers at the bottom of the staircase and heat up the tea kettle. It's like air is stuck in my lungs. I drop a bag of Calming Chamomile into a mug and gulp it down before the leaves even have a chance to color the water. It's like the old "Turn, turn, turn" song . . . "a time for everything under the sun"—even for letting go. Well, the sun's setting. Maybe it's time. In one swift move, I'm back upstairs, finger poised over "Stop the Luna Valley Dam," and I hit "Delete."

When my breathing returns, I reach for the phone and leave Jeff a message.

"Bring the large moving van. Let's start over."

Before I know it, I'm in my walking boots and out on the trail, hat smashed over my curls, nose dripping from crying. I charge up the hill to the west, dried leaves crackling beneath my feet. At the crest, two ravens let out a raucous call. I shout back at them, but they ignore me and resume their private conversation on an old snag. I stop to catch my breath before descending into the dark ravine where the ferns grow, then back up toward the ridgetop where acorns from all the oak trees around Great-Grandmother's old foundation roll beneath my boots. I pause briefly, then continue slower now, down to the little spring that despite the record-hot summer still trickles into a rocky pool where a small patch of wild mint grows. A flat stone invites me to sit, kick off my boots, slip my feet into the cold water, and dip my fingers into the pool. I sprinkle a few drops onto my forehead. "So be it," I whisper.

Back at the house I decide to light the old kerosene lamp instead of flipping on the harsh electric light. How fitting that it's autumn,

I think. A time of wrapping up, putting away, pulling back. I blow my nose into a tissue and take the lamp upstairs to my study. I know all things must end. But they say, "in every ending is the seed of a beginning." I stop at the little desk, now emptied of all my clutter. "Even you," I say as I pull up a chair and drop my head into my folded arms on the now-exposed heartwood.

The wick sputters.

It's time.

No, I shake my head. I'm done here.

I pull down the wick, and the flame disappears into darkness.

AMISHA
2076
Luna Valley, Northern California

The girl was intolerable! Amisha covered her ears, desperate to block the tapping and clicking from across the room. It was too early to get out of bed, but impossible to get back to sleep with Natalia's damn clattering. Amisha pulled the blanket over her head. This girl was driving everyone crazy, and some of the Silents were even threatening to leave. But the girl was her flesh and blood. She had no choice but to leave her small retreat and return to the house to share this room with Natalia.

Lying in bed with a pillow wrapped around her head, Amisha scoured her medical memory. When a baby actually made it to birth, she would know in the first hour which type of Pharm.food regimen to put it on. "Downer" babies were complacent with flaccid muscles and rarely cried. She'd put them on orange Pharm.food formula to give their gut the best chance of absorbing nutrients. On the other extreme, "Uppers" screamed at birth, their little arms and legs so rigid it was hard to dress them. They got the pastel pink formula. She'd heard babies had different Nibs inserted at birth, but that wasn't her department. Natalia probably was fed the pink formula.

To pass the time until it was time to get up, Amisha pulled one of Harmony's journals from the nearest box. It answered a lot of questions.

November 4, 2019

Four in the morning, and I can't sleep, can't think, can't even distract myself with emails since I deleted everything from my computer. Everything! I thought that's what I wanted. Jeff comes back in two days. I've got to get focused again. Maybe writing will help. I dusted off this green leather journal, the one I bought at Cody's Books the day I fell in love with Jeff. I was saving it for something special. Well, what's "special" now is that the life I thought I was going to live forever is all over. Everything I dreamed of, worked so hard for, done. San Francisco, ready or not, here I come.

November 5, 2019

I woke up with another stiff neck from napping all crumpled up at my desk. After an afternoon of packing books into boxes, I took a walk on the trail. It's about all I'm good for these days. Trees are filled with migrating robins and band-tailed pigeons pigging out on ripe madrone berries. A pileated woodpecker called from top of a pine. I couldn't locate it, my eyes were so blurred, but I called back anyway. Jeff comes tomorrow, and all I feel like doing is putting my head down on my desk and sleeping, letting my thoughts drop like leaves until my mind is as bare as the tree outside my window.

November 7, 2019

Well, yesterday morning Jeff pulled into the driveway with a huge moving van expecting, of course, that I'd be sitting next to him when we returned to San Francisco. Would it have been kinder to warn him before he arrived or face him at the door? I didn't have the courage to do either. I just waited in the kitchen when he opened the door and he noticed that only his belongings were packed and waiting.

I took a deep breath and announced that I've decided to stay. He stared at me for a long time, then pushed past the boxes into the kitchen where I had the soup pot heating on the stove and the table set for lunch. It hurt to see him so bewildered, especially since he thought we were starting over. I tried to be the calm one for once and said as softly as I could that this place won't let me leave. I tried to make our plan work, I really did, but even with the prospect of a dam, I can't leave the land, can't leave this homestead, can't take my little desk away from here.

There's no way I could have made this any easier. Jeff protested and threatened that I couldn't manage the homestead by myself. He said he'd been so happy and hopeful about starting a new chapter in the city. I cried. He cried. But I didn't change my mind. That night I sat at the desk with my hands resting on the desktop and felt a gentle warmth flowing into my open palms. I looked at all my reflections in the window. I swear, something had shifted.

"If Great-Grandmother Harmony had left, we wouldn't be here either," Amisha murmured. Just as she turned the page, Natalia jumped out of bed. "Pah!" She circled the room, tapping on the wall, on chairs, on whatever her hands landed on. "Pah pah ta pah pah pah." Amisha dropped the journal back in the box and rubbed her forehead. Another long day. She had to laugh—her first impulse was to find a good Pharm.food to calm Natalia down. Right. Pharm.food, the only relief for all the buzzed, confused children it was responsible for creating in the first place. She watched the agitated girl circle the room.

When had children's health started going off course? There was an official investigation made public, but Amisha had her own explanation—an insidious brew of inescapable contaminants. Like drinking water so tainted with hormone disrupters leached from old plastics that sperm and ova lost their instructions. Add to that the combination of air so blitzed with ash and nanometals that little bodies couldn't extract enough oxygen to live. Ever-present electromagnetic fields that wielded invisible destruction on anything alive. And food plant's DNA so manipulated that human's DNA couldn't process the nutrients. And there you have it—pah, pah, ta pah!

Nib.know's pat answer was *this is how life has always been.* But since being at the homestead, Amisha was understanding things differently. Lots of people, her own great-grandmother included, had warned and protested, but like the ocean that slowly encroached on the city's streets, the changes came on so slowly it was easy to dismiss the warnings as extremist or political. The easiest thing was to simply accommodate to the changes.

"Pah!"

"Good morning." Amisha waved to catch the girl's attention.

"Pah, pa, pa, pa, pah!"

Amisha couldn't wrap her head around Natalia as one of the family women. Up to now, she had Great-Grandmother Harmony, Grandmother Claire, her mother Zoey, and her sister, Isabelle. Natalia was a future she hadn't counted on, a future she clearly couldn't control. Amisha needed to consult the women and called an afternoon Council.

With her hat pulled down over her ears to block out sounds of Natalia tapping and storming through the house below, Amisha trudged up the hill. As she neared her retreat, she began to hear a new dissonance. Women were talking at once with an urgency she never allowed in her private space. During Council, Amisha set aside the rules of silence so every woman could speak as she felt guided. But this was chaos.

Outside the front door, she paused before entering. Why hadn't she given Natalia the same ultimatum she gave to other difficult travelers—respect their ways and perhaps be invited to stay, or move on? But she hadn't. She also hadn't insisted they remove Natalia's Nib. And why this elusive feeling that Natalia was important—perhaps more than they could even imagine?

The room quieted as she entered. Seated cross-legged around her room were the women she knew she could count on: Dar, Clarissa, Sharome, Principia, Montagna, India, Oceana, Africa, and the new woman, Nisena. She took a deep breath. This wasn't going to be easy. Perhaps after the opening ritual of communal silence she'd know what to say.

"She has to go!" India's demanding challenge broke the fragile silence. Suddenly everyone was talking at once. "She's driving us crazy! She rips around like a tornado, 'pam!pam!pam!'" Africa pounded the floor. "She's obliterated all peace. We can't escape her. Why, why is she still here?"

Amisha cautiously made her way through the women to sit at her desk and, with fingers spread wide, rubbed wide circles along the oak top, hoping she could stir up the right words. After a short silence, she turned and looked at the women.

"With every new person, we go through a time of adjustment," she said quietly. "Even with you, India." Africa nudged India as an amused ripple circled the room. "You refused to eat anything that came from the dirt. Now you're the one discovering new wild plants for us to eat."

India crossed her arms and pressed back against the wall. "But she's different."

"Yes, and we will be different with her," Amisha said.

Sensing the room was about to erupt again, Amisha quickly slid into meditation position and, with palms upturned on her thighs, closed her eyes and waited. One by one, the women joined her. After a prolonged silence, Amisha felt compelled to share more of her family's story. They already knew the homestead was built by her great-grandparents and kept in her family for generations. They knew of her Great-Gramma Harmy, of course, but they didn't know about Amisha's siblings, Isabelle and Luke. She filled in details about summer visits here with her sister and brother. She told about making the front deck into their fantasy kingdoms until Luke terrorized their make-believe world. When they returned home from their last summer at the homestead, things had changed. Her sister started hiding herself in her room until Luke caught on and paid her nightly visits. After that, Isabelle hid herself in her heavy clothes, wide hoodies that covered her sunken eyes, and long sleeves that covered the red marks along her thin arms. "I was young. I didn't know what was going on. But I could feel Isabelle drifting away."

"Go on," Oceana nodded.

Amisha looked down at her feet. "On Isabelle's fourteenth birthday, she disappeared. She even cut me off from menting, but a year later I picked up her trace in Michigan and three years later in Mexico. Once you've crossed the border, it's hard to return. After years of getting 'Unknown' from my Nib queries, I feared she had died."

"And this Natalia is Isabelle's daughter," Pacifica said quietly. "The niece you didn't know you had."

"I have no children of my own. Do you realize what this means to me? To us?" Amisha struggled to steady her voice, but it was quavering like wind blowing through dried grass.

Sharome opened her eyes partway and held up her hand to quiet the murmuring. "Natalia is the only connection left to your desk and to the future we're trying to build here. She must stay."

"Then make her live up here with Amisha," India demanded. There was a chorus of agreements.

Amisha pulled her worry beads from the drawer and rolled each bead between her fingers. When the room was quiet again, she continued.

"Natalia will live among all of us." She bowed her head and closed her eyes. "Our task now," she said, hands again resting on the desktop, "is to discover what Natalia needs in order to stay. I suggest we work in pairs, with Natalia making a threesome." She had no idea where this idea of triads came from but continued. "As one woman interacts with Natalia, the other observes. We will reconvene in three days."

At high noon three days later, Amisha sensed from the women's lively chatter that something had shifted. She opened the Council as she always did with a time of deep silence, asking the women to imagine their bare feet on the earthen floor merging into the web of rootlets that connected all of life within the earth.

"So," she said, opening her eyes, "what have we learned?"

"We'd like to speak first," Oceana said, slowly twirling a lock of her long, sandy hair in her fingers. "Clarissa and I have been observing Natalia. The girl's like a surging storm crashing wildly against the rocky shore." She held up her hand to quiet the room. "But, we can be a sandy beach for her. We can remove the rocks from her path, watch what calms her down, what dissipates her energy, like Clarissa noticed happened when I got down on the floor right next to Natalia. We can do this."

In turn, the other pairs offered their own observations. Several noticed that when they gave something for Natalia's mind to work on, even counting acorns, she almost stopped tapping and bobbing.

"Maybe with her Nib blocked by that goop, she's making up for not having any input," Pacifica said. "Maybe that's why Amisha hasn't ordered her Nib removed yet?" She looked to Amisha, who held up her hand in question.

"I don't know why. I only know it's not time yet." Amisha dismissed the thought that it might have something to do with finding Orion.

"I remember the feeling when my Nib was first out," Clarissa said. "It was all electric sparks, but no noise, just a vacuum. I was lucky my own thinking emerged. Sometimes it doesn't."

"It's not that simple," Amisha snapped. "She's been distorted like all the babies born out there. Everything she's had to eat, drink, and breathe—her entire world has short-circuited her nervous system. Some children do survive a few years." She pressed her hand to her eyes. "And I failed them all."

Oceana placed her hand on Amisha's shoulder. "Let me take the lead on Natalia then. I can be more detached." She turned back to the women. "I know you have other suggestions."

"Try drumming." Sharome slapped a steady beat onto the earthen floor. "Realign her circuits. First get them coordinated, then they can be slowed."

"She'll absorb the steady rhythms as if she were floating in an atmospheric sea," Oceana said, extending out her arms like she was floating.

"Tap on pots and doors, maybe even her body," Sharome demonstrated on Africa next to her. "Make it a game, only slow and steady . . . steady . . ." Sharome slowed her pace to a halt. "Steady, girl."

For the next three days the women took up the challenge of slowing Natalia's rhythm. For once, Amisha appreciated not being in charge. She thought about how easily Oceana had assumed the lead on Natalia. It was her nature. She'd have to give some thought about what else was better handled by others.

The second afternoon, Amisha watched Nisena and Natalia sorting acorns into baskets of those for storage and those too buggy to keep. How quietly they worked together! Natalia's head still bounced to whatever was happening inside, but she kept it together for a long time. It was like her fingers were sorting the pieces like a puzzle. That gave Amisha an idea.

The next morning as Natalia came bouncing down the stairs, Amisha pulled her aside. She handed Natalia a mug of herbal tea Clarissa made for her of nettle, Saint-John's wort, oats, and valerian—a blend Clarissa had made on her own because she hadn't yet walked Natalia through the forest to help the girl find her own herbs. Amisha nudged Natalia to the kitchen table, which was now extended to full length, and pointed to a small tattered cardboard box at the far end.

"Let's get to work." Amisha made sure Natalia finished her drink.

Natalia flicked her fingernails along the mug making a scratchy sound and handed it back to Amisha. "Huh, huh, huh?" she grunted as she spun around, arms stretched out like propellers. Amisha grabbed a wrist as it came flying by but found herself spinning as well. She followed Natalia as she bumped along the wall, mimicking her grunts and nonsense syllables.

"Hoofa, hoofa, hoof," Amisha laughed at her own silliness. She began tapping on the wall, trying first to outdo Natalia's pace, then slowly bringing her down like an unwinding clock. "Soosha, soosha, soo . . . sha, shooo . . . sha." She dragged the "s" sound out into a whisper, noting that Natalia was following her back to the table. As if unveiling a secret, Amisha lifted the lid of a fragile box to display the mound of small pieces of paper. She held one up. "Who's this?"

Natalia squinted at the black-and-white photograph as she waited for an answer to come, then shrugged. "I'm outta range," she said. Amisha ran her fingers through the papers then slowly started arranging them on the table.

"Some people lived long ago, some are younger. How can we tell who goes together?" Natalia quickly scanned the photos, then paired a male and female figure and set them off to the side.

"Well, yes, they could be a pair, but look how different they're dressed." She pointed to the woman's high lace collar and the man's bare-throated T-shirt. "How about this one?" Amisha found a woman with long straight hair flowing over her spaghetti-strapped shoulders.

Natalia's eyebrows shot up as she lunged into the box, first flipping all the papers upright, then setting them in lines along the table. When she came to a male with a high-buttoned shirt and bow tie, she placed it next to the woman in the lace collar. "Ta-da!"

Amisha turned the photos over and pointed out the matching years. "They're both 1870. Amazing, Natalia!"

Natalia easily grasped the matching game and went to work examining each picture for clues, then setting them into her own order. Amisha stepped back. "Call me when you've got it," she said. Natalia was too engrossed to respond.

Amisha herded everyone away from the table, making them eat outside on the patio while Natalia worked on her puzzle. She was heading out the door herself with a bowl of nuts and cut up apples, when she heard Natalia call, "Done!" It was one of the first words she hadn't made into a chain. Amisha returned to find the table covered from end to end with photographs, some singles, some in pairs, and a few groups. Amisha was thrilled, for there on the table was their family tree. Natalia turned away, one photograph clutched to her chest.

"May I see?"

Natalia refused to uncurl her fingers from around the photograph.

"It's your mother, isn't it?" Amisha said softly, as if coaxing a kitten from a tree.

Natalia nodded. A small tear formed in the corner of her eye.

"These pictures are different from the ones up here, aren't they?" Amisha tapped her head. "People used to print their images on paper like this. But then they stopped." She gently uncurled Natalia's fingers and looked into the face of her own sister—a beautiful blond woman in her early teens. Her eyes, though, were clouded over. Amisha turned away.

"Here." Amisha held up a candid photograph with a group seated around a dinner table. "Look at the one next to your mother with the droopy mustache." She waited as Natalia absorbed the image. "Keep it, if you'd like." Natalia's fingers curled as if getting ready to snap. Her toes were already tapping the floor. Amisha decided to go for one last thrust. She waved her hand along the table's length.

"This is your family, Natalia. All of them. From way, way back."

Natalia considered the photographs, looked at Amisha, then ran her hands through the collage, destroying the order she had created.

"Another day." Amisha bit her lower lip and helped her put the papers back into the box.

ELIZA

1915

San Francisco, California

By the time Eliza entered the Civic Auditorium, the Northern Caucus had nearly filled their designated section. The elaborate Beaux Arts auditorium still reeked of freshly painted walls and newly installed maroon carpet—final renovations after the 1906 earthquake decimated the building. The California Federation of Women's Clubs was one of the first to use the restored auditorium, and although delegates occupied two thousand chairs, they hardly covered a third of the massive open floor.

Eliza chose a seat in the last row although she knew a reserved chair awaited her in the first row. *The Examiner* tucked firmly under her arm declared, "Mrs. Jennings Alone Nominated." She looked up at the sudden burst of applause from the front of the auditorium, then returned to the smaller letters beneath the headline: "Wrangle at Club Women's Session—Mrs. Baxter's Name to Be Presented from the Floor Today."

Should I watch from back here or take my place up front? Mrs. Jennings was already seated in the front row, her signature hat with three pheasant feathers bobbed right and left. *They've wanted her all along,* Eliza thought. *I could easily slip out the back door and save embarrassment.* She removed the fox stole Mrs. Royles had wrapped over her shoulders for a touch of elegance and placed the two animal skins linked mouth to tail on the seat next to her, giving each little head a gentle pat. "What are you doing here in the city? Shoo! Get out to the meadow where you belong," she whispered.

The vice president gave Mrs. Lillian Parsons her arm and escorted her to the podium with slow, careful steps. After the standing ovation subsided, Mrs. Parsons addressed the delegation in her soft, quivering voice.

"As you know, health issues prohibit me from running for a second term." A murmur rose, but Mrs. Parsons held up her hand. "In a process determined by the state federation, the presidency now proceeds to the northern district. Next election it will return to the south, in rotation. Northern delegates consider the current president of the northern district to be in direct line for the state presidency." She waved the *San Francisco Examiner* at the crowd. "But it appears other sisters in the north have stirred things up, sending unprecedented waves of dissension and turmoil through our organization, distracting us from our purpose at hand."

"But newspapers have never covered us so well!" thundered a delegate from the center of the audience. "Women are finally being given serious notice on the front page."

"However," challenged a young red-haired woman toward the front wearing a modern-cut saffron-orange dress, "unless we change our approach, when this election is over you can be certain that once again, we will be relegated to small announcements on the back pages."

"Enough of this circus distraction," interrupted the woman to her right. "Let Mrs. Jennings take her rightful place as president and let us return to discussions of symbolism, art, and peace." The room erupted into waves of shrill conversations.

Eliza was appalled. This was not what she had envisioned when she agreed to run. Unable to suppress her instincts, she patted the foxes on the seat next to her and stepped into the aisle. As if in a dream, she swept up the center aisle until she was face-to-face with Mrs. Parsons. She turned to the now-silenced audience and spoke words not from her head, but from her heart.

"Ladies, forgive me for being the source of your consternation. We are all members of the Federation of Women's Clubs because we want our lives and our communities to be better, whether through books, gardens, Shakespeare, philosophy, or whatever club has brought us here. But I am here for reasons beyond that."

"Excuse me, Mrs. Baxter," Mrs. Parsons interrupted, pointing to the wall clock. "Your time to address the audience is at three this afternoon."

"No!" shouted the young woman in saffron from the third row. "We need to know what she has in mind."

Without waiting for Mrs. Parsons's response, Eliza stepped to the center aisle in front of the stage and continued.

"I have been called a simple farm woman. And indeed, that is what I am." She held out her unadorned linen skirt. "In the week preceding this convention, I have midwifed the difficult birth of twin lambs, written a paper on 'Diversified Farming' for the Woodland Farmers' Institute, sent fifty pounds of butter on the 4 a.m. train to the Palace Hotel, read the latest *New England Journal* cover to cover, helped my daughter memorize two Shakespeare sonnets, and laid out plans for next season's crops. And," she lowered her voice, "I'd rather chase those pesky foxes from my hen house than wear them draped around my neck!"

The audience rippled with laughter.

Eliza pretended to sweep a piece of lint from her skirt, blinking her eyes to keep them from tearing. *Lambs, foxes, dirt! I can't believe I said that. Get back to the point!*

Eliza moved along the front row to the other side of the audience. "Perhaps I bring something to the federation that has been lacking. For the farm woman knows she must scan the horizon for weather patterns and anticipate future trends in order to survive."

At this, Eliza stopped, seeing as if in a dream, a tall figure standing alone against the back row of seats. She was oddly dressed in men's clothing—light trousers and a long, cream-colored tunic covered with pockets, opened at the top to expose the sunburned wrinkles of her throat. The woman's long, sandy braid was not pinned atop her head but draped forward over her breast. A dream flashed, yes, last night, not quite a dream but something at her bedside. *California has dried up. Our water is nearly gone. Please . . .* A crackling like footsteps on dried leaves, and the figure was gone.

"Mrs. Baxter? Are you finished?"

Eliza shook her head to refocus her thoughts.

"You were talking of anticipating future trends," the woman in the saffron dress whispered out to her.

"Of course," Eliza paused, searching for a way back into her extemporaneous speech. "Imagine how a woman's arms encircle all that she loves—her family and her home, the very air she breathes, and the water she drinks. She takes nothing for granted and knows that any one of these can be taken away by man's unthinking actions." Heads turned toward each other, but the room was silent.

Eliza sensed the mood swaying from her. *I can't talk of the future or I'll lose hold of them. Yet I feel pressed inside to do so. Help me,* she pleaded.

Mrs. Parsons's stern voice broke the silence. "Mrs. Baxter, this is highly irregular. We shall consider this the address you would have given at three this afternoon. I can allow you only five more minutes."

"May I please have a glass of water?" Eliza asked, her voice trembling. Calmed by the soothing sound of water trickling into the empty glass, she took a sip and continued, having no idea what she was going to say.

"We are blessed to be living at a time of plenitude. When I arrived in the alluvial fields of the Sacramento Valley over forty years ago, I anticipated the promised beauty of our native land. Who wasn't beguiled by Albert Bierstadt's paintings? Instead, I found that men had already laid siege to the land. Their first ambition was to quickly reclaim the swamp lands that stretched across the valley and drain them of all life. What better way to control rivers than to straighten and dam them? Rather than protecting our water, men allowed rivers to be dumping grounds for factories and mining. Had not Judge Sawyer wisely passed his decision in 1884 to stop hydraulic mining, today's farmers would now be buried in silt, and cities would be drinking the poison sent downstream from gold mining in the foothills. What we do today matters to the future!"

"This has nothing to do with federation!" shouted a woman from the middle of the audience. Murmurs rose in agreement.

Keep going.

"As women, we know that everything we do or don't do has an impact that accumulates over time, like the sun that wrinkles our skin. Can you imagine there will be a time without water or, I daresay, without children?" Straightening to her full five feet three inches, Eliza walked slowly along the front row, looking each woman in the eye as she passed, Mrs. Jennings included.

"Our California Federation was founded upon the principle that *Strength United Is Stronger.* I ask you to come one step further with me. We are foremost an organization of women. And with the recent franchise gained here in California, and the power of our collective vote, we now have the clout to change the way we live in California. The future to which we are headed may be dry as a desert, but this doesn't have to be. Just as we encircle our homes and children to protect them, we will band together and fiercely protect the future of our home on this earth, not for the next election or even the next decade, but for our great-great-great-grandchildren."

After the applause diminished, Eliza steadied her voice and resumed. "Certainly, we will continue to work *for* education, literacy, and public health, and *against* the effects of alcohol, poverty, and . . ." A shadowy figure rose from a chair and paced along the back row. Eliza hesitated. Several ladies turned around to see what the distraction was. A man? Woman? Eliza couldn't tell. Certainly, the hair was too short above the shoulders to be a woman. But in a dress? In that brief second, Eliza lost her train of thought—another image took its place and she proceeded without losing a beat.

"May I ask one last indulgence as you sit here in this great hall? Please place your feet firmly on the floor in front of you." Eliza waited as delegates shuffled in their seats amid looks of confusion.

"What do your feet rest upon?"

"The floor, obviously," someone shouted.

"You are standing on pine planks that were once majestic trees in a California forest. I suggest *this* be the foundation of our federation. The earth! We must never lose sight of this. As a country woman, I propose we work equally diligently for our forests, our water, and our farmlands. And that, my sisters, is why I am here.

So that our children's children will live in peace and health on a land that provides for all living things. It is my uttermost hope and prayer that you will join me. And that is all I have to say."

A cautious silence ensued as women looked to one another. Then like an incoming storm, a few gentle claps at the back of the room swelled into a thunderous wave across the audience. Mrs. Jennings rose sharply and with a toss of her head gathered two rows of her supporters and angrily exited down the center aisle.

Mrs. Parsons pounded her gavel against the podium. "We will resume with the candidate forum at 2 p.m., at which time Mrs. Jennings will speak. Remember that voting is tomorrow, and results will be announced late afternoon before the banquet. Meeting is now dismissed." Mrs. Parsons brushed past Eliza and whispered under her breath, "It's a good thing I am retiring, for I would have had to answer for what you just did."

Was that a wink? Eliza wasn't sure. She also wasn't sure she saw two foxes scampering out of sight at the back of hall. Although she desperately wanted to retreat to her hotel room and put up her feet, she smiled, took a deep breath, and turned to the women waiting to speak with her.

Early the next morning, Eliza was roused from her deep sleep by a persistent rapping at her door. She had hardly thrown her robe over her shoulders when Mrs. Royce and Mrs. Fairchild burst into the room and thrust the *San Francisco Chronicle* into her hands.

"If you are wondering how your extemporaneous address went yesterday, read this!" Mrs. Fairchild opened to the second page and read aloud, "Another fact that many feel peculiarly fits Mrs. Baxter for the presidential chair is that she is considered one of the most brilliant women in the state and is said to be able not only to speak on any subject that may be presented at a state convention, but to be able to stop speaking when she has nothing further to say—and this is considered by those who know to be the rarest gift with which heaven ever endows a woman."

"Well?" The two women waited as Eliza reread the article.

"Knowing when to stop talking is my gift?"

"Perhaps they are obliquely referring to Mrs. Jennings's hour-and-a-half-long oration. She droned on incessantly with nothing new of substance to say." Mrs. Royce rolled her eyes.

"And you," Mrs. Fairchild wagged her finger, "you held court at every corner and hallway in the auditorium."

"Those women had so many questions, the janitors finally had to sweep us out," Eliza laughed.

"You are the older of the candidates, yet you attracted so many of the young women," Mrs. Royce said.

"Does anyone know the name of the young woman near the front, the one dressed in the color of the rising sun?" Eliza asked.

"I believe she is Miss Caitlin Lyons—delegate from the new student club at Mills College across the bay in Oakland."

"Well, I liked her attitude."

At two that afternoon, a white Peerless touring car purred into the circular driveway of the Civic Auditorium. The chauffeur emerged in his crisp brown uniform and paused long enough for news reporters to assemble before he opened the door and helped his passengers emerge.

With her gloved hand resting lightly upon her chauffeur's arm, Mrs. Jennings set her pointed black shoes onto the sidewalk and adjusted her hat's three pheasant feathers before stepping into the cool San Francisco fog. Escorted by a former federation president, she sauntered toward the front doors, giving time to amass a sizable crowd of women and reporters.

From her bench inside the lobby, Eliza watched the procession slowly make its way toward her.

"Mrs. Baxter," Mrs. Jennings nodded. "I don't believe we have had the pleasure of a personal word since this entire campaign began. No, no, please don't stand."

Eliza nodded. "Perhaps your women will continue on and give us a word together?"

Left alone, each woman searched for what would be appropriate to say. Mrs. Jennings stroked the pearl strands draped at her throat, then patted them back into place with her soft kidskin glove. "I was not anticipating this caliber of a campaign. I hope, as one of our most revered elders, that you are not being exhausted." Mrs. Jennings tilted her head with a look of concern. "I can certainly make it easy for you to reconsider your position."

Eliza straightened her back. "You forget that I've spent my life rising early and completing my work before the city woman has her first sip of morning tea." In the next breath, she added, "But I'm sure you felt that as the northern section's outgoing president you would be the natural selection for state president."

"Life is full of surprises, my dear. I only hope this distraction doesn't take up all the federation's time. We've hardly touched the arts and education agendas. You've heard that Mrs. Kendell will propose establishing five more county libraries. And I've not had the floor yet to offer my proposal to increase the diversity of trees in city parks, which I'm certain you would support. Yes? So much to be accomplished by the end of tomorrow," she sighed.

Eliza listened in silence. Yes, it was all worthy, but as always, dictated from a city woman's perspective.

"Not to be presumptuous," Mrs. Jennings said, looking over Eliza's shoulder at the delegates waiting for her down the hall. "I do hope I will have your pledge of allegiance when the election is over."

"And I yours," Eliza said, extending her white-cotton gloved hand, and with a firm handshake she added, "Mrs. Jennings, I run as a country woman so that country women have equal opportunity to offer their wisdom. But in the end, all women must work together."

"Of course, my dear," she absently agreed.

Mrs. Jennings sauntered down the hall to join her women, leaving Eliza with her arms crossed in her lap. This woman really doesn't understand. What's not important on the agenda: education, health, art, peace, legislation, civic involvement, natural resources? The difference is, I would put our earth's natural resources first. Because we must.

"Mrs. Baxter?" Eliza was roused from her short afternoon nap by a gentle rap at her hotel room door. "Mrs. Baxter, I have something for you. May I come in?"

Eliza opened the door. Holding a brown paper package against her saffron dress was the young delegate from the audience yesterday morning.

"From my parents." The young woman handed the package to Eliza. "I'm Caitlin Lyons. May I explain?"

"Please." Eliza nodded to the two chairs against the window, then with a pull of the string unrolled the contents from the outer wrapping, revealing a filmy white inner tissue package.

"Go ahead," Caitlin said, her eyes wide and inviting.

Eliza gently removed the tissue and lifted up several yards of fine white netting gathered at one end and topped with a row of white lace flowers. With a silent gasp, Eliza clutched it to her chest.

"One of father's strict conditions for allowing me to go to school in California," Caitlin said, "was that I should find you and give you this mysterious package. He said you would explain."

Eliza unfurled the full length of the veil across her lap. "Oh my. I honestly never expected to see my wedding veil again." She regarded the girl in a new light. What to tell her? "Your father . . ."

"Was a weasely old rascal," the young lady completed. "He used to say so himself."

Eliza nodded, relieved. "He was an old rascal and I was a miserable immigrant bride. Somehow our fates intertwined, and we gave one another something we each feared was lost forever."

"Please, continue." Caitlin leaned forward to Eliza, who seemed to be lost in thought.

"When your father pulled his wagon up to the house, he was nearly spitting nails. 'You the Eliza Baxter in this here note?' he yelled at me, waving a crumpled page in the air. But I knew the moment his wagon turned down the drive that my desk had returned. I've no words to explain it, but my desk is more than flesh and blood to me."

"And you gave him this wedding veil in exchange for a desk? How curious."

"Oh, we put him up for the night, seeing he went so far out of his usual route. After a shot or two of whiskey, he revealed to me his hopeless love for Meghan back in Ohio."

"My mother," Caitlin nodded.

"Yes, but her parents didn't think much of him—too much whiskey and wandering. How could he ever convince them he was a serious suitor, he asked me. I gave him my wedding veil and told him when he had fixed up his life a bit, he should find Meghan, place this wrapped gift in her hands, and wait for her answer. And you're living proof that he did."

"Father said he'd be indebted to you far beyond the end of time."

"I'd say he's a tad prone to exaggeration. All I gave him was a few words and this veil."

"But they were just the words he needed back then," Caitlin said. "They turned his life around. Today, most people know my father through his business, Charlie Lyons Great Western Moving and Storage Company. But I think 'Scrabby' suits him better!"

Eliza arranged the veil over Caitlin's modern bobbed hair. "I think you should have it now."

Caitlin laughed and folded it back into the tissue. "I have way too much to do before I settle down. It took me a year to find you. When you're elected president tomorrow, I plan on being close at your side."

AMISHA

2077
Luna Valley, Northern California

Orion hadn't intended on staying at the Third River site so long. In fact, he'd never conducted business as far north as the Third River, but when one of his regulars contacted him that this small band needed his help, he felt compelled to check them out. Most times he dropped off his cargo at concealed locations and quickly moved on, never knowing who picked up his boxes. Best that way. Third River was different. When he pulled up in Blue Sky, he knew immediately that a week wouldn't be near enough time. The dozen men greeted him with a slow-motion lethargy, unable to comprehend even the simplest details for setting up the illicit retro electronics he brought. The women weren't much better. The three older females and one young girl who moved between the cedar bark dwelling and the fire pit seemed unfocused and distracted. Orion turned down their offer of soup—a thin broth of unknown meat and roots—thankful for his supply of Pharm.food. He tried to keep his frustrations to himself, but something was very wrong. This small, ragged group needed more than help setting up an underground subnet for communicating with other groups hidden in the Sierra. They needed help with simple survival.

When he'd done as much as he could, he retraced his route for home, slowing Blue Sky around the wide curves that followed the riverbed, now hardly a trickle. Like the empty back of his truck, he felt light, but anxious to return to San Francisco. Here in the hills, his Nib was nothing but an annoying jumble of crackles and misguidance. Couldn't even update the cricket scores. He was ready to be back in touch with life.

After finishing off two Pharm.food packets, Orion rolled down the window. Maybe he'd catch scent of the river. Could have used Natalia back there. Took three days to find some corroded wires. She was good at that kind of thing. He felt a small pang. He didn't really dump her—she wanted to stay. Probably still hoping she'll find her aunt. Almost two years now, he'd cautiously asked about Amisha up and down the Sierra, but no trace. Amisha probably went farther south.

His Nib crackled half of the final score before going silent around the next bend. Blue Sky's motor was also faltering, but that was something he could fix. Orion pulled over and adjusted the loose solar panels, then resumed his travels back home, deep in thought. Amisha seemed to like, or at least tolerate cricket. Even went to a live match with him in South San Francisco. Just like he once went with her to one of those retro plays up on Nob Hill when she scored tickets to *Hair*. Kinda weird to see all that old-fashioned hippie dancing and singing right in front of you. He told her he didn't want her alone up on Nob Hill at night, but mainly he was curious how they lived beyond the gates—not that they could see anything in the surrounding darkness. His heart still ached when he thought of Amisha. Now that someone had moved into her apartment across the street, he'd lost hope she'd ever return. Still, he missed her.

Lost in thought, he didn't notice that he had turned right at Second River just before the crumbling old dam, but somehow Blue Sky was whining along the river road heading toward the old way station. OK, then, he'd just check to see if Natalia was still there. If she was, he'd even consider taking her back to wherever. Or maybe let her work with him. Hah! Maybe she was the missing something he'd been searching for. Like a partner.

Orion parked his truck in the clearing below the old house and climbed the stairs to the front deck. He rapped on the door.

Impatient, he rapped again. Maybe they didn't hear him with all the laughing and banging going on. He opened the door. Inside to the right, a rather large group was seated at a table quietly eating from bowls, while four or five children played a jump-and-tag game in the room to the left. The tallest child looked up with a start.

"Orion!" Natalia leaped over and tagged Orion on the shoulder. "Orion, Orion, Orion!" Then she was gone.

"Run!" yelled a short woman with frizzy blond hair. "Run fast!" The woman turned to the newcomer and looked him up and down. "So, you're Orion?"

He stepped back. "Where'd Natalia go? I came by to see how she's doing. That's all."

The rest of the group gathered silently behind the woman. Two other younger women stood on tiptoe to get a good look at him, while the children crowded in front, eyes set on him like he was a ghost. Orion stared back at the group. Forget the girl, he decided— just leave. Before his hand reached the front doorknob, the back door banged open. Breathless, Natalia pushed her way through the crowd, pulling a woman into the center of the circle.

The woman stopped, her chest rising and falling from her recent exertion. Long, silvery hair; enormous teal eyes in a thin face. His heart lurched.

Orion reached out with open arms and Amisha stepped close. "Oh, oh." She let go of Natalia's hand and threw herself at Orion, who quickly, naturally folded her into his embrace.

"Oh," he echoed.

If joy had a sound it was the clapping and squealing of the children, the teary sighs of the adults, the ripples of laughter from the entwined couple. In time, Amisha released her arms and turned to the group. "And *this* is Orion!"

"Don't worry about all their names," Amisha laughed as she introduced Orion to each in her community. "You'll learn them in time." Orion followed her around, taking in the new surroundings. Strange food on the table, more children than he'd ever seen— energetic too, and everyone had neck scars. Everyone except Natalia and himself. What a strange new life she'd found.

Amisha told Orion about the silence and the day's voice, then guided him through each of the rooms, describing how they were used—except for the fertility room—she'd save that for later. After an impromptu celebration of winter squash filled with applesauce and walnuts, Amisha tapped on her glass.

"If you will please excuse us now, I wish to bring Orion up to my retreat—alone."

Linked arm in arm on their way up the hill, Amisha pointed out the orchard, vegetable garden, tool shed, woodworking shop, drying racks, hand water pump, and the trail to the spring. She had so much to share.

"I see why you were in such a hurry to leave the city," Orion said. "I'd say you were damn lucky to find all this."

Amisha paused midstep. "Lucky to *find* all this? Orion, I didn't find this. I *created* this from the shell of an old house, a stone foundation, and a few old trees."

"Then who are all those people?"

"Until I arrived, those were travelers drifting in and out, using the house as a temporary wayside place. I've brought everyone together into a community."

"With no Nibs."

"No Nibs. And you and Natalia won't either."

Orion rubbed the bump behind his ear.

"Until you do, we better get you some of Natalia's goop. It's nearly gone, but we won't be needing it, will we?"

Orion didn't comment.

Outside the door to her retreat, Amisha kicked off her woven hemp sandals, took Orion by the hand, and invited him inside.

"It's even smaller than your apartment," Orion observed.

"I don't need much—just a place for silence and my desk."

"And the bed." Orion grinned and wrapped his arms around Amisha. These were not the tentative shoulders he last hugged at the dock, but firm and strong. Ignoring the crackling in his Nib, he pulled her in closer until he felt her heart beating next to his.

After so many years of heavy aching in her chest, Amisha's heart now beat strong and passionate. She was happier than she ever imagined she would be.

Just who was this man who swept Amisha away? Although the women, men, and children went through their daily activities at the homestead, their attention constantly drifted to the cabin at the top of the hill. Clarissa brought up trays of food. Montagna brought them back down half eaten. People still gathered and prepared food for eating. Men entered the fertility room and left with crossed fingers. Children did their chores and played. They knew everything would still function without Amisha, but they missed her.

Left to herself, Natalia regressed to her old pattern of filling the silence with the sound of her own tapping. It was weird here, a kind of weird she'd never known. The goop for her Nib was the only thing that helped her get through this, and she was running low. Natalia liked the women well enough, but with Orion and Amisha always together now, she kept her pack ready by the door.

The third night alone upstairs, Natalia awoke in a sweat. Someone was standing stark still across the dark room. Too short to be one of the women. She squeezed her eyes shut. The lid of a box scraped open. Books tumbled to the floor. Another box, more books. The figure worked its way closer, books scattered along the floor. Natalia loosened one eyelid. It was a short woman, amethyst jewel pinned to the lace collar around her neck, dark-purple skirt billowing to the floor, and squinty eyed, like her aunt when she was thinking hard. The woman straightened up with a large bound book clutched to her chest. With great care, she aligned all the loose pages, flicked off the crumbling edges, and set the book at the foot of Natalia's bed.

"For Amisha."

Then the figure dissipated into the dark.

ELIZA
1915
Yolo, California

Eliza returned home from San Francisco with the peculiar feeling of having awakened from a deep sleep. From the back seat of Mrs. Royles's automobile, she considered the headlines of yesterday's election: "Mrs. Baxter Wins Women's Federation Presidency in a Country Landslide." In one afternoon, her work was transformed from tending her farm to governing thousands of women in hundreds of clubs throughout California.

"Pardon me?" Eliza leaned forward as Mrs. Royles repeated her question. "Ah, yes," Eliza said, "There is so much I want to accomplish, but, no, I haven't determined where I will start. However, I am resolved on one thing—to break women free from our self-imposed restrictions and grow the federation into a new form of women's power." She leaned back into her private thoughts. It was well and good to utter these words, but how to enact them? An idea played at the edge of her thoughts, but as of yet, it had not come forward. Perhaps when she was more rested at home.

Dottie bounded down the farmhouse steps and, after greeting her mother with a kiss, snatched the *Chronicle* from under Eliza's arm.

"Ginny called me as soon as word was out. Oh, Mother, just look at you. Front page even!" Once settled inside, Eliza asked Dottie to read the entire article to her. She wanted to verify that the reporter had included her plans to reinforce women's role in protecting the earth's natural resources.

"Yes, it's all there, Mother." Dottie refolded the paper to the front page. "Who is the lady sitting next to you at the banquet table?" Eliza examined the photograph.

"Caitlin Lyons—a bright young woman who is going to be one of my first appointments."

Hardly two days after returning home, Eliza stood in her dining room, a thick stack of folders tucked in the crook of her arm. She dropped the files onto the already-crowded dining room table. "Time for a rest," she announced and retreated to her desk to enjoy the sweet tea Dottie made to get her through the afternoon.

The hallway phone rang for the fifth time since morning. Now who? She listened to Dottie take down the information and hopefully fend off yet another interview. Dottie—the only child not cut out for country life—was still here on the farm. She felt a tinge of remorse that her daughter wasn't off at finishing school like other seventeen-year-old girls, yet she needed Dottie now more than ever.

"If that's Elizabeth Whitford," Eliza yelled out to the hall, "tell her *yes*. She's one of the few reporters that understands how to give a meaningful interview." Eliza picked up her pen and signed *Eliza Baxter, President*, at the bottom of the first page, confirming her appointment of Florence Anderson as chair of Legislation, then Miss Caitlin Lyons as chair of Education.

"I know how a new president of the United States must feel with so many hundreds of appointments to make," she confided to Dottie, then decided that would be a perfect way to start her interview with Miss Whitford next week for the *Overland Monthly*. "And I do not intend to be content with less than the best possible woman for the head of each department. Women of California stand for fairness, for straightforwardness in politics, for measures and moral principles—not party lines."

"Mother, you don't have to campaign anymore—you've won." Dottie retreated to the kitchen with the empty teacups.

Eliza circled the dining table, where she had arranged files for each department in three long rows with each department chair reporting to her at the imaginary head of the table. Her most important department, Conservation of Forests and Water, was placed closest to her. The rest she placed in what seemed a logical order. She stood back, rearranged the order again, moved Women and Children closer to the top and Art and Music to the last row, always striving for a satisfying balance.

After working the entire day, Eliza threw her hands up in exasperation and plopped down at the kitchen table to watch Dottie put finishing touches on her triangle-pattern quilt.

"Here, let me help you," Eliza said as she poked a threaded needle into the edge of a blue triangle the color of sky on a crystal-clear day. "You are a godsend, Dottie, yet I fear I am going to wear you out."

Dottie shrugged and reached for the spool of blue thread. "I worry that you've taken on too much, Momma." Her jaw set tight as she pressed the edge of the blue triangle down with her thumbnail. "You say the farm has too many responsibilities, yet just look at what's on the dining table!"

Eliza reached for the pincushion, pulled out a needle with enough pink thread to work with, and started on the pink calico triangle. They continued stitching in a silence punctuated by needles slipping in and out of each triangle with a soft pop. Eliza thought back to all the times she and her mother had worked on quilts together. And the bowtie quilt her mother had hung on the back porch. Who would have guessed it was a signpost pointing the way to safety for escaping slaves? Hidden in plain sight, it was.

"Mother?"

Eliza didn't reply. Deep in thought, she drew her index finger along the seam lines, moving from color to color, edge to edge, triangle to triangle.

"Mother, are you finished sewing?"

Eliza held up her hand. She needed more time to think. After a few moments she rose abruptly.

"Of course!" she announced.

Dottie followed Eliza to the dining table and watched her rearrange the stacks of files from one side of the table then back again.

"Help me take these into the parlor, Dottie. This table is simply not the right shape."

After pushing the furniture back against the walls, Eliza worked trancelike for the next hour. She covered the carpet with her department files arranged into sets of three, each set forming a triangle by bordering with and connecting to the other two, each of those creating another triangle with its neighbors until the floor was like a quilt of interconnecting triangles. It was a bit awkward using rectangle files, but as she straightened her aching back, she saw what had been hidden in plain sight.

"Do you see how this works, Dottie? Each department head is connected to two other heads. They form a unit, help each other out, share resources. On either side of each woman is, in turn, another triad of women, making each woman and department stronger. You can go on and on, creating as many connections as you need. This is as stable as a three-legged stool. And no one woman has to bear all the weight."

"Including you?"

Eliza paused, scanning the floor for where to place herself. "Well, I hadn't thought that far. Maybe it doesn't matter. I can be everywhere."

"Or nowhere," Dottie said quietly.

Eliza opened her arms wide with excitement. "*This* is how women work—we reach out to each other. We set personal issues aside in order to strengthen the whole. *This* is women's power."

"Like a spiderweb or a fishing net," Dottie added.

"I'll unveil this at my first board meeting and let the women work on how they will arrange themselves, with the exception of this one." Eliza placed Conservation of Natural Resources in the center of the web. "If we don't make protecting our earth the heart of everything we do," she said, "then everything else we do will be in vain."

AMISHA

2077
Luna Valley, Northern California

Natalia kept the old scrapbook hidden under her bed. When she was sure she was alone, she pulled it out and turned each crumbling, yellow page carefully so it wouldn't dissolve beneath her fingertips. Every page had a smaller paper stuck on top of it filled with lines of odd, blocky letters easy enough to read even without being able to enlarge the print. Some words she recognized immediately, like "women," "farming," and "water." But "John Muir"? Maybe he was one of those relatives in the picture box.

She looked back at the pages. Much of the writing was crazy—like a secret code with long swirls, loops, and curlicues. She'd never seen a foreign language, but maybe this was one. Some squiggles were familiar—she could match them to what she knew, like "B" or "C." But the rest, who knew? She closed the book and decided to take it downstairs.

"I've seen this writing before," Clarissa said, holding the book very carefully. "It's old, old writing, but without our Nibs, it's lost to us." She turned to Sharome. "What do you think?"

Sharome motioned for Natalia to follow her back upstairs. She had seen something in one of the boxes that might help. She pulled a thin booklet from the box marked "Children's Books"—a primer for learning how to write by hand, both block and script.

"Ta-da! Your decoder," Sharome decreed.

Natalia's body came to a standstill. Got it! She knew without asking what that meant: a translator. She only had to match up the strange, swirly marks with the block letters she knew. Sharome handed her a pencil and paper and closed the door behind her. For the next two days, Natalia was lost in unraveling the mystery of the ancient book.

The house was unusually quiet with Amisha and Orion still up in the cabin and Natalia decoding the old scrapbook. It gave Clarissa time to work on her own ideas for Natalia. Whether she liked it or not, the girl had now attached herself to her. Today she'd try adding two pinches of wild hemp leaves she'd discovered growing around the old reservoir to Natalia's valerian, wild oats, and nettle tea. Using the secret knock she and Natalia had devised, she entered Natalia's paper-strewn room, found a place on the floor to sit across from Natalia, and offered her the tea. Natalia looked up, startled to see Clarissa also bobbing her head. "Read to me," Clarissa said.

Natalia started with the page in her hand, sounding out words she didn't know.

> *"Men gov . . . vern the country with their vote, but it is a total facade when most de . . . cisions are made in saloons the night before. Give women the vote and we will show how to rule with fairness and respect for all."*

"What's 'vote'?"
"I'm not sure," Clarissa said. "Read something else."
Natalia turned to her two-sided page of blocky scribbles.

> *"May 23, 1909. After my address to the Fed . . . er . . . ation on state forests yesterday, a very pec . . . pec . . . peculiar man spoke after me, looking for all the world as if he just e . . . merged from living in the wilds. Very fitting that he called himself a naturalist. He spoke elo . . . quen . . . tly about the great beauty of Hetch Hetchy . . .*

Natalia looked to Clarissa, who shrugged back.

. . . Valley and pleaded with the women's Federation that it must not be buried under water when there were many other places for San Francisco to obtain water. His voice fairly quiv . . . vered as he pro . . . noun . . . ced that what we do today will matter to the future. That I understood, and recommended we endorse Mr. Muir's reso . . . lution that congress delay action until the matter could be further investigated. With no requests for further discussion, we passed the motion."

"You're amazing," Clarissa said. "You not only translated it, but read two whole pages aloud!" With a slow, deliberate nod, Natalia reached for her other pages, but Clarissa stopped her. "Enough for now. Got to get ready for Amisha. I think they're finally coming down this afternoon."

Natalia scooped up her pages of translations, thrust them into an empty box along with the scrapbook, and hid the box in the back of the closet.

"Don't you want to show your aunt? She'll be amazed too." At the mention of Amisha, Natalia's shoulders began anxiously pumping up and down like a churn, and Clarissa realized that she had spoken too soon.

When Amisha and Orion reentered the household from their cocoon on the hill, people knew by the softness in Amisha's voice and by the ease with which she and Orion touched that the delicate balance of the Luna Valley homestead was going to shift. Amisha's face radiated happiness, but Dar also detected a tension between the couple.

The women had questions about the addition of two more people, first Natalia, and now Orion.

"Our population is already maxed out," Dar protested to Clarissa, who was taking longer than usual to pump up a bowl of water. "How can Amisha think we have water and food to absorb two more?"

"If a man stays, he needs to be part of the fertility cycle," Clarissa replied.

"And the girl. Did you notice?"

Clarissa nodded. "I wonder what Amisha's going to do."

Life at the Luna homestead was always tenuously balanced, but now with Orion's descriptions of widespread deterioration below, there was a new urgency. California was parched black from endless firestorms, he said, and the sea was engulfing entire communities built on landfill around the San Francisco Bay and even upriver as far as Sacramento and Marysville. It was like Mother Earth was on a rampage. Then there were the refugees. Orion reported that those who hadn't already fled north or east were directed straight to the ocean by their failing Nibs. The few glassy-eyed, confused travelers who wandered into the mountains described long, paralyzing blackouts as their Nibs faded, rebooted with confusing results, then—worst of all—sputtered into oblivion. Unsure what to do, they retraced their steps back to the only life they knew back in the city.

Amisha felt a growing certainty she had been guided up to the homestead for a reason. It was from the silence, the earth, and the women that she knew what to do. Mankind must hold on, live lightly, give the earth a chance to calm down.

Orion and Natalia's arrival presented three new obstacles, and Orion was unwilling to negotiate the first two. He needed his Nib, and he needed Natalia's help. Give him one week, he promised; his own work would be in place and Amisha could destroy both their Nibs. Those were her first two challenges. The third came from the men. She'd try to put that one off as long as possible.

Amisha reluctantly gave over the old woodshed for Orion's project and, for days, Orion and Natalia disappeared from sight. With the last of his cargo safely loaded into the shed, Orion had Natalia organize old motherboards, integrated circuits, and other electronic components onto the makeshift shelves of sheet metal and weathered siding. The pair worked hours behind the closed door, leaving Amisha outside to wonder what was going on. Amisha brought Natalia her tea, hoping she could peek inside.

"Not 'til we're all connected," Orion shouted from the back corner, and, with a childish giggle, Natalia closed the door. A few days later, Amisha was startled to hear sounds like a woodpecker inside—bursts of tapping and intermittent silence. With Natalia's help, Orion turned his collection of old electronics into an underground communication network that no Nib or dronefly could detect.

On the next sun-filled day, with Blue Sky once again loaded with boxes, Orion and Natalia left with no explanation other than they would return as soon as the last site was set up. Amisha's heart sank as the truck disappeared down the road. She knew what she would face at supper that evening.

Trev pushed back from the table, his arms crossed over his long torso. "You see it. Everyone here sees it." He looked to Dar for confirmation.

"Rooster's right. We haven't had a baby born in over a year," Dar agreed.

"The girl's breasts are filling out. So are her hips. It's time for us to start Natalia," Trev challenged.

Natalia? Amisha's vision clouded with tears. She'd just seen the girl drive away, arms and head dangling out the window, giggling like a child with a secret. Now that she was understanding how to work with Natalia, she wouldn't have insensitive hands undo all her progress.

"There's no way." Amisha rose to leave, but Dar held her back.

"You know our men need every fertility cycle women can produce," Dar pleaded. "Henri and Xeri haven't been in the fertility room for two full moons now. Jacob in three. They occupy their time keeping the water system going, repairing fences, even help with planting. And now we're adding another male. We can't have men's seed wither away—we need Natalia!"

Orion? Amisha blanched at the suggestion that he too would be waiting his turn at the fertility room door. "No. Not this time," Amisha said. "This is where I draw the line." As the door banged behind her, Amisha knew they'd be talking about how to get around her. She needed to get away.

Up in her retreat, Amisha spread her fingers out on the desktop until she felt heat build beneath. She fixed her gaze out into the sparse canopy of oak and pine and inhaled deeply. It was all such a delicate balance of people, food, and water. They needed Natalia to help replenish their diminishing numbers, but she needed Natalia to help with a much deeper level of survival. She couldn't put it into words just yet. Amisha blinked, but her eyes wouldn't focus. Out in the forest, seated under a wide-spreading oak, was an older Natalia, her arms wrapped around her full belly, Orion at her side. Amisha swallowed hard.

Is this to be my sacrifice then? Amisha wondered.

No, it will be your greatest gift.

ELIZA

1915

Berkeley and Yolo, California

August 1st

Forehead pressed against the train window, Eliza hardly noticed the rows of workingman's Victorian houses slowly gliding past. She usually enjoyed unpretentious Oakland and Berkeley—San Francisco's younger (and harder-working) sisters across the bay. But this afternoon she was too exhausted to appreciate anything. Inside the wicker box that Mrs. Barrie had packed for her trip home was a lamb chop set in a dish of sautéed onions. The smell filled her with nausea. Though it was a kind gesture by Berkeley's club president, Eliza rewrapped the meat and returned it to the box. The coal and oil fumes permeating her cabin left her with no appetite.

For all her anxiety, her first federation board meeting in Berkeley had gone exceptionally well. She had formulated her opening remarks carefully so they could be easily quoted. As she had hoped, this morning's headline read: "Women of the Federation Will Make Caring for Our Natural Resources Central to All They Do."

Next, she had introduced her carefully selected department heads, noting how each woman scrambled to demonstrate the "country perspective" in her agenda. Well, that's a start, she thought. However, the triangle quilt idea perplexed the women more than she had anticipated.

"We're all so accustomed to the organizing structure that men have handed to us," she told them. "But theirs is a structure that keeps women from our power. I propose we try something more aligned to our female nature: a structure that facilitates sharing connections and power, not merely an exclusive hierarchy of power; one that promotes the integrity of our planet, not one that destroys the planet for man's selfish gain." This, the women understood.

After the spontaneous applause quieted down, President Baxter set the women to work. Using the outline of a triangle quilt taped to the wall, she watched them confer how to arrange their departments around the central Conservation of Natural Resources. After initial reticence, they began to grasp the concept and worked until they had placed all the departments within a triangle: Education, Legislation, Philanthropy, Public Health, Home Economics, and so forth.

With a deep cough, Eliza settled back onto the train cushion. Her eyelids fluttered closed. The train clicked and swayed along the tracks. An hour later, the train lurched to a stop. Eliza glanced outside expecting to see passengers waiting on the platform but was surprised that, except for a hunched figure of an old woman, the platform was deserted. The old woman, hair like strands of gray moss, fumbled in her basket, then, drawing Eliza deep into her gaze, offered a small bag.

Eliza's arms flushed with goose bumps. The old woman approached the window and, like the Patwin woman with her acorn cakes, held out the pouch to Eliza. Maybe I do need to eat, Eliza thought. She lowered the windowpane and extended her hand. The old woman dropped a soft leather pouch into her palm.

"How much?" Eliza reached into her purse for coins, but when she looked up, there was no one to answer, only a vacant platform and a lingering scent of smoke.

Eliza rubbed her forehead and searched her purse for something for her headache. "I must be more tired than I realize." She dropped the pouch into her purse and snapped the clasp closed. Overcome by a pervasive heaviness and a coughing fit that made her ribs ache, Eliza drifted back into an uneasy slumber.

She awoke an hour later, refreshed enough to take notes on what she would report to her federation friends at home. The day before, she had been south of San Francisco giving a speech at the university in Palo Alto. Although it was across the Bay, she had accepted the invitation in order to lend support to Leland and Jane Stanford's vision of a university that supported women's rights to participate in suffrage, politics, and education.

In San Francisco the day before that, she had received a standing ovation for her speech at the Fruit Growers Association, where she talked of "Women as Farmers in California." It wasn't the speech the men had asked for, but it was the one they needed to hear.

She closed her notebook and rested her head between the window and seat back. Cigars, soot, smoke—it was becoming hard to breathe. Beneath the clacking of train wheels, her breathing gurgled and rattled.

"Mrs. Baxter?" A short Chinese porter in a white jacket and long black queue nudged her shoulder. "Woodland your stop, yes?" Eliza struggled to her feet and directed him to carry her valise. Her forehead glistened with sweat.

A hollow tapping at the window. Dottie? Her vision dimmed briefly. Yes, and Rossiter. Then she was standing on the platform, questions coming from all sides. Someone tall held her arm. Can't catch my breath. She searched for the buggy.

Rossiter slapped the reins hard, and the horses pulled into the dusty street. On the bench behind him, Dottie and Berta supported Eliza between them like a sack of flour.

"Get home fast," Dottie urged, searching her mother's face for answers her mother would not reveal.

AMISHA

2082

Luna Valley, Northern California

The light was getting dim, or was it her eyes? Amisha held Harmony's journal up to the window to capture the last bit of light. There was so much she didn't know about her Great-Grandmother. She would never get through all of Harmony's journals even if she read full-time, so she skipped around—a starving woman at a buffet. This evening she learned that there was once a dam here.

> *September 1, 2025*
> *What County asshole sent me this? I'm "Cordially Invited to Celebrate the Completion of the Luna Valley Dam with a Ribbon Cutting Friday, September 15th, at the Lakeview Parking Lot." Lakeview? Hah! I've seen their water. Nothing more than leftovers from a kid's overturned wading pool. If they're expecting this winter's storms to start filling it, good luck!!!*
>
> > *They boast the dam was built way under time and under budget. They don't mention how quickly the new "Agricultural Endeavors" also started stripping away the forest for their pot plantations. From my chair on the deck, I look across the valley and instead of forest, I see massive sores of brown earth. It breaks my heart. Dora says since the feds have relaxed pesticide and herbicide restrictions, the agri-grows are free to use their coveted poisons. And just where is their polluted run-off going to go? Yeah, into the wading pool of the purported lake.*

August 7, 2027
The reservoir is only filled halfway up to the spillway. Heard
rumor of new diversion tunnels up higher in the Sierra. After all,
the County must make up for all the water being pumped out for the
marijuana plantations if there's going to be anything left for people
to drink. Let's see, if each pot plant sucks up 10 gallons of water a
day, times, who knows, 100,000 plants? It's crazy.

I'm not against marijuana. Mark's cream was the only thing
that helped my arthritic fingers. But oh, how I miss my neighbors
and their small organic gardens. I could trust them. I'm so thankful
my land is uphill and somewhat away from the reservoir.

From the overlook parking area, I can see so much. Today,
maintenance workers in brown shirts were milling around the base
of the dam. I flagged them down as they drove back up. They told
me they were just checking on a few tiny cracks. Nothing to worry
about. I asked them why nothing green grows around the water's
edge. No dragonflies or bees either. Probably too early in the season,
they shrugged, as if they hadn't bothered to look into the absence of
life. I know, not in their job description.

May 13, 2028
Two grandchildren and I still have enough energy to keep up with
them! Claire and Auggie drop them off for the weekend. Little Robbie
takes after his father—nose deep in his father's old ebook. But sweet,
sprightly Zoey is my adventure partner. She knows every inch of the
trails, where the wild plants grow, bird calls, she even knows where
my secret garden patch is. Last year I came across that old box of
seeds Dr. M. wanted me to grow for their "save the planet" project.
I didn't have the heart to tell her I wasn't interested and left the seed
packs at the back of the pantry shelf for years. In one of my rare fits
of housecleaning, I took the box up to the clearing above the spring
and sprinkled some of the seeds around. I even made a little map so I
wouldn't forget to check on them. Who knows how long seeds last? I
fear my memory's beginning to fail, but then, living alone, who's to
notice!

On the other hand, I wish Sage and her partner Francesca had been able to conceive. I don't get it—two healthy women and none of their fancy fertilization efforts took. You'd think with all the money this couple spent on the latest biogenetic manipulation and fertilization, they could produce at least one baby. They tell me it's just getting harder and harder for anyone to conceive. Anyway, they seem to be happy being the doting aunties from San Francisco. They have a cute bungalow at the end of Golden Gate Park—they like to smell the ocean.

April 1, 2033
Can't understand that black cord around everyone's necks—even the grandchildren's. Never off. What's a Unity? Zoey tells me in the slow, loud voice she now uses on me that a Unity is what they call a Universal Information Tech. These information devices are permanently corded around children's necks now. I notice when Zoey gets enthusiastic about her new tech, Claire gets up and leaves the room. Zoey lifts her own cord from under her shirt collar and raves about all she can do with hers. Shows me the thin metallic square about the size of my thumb, dangling in front. She asks a question, it answers (she pulls out her ear amp, which she's thinking of installing permanently). News coms are announced in her ear as they come in, she tracks what all her friends are doing, and has anything she wants delivered to her house within the hour. She'd never go back to a handheld one. Claire sets her scratched-up silver handheld device facedown on the table, grumbling that it looks like the children all have nooses around their necks. "Universal Information Tyrants," she calls them. At least she can walk away from hers.

June 20, 2035
Zoey's here again for the summer. Bay Area is sweltering hot, but the mountains aren't much better with the perpetual wildfire smoke. Too bad there's no water in the reservoir, not that I would let my

grandchildren swim in that contamination. Last big quake took care of that. I just feel sorry for the people living downstream when the dam cracked.

For my seventieth birthday, Zoey brought me a fancy chair that lets me float between my bed, desk, and bathroom down the hall. What more do I need, except to walk outside? Mornings, she helps me outside, but just getting to the garden gate leaves me out of breath.

Zoey tells me it's a miracle my old apple orchard is thriving because most California agriculture is gasping for life. Too hot and dry. Her new husband Tim is working for a small pharmaceutical start-up that makes packaged whole-spectrum foods. He's certain the future is in creating customized, self-contained food packs for people with special needs. Patients send in a swab of their saliva and his lab will identify specific allergens, then manufacture foods customized for their special dietary needs. I'm not so sure. If it's not grown with earth and water, can it really be food? Zoey says it's a good thing: no restaurant or grocery store could ever keep up with the growing types of food intolerances people have. Pharma will help people lead a normal life.

A shiver coursed down Amisha's spine. This sounded like the beginnings of Pharm.food—developed to help mankind, then quickly turned against them. Amisha had been too young to remember when her father's company was overtaken by a nameless corporation, but she did remember the hurt in her stomach listening to her parents argue behind closed doors. She was too young to know the economy was sliding downhill into the great collapse, but she did know her parents were too distracted to notice what was happening to their three children, especially Luke and Isabelle. She sympathized when Isabelle packed her bag and disappeared one night. She just wished she could have done more to help her. After that, she spent her whole career trying to keep children alive, but it was only here in Luna Valley that she finally began to understand how.

ELIZA
1915
Yolo, California

August 1st

Eliza yanked Dr. Lawhead's stethoscope away from her chest. "I caught something foul from all those people crowded into small rooms."

"She's exhausted from doing too much," Dottie said firmly. "Tell her she must stay home and rest."

"Your lungs are filled with gurgling rales. I'd say pneumonia, but you've no fever." Dr. Lawhead handed Dottie a list of orders. "Bed rest. She is absolutely not to lift a finger. And I want a full-time nurse here or I am sending your mother to the hospital."

Eliza rocked her head vehemently. "I'm staying right here." She motioned Dottie to her bedside. "Send for my attorney. I want the right-of-way through Edith's land settled. I mean, right now." She lay back, exhausted.

"Mother, it can wait." Dottie gave Dr. Lawhead an exasperated look.

"No, today! No neighbor's going to contest the water to any of your parcels. Should have done it long ago."

Dr. Lawhead checked the bluish hue of Eliza's fingernails. "If she stops directing everything from her bed, she might recover after a good rest, but call me right away if you have any concerns."

Dottie walked the doctor to the front door. "Should I send for the rest of the family?"

"No need. She's a hearty lady. But she absolutely must rest and let her body recover."

August 2nd

Miss McCloud, the registered nurse from Sacramento, arrived late the next day, grumbling under her breath about *farm* positions. With a curt nod hello, she set up her nursing station in a corner of the sitting room downstairs where it was cool.

Scottish and almost as old as Momma, Dottie assessed. The nurse removed her dark-blue nurse's cape and set it next to her satchel.

"I suppose you'll want to see Mother first?"

"I would like to review Doctor Lawhead's orders first." Miss McCloud unfolded a crisp white apron and slipped it over her charcoal-gray uniform, then perused the list of instructions for her patient.

"I was told she is suffering from exhaustion," Miss McCloud questioned, "but these orders look more like heart failure."

"All I know is she's not to be let out of bed, but you'll soon see how hard that is. She won't even let me tell my sisters and brothers she's sick."

Dottie brought Miss McCloud to the bedside. "Mother, Miss McCloud is here to help."

"I don't need her kind of help," Eliza snapped. "My next board meeting is Tuesday. Who's going to write up the agenda? This nurse?"

Hattie came by for her weekly visit, shocked not to have been informed of the turn of events. Without asking, she telephoned Rossiter, Edward, and Edith, assuring that most of Yolo would soon know that Mrs. Baxter was laid up in bed, not to be bothered, and whatever else Ginny the operator, decided to pass along.

August 3rd

As the third day progressed, Eliza regained enough clarity to think about her situation. Physically, she was severely tired, and even though well supported with pillows, she couldn't gasp enough air to relieve the feeling of drowning. But she had time to think.

She had to draft the meeting agenda in her mind because that old nurse wouldn't give her pen and paper. But figuring out strategies for getting more women appointments to California's state boards left her frustrated and tired. As her agitation rose, Miss McCloud called for Dottie.

Eliza pulled Dottie close to her lips and whispered between coughs. "She forbids me to write instructions to my women!"

"Then let me write," Dottie said as she replaced her mother's blood-tinged handkerchief with a clean one. By the time she returned with paper and pen, her mother had drifted off into a stupor.

August 4th

Dottie was pulled out of her exhausted sleep by a loud knock on her bedroom door. Miss McCloud stood outside wringing her hands.

"She's been up all night, cryin' and complainin'. Doesn't make much sense at'all—arguing with the wallpaper as if the flowers could answer, talkin' about Indians and someone called 'Amnesia.'"

Dottie pulled on her robe and followed the nurse down the hall.

"I think it's the laudanum Dr. Lawhead ordered to help her rest," Miss McCloud said. "It's only servin' to make her more confused."

"Then stop giving it to her," Dottie commanded as she rushed to the bed.

"Mother, there is no one else in the room. No 'Amnesia' and certainly not an Indian." Eliza's breath bubbled and rattled. Dottie turned to Miss McCloud, deeply afraid for the first time. "Is she going to be all right?"

"If you ask me, she should be in the hospital." The nurse placed her hand on Dottie's shoulder. "It's possible she may not survive."

Dottie pulled up a chair and lifted her mother's cool hand to her cheek.

"Mother," she said, choosing her words carefully. "You should be in the hospital in Woodland, where they can take better care of you."

"Why? You and the nurse take good care of me here."

Dottie turned her head to hide the tears streaming down her cheeks. Downstairs, the front door flung open and Dr. Lawhead stormed into the house. Without so much as a hello, he entered the room and placed his stethoscope on Eliza's chest. For once, Eliza did not protest. "I should have been called long before now," Dr. Lawhead said, his voice shaking. "I'm calling for an ambulance. Notify the rest of the family to meet us at the hospital immediately!"

"Mother," Dottie's lips quivered. "We're taking you now. You have no choice."

"Am I dying?" Eliza asked, searching Dottie's face.

Dottie nodded.

Lost in a deep silence, Eliza released her grip. She looked to the wall behind Dottie, then to the other side of the room. Her face relaxed into a soft smile.

"If this is death, then this is where I shall remain," she whispered. "Where you took your first breath and Silas, his last. I will be among my women."

"No, mother, you must go . . ."

"Go away," Eliza waved her hand at Dr. Lawhead and the nurse. "I have no further need of you." She turned back to Dottie. "Tell my women . . . look on . . . my desk . . . a file for every . . ."

"Momma, you don't have to explain. I'm sure they can find everything."

Eliza gasped for air several times. "Tell them . . ." she stopped, each word now a measured effort. "To do what . . . must . . . be done."

"Do what must be done? Will they understand?"

Eliza nodded, then drifted into a shallow sleep, where her breaths stretched out interminably.

By eight o'clock that night, Edith arrived out of breath. Rossiter, Edward, and Hattie followed soon after. All were stunned at the sight of their mother on her deathbed. "You should have called us sooner," screamed Edith. "She should have been sent to a San Francisco hospital."

Eliza waved them closer. "Let Dottie be."

Huddled in the corner, Dottie buried her face in her hands. She had struggled to hold up for so long, but with everyone here, she gave in to her uncontrollable anguish. Hattie moved to her side, held her close, smoothing strands of damp hair away from her face.

"Oh, my dear Dottie. You'll live with us, then. We'll take care of you."

Dottie pulled away.

In the late afternoon, surprisingly awake and alert, Eliza looked at the family gathered around her and demanded to be dressed in a clean house dress and apron—now, before she was too stiff and heavy to move. "Let them pass by my body and make no mistake that I am a country woman."

"Mother, please," Dottie winced.

"My amethyst broach, Dottie. I want it at my throat when I die. Then it will be yours. Are you sixteen yet?"

"I turned seventeen two months ago, but I think you forgot."

"Well, then, it's time you had it." Eliza relaxed back under the blanket and drifted in and out of sleep. For the next few hours, she conversed with unseen entities. Dottie recognized her father's name and the familiar smile that spread across her mother's face when her husband came in for supper long ago. But she was baffled by the strange tearful pleas. *It isn't fair. I need more time. I had plans to do so much. Amnesia?*

Eleven o'clock that night, when Dottie took her turn at her mother's side, she noticed something different emanating from her mother, like the dank odor of molding oak leaves after an autumn rain. Yet her mother's mind continued alert as ever in spite of her failing body.

"What will you do?" Eliza's lips hardly moved as she whispered the words.

"I don't want farming, so college, I suppose."

"You'd make a terrible farmer," Eliza whispered. "Still no man?"

"No, Momma. I've been too busy running the farm."

"Well, that will change." Eliza opened her mouth as if to continue but stopped short and clutched Dottie's arm as if she had just remembered something.

"The desk. You will do as I told you?"

Dottie nodded.

"Then nothing else is important."

> *August 4, 1915, 11:30 p.m.*
> *Yolo, California*
> *Age: 66 Years. Cause of Death: Heart Failure*
> *Signed, Doctor E. B. Lawhead*

AMISHA

2087
Luna Valley, Northern California

The pathway up to her cabin hadn't grown longer and steeper, it just felt that way. Catching her breath, Amisha leaned on the walking staff Orion had carved for her out of a long cedar branch. He would be waiting for her, pull back the quilt, rub her shoulders, settle next to her for the night, keep her warm. She opened the door into the shadowed room and knew at once that Orion was not there. Amisha crawled onto the mattress, pulled the old blue quilt up to her neck. Orion was with Natalia. She remembered now.

She never used to get cold at night—used to sleep naked under the stars. But even as nights grew hotter, her body was growing colder. The years were beginning to wear on her and she feared her time was running out. She loved Orion as her friend and lover but knew there was something more she must do.

For months, she listened to the night, to the owls in distant trees, to the dreams that interrupted her sleep. In morning's early light, she listened to the silence of her desk, palms spread wide on the desktop. She walked the forest, attentive to the sensations that arose along the trail. She recalled her vision of Orion and a pregnant Natalia resting on the blanket. When she returned, she called them up to her cabin.

Amisha felt strangely calm as she shared her vision with them. Natalia was no longer the tightly wound spring, the tap-tapping

405

gyroscope who appeared in her life eleven years ago. With great patience, the women and men had calmed Natalia's erratic impulses, fed her the earth's food, showed her how to walk the forest, touch the wood, ask for what she needed, and to listen. Now, standing with their arms around each other, Natalia and Orion would try to continue her family's lineage with what fertility remained. Amisha would help the others understand, but even as her own mind understood, her heart ached.

Natalia and Orion had always had an unusual closeness, Amisha realized. She recalled the days the two spent secretly working in his shed making something out of the hodgepodge of electronics, and the way Natalia looked to Orion with an irrepressible grin when she figured out a difficult problem. Orion responded with a spontaneous high-five that over time became a lingering hug. When the two were ready to have their Nibs removed a year after arriving, Amisha had held her blade into the flame until it glowed red, let it cool, then quickly dug deep into their flesh, one at a time, to pry the Nib's bioelectric tendrils from its interface within their nervous systems. Prepared for the firestorm of pain, Natalia and Orion held each other close. Clarissa pressed a paste of yarrow and plantain leaves over their wounds to stem the bleeding. Amisha ground the Nib's quivering circuitry between two rocks and gave them to Trev to bury in a dozen places by the old dam. Even without her blessing, Amisha suspected the two of them would have come together naturally. It was right that Orion now kept Natalia warm at night. But it made her own nights so much colder.

Upon waking alone the next morning, Amisha waited until the sun warmed the cabin and her cold, stiff joints. She pulled one of Harmony's boxes from the shelf and set it next to Eliza's fragile scrapbook that Natalia had quietly placed on her desk one day. Amisha opened the flap and pulled out "2038." Both family women had given her a crucial key to survival although it may have seemed insignificant in their time. Had they known?

Harmony's handwriting wobbled all over the page, making it hard to decipher.

March 7, 2038
Claire, my oldest, announced she and Auggie are moving in with
me. Do I really need babysitting? I think they're tired of driving
six hours from the north coast whenever I hurt my back wrangling
with heavy garden hoses. She tried to convince me they can do their
engineering and editing jobs just as well here, but she was never
good at lying. It's when she said, "I just want to spend what time
we still have together, Mom," it got to me. Anyway, this old house is
too big for one person. I gathered all my books and random notes
strewn around the house and had Auggie haul them in boxes up to
my study. All I need is a bed, this journal, a bright lamp, and
my desk.

July 20, 2039
Sage and Francesca are visiting from their new home in central
Sacramento, relieved to be away from the saltwater lapping at
their doorstep in San Francisco. Can't believe I've got a daughter
in politics. Both of them! She and Francesca are now part of the
seventy percent of elected offices held by women. Men got to set up
our political system and run the country for hundreds of years, Sage
says. Now women are redesigning it for how women make decisions.
Long ago the Dalai Lama foretold the world would be saved by
western women. I hope he's right.

September 17, 2040
Yesterday, when I hobbled my way down the stairs for coffee (I
refuse to be carried!), Claire couldn't wait to show me the news, even
though she knows I gave up on news reports decades ago. She still
uses the old-style handheld, which is fine with me. I won't tolerate
having a perpetual newsfeed flashing from the wall. I listen as she
reads that San Francisco is on the brink of closing down. Saltwater
flows in the streets but drinking water is all gone after they siphoned
the last drop from Hetch Hetchy Reservoir. "You'll like this, Mom,"
she told me, and enlarged the photo of a waterlogged Hetch Hetchy
Valley re-emerging like a Phoenix from behind a gigantic dam.

February 7, 2041
My eyes are getting old. I sit at the desk and look out the window.
Images blur into the night like a hall of mirrors. How many times
have I sat here? How many of me are there? I get shivers trying to
count. My closet is filled with boxes of books. I'm in my twenty-
second journal—one book for every year I've lived here alone. I've
had a lot of time to think. Who'd have thought I'd make it this far?
And without a piano? No mind, the music is rooted in my fingers,
no—in my soul.

Amisha closed Harmony's journal and pushed back from the desk. There were times she had felt deeply alone, even when surrounded by people—until that night curled up in a bed of forest leaves when she felt life tingling all around her. Now everywhere she went, she was intimately aware of the communion of leaves and stems and roots sharing water, nutrients, and warnings. Orion's MycoNet was like that in some ways—so simple, so brilliant, like a Morse code of woodpeckers tapping on hollow trees, or an underground intranet of root tips and mycorrhizal fungi. Who'd have thought there were other scattered groups of people up here working out their own subsistence, for better or worse? Connected now through Orion's MycoNet, we can reach out to each other.

When Third River transmitted the first call for help, Luna Valley sent India, Nisena, and Henri up to live with them and share Luna Valley's simple means of survival. The triad brought with them a cross section of an oak tree. India pointed to the circle of heartwood at the center.

"This is our earth. For us to survive, we must be like the rings that surround and protect the heartwood," India said. "Listen to the earth's voice in the silence, in the wood, in the soil, in the wind. Listen to know what must be done."

Orion and Natalia had coupled nearly two years ago, and although Amisha's aging body gave signs of wanting to let go, she couldn't. Natalia had conceived only once, ending in a miscarriage. Was it

Orion? The thin beard he now grew on his chin was tinged with gray. Was he beyond fertility already? Or had they not taken Natalia's grounding deep enough? She wondered if she should have opened Natalia to the fertility room. Yet Amisha knew she wasn't waiting for just any baby. Maybe that was the problem.

Amisha returned to her desk, spread her hands wide along the top. Breathe in deeply . . . out slowly . . . deeply . . . slowly . . . in . . . out . . . she waited for the heat to build beneath her fingers. With every breath, she sank deeper into the earth's currents, drifting until she came at long last to the fire. Wavering behind the rising smoke stood the old woman, animal skins draped softly against her bony frailness. The old woman extended her arm through the pelts and opened her palm. It was empty. Amisha understood it was not she who should be here, but Natalia.

Soon after, Amisha summoned Natalia to the cabin, gave her teas, and calmed her breathing. She placed Natalia's hands upon the desk, told her stories of the oak, the acorn, the desk, and their family's women. Was Natalia ready for more? Natalia's movements quieted; her breathing deepened. Amisha guided her into the earth, to the fire.

"Did you see the old woman?" Amisha asked when Natalia returned.

"No," Natalia shook her head.

"Then you must return."

For three days, Natalia entered the silence, abstaining from food, drinking only sips of tea. Guided by a web of fine currents surrounding the living earth, Natalia dropped deeply into the flow, floating as mist above the river of time, until time held still. Beyond the river, behind the rising smoke of the fire, stood an old woman. She extended her long, birdlike arm and opened her hand. In her palm, she offered Natalia an acorn.

ELIZA
1915
Yolo, California

Eliza Osborne Baxter never believed in rumors that the dead hung around the living for three days, occasionally attending their own funeral. Yet here she was, inspecting every detail from afar with detached scrutiny. Why, it didn't feel the least bit like haunting.

"Seems like the whole town has come to see you off," said Amisha, flinging her long silver braid over her shoulder. But the newly deceased was too distracted with all the black coats and veils entering her front door.

"And my house is such a mess! Mrs. Archer doesn't clean until next week," Eliza moaned.

"Bad timing," said Harmony. "And you, with all your silver unpolished."

"Maybe you should have followed your instinct and polished them yourself." Amisha shook her head. "We all think we'll have more time, but then sometimes, poof—you're gone."

"Oh, look, Mrs. Barrie is taking her turn sitting with me." The aged but spry French seamstress, enveloped within a black cape and feathers, kissed Dottie's cheek, then collapsed in tears in Dottie's arms.

For the next twenty-four hours, a steady stream of women sat with Eliza's body laid to rest on the dining room table. As requested, Eliza still wore the unadorned beige linen dress and her favorite green apron appliqued with flowers.

"Berta, Sarah, Emma, Rachel, Claire, Edith. And who'd have thought, even Ginny. When she gets back to the switchboard, the whole town will be wagging their tongues about what they dressed me in!"

"Well, my dear Great-Grandmother, newspapers wrote about you for months. Dottie must have clipped out the articles and pasted them in your scrapbook. It's my most treasured possession," Harmony said.

"You have it still?"

"Even I got to peek at it," Amisha said.

"I never imagined."

"Every word you wrote, every speech you spoke." Harmony laughed. "The reporter from *The Home Alliance* wrote that 'you died in the harness.'"

"Well, that's an image if I ever saw one! Beaten to death like an old workhorse." Eliza viewed the mourners descending from the automobile at the farmhouse's carriage entrance. "How could I die when I was getting to the most important work of my life? It must have been a mistake."

"I don't know. Are there mistakes?" Amisha turned to Harmony.

Harmony shrugged, and the three women settled into a prolonged silence.

At last, Amisha spoke. "You saw her, of course?"

Eliza didn't reply.

"The old woman who placed the acorn there beneath your crossed hands. See how Dottie lifted and reset your hands just now?"

"I don't believe Dottie saw it," Harmony said.

"No, she couldn't have."

"I've seen that woman before," Eliza said, as if unraveling a dream.

"We all have."

Horse buggies and automobiles rolled in for three days as the line of people paying tribute to Eliza Baxter grew to unimaginable lengths. While the workman was busy with the ice deliveries, Dottie directed Edward to carry mother's little desk from the parlor window to the entry hall, so mourners could write in the guest book as they entered.

Eliza beamed with such love for everyone there—her family, neighbors, townspeople, federation and farm women, merchants, journalists. Even old Jeb Vardell.

"Had to see for himself I was dead!" she chuckled.

"They say he respected you," Harmony said.

"What? For putting him out of business?"

"No, Grandma Dottie told me when you and the other Musketeers showed up at his mercantile that night, he knew he was in trouble. He didn't agree with you, but he respected your integrity."

By late morning the third day, vast numbers of Federation Club women had arrived from as far south as San Diego. They were inconsolable, speaking of their leader's vision, inspiration, eloquence as a speaker and writer. They vowed to carry out the new structure of women's power she had introduced so recently. The gift of this country woman will not be forgotten!

"But did anything change?" Eliza's mood was decidedly dampened.

Harmony lowered her eyes. "It was an opportunity. Some ideas take years, decades, even centuries to come to fruition. And still, old ways run deep. Who'd have thought a hundred years after Emancipation we'd still be struggling with attitudes leftover from slavery. If your women had persevered, who knows, women might now have a stronger voice in how things get done. Even with the rise of feminism and eco-consciousness in my time, the earth still suffers from man's greed for power and control."

"Do you really think one person can make a difference?" Eliza asked.

"It happens all the time," Harmony said.

"Although it may not become apparent until much later," Amisha added.

"When I sat at my desk, I simply knew what must be done," Eliza said.

Amisha and Harmony glanced at each other. *The desk does that.*

"I was the first one the desk called to," Eliza said.

"I didn't ask for the desk, didn't want it, and when it showed up, I ignored it," Harmony admitted. "Until I couldn't anymore."

"And I almost gave up my life to find it," Amisha said. "But in the end, it made all the difference in the world."

HARMONY

2042
Luna Valley, Northern California

Harmony lit the sage candle on top of her desk, mindful that open flames were absolutely prohibited. Even candles were considered too dangerous during high-fire season in the Sierra—the only season that remained. She closed her eyes, pressed her open palms onto the desk, and slowly inhaled. The flame wavered.

A knock at the door of her study: "Miss Harmony, five minutes."

She extended her arthritic fingers and moved them in familiar patterns along the length of the desktop.

The door opened behind her.

"It's time."

With a nod, Harmony rose. Her translucent dress cascaded to her ankles; sapphire-blue silk shimmered in the candle flame.

"We're ready," whispered Eliza.

"Are you?" asked Amisha.

Harmony shook her head. "Is one ever ready when your time comes?"

Harmony clasped her abdomen then, gathering the soft, sapphire folds of her gown, followed the candlelight down the stairs to the darkened living room. Shimmering within the flickering flame of the candelabra awaited her grand piano.

The room hushed. Harmony lowered herself onto the bench before the deep ebony and ivory keys and adjusted the drapes of her dress. She sensed the familiar faces of family and friends waiting for her in the shadows and, from the corner of her eye, noticed Eliza's hand resting atop Amisha's. She would play just for them.

"*Nocturne in E Minor, Opus 72, Number 1* by Frédéric Chopin," Harmony announced. "Possibly the first nocturne he wrote as he mourned the death of his sister, or his last nocturne published after his death in 1855. Although he composed this centuries ago, his music is timeless, like the silence between the notes, like the silence between our breaths."

Harmony lifted her left hand in a graceful arch and opened the nocturne with a steady flow of unbroken triplets. Imperceptibly, her right hand entered with the slow, haunting melody. She leaned into the crescendos, withheld all but the slightest resonance in the diminuendos as she soared into the timelessness of the universe. On through the night she played, until it was more than she could hold in one lifetime and she was transformed into a million blazing stars.

Look up, her children would tell their grandchildren. *See how she lights the heavens.*

AMISHA

2090
Luna Valley, Northern California

Amisha rubbed Clarissa's kit-kit-dizze liniment into her swollen, aching knees then, leaning on Orion's staff, slowly rose from her desk. All was in order. She left the door to her cabin ajar to make it easier when she returned for the last time. With small, careful steps, she shuffled down to the house. As she entered the kitchen, the hallway clock chimed one, two, three times. It would soon be time to begin supper preparations. The youngest children were already seated at the table drawing animal figures with charcoal on scraps of hemp paper under the tutelage of Arctic and Malibu. Amisha sighed. How quickly time has passed. Soon even little Tibet will be part of the fertility cycle.

Though her vision was becoming clouded and dim, she could tell that Clarissa and Montagna were cracking walnuts for tonight's loaf, first separating the nutmeats from the shells with their arthritic fingers, then chopping them with a short blade. Sharome stood hunched over the table, encouraging the young artists in their creations, relying more on her inner vision than what she could see. Trev, his sideburns tinged with gray, bent over the woodstove banking the fire for cooking. On the other counter, Africa and a younger woman she did not recognize chopped pungent garlic and greens for the soup pot. Was that Glory? Her twins must be walking by now. A smoky layer suffused the room, giving their hair a silvery sheen. Not so long ago, she was the only one with gray hair. When had all that changed? Amisha circled the table, laying her gnarled hands atop the head or shoulder of each precious young artist.

"May I have a piece of paper, too?" Amisha asked. "Like this one, where you drew seeds with your charcoal all along the top?" She folded the page in thirds and put it in her pocket. With a nod of thanks to the children and a deep, lingering bow to each of the adults, she slipped out the back door—past the sounds of laughter and pans clanging in the kitchen, past the wind chime on the garden gate, and past the small meadow where Natalia napped on a blanket, Orion resting at her side, baby Azile at her breast.

Time flowed backward to Orion's breathless knock at her door.

"Amisha! It's time! Clarissa says to bring you down. It's Natalia. She's . . ."

Amisha grabbed the small bag she had packed for this moment and leaned on Orion all the way down to the front deck of the house. The women parted to make room for her. Sweat glistened on Natalia's forehead as another contraction came upon her. When Natalia relaxed back into Orion's arms, Amisha spread her hands wide over Natalia's pregnant belly as if deep in a private conversation. Smiling, she looked up.

"It's time."

Natalia held her breath and pushed once, twice, and, on the third push, her baby slid into Amisha's waiting hands.

"Welcome," Amisha whispered as she lifted the caul, the thin veil of amniotic sac from the infant's pink face. "I've been waiting for you." Baby Azile opened her deep, dark eyes and looked into the shadows of her Great-Aunt's face . . . as if she knew.

Seated back at her desk in the cabin, Amisha knew that her own time had come. She withdrew the paper from her pocket and smoothed it out on top of the desk. Though her fingers could scarcely hold the pencil, she slowly filled the page with the flowing script that Natalia had taught her long ago. When the sun dropped below the trees and she could no longer see to write, she took a yellowed envelope and wrote "Azile" on the outside, then folded her letter, sealed it inside, and slipped the envelope into the back of the desk drawer.

Only one last thing remained. It was resting in the pine needle basket on her shelf. She didn't need light to know when her fingers found what she searched for. With the small acorn clutched in one hand and her walking staff in the other, Amisha closed the door behind her. Like a deer migrating on a well-known trail, she knew the way back: past Natalia telling Azile one of the family stories, past the vision of Harmony filling her bucket with water at the hand pump, past the wavering image of Eliza digging a hole for her apple tree on the hillside. Instead of stopping at the top of the ridge as she usually did, she continued on.

Come, the forest beckoned. *Come rest beneath this great oak.*

NATALIA

2091
Luna Valley, Northern California

"Come here, you wiggly little girl. Climb up on my lap. If you sit still, I'll tell you our special story." Natalia grasped Azile's pudgy arm before she could get away, settled her into her lap, and smoothed the brown curls away from her daughter's inquisitive blue eyes. It was unusually cool that morning up in the cabin. She wrapped Amisha's worn blue quilt around them both and pulled the chair close to the desk. Hands spread upon the desktop, Natalia inhaled deeply, exhaled slowly as she had learned from the women, then began the story as Amisha had told her.

"Once upon a time, long, long ago, almost before time, an old woman kneeled by a shallow grave on the bank of the great river. She had dug it herself, because she knew it was her time. Her name was Shima'a, and she had magic." Natalia drew out the "Mmm" for emphasis. "Shima'a lived on the great river her whole life, and she watched the mist rise like another river floating above it. Shima'a gathered her people's stories to her breast like wildflowers in a meadow."

"Mmmm," Azile gave her mother's breast an insistent pat.

"OK, OK, a short nip then." Natalia lifted her tunic top and let Azile nurse. When her daughter was relaxed and quiet enough to listen again, Natalia resumed.

421

"Even when this old woman was a baby like you, she was different. She could hear things and see and know things that were invisible. But her own people grew tired of her stories. Over and over, she told the same old story: someday the whole land would be burned by fire; water would be dried up; there'd be no food to eat; and no animals for company . . . how did she know?"

Azile cupped her chubby hands over her ears.

"Right! No one wanted to listen. Then she said her magic words, the same ones Amisha used to tell us: *Listen to the silence, hold the earth in your hands, gather women together, then, bam! Just do it!*"

Azile opened her eyes with a start and stopped suckling. "B . . . b . . . bam?"

"Just like that—bam!" Natalia let out an explosive "B." Azile giggled, reached for the other breast, and twirled a strand of her mother's long black hair as she nursed. "Now we've learned that when the old woman shows up, you better pay attention!" Natalia smoothed the quilt over Azile's bare legs. *I've seen the old woman once,* she thought. *Would she appear again?*

"If you know you're going to die, what will you need?" Natalia asked. "Well, Shima'a tied raven feathers in her hair, made a circle of stones perfect for curling up inside, and here's where the magic begins. She found a very special acorn and told it everything she knew. Especially her magic! Then she tied the acorn over her heart with a long strip of deer skin and laid down in her grave to die."

Natalia shifted Azile in her lap, now heavy against her chest with the weight of sleep.

"Should I continue, little one? Even with closed eyes, I know you'll hear. It's important that you do." With a hushed voice, Natalia resumed the story.

"In that long-ago time, it got so cold the ground froze and everything seemed to stop."

Azile shifted and opened one eye.

"The acorn waited. Even the sun waited until it was time to grow stronger. At just the right moment, the sun began to warm the earth, and when it did, something inside that little acorn ignited."

Both eyes open, Azile regarded her mother, taking in every word.

"First a tiny root curled back and forth inside the shell, searching for a way out. Then it found the tiniest crack and pushed its way through. It knew what to do—go deep into the earth. But uh-oh, something was in its way. The root traveled along the long, hard breastbone of the old woman until it found a passage between two curved ribs and spiraled right down to settle in the old woman's heart."

Azile struggled to sit. Natalia helped her up on her lap, facing the desk. The child spread out her little hands and patted the heartwood. Outside, leaves flickered as the wind passed through. Natalia took a deep breath and continued.

"Another tiny tendril grew upward, searching for the sun. It pushed and pushed away the dirt and when it reached the top, it unfolded two green leaves to soak up the light.

Azile squirmed free of Natalia's arms and reached for the narrow drawer. Natalia drew her back.

"Hey, when it's time, little one. When it's time."

Undeterred, Azile slid the drawer open, revealing the bottom where a knot had been split open then realigned into an imperfectly shaped heart. Natalia pulled Azile's arm away before she could reach the yellowed paper in the back.

"Like you," Natalia continued, "this little acorn grew and grew from a tiny sapling into an amazing oak tree. She was called Grandmother. . . ."

The toddler spread her fingers on the desk before her.

"Azile?"

The child cocked her head, her hand patting out a gentle rhythm on the ancient heartwood.

A vibration moved through the desk, into the earth, and spread out across the forest floor. Azile slid down to the ground and, after two unsteady steps, dropped back on her haunches. Far across the forest floor, currents flowed, roots quivered, and leaves shimmered in welcome.

ENDNOTES

Historical References

Heart Wood is a work of fiction inspired by many real-life people, organizations, and events. For those interested in reading the primary sources of the historical references, I have listed them on the next page. Complete documents and further information can be found on my website: www.shirleydickard.com.

The fictional characters of Eliza and Silas Baxter were inspired by my great-grandparents, Emily Anna and Charles Rossiter Hoppin. Charles came to California with the 1849 Gold Rush, then returned to Niles, Michigan, twenty-five years later to marry Emily and bring her to his Yolo ranch in the Sacramento Valley of California. After his death in 1903, Emily not only ran the eight-hundred-acre ranch, but rose to power, both locally and on the state level, fighting for women, farming, water and land use, and prohibition. What I know of their lives comes from a legacy of hearing family stories and reading news clippings of Emily's speeches (always eloquently laced with poetry) and of her hotly contested election as president of the California Federation of Women's Clubs, 1915. Sadly, she died two months after taking office.

The following original documents have been scanned and are posted on www.shirleydickard.com.

1. Charles Rossiter Hoppin, *Some of His Letters Home, 1849–1863. As written to his family in Niles, Michigan, following his immigration to California in 1849*. Privately printed by James Hamilton Moffett (son-in-law), 1948.

2. The personal scrapbook of Emily Anna Bacon Hoppin, 1854–1915. A selection of her speeches about women and farming, news clippings of her successful election as president of the California Federation of Women's Clubs, 1915, and family obituaries.

3. "Country Life" speech given by Emily Hoppin at the California State Fruit Growers Convention, June 1914.

4. "Women as Farmers in California," by Emily Hoppin. *California Magazine Quarterly*, 1915.

5. "The New Executive in Feminine Clubdom." Interview with Emily Hoppin, newly elected California Federation of Women's Club's President, *Overland Monthly Magazine*, July–December 1915. (Includes University of California's consideration of Hoppin farm for new experimental farm campus.)

6. "The Home Place, Growing Up on the Yolo Ranch." Interview with Emily Hoppin's daughter, Dorothea Hoppin Moffett, conducted by granddaughters, Shirley Jensen DicKard and Emily Jensen Elliott, 1976.

References relevant to the 1980–2020 era in which the fictional character Harmony lived are also posted on www.shirleydickard.com.

ACKNOWLEDGEMENTS

Heart Wood has been a collaboration of those who came before, are with me now, and are yet to come.

To the past, I honor the inspiration for this book, my ancestors great-grandparents Emily and Charles Hoppin, who came to California in the 1800s and left a legacy of family stories and written records.

In present time, I am grateful for the wide circle of friends, family, and enthusiastic supporters who have followed the journey of *Heart Wood* since it was originally conceived ten years ago as a book about family women.

To the future, I honor the apparition of my great-granddaughter Amisha, who reached through time to insist that I include the future in this story, for we are now collectively creating the world she lives in.

First and foremost, I am deeply grateful to my husband for believing in this story, for his daily encouragement, first edits, morning lattes decorated with lopsided hearts, hot homemade bread, and evening glasses of wine. Thank you, Dick, for your heart truly nourished this novel.

To my family women: daughter Crystal Sevier for her grasp of this story's significance and her perceptive suggestions; daughter Mariah Lander for her beautifully insightful graphic design; and my sister Emily Jensen Elliott who years ago passed the family desk on to me, never dreaming that such a story would arise from it.

To Gary Snyder, poet and community neighbor, for tea on a rainy afternoon, and for reminding us all to live in place, listen, and notice.

To Kurt Lorenz, who transmitted his first edits from his sailboat *Raven* along the Pacific coast. Thank you for your confidence in this story, your critical questioning, and for being the catalyst that connected me to just the right people.

My deep appreciation to writing coach, Catharine Bramkamp, who helped me weave an array of chapters into a book ready for publication. Her extensive knowledge and patient guidance gave me, as a first-time author, the tools and confidence to make my book a reality.

For support of my journey from retirement to becoming a writer, I thank Patricia Dove Miller (writing teacher); Heather Donahue; Nicole Bowden; and especially the dear women of the Sierra Muses Press: Jenifer Bliss, Mila Johansen, and Leslie Rivers.

Thank you to Mark Jokerst for helping craft futuristic terminology and river-route mapping, to Diane Pendola and the indigenous wisdom at Skyline Harvest Eco-Contemplative Retreat for their earth-centered spiritual guidance, and to Teresa Hahn who kept me fueled with her chocolate chip cookies.

For technical assistance: Jenifer Bliss (Felix Gillet Institute), Debra Bushnell (California Federation of Women's Clubs), Sarah Cahill (performing artist, piano), Susan Drew (horse woman), Robert Mumm (artisan woodsman), Dr. Christine Newsom, (retired MD and environmental activist), Ashly Overhouse (South Yuba River Citizens League/SYRCL), Shabda Owens (piano technician), Jason Sevier (school psychologist), Traci Sheehan (Foothills Water Network), Ross Trotter (retired US Forest Service naturalist), and DJ Worley (Patwin language and history manager, Yocha Dehe Wintun Nation).

I'm grateful for my Beta Readers' invaluable early suggestions and edits: Shirley Benedick, John Deaderick, Dick DicKard, Emily Elliott, Lee Good, Kurt Lorenz, Sushila Mertens, Sky Schual, Crystal Sevier, Alicia Vandervorst, Cynthia Yaguda; to Linda Brown for final edits, and Yakshi Vadeboncoeur for her on-going support.

Thank you to the many local, professional women who have worked their magic on *Heart Wood*: Catharine Bramkamp (writing coach, editor); Betsy Graziani Fasbinder MFT (editor); Joan Keyes of Dovetail Publishing Services (copy editing, interior design); Mariah Lander of Blue Avocado Design (cover design, family tree, and map design); Barrett Briske Editing (proofreading, research); and Lisa Redfern of Redfern Studio (photography).

About the Author

A fourth-generation Californian, Shirley has always been passionate about living close to the land and protecting the earth. Her first novel, *Heart Wood*, was written from the homestead that she and her husband built in the 1970s in the Sierra Nevada, Northern California.

Lisa Redfern, Redfern Studio

Shirley earned her RN degree from the University of California, San Francisco, and draws on her background as a pediatric nurse and as former executive director of a rural nonprofit, where she promoted community-building as a means of improving children's health. She served as the coproducer of the Nevada County Women's Writing Salon and is a founding member of the Sierra Muses Writing Workshop and Press in Nevada City. Shirley is the senior editor of a community newspaper, the family's historian, and an avid naturalist.

When she is not writing, Shirley is walking in the woods with her husband and dog, spending time with their two daughters' families, volunteering in the community, and tending their large homestead garden and orchard.

Website: www.shirleydickard.com